Stories for the (URBAN) SOUL

A Compilation of Short Stories, Novellas & Poetry

Nicole D. Miller

This is a work of fiction. Names, characters, places, and incidents either are the product of the author's imagination or are used fictitiously. Any resemblance to actual persons, living or dead, events, or locales is entirely coincidental.

Copyright © 2021 by Nicole D. Miller

All rights reserved. No part of this book may be reproduced or used in any manner without written permission of the copyright owner except for the use of quotations in a book review. For more information, address: strgtower7@gmail.com.

Editing by Clotea Mack
Book cover design by Meredith Rucker
Book interior design by Anointing Productions

ISBN: 978-1-7369429-0-1

For the woman who taught me how to be "fly". And the woman who taught me how to be a disciple. May your legacies live always...

ACKNOWLEDGEMENTS

To the Sharpley (and Welchans) clan, thank you. Thank you for lending me your beloved Chris and Rhonda who have been everything to me. From Papa on down, you have been the very hands of God in my life; nurturing, encouraging, giving, supporting, loving. Even if you were unaware, know that you have been used and I aim to be good ground for the seeds you have sown in my life.

To my sisters, what words are there for you? I was alone and you found me. You are the very answers to the prayers that were prayed on my behalf, and on that fateful day when I had to walk down the aisle and do the hardest thing I've ever had to do, you were there. Walking beside me, behind me, surrounding me, so that the fires that threatened to consume my being were forced to stay at bay. Your love has been protection, and I don't deserve the devotion you have lavished but I have desperately needed it, so thank you.

To my community and loved ones, thank you. For every moment of acceptance, every word of affirmation, every prayer you gave in intercession on my behalf, every prompting on your heart that you heeded and obeyed to war for me, thank you.

To the women who raised me, the ones that now cheer for me eternally, I will spend my life sharing with the world the magnificent truths you taught: that God is real, and I am His, and you are mine, and He is ours, and we are forever, together. Without you, there is no me. Thank you.

To my Father, the one who taught me true love. You swept me off my feet and I could not resist. Your passion, Your zeal, Your jealousy! It overcame me. You are relentless and I am grateful. Thank You for seeing *me* when I could not. For scrubbing and rubbing and removing the coal that was stubbornly hiding the jewel that was inside, even when it hurt. Especially when it hurt. You are still working, and I am glad to have finally learned (and I am still learning) that *You* are the one that completes the work, not me. And in fact, it is already finished. Thank you.

TABLE OF CONTENTS

Lisa	1
Joe	51
Vanessa	103
Calvin & Monica	161
A Real Love: Asia	201
Carly	215
Dante's Joy	239
Jasmyne	279
For George (A Poem)	315
Tyrone	319
Nikki	361
Lessons from Characters	393
A Note from the Author	429

LISA

Lisa rocked back in her chair, let out a sigh, and tapped a pencil on the desk.

"Where *is* he?" she said out loud. It wasn't enough that this was her *ex's* weekend to keep their daughter, and due to some supposed emergency, he was dropping her back off—now he was late! She checked her cell again. Nope, nothing. She stood and looked out the five-story window at the city. Cabs and people bustled down Manhattan's streets, signifying five o'clock. A few moments later, her work phone rang.

"This is Mrs.— er, uh *Miz* Doris."

"Lisa, I'm stuck in traffic, but I'll be there soon." Michael's voice was stressed.

"Ok, how long will you be?" she asked, trying to be calm. "How's Michelle?" she added, referring to their 5-year-old.

"She's knocked out in the back seat. I'm on my way."

Lisa shuffled some papers around on her desk in an attempt to focus. She had a deadline to meet but wasn't sure if she could, given the change in plans.

"Maybe I can get Aunt Sylvia to watch her," she said out loud, and with a sigh. Aunt Sylvia was a dear older woman who lived upstairs. Her smooth brown skin always seemed to glow and she had a proclivity for smiling. Frequently, her eyes twinkled with mischief, and for that reason alone Michelle had quickly grown fond of her, adopting her as "Auntie Sylvie."

Lisa had really leaned on Sylvia through the divorce. She had no family in the city and Sylvia had much wisdom to offer, even though she herself had been happily married 30 years. Unfortunately, her Richard had passed in his sleep after a long gruesome battle with lung cancer.

Lisa had moved to Manhattan for one reason and one reason alone: Michael. One look at those light browns and she couldn't refuse his offer. Maybe she had rushed into things? She knew she was ready for a strong family structure when they had started dating. Since she was in love, when he had asked, she hadn't hesitated.

They had been dating for eight months when Michael had taken her to their favorite restaurant, Devonte's. She wore a spaghetti strap dress, which, at the time, hugged every inch of her. After Michelle, she couldn't even think about getting into it. He looked at her with hunger in his eyes while they chewed their stake and indulged in their Champagne.

"Can I have you, Lisa?" He studied her over their meal as she felt her face flush. No man had ever asked her that before. She gazed downward, then leaned slightly to the side, resting her chin in one hand delicately.

"You already do," she answered in an honest tone. As she met his eyes, she felt safe with a man for the first time in her life.

She asked him why he ordered the Champagne. "Because, we have something to celebrate," he responded softly. It wasn't long after that he was kneeling on one knee with a fat diamond glaring up at her. She heard the "ooo's and ahh's" surrounding them, her heart beating a mile a minute.

"Yes," she said breathlessly, even though she felt like there was no need to answer. She had been his' for a while now. She watched his hand slightly tremble as he put the ring on. Promptly, his lips were on hers, his arms a protective shield from the world, from her past, from her fears.

Guess I was wrong, Lisa thought bitterly at the memory and glanced down at her bare ring finger; only a tan line remained. She gave up on trying to write, then checked her email, letting out another sigh. About 30 minutes later her office door opened.

"Hey, sorry I'm late." Michael rushed in with a sleeping Michelle in his arms; her secretary must have let him in. Even after all they had been through, the sight of him still made Lisa catch her breath. He was dressed in grey khakis, brown suede shoes, a white collar, oxford shirt, and a burgundy vest. She could smell his cologne across the room.

"That's fine. Put her on the couch," Lisa said, getting up to greet him. He gently laid their daughter down and met her eyes for the first time. She assumed he was feeling some kind of way for dropping their daughter back off. *Well, that's his problem*, she thought to herself.

"I'm sorry to do this to you. I know it's my weekend to watch her, but the firm just lost this huge account and they want me to fly out to Denver to try to win it back," he said in a rush.

"Michael, you mean to tell me your emergency is work-related?" Lisa asked through gritted teeth. She knew how important his work was, but sometimes it was too important.

"Now don't start. This account is major, and this is *huge* that the partners would trust me enough to reel it back in all by myself," Michael refuted. He crossed his arms and stood, legs spread, ready for battle. Lisa bit her tongue to keep from spewing venom.

"But, Michael, you only see your daughter every *other* weekend. You know how much these weekends mean to her. She asks about you every day during the week, and those night time phone calls are not enough for her." She crossed her arms, and sighed heavily. Michael let out a breath of his own and rubbed the back of his neck.

"Look, Lis, don't make me feel worse than I already do. You know I don't want to miss out on my time with her, but I won't be any good to her if I'm out of a job. You *know* I can *give* her more if I *get* more." That was his favorite line, and Lisa had heard it one too many times. She decided to keep quiet.

Michael looked over at their sleeping daughter, who was sprawled out on her stomach on the leather sofa. She was lovely as ever and had no idea the tension that was building in the room. Lisa went to remove her daughter's shoes and put a loose leg that had fallen, back in its place. Michael came over to join her and both adults' hearts softened while gazing down.

"Well, maybe we weren't the best for each other, but at least we did one thing right," Lisa said. Michael gave her a sorrowful gaze.

"Yea, Michelle was worth all of it," he responded. After a minute of silence, he interrupted their moment. "Look, uh, I got to go. The firm has my flight scheduled, and I'll be leaving tonight. I need to go home and pack."

"Alright then," Lisa said, not looking up. She was already feeling angry again and did not want to ruin the mood. "Give us a call when you land. You know she'll want her bedtime call."

"Of course." Michael turned to head out of the small, but stylish office. "And Lisa," he stood in the doorway with his hand on the knob.

She finally looked up. "Yeah?"

"Thank you." He gave her a boyish grin that belied his 30 years and left before she could respond.

* * *

Devon's was a hip, local coffee shop around the corner from Lisa's apartment complex. She loved going there to write. On any given day one would hear the soothing sounds of Erykah Badu, Jill Scott or Anthony Hamilton oozing over the speakers. The back wall, hugged in hues of violet, displayed a large picture of Martin Luther King Jr. and Malcolm X, shaking hands. The first Friday of the month was open mic night. Poets and artists graced the platform with original creations. This Friday was no exception.

Lisa sat in her favorite corner and looked up from her laptop. Customers in various tones of brown were conversing quietly with cups of steaming liquid in the large, comfy chairs near the back. Some hovered over laptops pounding feverishly on keys, while others were enjoying the latest read of urban literature on the charming, tall stools at the coffee bar. Devon himself was working the bar along with three of her favorite servers: Alice, Denise, and Chuck. All four were on the move as the front door jangled with incoming business every few minutes. Devon's was booming.

Lisa breathed in deeply the familiar smell of coffee beans. Her article for *Jazz* magazine was coming along nicely. She had done her interviews and taken her notes the week before and as was her normal, she had everything she needed to create a superior piece.

Maybe I can get done in time to enjoy some of the acts tonight, she thought. She had a good hour before open mic night began.

"Hey, girl! How you doin'?" Denise stood by the table where Lisa was working, and gave her a winning smile.

"I'm alright, girl. You know it's Friday but for us *real* adults, we have to work on the weekend," Lisa replied, grinning.

"Oh, so I'm not a *real* adult yet, huh?" Denise laughed, pulling a loc and twisting it. Neat, perfectly sized and spaced, her locs were flawless. "I pay my bills *and* my taxes! That's gotta count for something!" She planted a hand on her hip in mock offense.

"Hehe! Yea, well one day, when you settle down and have a family, you'll see *these* are the years you had it easy." Lisa smiled, feeling like an old woman.

"Girl, you are not that much older than me and you *still* look good! Get you a nice dude who's ballin' and let him spoil your ass and that adorable little girl of yours!"

Lisa shook her head, still smiling. "Umm, honey, I am not a gold digger."

"Yea, yea. Well, you ain't gotta do all *that* but you can at least have you some fun! Men do it all the time, so why can't we?"

"Because, we have to have *some* type of standard. You know men go as far as we *let* them. *We* need to be about something so *they* will be about something." Lisa crossed one leg over the other and cupped her chin in her hand; a thoughtful expression settling over her attractive features.

"Hmmm. I mean, I definitely get the whole standard thing. My daddy did my mom all kinds a ways, but that's why I vowed it won't ever happen to me!" Denise's expression was determined. "I can't afford to be out here like that." She crossed her arms, balancing the tray firmly in her right hand like a pro.

Lisa understood. "Well, using others goes both ways, Denise. Two wrongs don't make a right." Lisa looked at her, and Denise seemed to be listening, but then her face clouded over and she shrugged off her elder's words.

"Look, you do what works for *you,* and I'll do what works for *me*. You can keep right on with yo standard and we'll see how many *something's* ask for your number tonight!" Denise joked, before leaving to serve the next customer.

Lisa just shook her head again in response. It wasn't too long ago where she had similar views as Denise. Young and carefree, her caramel brown skin and curvy frame brought her plenty of attention, and she was never one to turn down good company. It wasn't until Michael that she literally felt butterflies.

"Alright, girl, get to work," Lisa muttered to herself. She didn't know how much time had passed, but in the midst of concluding her article, she heard the facilitator step to the mic.

"Wuz up, everybody? It's so good to see y'all lovely faces tonight! I see we have some newcomers as well as our regulars. We are always so happy to have a great crowd on open mic night!" Chuck began. He held the mic up closer to his lips so that the sound reverberated through the whole cafe.

"Tonight we have a special treat for y'all! Our first act is a newbie, but I want y'all to make him feel good 'cuz he really means a lot to me! It's my cousin Joe. Come on y'all, now give him a hand!" The crowd immediately applauded, and some even hollered their encouragement.

"Ok, Joe!"

The lights dimmed, and Joe made his way from a stool at the bar to the front where the mic was. Lisa was so focused on her work that she hadn't bothered to look up. Her concentration was interrupted by the deep, riveting voice that flowed through the mic.

"How is everybody doing tonight?" Joe asked. The crowd responded and nodded in assurance that they were on his side. It took a lot of guts for people to bare their souls, and Devon's was a safe place to do it. Most of the crowd were artists and understood the vulnerability in artistic expression.

"That's good," Joe responded. "I want to share a piece that really captured a period of time I went through a while back. I was going through some hard things and didn't think I would make it out, but the fact that I'm standing here today says otherwise. I want to share this in case anyone else is going through something similar." He cleared his throat. "So here goes."

If he was nervous Lisa couldn't tell. The steadiness and confidence in Joe's voice seemed to match his physique. Joe's tall, muscular frame and dark, glistening skin screamed strength. His eyes were intense as he recited from his soul words that had been etched there undoubtedly from a difficult experience.

> I don't know about you, but I feel the pain
>
> It wraps around my heart, invading each artery
>
> Coursing through each vein
>
> And how does one combat an unseen foe?
>
> I thought I knew, but I really didn't know
>
> The ebb and flow of this life is unreal
>
> One day you are high and lifted up
>
> The next, you are stumbling downhill
>
> Its' fists, its' kicks, they hold and grip
>
> And gut you out 'til you just can't take it any longer
>
> If only I had an arm that was stronger
>
> If only I had a right hand that could slaughter

Lisa

If only the dark would hide under the covers of the crevices of my mind, in kind, I would thank Him for coming to my rescue

For being Light *and* Truth

For invading my heart with joy and teaching me that, yes I am a man, but I will always be His boy

His son

And His Son went through all the pain *I* feel

So that the victory He once experienced, I could partake in

These fists from bullies that try to dominate

They not gon' win

They are only the illusion of an enemy that is afraid

Now I stand unafraid

Now I stand, no longer in pain

Now I stand the exemplary testament of more than a survivor,

but an overcomer

A first-generation trendsetter

A young Black go-getter

A force to be reckoned with in this generation

The light of the world

And a conqueror of nations.

Lisa was in awe. She had never in her life come across a man with such depth and an ability to articulate that depth. The crowd was equally pleased as the room filled with applause and snapping.

"Thank you all!" Joe said gratefully. He made his exit from the front so Chuck could introduce the next artist. Lisa followed him with her eyes in the dimly lit room. His large frame walked purposely with each step. Random people from the audience stopped him to share their approval of his poem, and he thanked each one. She noticed a woman with low cleavage and a short jean skirt grab his hand as he passed by. After a few words he disentangled himself from her grasp, then quickly got seated again at the coffee bar.

After about the fifth person to share, Lisa started feeling drowsy and knew she was out past her bedtime. She would need to get up early to get Michelle who was spending the evening at Sylvia's. Taking care of her that weekend would use up enough of her energy. She packed her laptop and purse, using the intermission as a stopping point to make her exit.

"Hey, Lis! How you doin'?" Devon greeted her as she neared the coffee bar. He was wiping down some mugs that he had just washed.

"Oh, I'm alright. I had to get some work done and you know this atmosphere is a great muse for me!" Lisa responded with a smile, her left dimple peeking through.

"Well, you know we are always happy when you bless us with your presence!"

"Hey, y'all keep providing the coffee and sounds and I'll keep visiting!"

Devon laughed. "Where's your 'mini-me'?" He put the rag back on his shoulder after finishing the last mug.

"Oh, she's with Aunt Sylvia, probably terrorizing the cat and running around buck naked!" Lisa joked and leaned in, lightly touching his arm.

Devon chuckled again. "Yeah, it's good to have people who love your loved ones like you do when you can't be there."

"Hey, man, I'mma get out of here, but thanks so much for the opportunity!" Joe walked up beside Lisa and greeted Devon.

"Oh yea! No doubt! I definitely appreciated yo piece, man." Devon gave Joe dap and Lisa had to step out of the way for him to do it.

"Oh, I'm sorry, Miss! Did I interrupt you?" Joe asked Lisa, turning towards her while holding up his hands apologetically.

"That's alright, I'm out of here anyway," Lisa replied, offering a smile. Her dimple peeked through again as she looked up to meet his eyes. "I did appreciate your poem also by the way," she added, then hugged her belongings closer to her.

"Awe, thank you! This is the first time I shared that piece, and I was a little nervous," Joe admitted.

"Wow, I sure couldn't tell! You seemed like a natural!" she said, with a look of surprise.

"Yea, I have a few tricks I use to channel my nervous energy, but it's still there." Joe smiled and his smooth, deep voice seemed to dance around her heart. Lisa was startled by her response to him.

"You know, Lisa is a writer too," Devon jumped in, gesturing in her direction.

"Wow, is that right?" Joe looked intrigued. He turned towards her to give his full attention.

"Yea, I write for a local magazine. Usually covering happenings in the city–events and such," Lisa said.

"Not just a local magazine!" Devon interrupted. "She works for *Jazz,* man. That mag is fire!"

"Oh yea, I'm hip! I'm always interested in their stories on Black families, businesses, and culture," Joe said. He looked at her impressed.

"Yea, I appreciate their style. Their voice really compliments my views and what I'm passionate about," Lisa responded. Joe nodded his head and looked at her admiringly.

"Well, boys, I've gotta run," Lisa announced, breaking Joe's stare. "It's getting late and I need to make sure I get a good night's sleep." She began backing away from the intimate group and turned towards the door which was now propped open. The cafe was so full it was standing room only, and some were even loitering in the opening just to hear the acts.

"Umm, maybe I can split a cab wit' chew'? I'm 'bout to be out myself," Joe offered. He took a few steps closer to Lisa.

"Actually, I don't live too far away. I'll be fine walking."

"In this city?" Joe looked alarmed. "I don't think so. I'll definitely walk you!"

Lisa glanced quickly at Devon, not sure if she should take Joe up on his offer. His poetry was good and all, but she didn't really know him like that. Devon understood her hesitancy and vouched for him.

"Yo. Joe is cool peoples. Me, him and Chuck have hung out a few times."

"Yea, I ain't no serial killer!" Joe smiled.

Lisa chuckled at his humor. "Alright then."

Joe and Lisa made their way into the spring night air. The temperature had cooled some from earlier that day but it was still pleasant enough for her red trench coat and low open-toed pumps.

"So, how long have you been with *Jazz*?" Joe asked.

"About two years now. I started out being an editorial assistant but moved into covering stories. How about you? Are you a full-time poet?" Lisa asked half-joking, half-serious.

Joe laughed. "I wish! Naw, not at all. I work at a consulting firm full-time in Marketing. We help businesses transform their brand to keep up with industry trends. So often a business will start out with a certain group of values, mission statement, and work culture, but when technology or other industry factors shift, they don't shift with them. Then they lose revenue, all because they're no longer relevant," Joe said.

"Wow. So, you're like a business makeover consultant," Lisa said. She tilted her head up at him, impressed.

Joe laughed. "Yea, something like that! Anyways, it pays the bills, and it's something I enjoy. It gives me a creative outlet, but not the kind I get with doing poetry." Joe and Lisa stopped at an intersection.

A boy on a bike—no doubt a bike messenger— zoomed between cars and was nearly hit by a cab, but made it safely across. Joe moved in closer to Lisa and held her lower back as the boy rode past them so fast his hat flew off his head. The youngin' kept on moving.

"That boy is nuts!" Lisa said.

Joe shook his head. "N-Y-C is hardcore!"

"So, have you lived here all your life?" she asked.

"Nah, I'm from the Midwest. St. Louis actually."

"Nice. I have family there," Lisa said. She hadn't seen her cousins in years and didn't really keep in contact with them, but they were family nonetheless.

"Yep, born and raised. I only came to New York a few years ago for work." Joe kept his hand against her back as they crossed the street. Lisa admitted to herself it felt so good that she was disappointed when he finally let go. The two walked in silence for a moment, but it was a peaceful silence, one it normally took years to acquire.

"Well, here's my stop." Lisa stood in front of a multi-family duplex and clutched her laptop. The building was brick and old on the outside but surprisingly modern on the inside. Joe looked up at the duplex while putting his hands in his pockets. He turned towards Lisa and took in her fullness. She had on a knee-length, black, pencil skirt and a white, collar shirt underneath her partially opened trench. Her frame was accentuated through the business attire. Multi colored ethnic earrings dangled on her delicate ears and her hair was braided and pulled up into a bun. He liked what he saw.

"So, I don't normally do this, Lisa, but you seem like a beautiful and intelligent woman. I would like to get to know you better. Is it possible for me to get your number so I can make that happen?"

Lisa smiled, refreshed by his approach.

"Yea, that would be nice," she said. Joe pulled out his cell and sent her a text with his info. When she pulled out her phone to review the text, she saw that she had three missed calls from Michael, and a text from him as well.

"Dag," she said out loud.

"What? You wish you hadn't given me yo number already?" Joe joked, his eyes sparkling.

"Naw, it's not that. Sorry. I just saw I missed an important call."

"Ok, cool. As long as it's not me!" Joe flashed his beautiful pearly whites and leaned in to hug her, his cologne teasing her nostrils.

Girl, get a grip! she told herself.

"Well, I'll let you get to the rest of your evening, and I hope we can see each other again real soon," Joe said. He looked down at her as if she were a prize he had just won.

"Yea, I hope so too," Lisa responded. She was already feeling the attraction between them intensifying and needed to clear her head. She quickly turned and made her way up the steps, pulling out her keys. She sensed his gaze on her back as she unlocked the door.

"It was nice meeting you, Joe," she said, before going inside.

"Trust me, the pleasure was all mine."

* * *

It had been a week since their phone number exchange and Lisa hadn't had a call from Joe. Not even a text.

"So, what's happening with that young man from open mic night at Devon's?" Sylvia asked. Lisa was seated at Sylvia's dinner table with a mug of hot decaf and her favorite creamer. Truth be told she didn't like coffee too much; it was the creamer she enjoyed. She drew the large mug to her lips and blew softly before taking a sip.

"Nothin'. I haven't heard from him," she answered with a shrug.

"Now, honey, you know men these days like to wait before they call. They not on that whole, 'let me let her know I'm really feelin' her' like they used to be! Back in the day, a man would let the *world* know he liked a sista, but now, naw, that's called bein' *thirsty* as you kids say!" Sylvia grinned and stirred in a heap of sugar in her own mug of black tea.

Lisa laughed. "Oh, I'm good, Aunt Sylvia! I got so much goin' on, it don't phase me none. But what I *will* say is, Joe really didn't seem like he was on games. He seemed like a *real* man, not one of these fake players rackin' up numbers–though I'm sure he could if he wanted that." She frowned, thinking about their brief interaction.

"Well, honey, time will reveal all things. A man's character and mindset will show itself in time. If he's the real deal —as you say— he'll call." Sylvia gave her a knowing look, then leaned back in her chair and took another sip of tea. Lisa glanced over at Michelle sleeping on the couch; Snowball the cat laid contentedly at her feet. Lisa had come just to pick her daughter up but ended up in conversation at Sylvia's insistence. She was grateful for the fellowship, as it had been a long week. According to the new editor, her article that she'd worked so hard on needed revisions, she and Michael had been going at it, and Michelle had been battling a cold the last few days. Lisa's mood was not the best, and Sylvia knew her well enough to see it.

"So, how is *your* love life?" Lisa grinned at the older woman.

"Well, that date I had last week with "Milk Chocolate" was so good I let him court me some more!" Sylvia's eyes twinkled with mischief. "So far we have gone to the movies *and* took a ride on the Staten Island Ferry. Next week he wants to take me to a musical on Broadway." She shifted her full figured-frame on the chair and adjusted the sleeve to her blouse, looking pleased.

"Nice! Milk Chocolate is fine *and* has bank!" Lisa joked.

"Yes, honey. And he's a man of faith which means he has *potential*." Lisa had heard Sylvia reference her spiritual beliefs before and knew she was a churchgoer, but she hadn't considered it to be a *need* in a relationship with a man.

"So, why is that potential?" She cocked her head to the side. "I mean, what's the big deal if he didn't have a faith?" she asked out of curiosity.

"Well, if I were to get serious with anyone, they would definitely have to be in agreement with my core values," Sylvia said thoughtfully. "I mean, I could enjoy someone's company for a while without it, but I wouldn't expect them to be able to enhance me in the area that is most important to me, and that would be a disappointment."

Lisa was quiet and thought about her elder's viewpoint. She felt spirituality was cool, and people believed different things, but she didn't think it was a need in a relationship. But then again, she didn't have a successful relationship herself, so maybe she was missing something?

"How do you know that what you believe is the *right* thing? I mean, so many people have different beliefs. How can there be just *one* right belief?" Lisa looked at her, her facial expression perplexed.

"Well, because of the *evidence*. When you are living in a world with so much hate and darkness, and you experience a light that defies that darkness, there is no other way to believe." There was that certainty again. Lisa figured Sylvia's experience with the light must have led her to believe so strongly. She knew that she herself did not have such an experience, or maybe she hadn't recognized it as such.

I do however believe in the supernatural, Lisa thought to herself. *It's just too egotistical to think we humans are the highest form of life in existence.* She glanced at Michelle again. *I would at least like to give her a strong foundation of faith, if it will help her be as full of hope as Sylvia is.*

"I wasn't raised in a faith," Lisa shared. My parents felt that people who leaned on spirituality were weak. Growing up, it was about working hard and doing it yourself." She looked down into her mug and clasped her hands more tightly around it, trying to absorb the warmth it emanated.

"Ah, I see. And how did that work for them?" Sylvia asked. Her thick curls peppered with grey were shimmering in the light of the room, and to Lisa —if such a thing existed— she looked like an angel.

"Well, probably not good," Lisa said, thinking about it. "They ended up divorced when I was 12. My mom took up drinking, and I hardly saw my father. He started a new life with a new family." Lisa's heart tugged at the memories and she gazed downward once again. She hadn't really shared that with anyone here in New York, other than Michael.

"I'm sorry to hear that, honey. We all face loss and hard things in this world. Christ has not been a crutch for me, but instead, a strong arm to fight with." Sylvia nursed her tea and peered over the mug at Lisa, staring intently.

Lisa met her gaze and nodded in response. *I sure could use some strength,* Lisa thought. She heard her cell phone ring.

"I'm sorry. It's probably Michael. I need to get that." She stood up to fish out her phone in her purse and answered it. "Hello, Michael," she said, turning her back to the kitchen and glancing over at Michelle.

"Hey, sorry I'm calling so late. Is Michelle still up?"

"No, she's been sleeping for a while. This cold is kicking her butt so Aunt Sylvia gave her something to help her sleep. Why don't you try back tomorrow?"

"Oh, ok. My bad. Look uh- I just want to apologize for how stressed it's been with us this week. I know I overreacted when you missed my calls the other day." He paused. "Sometimes my temper gets the best of me..."

Lisa was touched. "It's cool, Michael. I know we're not going to do this perfectly. We all have our moments."

"Thanks, Lis. I appreciate that. Look, I know it's not my weekend, but my dad will be in town and I wanted to know if you and Michelle would want to visit with my dad? He's been asking about her, and you know he don't usually stay long when he's in town visiting. I was hoping we could hang out for a while."

"Oh, well let me look at our schedule and get back to you. Right now I'm actually at Aunt Sylvia's and I'm being rude." She pivoted slightly to glance at Sylvia over her shoulder.

"No you not, honey! You fine!" Sylvia shouted from the kitchen.

Lisa laughed. "Well, I *feel* like I am, so I'm gonna get back to you on that."

"Ok, Lis. I'll talk to you soon." Lisa reflected on the call. It was big for Michael to make the first move and apologize.

"When do you think you ever get over someone, Aunt Sylvia?" Lisa asked with a sigh while moving back to the table to join her elder.

Sylvia gave Lisa a sympathetic look. "The heart is the wellspring of life, honey. It is the key to the depths of who we are. When we give someone access to that key, they can leave the heart in a better state, or a worse state than how it was when they first entered. When it's left in a worse state, well, it takes time to get it cleaned back up. Just like with a house."

"Yea...but how much time?" Lisa bit her lip frustrated. Why did she still love this man when things clearly didn't work out?

"Only God knows *that,* honey. Maybe you should ask *Him.*"

Lisa sighed again and instead of responding, got back up to gather her things. "Alright, it's time for me to get us out of here. Michael wants us to meet with him and his dad this weekend which means I've got to try to get my errands done beforehand."

"Ok, honey. You take care." Sylvia continued drying dishes while Lisa picked up a heavy, sleeping Michelle. Snowball looked up at her in confusion, and she offered him a gentle pet on thehead with her free hand.

"I really appreciate you, Aunt Sylvia. I can't entrust Michelle to too many folks."

"Oh, you know it ain't nothing but a thang. You know I love that girl!" Sylvia's eyes twinkled in their usual way as she dried off her hands to see out her guests. Lisa had Michelle draped over one side of her body and her purse on the other.

"Whew! This girl is getting big! Good thing we only going down one flight!"

"Yes, honey! You ain't gone be able to do that much longer!"

Lisa laughed in agreement. Sylvia opened the door as Lisa made her way into the hallway.

"And Lisa?"

"Yes ma'am?"

"You oughta think about what I said now."

Lisa gave her a quizzical look.

"God created your heart. He knows how long it will take to heal it."

Lisa smiled politely and turned to make her short walk downstairs. She would have to think about that. She had never tried to talk to God before.

* * *

"Mommy, I can't find my pink swimsuit!" Michelle yelled from her room. It was decorated in various shades of pinks with dalmatians everywhere. Whether they were painted on the walls, stuffed animals on her bed, or adorning her sheets, the spotted creatures were lurking near. The child had so many dalmatians that Lisa was counting the days when this phase would *end*. If she saw *101 Dalmatians* one more time it would be too soon!

"Michelle, when was the last time you had it?" Lisa yelled back from the living room. Al Green was playing in the background, and she had finally gotten settled on the couch with the laundry basket. She did not want to have to go help her find it when she was trying to finish folding their laundry.

"Umm, I think when I went to the rec with Danielle?" Michelle said.

"Oh, well I would have washed it by then," Lisa said, thinking back. *That had to be like three weeks ago*. "It has to be in one of your drawers."

"But it's not, Mommy. I looked!"

"Then why don't you just wear the purple one, sweetie? It's just as cute." She shook out some wrinkles on a light blue blouse.

"Cuz, the pink one is my favorite! And Papa needs to see me in my fa-vor-ite!" Michelle said, pronouncing each syllable in frustration. Lisa puffed out air while putting the clothing to the side and pushed herself off the couch. This child was not about to let her get away with getting the chores done. It was Saturday afternoon, and she told Michael they would be over to see him and his dad that evening for dinner. His apartment complex had an indoor swimming pool that Michelle loved. She was like a fish in that thing.

"Ok, I'm comin'," Lisa said, making her way down the hall to her daughter's bedroom. She appreciated their home. It was cozy and perfect for the two of them but she still missed the larger space they had when she was with Michael. "Oh well, that's life," Lisa told herself. When she made her way to Michelle, she found her daughter on all fours, head hidden in the closet and her rear poking out of the opening. She smiled warmly at the sight.

"Mommy, I can't find it!" Michelle exclaimed as Lisa's familiar footsteps approached. Her voice sounded muffled coming from inside the closet. When Lisa finally made it into the room, she knelt down next to her daughter and realized Michelle had a pile of clothes sitting on top of her head like a hat. She let out a laugh.

"Girl, what are you doin'? And what is on your head?" She started grabbing articles of clothing off her daughter to uncover her face, all the while laughing.

"I was looking for my swimsuit! I dug and dug and can't find it."

"Alright, well let me try. I told you to look in the drawers but you lookin' in the closet."

"That's cuz I already looked in the drawers!" Michelle was upset but Lisa couldn't get over how cute she looked. Lisa continued unmasking her daughter until finally her beautiful brown skin was no longer covered.

"There. Now we can make some real progress." Lisa smiled and kissed Michelle on the tip of her nose, soothing her. She was her spitting image. From her caramel skin to the dimple in her left cheek, nobody couldn't tell her that wasn't her baby. The only thing Michelle had from Michael were those big, light brown eyes, and Lisa was glad she did. They were what attracted her to him in the first place.

"Why don't you help me by folding the clothes, and I'll look for the swimsuit?" she suggested to a sulking Michelle. Immediately, her child's disposition changed.

"Ok!" Michelle took off running towards the hall to make her way to the living room, her long, poofy pigtails bouncing behind her.

"Don't run in the hall!" Lisa called, and heard her daughter's feet slow down instantly.

At least she still listens to me, Lisa thought, feeling a wave of gratefulness. After she made her way through each drawer, she still couldn't find the missing item. A half-hour later Lisa realized that there was no way she could afford to spend any more time on this foolishness.

"Mommy, I found it!" Michelle suddenly screamed.

"Thank God," Lisa muttered to herself. She got up from her cramped position on the floor and stretched her side. "Where was it, baby?" Michelle ran into the hallway holding up her prize.

"It was in the laundry!" Michelle announced, her hands clasped tightly around the suit in victory.

Lisa shook her head. "Of course it was!" *I guess it has been a while since I did laundry!* she said to herself. She made her way to the living room and discovered that though most of the clothes had been folded, they were in need of some serious tidying up.

"Good job, baby, folding those clothes! You are getting so good at being Mommy's helper!"

Michelle glowed under her mother's praise. "Yep. I been practicing!" Lisa kissed her on the forehead, dodging the baby hair that was poking in every which way, and smoothed her hand over her pigtails.

"Alright, why don't you get out of your play clothes and change into your evening clothes for dinner."

"Ok, Mommy!" Michelle dashed back to her room, but halfway there she caught herself and slowed down. The music on Lisa's playlist had changed to Marvin Gaye. "*Like the sweet morning dew, I took one look at you, and it was plain to see, you were my destiny..."* The lyrics floated through the room, and Lisa hummed right along with her tunes as she straightened up her daughter's efforts. It wasn't until her cell rang that her chores were interrupted. She figured it was Michael checking in, so she didn't bother to look to see who it was.

"Hi–uh, Lisa?" Though the voice was male, it wasn't that of her ex-husband. Caught off guard, she quickly glanced at her screen, and surprisingly realized, it was Joe.

"Uh, yes. This is her," she stumbled out.

"Hey, how you doin'? It's Joe." She could hear him smiling on the other end. A warm feeling moved through her at the sound of his voice. She had to remind herself he had taken his time calling.

"I'm well. How are you, Joe?" she responded in an even tone.

"I'm good. I was just thinking about you and wanted to connect. It's been a crazy week, but I finally have some time on my hands."

"Oh, is that right? What's been goin' on then?" Lisa continued straightening up the laundry while balancing her phone on her shoulder. *This better be good since you took five days to call,* she thought to herself.

"Well, our company had a huge client I had to take the lead on. Thankfully, I did well and finished the project!"

"Well, that's great. I'm glad you did well," Lisa responded. She was playing it cool, though she was genuinely happy for him. It was always good to see a brother doing well for himself.

"Yea. It was pretty intense, but I'm definitely glad I took the opportunity. They actually gave me a choice in whether or not I wanted the lead," he shared, his voice lively and stimulated.

"Cool. I'm sure it will do wonders for your career," she said, kindly.

"Yea, but I didn't call to talk about work. I wanted to talk about *you*. What's goin' on wit' chew'?"

"Mommy, I got my dress on!" Michelle stood in the living room and twirled for Lisa.

Lisa looked up and turned to face Michelle. She placed a hand over the speaker, "You look pretty baby!" Michelle did a curtsy as if she were on stage, then swung from side to side to show off each angle.

"Oh, well, it sounds like you busy." Joe said on the other end, sounding unsure. "Maybe this isn't a good time?"

"Uh, no you're fine. I mean, I am kind of in the middle of something, but I'll be free tomorrow if you want to call back."

"Yea, no problem. Actually, if you're free, I was gonna head to this little spot I like to go to Sunday evenings. Maybe you'd like to join me?"

Lisa smiled, but didn't let him know it. "Sure, what time?" she answered, trying to sound noncommittal.

"How about 6PM? That will give me time to unwind after church. They have great music."

"Ok. I'll see if I can get a sitter and let you know," Lisa said. She assumed he had heard her daughter in the background.

"Sounds good. Talk to you later."

"Mommy, can I stay with Daddy tonight?" Michelle had made a seat between her legs so Lisa could comb through her hair.

"Honey, it's not Daddy's weekend. You'll stay next weekend."

"But I want to stay *this* weekend!" Michelle whined.

"I know, sweetie, but that's not the deal we have." Lisa had gone through this routine too many times and it was never easy. She stopped believing her child would ever get used to the idea of having her parents live separately. Michelle tightly folded her arms across her chest and pouted while Lisa struggled to untangle the knots that had formed.

"Hold still, Michelle," Lisa said, trying to be patient.

"Why can't we live with Daddy? Why can't we just all live together?"

Lisa's heart broke. *I wish it were that easy.* "Because sometimes daddies and mommies fall out of love with each other, honey. Sometimes it's best if they don't stay together." Stevie Wonder's *Ribbon In The Sky* hit the speaker as if to argue against her previous statement.

Oh so long for this night I prayed

That a star would guide you my way

To share with me this special day

There's a ribbon in the sky for our love

"I don't understand, Mommy," Michelle said in her innocence.

Lisa bit her lip to keep tears from falling. She pumped the spray bottle of water on Michelle's hair to help with the detangling. "I don't either, honey. I don't either."

* * *

"And then he had the nerve to tell *me* that *I'm* old!" Mr. Doris grinned while using his large hands to cut the well-done steak on his plate. "How can *I* be old if you 80? Last time I checked, 65 was younger than 80!" His laugh was as boisterous as a five-year old's birthday party. Lisa and Michael laughed with him. Michelle laughed too, not because she understood the humor, but simply because her favorite people in the world were happy.

"Hey, Pops. You want more mashed potatoes?" Michael reached over the table to grab the large china bowl to serve his dad before he had even responded; he knew his father liked his seconds.

"Sure, son. You know I need my seconds!" He gave a quick wink at Michelle before stuffing a chunk of meat in his mouth.

"Papa, am I going to be big and strong like you when I grow up?" Michelle's shiny eyes complimented the hopeful smile plastered on her face.

"Oh, darlin'! You don't wanna be big like me! You want to be small like your momma!"

Michelle looked at her mom and then at her grandfather. "But isn't it better to be big so I can be strong?" she questioned.

"Well, strength isn't always in a size, sweetie," Lisa chimed in. "People can be strong in different ways." Michelle looked at her, confused.

"That's right. Like your mommy is a great writer. She is strong at putting feelings and circumstances into words for others to understand," Michael said. Lisa was touched and caught off guard by Michael's generosity. *When was the last time he complimented me?* she thought.

"Yea, and your daddy is strong in how he gets those sales at work!" Mr. Doris expelled a chuckle while stuffing several green beans into his mouth.

"Oh, ok," Michelle said, not really understanding but wanting to fit in. She kicked her feet back and forth under the table while pushing around the green beans on her plate.

"Honey, one way to be big and strong is to eat your vegetables," Lisa said, observing her daughter's lack of enthusiasm with her meal. Michelle took a small bite and then sighed.

"Can I go swimming now?"

"Not until you finish your dinner," Michael responded. Lisa appreciated his help in backing her up. She remembered too many times where that didn't happen. She gave Michael a grateful smile, and he returned the favor. Michelle slowly chewed the rest of her food until it seemed she couldn't take it anymore.

"I'm done!" she said, and held up her plate for all adults to see.

"Good job, Buggy!" her grandfather said. "How 'bout I join you in the pool?" he suggested. "I brought my trunks!"

Michelle's eyes lit up. "Yay!!!" she exclaimed. She pushed herself from the table and hopped up and down.

"Honey, why don't you go change into your swimsuit, and I'll help Daddy clear the table," Lisa said. She was so happy her daughter had a bond with her grandfather. She could count the number of times on her hand that her own mother had traveled to see them.

"Ok!" Michelle took off running to Michael's room to get her backpack with her clothes in it. Lisa then heard little footsteps make their way to the bathroom.

"Guess I need to change too!" Mr. Doris said, and smiled. He headed towards the guest room and Lisa started gathering plates.

"You don't have to do that, Lis. I got it." Michael placed his hand over hers, and she felt a current of electricity shoot through it. Did he feel it too?

"Don't be silly. You cook, I wash. Remember?"

"Well, you'll have it pretty easy since the dishwasher will be assisting you!" Michael laughed.

"Hey, I'm going to *hand wash* this china boy! I know better than to put these priceless jewels in the dishwasher!" She held up two china bowls he had served from as examples. Pain hit her in the gut: she recognized them as wedding gifts.

"Yea yea," Michael said. He followed her to the kitchen. Lisa's figure was enhanced in the off-shoulder black lace dress she wore. Her silver stilettos clicked on the tile as she switched her hips from side to side. "Now you know you lookin' good in that dress, Lis," Michael commented.

Lisa blushed. Was it just her, or was it getting hot in here?

"Why, thank you, Mr. Doris," she answered with a smile. *Oh Lawd, now I'm flirting with him!* She moved a few inches away under the pretense of grabbing the dish soap, but really it was to calm herself down.

"I'm ready to swim!" Michelle burst into the living room in her pink, one-piece bathing suit. It had a picture of a dalmatian's face on the front made out of glitter, and large, floppy frills around the waist. She raised a yellow inflatable water tube with both hands above her head in excitement. Her grandfather stood right behind her, dressed in a plain white t-shirt and some blue baggy trunks. His large belly fought against the inside of the shirt material, but the elasticity from his trunks helped him win the fight.

"Alright, Buggy! You lead the way!" he said, and Michelle jumped with joy.

"Now, you be good for Papa, Michelle. Your dad and I will be down shortly once we finish cleaning up here."

"Ok, Mommy!" Her grandfather's large hand swallowed her own and the two left the apartment, practically skipping. Lisa started rinsing and felt Michael's eyes on her.

"Something wrong?" she said, not looking up, too afraid of his big light browns.

Legs crossed with his back leaned against the counter, Michael placed both hands behind him and rested them on the counter's edge. Lisa couldn't help admiring him. Tan slacks, a cashmere cream turtleneck and cream leather shoes. She had bought those shoes for his birthday.

"Why don't we have a glass of wine before heading down to the pool, Lis?" Michael asked, instead of answering her. He moved swiftly from his stance and was already pulling out the bottle from the fridge and popping it open.

"Umm, ok." Lisa licked her lips nervously. She continued rinsing while he poured two glasses. They then made their way to the sofa in front of the fireplace. Michael clicked a button on his phone, and John Coltrane started playing through some hidden speakers she couldn't seem to locate.

"Now, Mr. Doris, I know you not trying to make a move on me?" Lisa took a drink of her Merlot, her eyes dancing humorously.

Michael smiled. "No, ma'am! I just want you to relax. I know it's been difficult between us, and I want you to know that I am working on myself." He rested his arm on the couch and shifted his weight to face her head on. His tone grew serious. "I been going to counseling, Lis. And I know it's something you wanted me to do while we were together, but I honestly was too afraid. I was too afraid to admit to myself my own weaknesses. It was easier for me to put the blame on you." He stopped talking and took a sip of his wine, gathering courage. Lisa was shocked. Michael had never been open to getting outside help during their six-year marriage. She really didn't even know how to respond.

"I know it's probably not what you want to hear since it's kind of after the fact, but I'm doing some work on myself, and I'm hoping it will make me a better father." He paused. "And maybe one day a better husband." He looked at her, searching her face. Was he alluding to them getting back together? She was too afraid to ask.

"Well, that's great, Michael. I mean, *really*. I just did not expect you to say that," Lisa managed. She took another sip and played with the liquid on the rim with her manicured finger, looking down. Michael reached over, tilted her head upward, and stared into her eyes.

"I want you to know that I still love you, Lis. As much as we fight. As hard as it's been. I still...." His voice broke with emotion and trailed off. "And I'm hoping that at some point I'll be a better man so that I can commit to you again." He caressed her chin gently.

Lisa's stomach dropped. This was what she had been wanting. She had wanted Michael for so long she couldn't remember a time *not* wanting him. But what had changed between them? She needed to move slowly.

"I don't want you to respond now. I just want you to know where I'm at, and when the time is right, you can let me know how you feel." Michael tucked a loose braid behind her ear. She had pulled all of her hair to the side so that the off-shoulder part of the dress revealed her skin. She took another sip and slowly nodded her head. She had a lot to think about. Could Michael and she really have a future together? It would take a lot more than a few compliments and counseling sessions for her to really believe it. She would need a sign from God Himself.

* * *

They walked into the night club, and Joe held her close to him, protectively, as if nothing in the world could get between them.

"They play Jazz Sunday evenings," he had told her, so she had dressed appropriately. A fitted purple dress, shear at the top, slits down the arms and cinched at the wrists. Lisa's large gold hoop earrings and a cute black clutch complimented well. Her shoes were the open-toed black Louboutin's that had come out that season. It had been a while since she'd been on a date.

"Definitely a nice vibe!" Lisa said over the music. They were already being escorted to their table which was seated in a corner, close enough to watch the action, but far enough to have a good conversation.

"Yea. I love coming here to unwind before the Monday grind begins," Joe said, whispering into her ear. She enjoyed his nearness and indulged in a whiff of his cologne. The waitress, a young hip thing who looked more like an actress than a college student (she was probably both), poured two glasses with water and lemon then left them to view their menus. The menu was full of items Lisa could barely pronounce, even as a journalism major. The music was soothing and people of all shades were filling the room. She was impressed. If this was the first date what in the world would he do on the second?

"How did you find out about this place?" she asked him out of pure curiosity. *I don't know too many brothers that have this kind of taste,* she thought.

"Oh, a client of mine. We do a lot of out of office work meetings, so I get around the city." Lisa nodded, impressed.

"Gotcha. So, what do you recommend?" That was her way of seeing how much she should be ordering. She didn't want to kill the man's pockets.

"Well, the shrimp is phenomenal, but if you like spicy, I would definitely try the goat." He leaned back, laying his arm on the top of the booth's seat. Lisa couldn't help but notice his muscles flex under the blazer he wore. They locked eyes for a moment until she felt her face flush and looked down to study the menu. It wasn't long before they placed their order; she decided to go with the goat.

"So, Lisa, tell me more about yourself. Where you from?" He took a drink of his water and leaned back, getting comfortable.

"I'm from Atlanta. But I went away to school in North Carolina."

"Ah, so you're a southern girl. Funny I didn't notice an accent," he teased.

"Yea, I've practiced a lot to hide it. I figured it would be beneficial in my career if I ever moved out of the south. I was right." Lisa placed her chin in her hand and smiled.

"Oh, so New Yorkers are hard on southerners, huh?" Joe asked playfully.

"New Yorkers are hard on everybody!"

Joe laughed. "Yea, you right. They can be rough." He nodded in agreement, rubbing a spot on the linen tablecloth.

"But I will say I've found some beautiful people here. Good people who are like family." Lisa was thinking of Sylvia and her friends at Devon's.

"That's definitely a blessing. I've had a hard time meeting people. I was excited when I finally found someone who seemed to have it together like yourself," Joe said. She was touched by his compliment.

"Yeah, well, I'm definitely not perfect. But I want to be a good example for my daughter."

"Tell me more about her. How old is she?" He looked genuinely interested while leaning in closer.

"Five going on 15!" Lisa said, rolling her eyes. Joe laughed. "But seriously though, she is the apple of my eye. It's like every day I see her is a reminder there is hope." Lisa didn't want to get too deep. She didn't want to scare the man away, but she had to be honest about how she felt.

Joe grew serious. "Yea, I know what you mean. It's easy to lose hope sometimes." Joe looked away, and she could tell his mind was elsewhere.

"Well, of course I'm sure you know since that's what you shared about in your poem," she offered. Joe nodded in agreement and the waitress appeared with their meals. They grew quiet while eating and enjoyed the band. Lisa glanced around and saw a few couples move to the dance floor as an upbeat number played. She smiled at an older couple, rocking and swaying slowly to a melody only they could hear. Joe followed her gaze and took the initiative.

"Alright, Ms. Doris. Show me what chew' workin' with!" He rose to his full height and held out his hand. Lisa smiled and let him assist her on the floor. The two became one as they flowed in sync with the music. Lisa let herself relax and have fun, allowing the tension of life to leave her body. Joe held her lower back and smoothly rubbed it with his strong, yet gentle hands.

I could stay here forever, she thought, but eventually, the music ended. The band took a break, and she and Joe took their seats again.

"Well, I'm ready for dessert! How about you?" Joe asked, handing her the dessert menu. He gave her a smile, his dark eyes bright. Lisa accepted it, but knew she had already had her fill.

"I think I'll pass. I'll have a cup of tea though." Joe signaled the waitress and placed their orders. He looked at her thoughtfully.

"You seem like you've had a difficult time lately, Lisa." He stroked the hair on his chin while watching her.

Lisa was surprised at his sensitivity.

"Yeah, well, it's been an interesting year," she said, not making eye contact. "But things are looking up." She added, "I met *you,* didn't I?" She grinned at him, dimple flashing.

"Yea, you *do* have a point!" Joe joked. "I have been told that I'm the highlight on more than one occasion." He looked at her smugly, puffing out his chest in jest.

They both smiled at each other like two high schoolers with a crush. "But seriously, what has helped me through some hard times is my writing and my church community. Do you have a church community, Lisa?"

Lisa was caught off guard by the question. She had never been asked something like that on a date. "Umm, no I don't. I actually haven't been to church since I was a kid," she admitted. With her hands under the table, she smoothed the linen napkin on her lap, thinking for a moment of her previous conversation with Sylvia.

Lisa

Joe nodded, understanding. "Yea, I've found that to be so helpful when I don't know what direction to go in, or I simply need support dealing with life." Their order had arrived, and Lisa let his words sink in as she enjoyed her tea.

"So, why is church helpful for you?" she asked curiously.

Joe smiled, and his face lit up when he talked about church the same way she was sure her face lit up when she talked about Michelle.

"Well, it's encouraging. It gives me the strength and the hope I need to keep moving forward and more importantly, it helps me learn more about this relationship I have with God."

"So, you feel you have a relationship with God?" she asked. Lisa's interest was aroused.

"Yes, definitely. I feel like God is a Person, and He talks to me the way that we are talking right now." Joe gestured to her. To Lisa, he appeared confident without appearing arrogant. It was an attractive quality.

"That sounds like something my friend Sylvia has told me before–that God is a *Person*." Lisa ran her fingers up and down the tea mug slowly, deep in thought.

Joe smiled and finished his German chocolate cake, then wiped his mouth with his napkin, dispensing a few dark crumbs in the process.

"Let me put it this way. I've been through some things, and if it wasn't for my relationship with God, I wouldn't have made it through." Joe found her hand and lightly touched her fingertips, then studied her with his dark eyes.

Lisa felt a warm feeling grow in her belly and move throughout the rest of her body. She didn't know if it was the man or the wine she had earlier, but she felt as if she were being–*hugged*. She exhaled.

"I'd like to go to church with you sometime," she heard herself say.

Joe's face lit up. "I would love that," he said, removing his hand from hers and sitting upright.

Lisa wondered what had gotten into her. *I must really like this dude,* she thought, and decided that one church service couldn't hurt too much.

* * *

Lisa was at Devon's trying to finish up some last-minute touches on her piece, but her mind kept drifting to the two men in her life. For the last three weeks, Michael had been steady in his approach, even though he knew, per Michelle, about "Mommy's friend". Every night after he would talk to Michelle and read her a bedtime story over the phone, he would talk to Lisa. It was like when they were dating again. They had met up a few times for coffee just to talk and he even took off work last Saturday to meet up with her and Michelle at the park. But then

Lisa

she had Joe, who was wining and dining her around the city, taking her to museums, parties, bike rides, and of course, church. Michelle was finally building the spiritual foundation Lisa had desired for her to have. She herself was growing spiritually, *and* she was having a blast. How did she go from not having one man, to having two?

"Lord, what in the world should I do?" she heard herself say. She had been doing that lately–asking God for guidance. That warm feeling in her stomach appeared again, and she felt a peace she couldn't explain, so she decided to pull out the small Bible Joe had given her. She thought it was a very touching gift at the time, but hadn't expected to really use it. So much had changed. She flipped it open, not really knowing where to begin, but her eyes landed on a scripture that seemed to be illuminated:

"Trust in the Lord with all your heart and lean not to your own understanding"- Proverbs 3:5-6.

"Hmmm, I wonder what that means?" she said. She went back to her work but kept the scripture in her heart. Maybe she could ask the Pastor at Joe's church about it tomorrow after service.

* * *

Lisa, Joe and Michelle gathered in front of the church steps with the other congregants. Service had let out and it was nice enough outside for people to chit chat, instead of being cooped up in the foyer.

"Honey, why don't you go play with Andrea's little girl, Dominique?" Lisa suggested. She knew Dominique was a good girl, and it was always nice when Michelle made new friends. She worried about her sometimes being an only child.

"Ok, Mommy!" Lisa watched Michelle run over to the other little girl, and they made up a game of chasing each other by the large maple a few yards away.

"She's adorable," Joe said. "She takes after her momma." He grinned at her. Lisa smiled back, but her smile didn't quite reach her eyes.

"Something wrong?" Joe looked concerned. He was striking in a sharp, navy blue suit and cream tie. His dark skin sparkled like fireworks in the afternoon sun.

"Joe, how do you know that you are hearing the Lord?" Lisa asked hesitantly.

Joe smiled, relieved at her question. "Well, He speaks in many ways, Lisa. He speaks through His Word, in our hearts, through people, through circumstances, even through nature. In fact, I know He told me to connect with you," he revealed. She raised her eyebrows in surprise.

"Really? How do you know that?"

"Well, I didn't know right away, but when I walked you home that night, I felt drawn towards you in a way I'm used to experiencing when I'm supposed to connect with someone.

Also, of course, I was very attracted to you." He smiled at her in uncharacteristic shyness.

Lisa was silent and played with the hem of her yellow, sheath dress. "Why do you think He wanted us to connect, Joe?" She was almost too afraid to ask. What if his thoughts didn't match hers?

Joe grew serious and looked at her pensively. "Well, I stopped a long time ago being presumptuous with God. If I were younger, I would have automatically responded that we were to have a romantic relationship. But I know you have a lot going on and so I've been careful about crossing those boundaries with you." She knew he was right. He had barely kissed her, though he had the opportunity to do more on more than one occasion.

"And I appreciate that, Joe. I really do." The fact that he was such a gentleman and so caring made the choice she knew she had to make even more difficult.

"So, what is it you're hearing from God, Lisa?" He looked at her openly, and she knew that whatever she told him he would respect. "What's on your heart?"

"Lean not to your own understanding but in all your ways acknowledge Him," Lisa said. Joe was both surprised and impressed that she had memorized a passage of scripture.

"Wow! That was in today's sermon," he responded. Lisa nodded slowly, almost painfully. "And what does that mean to you, Lisa?" After her silence he then added, "What does that mean for *us*?" He looked expectantly at her, and she felt her stomach drop. She peered into his charcoal eyes and studied his face, biting her lip.

"It means I need to go back to my husband. I need to work on my marriage." There. She had said it. It was the truth she had been wrestling with for the last few weeks. It was the thing that rested on her heart like a newborn on a mother's chest, soft and endearing, but still weighty.

Joe's eyes lost a little bit of light, but he was more impressed by the maturity she was displaying in her faith. "Well, look at you Lisa! You are hearing God." He touched her chin and smiled reassuringly, though his eyes were dim.

"Yea," she said. "I guess I am."

The two parted ways that day, and Lisa learned to keep not leaning to her own understanding. She didn't understand why God would bring a man into her life as great as Joe when she was going to end up with Michael, but she was learning to trust that warm feeling in the pit of her stomach. She was learning that He always led her in the direction that was in her best interest, and she continued to feel those invisible arms wrapping around her as she walked an unseen path alongside those on a similar journey.

JOE

"Aye, man! Pass the ball!" Joe yelled at the new dude who had joined their team for the first time that day. *Man, this Chris Brown-lookin' dude is killin' it!* Joe thought.

The new guy, aka Chris Brown's look-alike, did a quick pump fake and side-passed the ball to Joe, not even looking in his direction. Nice! Joe caught it and made an easy layup, his long legs carrying him to the net. Swish!

"Dope!" His teammates congratulated him and New Dude slapped him on the butt.

They were up 3-0 but Joe knew the guys they were playing were serious. It was anybody's game. Big Rob was king on the court and was playing center for their opponents. He grabbed the ball in mid-dribble from Ricky.

Joe, seeing Duck open, yelled, "Duck, get him!" But Duck was too slow. Big Rob dunked his 6-foot frame, putting his team on the board.

Joe bent over and wiped sweat from his forehead, using the back of his jersey. He was not the best player on the court, but he was definitely one of the top three. Dave ran the play, and Joe saw that Dave wanted him to set a pick, where he stood behind the point's opposer and planted his feet offensively, acting as an obstacle for the point to run around and also to block the opponent. Dave was point, and he was relying on Joe to come through. Only problem was, when Joe set the pick, Johnny from the other team saw it coming. He easily sidestepped it, staying on his man and knocked the ball out of Dave's hand when he went for the shot.

"Damn!" Joe heard Dave swear, and he ran to the hoop to try to catch the rebound along with a few others, but Big Rob beat them all and was already making his shot. 2-3. The game was first to 10 wins, but it was so competitive that the boys ended up playing for almost an hour until Joe's team finally made it to 10.

"Man, that was raw!" Dave said. He gave Joe a high five.

"Good game, y'all! Fa sho!" Joe, Duck, Dave, Ricky and New Dude (Joe still couldn't remember his name, even after winning) all gave daps and head nods to their competitors. They left the court wearing the grins of victors.

The group decided to do their usual and have lunch at the burger joint down the street. They were musty and sweating something fierce in the hot June heat, but they didn't care one bit. They were winners.

"Yo, son. Did you see that spin Earl did around Chris? He nailed it!" Dave said, giving Earl, aka Chris Brown's look alike, credit for his basketball skills.

Man, I'm glad somebody *finally said that dude's name!* Joe thought to himself.

"Yea, did you see that pass tho? He whipped it like Lebron!" Joe jumped in, giving his own imitation of a Lebron pass.

Earl grinned and lifted his long arms in a shrug. "Aww, you know! I do what I do!"

The young men ambled their way down the street, joking and reliving their game. Joe loved Saturday afternoons like these. It was nothing like time with his boys and getting a good workout to relieve a stressful work week. It had taken him a minute to meet some people in Manhattan, but he started going to the basketball court near his house a few months ago when Dave had invited him to join their team. The group made an effort to play at least twice a month, and they usually faced off against Big Rob and whoever he was rolling with.

Joe breathed in deeply and smiled upward. Life was good. He had a good home, a good job, and some cool people to hang with. He hardly missed home, but when he did, he remembered why he was there: purpose.

"Yo, son. You bet not order those onion rings! You know they be stankin'!" Ricky was giving Duck a hard time once again. They were brothers and always going at it.

"Dawg, quit ridin' me, and don't worry 'bout what I do! I'm sayin'. Let me do me," Duck retorted.

Joe smiled and chuckled to himself. They were seated in their normal booth that looked out the window towards MLK Boulevard. The restaurant had a 1960's theme, which was accentuated with red-top stools and waitresses who skated over to take customer's orders. James Brown's *Papas' Got a Brand New Bag* played over the speaker.

"Hey, what y'all want today?" Latisha sashayed over on skates, popping her gum and positioning her pen to take the regulars' orders. She cocked her head to the side, her long braids cascading over her shoulder.

"Aye, Tish! Let me get a chocolate shake," Duck said.

"Yo, I want one too!" Dave said

"Yea, me too!" Ricky joined in.

"Ok, make that *five* chocolate shakes," Duck said, holding up his hand. "And uh... five double mega burgers, four orders of fries..." He paused, before looking at his brother out of the corner of his eye. "And an order of onion rings!"

"Aww man!" Ricky said, causing the table to erupt with laughter.

Latisha laughed too. She figured they must have won their game since they were in such a good mood. "Aight' y'all. I'll be back in a sec." She skated off towards the counter to put in their orders.

"Man, baby girl is *thick*!" Earl said, once Latisha was out of earshot. Three heads simultaneously turned in her direction to check out her backside. It took everything in Joe not to take a peek himself.

"Ohhh, he comin' for yo giiiiiirl!" Dave said to Ricky. He cupped his hand over his mouth as if he were an announcer at a sports game.

"My bad, dawg! I didn't know," Earl quickly said to Ricky.

"Awe, man! He *wish* he could get wit' Tish!" Duck said. "He been hollerin' at shawty for two years and *still* ain't got no play!"

"Bruh, really? You gon' play me like that? You know I got those digits!" Ricky said, giving his brother the side eye.

"Yea, but chew' ain't did nothin' wit em'!" Duck responded.

"That's cuz I'm takin' my time, fam!" Ricky slouched back in his seat and folded his arms, placing his hands under his sweaty armpits.

"Man, you a lie. You know she hooked on Marcus down the way, and she ain't *never* gon' give it up for nobody else!" Dave said, and the boys started laughing again.

"Ain't nobody thinking about Marcus." Ricky smacked his teeth, his light brown skin turning red. Joe felt bad for the brother, even though he was enjoying the banter.

"So, where you come from, man? I never seen you before today," Joe asked Earl to take the heat off Ricky.

"Yea, I live down the way. I just hadn't been to the court yet. I used to stay in Brooklyn and so that's where I would hoop," Earl explained.

"Well, you got mad game. You should join us in the tournament this summer. We could always use some fresh talent," Dave said, giving Earl an appreciative look.

"Dope. When is it?" Earl asked.

"Next month. First place is a cash prize and a percentage goes to the Urban Youth Center," Joe answered, while rubbing his six pack underneath his Knicks jersey. He was so hungry, he could feel his stomach rumbling through his shirt.

Earl grabbed his chest and leaned over the table excitedly. "Cool, I'm down. I could always use some cash!" Latisha came back with their shakes, and Joe noticed Earl keeping his eyes to himself.

"Thanks, Tish," Ricky said, his butterscotch face breaking into a huge grin.

Latisha smiled, "You welcome, Ricky." She went about her business.

"See!" Duck said. "No play!" He shook his head.

"Man, whateva!" Ricky proclaimed, swatting his hand at Duck. "Yo, my boy T. P is spinning tonight," he added, changing the subject.

"Aww, that dude is a beast!" Duck said, "I'm fa sho' down."

"Now you know I got the Mrs. I gotta check wit," Dave said. "Tina probably ain't gone want me out tonight since I was out last weekend." He gave the group a look, indicating he didn't think it was likely he could make it out.

"Aww, you on lock!" Ricky taunted.

"Yea, and proud of it!" Dave shot back.

Joe laughed with the rest of them, but there was a dull ache in his heart. He wouldn't mind being committed to someone himself. He drank his chocolate milkshake and stretched his long, dark legs under the table. He felt his high from the win coming down but didn't want to bring the others down with him.

Latisha showed up with their order, and the men grew quiet as they dug into their food. No silverware was needed.

Their appetites wouldn't allow them to even take a break from inhaling one item after another. Earl let out a loud belch, and everybody started laughing.

"My bad! Guess I was hungrier than I thought!" he said, looking embarrassed.

"It's cool my man! You in good company," Joe said for the group. He assessed Earl and saw the young man had several tattoos on each arm that looked to have been homemade.

He probably had a friend do 'em, Joe thought.

Everybody had on Jordans and Air Force 1's, but Earl had regular shoes on, probably from Walmart.

That didn't seem to stop his whip skills tho', Joe thought to himself. *I bet he could really do some damage if he had a good pair of sneakers!*

"So, Joe, you down tonight, brotha?" Ricky resurfaced their earlier topic. Joe didn't normally hang out with these guys in that scene, but for some reason he was feeling a little lonely and he didn't have any plans for the evening.

"What time?" he heard himself say.

"Whaaaat!! Joe comin' out tonight?" Dave looked surprised. "I might have to turn up wit' y'all then!" he said. Another round of laughter hit the table.

"About 10PM. We can get there early to get some seats in the VIP area. T.P will hook us up," Ricky said.

"Alright, that's cool. I'll let you know if my plans change," Joe said, not wanting to fully commit.

"Aight', bet!" Ricky answered.

* * *

Joe looked in his bathroom mirror while he shaved. *Not bad*, he thought, rubbing the short stubs on his chin. His dark complexion was adorned with thick brows, a slender nose (inherited from his Seminole ancestors), and full lips. He liked his fade just right and regardless of what his boys said, he made sure to keep his nails manicured. He had no problem getting women, it was just the right woman that seemed difficult to find.

"Lord, what is the deal?" He looked up at the ceiling. No response. He didn't really expect one. In every single area of his life, he felt God's leading, but when it came to *this* one—crickets. He had hoped Lisa was the one, especially when she started growing in her faith, but he had to respect the choice she made. He wiped off the remaining water on his back and tied the white towel closer to his waist. He would need to hurry up if he didn't want to be late. His phone blared Neo-Soul as he fingered through his fully stocked closet. Anthony Hamilton's smooth baritone flooded the airwaves while he searched:

It's simple, I love it, having you near me, having you here

Our conversations, outrageous

You smile, and I smile then I say

Now, what am I going to wear? Joe thought to himself.

He settled on light, distressed jean shorts, a pink collared shirt rolled up at the elbows and unbuttoned at the neck, a thick herringbone chain, and his favorite Prada shoes. He made his way down three flights of stairs and onto the sidewalk leading out of his apartment. It was Saturday night and everybody knew it. Cars drove by blasting loud music, young women scantily dressed switched by, and street artists were out doing their thing. Joe loved New York most of the time for this very reason. "It's poppin'!" he observed, looking around. He started walking the 20 minutes it took to get to the club, lost in his thoughts. For some reason the young man that he had met earlier that day, Earl, was heavy on his heart.

"Aye, look who's here!" Joe could hear Ricky's voice before he saw him. Their group was posted up in a spacious corner booth. A large bucket with ice and drinks was positioned in the center of the table.

"Hey! How y'all doin'?" Joe's spirits lifted when he saw the warm welcome everyone gave him. All the boys from their team were there and then some. Even Dave had made it out.

"Man, we didn't think you was comin'!" Dave said, standing to give him dap.

"I didn't think *you* was comin'!" Joe joked. "Tina know you out past yo bedtime?"

Everybody laughed.

Ricky introduced the rest of the crew. Joe gave head nods to the fellas and took in their clothes. *Everybody has on their grown man wear*, he observed, and he was glad he had picked what he had. *I definitely need to up my game tho*, he thought to himself, as he took in Donte's gold and leather Versace watch. *That's gotta be the newest one!*

The place was filling up, and the loc wearing DJ, who Joe guessed must be T.P, was starting to change up the style from laid back to new school hip hop. After a few drinks, some of the guys started getting their courage to ask some ladies to the dance floor. Joe stayed in the booth, taking inventory and watched his surroundings.

"So, you think you gon' get out there?" A seductive voice whispered in his ear. He looked up to see an equally seductive woman. Light skin, slender, and wearing a pleather jumper that revealed her butt cheeks, she crouched over him like a cat does its prey.

Joe smiled politely. "Aww, you know I'm just waiting for my song."

Instead of backing off, she pushed harder, crawling her long, oval-shaped nails over his arm.

"Oh, come on now. This is *my* song, and I need a dance partner." She gave him a fake pout thinking it was attractive. It wasn't.

"Yo, I'll dance wit' chew!" Earl piped up. He had just strolled in and sat down by Joe in the midst of their exchange. The woman turned her gaze toward Earl, took in his plain white T and knock-off jeans, and decided he wasn't worth the twerk she had planned on giving.

"That's cool, honey. I'm good." She lifted her chin and walked off with a delusional air of arrogance.

Earl smacked his teeth, angrily. "I didn't want her ass anyway! I was tryin' to help *her* out," he said, obviously trying to save face.

"Yo, man, that woman is not the type of female you want to kick it with. Any woman that approaches *you*—especially in a group of men— is too brazen for her own good," Joe said. He reached over and grabbed his drink from the table, taking a long appreciative sip.

Earl thought about what Joe said, and nodded slowly. He had never been taught to have standards with women. It was all about getting with whoever would say 'yes' to what he was offering, which was usually a fun night with no strings attached.

The mood changed in the atmosphere when a slow song hit, and Joe looked around. *Everybody bumpin' and grindin'*, he observed with a sigh, and decided this was a good time to go use the bathroom. On his way out of the stall, he was thinking about leaving, when all of a sudden, he ran smack dab into a young woman leaving the ladies' room.

"Oh, my bad! I'm so sorry!" Joe saw that he had knocked over the drink in her hand, and it was already staining her white dress. His eyes grew wide in horror as he watched her bend over and shake the top of her dress away from her skin, trying to keep the liquid from running down the rest of it.

"Here, let me help you with that!" He immediately ran into the men's room and came out with a hand full of paper towels. She looked up to meet his eyes for the first time. She was beautiful. Hazel eyes with honey brown skin and a petite frame.

"Thank you." She held out her hands for the paper towels and Joe, for the first time in his life, was at a loss for words. He couldn't stop staring. "Let me get some club soda for you. I'm sure we can get that stain out," he finally managed.

"Good idea," she muttered with a heavy breath, clearly annoyed.

She followed his lead, and they made their way to the bar. Joe kept glancing out of the corner of his eye to make sure she was behind him. It was so crowded, and he didn't want to lose her. When the bartender finally got open, Joe ordered the drink.

"You want anything else besides the club soda?" He was hoping she would say 'yes'. Anything to stay in her presence.

"Umm, I think I'm ok, but thanks." Joe tried not to show his disappointment. The young woman worked feverishly to scrub the club soda into her dress. Joe wanted to help, but the bulk of the stain was near her chest area, and he had already had one slip up that night, he didn't need another.

"Well, thanks for the help." She offered him a polite smile after a few minutes of scrubbing, but was already turning away. A current shot through him, and he knew he had to get to know her.

"So, what's your name?" he ventured. She took a second before answering, probably trying to decide if she wanted to spark up a conversation with some random dude in the club who spilled her drink on her.

"Nina. My name is Nina." His attempt at helping her must have given him points, Joe decided.

"Nice to meet you, Nina. My name is Joe." He held out a hand, and she half-smiled when taking it, but her eyes still seemed guarded.

"Look, my friends are waiting for me, so I should probably get back to them," she said, while trying to peer on the other side of the club. There were so many people, and she was so short, Joe doubted she could see them.

"Well, I would definitely like to redeem myself and make it up to you for my awful mishap tonight. Could I at least get one dance out of the deal?"

"Oh, so you gon' pay me with dance moves? You must be a really good dancer!" Nina shot back. She was quick.

"Yea, you know. I do my 1-2." Joe moved from side to side to demonstrate, inducing a laugh from her. It was music to his ears.

Nina was hesitant. "Umm, yea…I guess *one* dance won't hurt. I'm just hoping this stain doesn't set in. I probably won't stay too long if it does." She looked down at her dress.

Joe's eyes pleaded with her to believe him, while he held up his hands in front of him. "My bad about that. I didn't see you at all."

"It's cool." She gave in to his persistence. "Come on, let's dance." She grabbed his hand, and the pair made their way on the floor. It was right on time too because Joe's song from back in the day came on: Notorious B.I.G's "Hypnotize".

That was my jam! Joe thought, then let loose on the floor with Nina. They danced so well together they ended up staying on the floor for another couple of 90's hits.

"Man, it's been a while since I got it in like that! And I guess you did pay me back with those moves!" Nina said. She pulled her loose waves from around her neck and wiped sweat from her brow. The couple leaned up against a wall while the party kept going.

Joe chuckled. "Thanks! I feel you! Same for me!" Joe dazzled her with a smile and admired her features: large, round brown eyes, cute little button nose, and a heart-shaped face. "How 'bout we go outside to get some air and cool off?" he offered, trying to be heard over the music. She once again looked for her friends, and after figuring that finding them was an impossible feat, she decided to text them instead.

"Ok. Let me just let my girls know what I'm up to." She revealed her phone from a secret compartment in her dress (Joe didn't know how women did stuff like that) and swiftly sent a message. He led her outside and they found a bench near the front of the club. Joe cleared off some dirt he saw on the bench, not wanting her to do more damage to her dress. He was relieved to see that the stain was fading.

"So, Nina. Tell me about yourself." He swung an arm on the bench, leaning back as she crossed her legs. A slight breeze emerged and kissed them both.

"Well, I'm a nurse. I work at St. Vincent's hospital, and I've been there five years."

"That's dope. That means you're selfless and caring." Nina raised her eyebrows in surprise.

"Yea, I definitely love taking care of people and helping them heal." While listening to Nina, Joe started feeling something he hadn't felt before with a woman. It felt like— familiarity.

Joe

"Healing is needed, both internally and externally," he offered.

Nina's brown eyes widened. "I completely agree. I can only do so much for the outside of a person, but I always hope that my presence in my job will help to bring much more than that. I believe we need faith to get that full healing," Nina said.

Joe got excited but didn't want to scare her away. "Yea, I agree. My faith is very important to me, and I don't know where I would be without it," he shared.

She looked at him pleased, and he knew there was going to be so much more to look forward to in getting to know Ms. Nina.

* * *

"So, what you're saying, is that the last five fiscal years' revenues have a steady decline?" Joe asked his client. The balding man placed both pudgy hands over his belly after smoothing down his red tie. He was embarrassed, and Joe knew it simply because many of his clients were. They came to him, unfortunately, when all else had failed.

Mr. Wells took a drink of water from a glass and swallowed his pride. "Er, umm, yea. We've seen a decrease, and we're just not sure where to take it from here," he sputtered out.

Joe admired the corner office with its glistening, mahogany wood and immaculate view of the city. 20 stories high in any building normally depicts vision and drive. Mr. Wells seemed to be running out of both.

"Honestly, Mr. Wells, I have seen companies with worse figures," Joe said, glancing over the financial reports. "And you'll be glad to know that we have been able to cause sinking ships to once again, get afloat."

Mr. Wells raised both thin eyebrows and leaned in across the desk. "Is that so?" he asked thoughtfully.

"Yes, sir," Joe responded with confidence. "We have a great team who can analyze not only your industry's challenges, business structure and future desired projections, but we can assist you in meeting those numbers. We want your company's values and vision to reflect the heart behind its purpose." For the first time since Joe entered his office, Mr. Wells seemed hopeful.

"Now, what I'm going to do is take your file and create a portfolio of recommendations. If you're interested, you can hire us to implement our proposal, or another team can do it. We will charge two separate fees. It's up to you."

"Well now, that sounds fair. You know my guys over at the golf course recommended your company and said you were one of the most reputable firms in the city!" Mr. Wells stood to his feet with a smile.

"That's great to hear, sir. We do aim to please!" Joe smiled in return.

After the meeting, Joe was led down the hallway by Mr. Wells' secretary. A tall redhead with cat eye glasses. She gave him a flirtatious smile as he maneuvered onto the elevator. Joe chuckled, feeling flattered. When he stepped out of the swanky building, he finally let himself rejoice.

"Yes!" he let out, and gained a few stares from fellow New Yorkers. Unbothered, he walked with a pep in his step all the way back to the office.

"So, how did it go?" Wendy, the new hire asked him.

"It's in the bag." Joe smiled at her excitedly. He was certain Mr. Wells was on board. *I just need to kill the portfolio*, he thought while heading back to his cubicle. Once there, he started typing immediately. It wasn't until an hour later that he took a break and checked his cell.

Joe, was wondering if I could get some advice from you. Hit me up when you get a chance.

He had received a text from Earl. For some reason the young man had been on his heart heavy, so he wasn't that surprised to hear from him.

Bet! He replied. Then he saw another one that perked him up.

I had a great time last night. Just wanted to thank you for the great conversation.

Nina. They had met last night for a night cap, and it went really well. He found out she was living in New York to help out her mother who was sick. His heart went out to her.

I thoroughly enjoyed your company! I'll be calling soon. He sent the smiley face emoji. The rest of the day flew by as he worked diligently on his portfolio. By five o'clock he felt satisfied.

"How'd that meeting go today with Mr. Wells?" His boss, Dick, was standing over the cubicle in expectancy. Overly anal and always business, Dick was typically difficult to please, but Joe seemed to have won him over.

"It went great, sir. I'm finishing up our proposal now and will have it on your desk ASAP to review." Joe looked up and gave him a thumbs up sign.

"Excellent! I knew I could count on you, Joe! One of our best!" Dick was already walking away before Joe could acknowledge his praise. The man was a firecracker.

Joe smiled, swiveled in his chair, and cocked his head back in satisfaction.

* * *

That evening Joe came home and immediately started to get ready to hook up with Earl.

I wonder wuz up with him? he thought to himself, while removing his blue-grey, plaid Brooks Brothers suit and tie. The only sense he could get was that something was wrong. He told Earl he would meet him at Devon's, and, true to his word, he made it there a few minutes early.

"Hey, wuz up, Joe!" Devon was working the cash register and welcomed him with a smile.

"Wuz up, man!" Joe said, giving him dap.

"Haven't seen you in a while! How you been?"

"I'm hanging, man. Doing my thing. Stayin' busy." Joe took a seat at the counter. It was a quiet Monday night and not too many people were there. Slow, cool jazz flowed through the speaker, easing Joe's mind.

"Oh yea? When you gon' lace us wit' some of that good good?" Devon asked, referring to how good Joe's poetry was. He proceeded to wipe down a spot behind the bar.

"When's y'all's next open mic?" Joe asked, resting an arm on the bar and loosely clasping one hand over the other.

"Oh, it's still first Fridays. We definitely wanna hear what you spittin',' man." Devon smiled with kind eyes. He had a medium build with brown skin and a streak of grey that gave him a distinguished look.

"Aight', this Friday then."

"Cool. Can I get you something?" Devon waved a hand behind the coffee bar. Just then, Earl shuffled through the door. Joe met his eyes and nodded him over to the counter.

"Yea, uh, lemme holla at my man first," Joe said to Devon.

"Ok. Cool."

"Aye, wuz up, bruh?" Joe stood as Earl made his way to him.

"Yo, man. You think we could sit in the back somewhere?" The young man had a cap pulled low over his face and was shifting from side to side with his hands jammed in his pockets. His jeans had a hole in them and not the kind that were fashionable. Upon closer inspection, Joe saw he had a black eye.

"Yea, bruh. Whatever you want." Joe led him to a table in the back that was more private.

"So, how you doin'?" Joe evaluated him. *This dude looks bad.* Earl folded his hands on the table, keeping his head down and Joe noticed the scars on his knuckles.

"I been better. Thanks for meeting with me."

"No doubt." Joe waited for Earl to share, but when he didn't, he figured he may need a little help in opening up.

"Why don't I get us some coffee?" he suggested.

Earl looked relieved. "Yea, that a be good."

Joe got up and put in their order. A few minutes later he came back with two steaming cups. Earl began fiddling with the sugar packs, then dumped in the contents. "I'm not sure what to do," he finally said. "I got myself into some trouble, and I need money. Bad." Joe nodded for him to continue.

"Remember when I said I moved from Brooklyn?" the younger man asked.

"Yeah, I remember."

"Well, I actually moved from Brooklyn Penitentiary." Earl lowered his gaze and played with the black and silver mug on the table that read "Devon's" in large cursive lettering. Earl snuck a peak at Joe's face, fearful of rejection. Understanding flooded Joe, and all the pieces were starting to come together. He nodded his head for Earl to continue.

"I was locked up and just got out. That's when I moved to Manhattan. I been trying to stay clean, but now…" His voice trailed off, and he looked away. Joe gave him time. Both men sipped their coffee and let the soothing atmosphere of Devon's wash over them.

"Some dudes I owed came after me. They ruffed me up, and they want what I owe. I don't know what to do." He kept his gaze low and slumped his shoulders, all the while drumming his fingers on the table nervously.

"You working?" Joe asked.

Earl looked at him with frustration. "You know how hard it is to get a job with a record? I do little odds and ends here and there, but nothin' stable."

Joe's mind was racing. "What you good at? What you like to do?"

"Fixing cars. I'm good at that. And pretty much anything with my hands. I can build and fix almost anything."

"Ok. Well, I'm a look into some contacts and see what I can do." Joe looked at him encouragingly.

Earl's eyes flooded with gratitude. "Thanks, man. I really wasn't sure if I should reach out. I mean, I know we don't know each other all like that, but I felt like I needed some type of guidance 'cuz everybody I know is on what I used to be on. You know?"

"Oh, I know. I definitely know. I'm glad you did too. We need to have each other's backs in this society. If we don't, who will?" Joe said reassuringly.

Earl slowly nodded. "Yea, I guess you right. I'm just not sure of what to do in the meantime. I mean, even if I get something steady, it'll take me awhile to get the kind of money I need."

"How much you need?" Joe said, taking a sip.

Earl hesitated. "Five stacks," he mumbled.

Joe nearly choked on his coffee. "Five thousand dollars?"

"Keep it down, man!" Earl looked around anxiously at the nearly empty cafe. "Yea, I mean, that's what it is." He shrugged his shoulders and bowed his head like a puppy being chastised.

"Dawg, I don't know. That's a lot of money." Joe's mind was racing. How could he help his friend get that kind of money? Legally?

"Yea. I'm in a bind. I had some product, and since I got caught, the police impounded it so I couldn't sell it. Now I owe it."

"Man. I'ma think about that and see what I can do. It's gon' be aight' tho. When you need it by?" Joe scrunched up his lips in thought and furrowed his brows deeply.

"As soon as possible. These dudes ain't no joke. If I don't get it ASAP, you might not see me again." Joe let that resonate, and the two young men sat in silence until both cups were empty.

Lord, what should I do? he thought. The answer came to him fast and clear.

* * *

Devon's was at its normally full capacity for a Friday night. People loitered in the front door or chit chatted on the sidewalk,

Stories For the (Urban) Soul

waiting for the show to begin. Joe walked in holding Nina's hand. She looked good, dressed in a black romper with a thick silver belt and silver open-toed heels. Joe had on a black tee, gold chain with a cross on it, and calf length white shorts. He guided her inside and introduced her to a few regulars, many of whom he hadn't seen in a while, since he had taken a break from Devon's after the whole Lisa thing.

"Let me get that for you," Joe said, pulling out a chair for Nina. It was one of the few available.

"Thanks." She smiled and sat down. She was a beauty, and he was enjoying their budding relationship.

"So, do you come here often?" she asked him innocently.

"Umm, I used to, but it's been a while. You want me to get you somethin'?" Joe asked, changing the subject. "Yea,

I'll take an iced chai tea latte."

"One chai comin' right up!" He stood to make his way to the counter and noticed that the cutie with the big mouth was working tonight.

"Excuse me, Miss. Can I put in an order?" Joe asked her. She started to turn around from her post of putting away mugs.

"Sure, what can I..." Her voice trailed off. She clearly recognized him. "I'm sorry, what can I get chew'? Joe, right?"

"Yea, that's right." He was surprised she remembered him. "How about two iced chai tea lattes please."

"Ok, no doubt." She turned her back and started working on the drinks. "So, you talked to Lisa lately?" she asked, when presenting him with his order.

Joe stole a glance at her name tag and shifted from one foot to the other, doing an uncomfortable dance. "Uh, naw, Denise. Not really. You?" *No this chick didn't,* he thought to himself. The audacity to bring up his ex like that. *Petty.*

"Yea, actually she was in here last week. But apparently she won't be making it tonight." Denise gave him a facetious half-smile while studying his reaction.

Joe sighed inwardly and tried not to look relieved. "Oh, ok, cool. Well, tell her I said 'hi'." He swiftly confiscated the finished drinks before turning away. He heard Denise chuckle, but was too nervous to even acknowledge any response she had given.

"Here you go, Ms. Lady." Joe slid the cups onto their table and Nina cupped her chai.

"Thanks. I'm excited to see you do your thing tonight!" She looked at him eagerly and Joe felt his heartbeat speed up.

"Yea. I'm a little nervous, but I love the release poetry gives me."

"Cool. I haven't written since I was a kid, but maybe you will inspire me tonight."

"You already inspire me," he couldn't help saying. The site of her lips curling upward put him at ease and he breathed out deeply. *Lisa who?* he thought with an internal grin.

"How y'all doin' tonight?" Chuck was at the front greeting the audience who, in turn, clapped and cheered. "Good, good. Y'all know what time it is! It's poetry night here at Devon's, and we only have a few rules. 1. Be respectful. Everybody deserves a chance to be heard. 2. Snap don't clap. And 3. Buy some more coffee while you enjoy the talent!" The audience laughed.

The first poet was an older woman with a sweet smile. She was clearly a beginner, but her charm was infectious. Joe snapped along with everyone else when she was done. It went on like that for a while with one poet after another, until finally he was up.

"Hey y'all, I'm Joe!" He beamed at the crowd as his eyes searched for Nina's. "I want to share this poem that was recently written about someone special." He cleared his throat before beginning.

I think I was a sojourner on the way

And then I stopped to see the Master forming you, and I could not look a-way

I was compelled to admire the working, working, working of your inner man

Joe

Birthed out of love

Clothed with beauty

You are a sight

You are the sky and I am a flight

You are a dream and I am the night

You are a Queen and I am a Knight

How can I fight for you my lady?

How can I cause the downfall of your enemies to make myself worthy of serving in your court?

What courageous gesture qualifies one of your love?

Fascination and Intrigue guide me by the hand

I walk slowly

I transform

My battle-ridden armor falls, by the wayside

A crown is placed upon my head

I am positioned, by your side

I am hidden–in your smile

I am lost—in your thoughts

And swim happily there

No longer am I a sojourner

I am a man

I am your king

He heard the snaps and encouraging comments but really only wanted to see Nina's reaction. Her smile was huge, and he knew she was pleased.

"You did so good!" Nina greeted him when he made it back to the table. She stretched her 5-foot 1 frame and captured him in a warm hug.

"Thank you!" His chocolate features were grinning from ear to ear. The couple enjoyed the rest of the night talking and hearing the other poets. They went for ice cream after and Joe took her to his favorite spot. On the walk home he kept her near him, not wanting the evening to end.

"This is me," she said, as they stood in front of a large apartment complex. Joe wasn't sure which floor she was on, but he guessed it would come off presumptuous if he offered to walk her inside, so he refrained.

"Well, I had a good time." He peered down into her eyes. A few young teenagers stood down the street rapping about God knows what, but to Joe, it felt like they were the only ones on the planet.

"Yea, me too," Nina said, smiling coyly. She looked at him in that way a woman looks at a man, and he knew what to do. He lifted her chin gently and drew her lips to his.

* * *

Joe was in his living room decked in a navy-blue suit, yellow shirt and solid grey tie.

I hope she likes these flowers, he thought, and swiped the dozen yellow roses off his dinner table. Nina said her mom loved yellow. He steadied his hand while turning off the bedroom light. It had been a while since he had met a girl's parents, but he felt confident in the direction he and Nina were headed in. It was a good half hour to Joe's destination and he didn't want to perspire before he made it there, so he hailed a cab.

"**On my way,**" he texted Nina.

"**Great! Can't wait!**" Nina texted back with the heart emoji.

Joe made it to the restaurant in record time and hopped out of the cab.

"There you are!" Nina greeted him at the door, and he was once again smitten. She had on a beige A-line skirt that reached mid-calf, a V-neck pink top that crossed at the chest, and pearl-colored high heeled sandals. Her light brown hair was piled high on top of her head in loose curls and her ears dangled with large hoops. He embraced her.

"And you must be Nina's sister," Joe said, addressing an older-looking version of Nina. Mrs. Cole, dressed in a loose navy dress with low heels, poured out a hearty laugh.

"Ah, Nina, you said he was handsome, but I didn't know he was blind!" Joe laughed and handed her the flowers.

"These are for you, Mrs. Cole."

"Why thank you, Joe. It's a pleasure to meet you!" Mrs. Cole replied, eyes sparkling. She hugged the flowers close and inhaled deeply, running her nostrils over the tops. Her face filled with pleasure and Joe was glad he had bought them.

They were led by the hostess to a booth with a white tablecloth and candle. Joe let the ladies slide in before he joined them; Nina sat in the middle. The trio was greeted quickly by a server and placed an order for drinks and appetizers which came in record time.

"So, Joe, how is it that you have come to know my little girl?" Mrs. Cole asked, looking at Nina fondly. Joe and Nina locked eyes and shared a smile, as if they had a secret only they knew.

"Oh, she didn't tell you?" Joe replied in a humorous tone.

"Well, it's not a story I'm super excited to tell!" Nina said.

"What? You embarrassed we met at a club?" he asked, giving her a hard time.

"Whaaat? My baby girl was at a club?" Mrs. Cole feigned shock.

"Momma, you know I don't be out there like that!" Nina laughed.

"Yea, she be at the club every night!" Joe joked.

The server arrived with plates full of steak, salmon and veggies, so everyone started to partake. Joe noticed that even with the physical resemblance between the two women, he could still see touches of Mrs. Cole's illness. Her movements were slower and a corner of her mouth drooped.

"Mind if I help you with that, Momma?" Nina offered, already moving to do just that. Her mother was having a hard time opening some packets of sugar for her coffee due to a tremor in her left hand.

"Yes, honey. Thank you." Nina was in caregiving mode and Joe saw the ease with which she transitioned into it. This made her even more attractive to him.

"Now, what's this about a club?" Mrs. Cole had not forgotten their discussion.

"Umm, yea. So, we met at a club," Joe started.

"And actually, I was just thinking about leaving," Nina interjected.

"Naw! I was about to leave myself!" Joe said, shocked.

"But this brotha runs smack dab into me and knocks my drink all over my dress!" Nina said, shaking her head emphatically.

"Umm, I'm pretty sure she set me up. See, she knew I was coming out the bathroom just at that time, and she positioned herself just so she could play damsel in distress!" Joe jumped in. Nina's eyes grew wide and Mrs. Cole was so tickled by their interaction that she accidently kicked her daughter under the table. Joe laughed happily, his deep smooth voice caressing the airwaves over their intimate table.

"You know you ain't right, Joe Banks!" Nina said.

"Ok, ok. She's right. I knocked over her drink and we went to get some club soda to clean her up."

"Then he offers to pay me with his dance moves." Nina was shaking her head vigorously now and grinning.

"And then what happened?" Mrs. Cole looked intrigued at the two and took a sip of coffee.

"Then she swept me off my feet," Joe said matter of factly. He reached over the table and captured Nina's hand in his. "AndI haven't been the same since."

* * *

Later on that evening, Joe and Nina walked hand in hand at the park across from her house. They had gotten her mom settled in the house after dinner.

"I think she likes you," Nina said. She smiled up at him, her honey skin radiant under the stars.

"Yea, I'm sure she likes all yo dudes," Joe teased her.

"Yea, she does," Nina shot back.

"Hey!" Joe stopped walking and picked her up around the waist, pretending to be upset. Nina laughed and wiggled out of his grasp.

"Ok, ok! I'm just playin'!" She grinned at him. "You the only one in my life, Joe." she said huskily, her voice thick with emotion. Joe's heart melted, then he looked down at Nina and stroked her cheek.

"Same here." He was just contemplating making a move when her cell rang.

Nina looked down at the screen and picked up. "Hey, Momma. Yea, we outside across the street. Yea, I'm 'bout to be up in a few. Ok. Bye."

"She needs help with her bath." She looked at Joe apologetically.

"No worries. I had a good time tonight, Nina." He turned in the direction of her apartment as they walked, still hand in hand. For Joe, touching Nina felt like being able to touch a star in the sky.

"Me too," she sighed. "Call me when you make it home. I should be free."

"Definitely." Joe kissed her forehead, feeling the moment had passed for more, and watched her walk inside the building. *Yes*! He couldn't resist doing a little dance on the sidewalk then looked around to see if anyone noticed. Only a few young men down the way were blaring their music and loitering outside the liquor store. He decided to walk the rest of the way home since he was full of energy. Checking his phone, he saw he had a few missed phone calls from Earl, as well as a text.

Man, when you get this holla at me ASAP.

Joe gave Earl a call. "Yo, dawg, wuz up?"

"Aye, man. Remember that stuff I told you about last month?"

"Yea. How could I forget? Wuz up with it?"

"Well, you know I been working for the Robertsons repairing cars which, thank you for that gig by the way, and I been saving. I got about half saved. But umm, these dudes is expecting the rest by tomorrow. You think you could spot me a loan? I'm good for it, man. I promise I'll pay you back ASAP. You can even work it out with the Robertsons to take it straight outta my checks!" Earl was talking a mile a minute and it was taking Joe a moment to process and switch gears.

"My dude, that's some heavy cash. Ima have to think about it."

"Yea. I understand. Thanks anyway," Earl said, sounding disappointed.

"Aye, I didn't say 'no'. I just mean I gotta think about it. When you need it by?" Joe asked quickly.

"By one o'clock. I'm supposed to make the drop by then."

"Aight'. Let me hit you up tomorrow then." Joe scrolled through his phone calendar to set a reminder.

"Ok. And thanks, man. I really appreciate everything you've done for me." Joe hung up and made the rest of his journey. He knew what was on his heart as far as what he should do. He just hoped it was the right thing.

* * *

"Mr. Banks, don't forget our two o'clock today with Mr. Wells. This baby is ready to be born!" Dick peeked into Joe's cubicle and gave him a good 'ol boys wink.

"Yes, sir! I'm ready for delivery!" Joe responded.

Dick was already halfway down the hall. Joe was looking forward to the meeting. The client loved his portfolio and decided to go with his firm to implement it. Because of their decision, Joe would see a nice bonus in his next paycheck. They were on stage two of the business plan and if all went well, he would move from second in command on the project to lead.

"Hey, Wendy. Can you let me know if anything changes with our meeting today? I need to make a run on lunch, and I'll just meet Dick at the client's." Wendy instantly perked up at his attention.

"Sure, Joe! I'll shoot you a text if that's the case." She pulled a few strands of her blunt, red haircut behind her ear and smiled shyly.

"Thanks! I appreciate that." Joe was grateful that Wendy seemed to always be reliable. *I'm gonna have to look out for her when the time comes,* he thought to himself. Briefcase in one hand and his suit jacket in the other, he took long, decisive strides out of the building. It was a warm day; the sun was shining, and Joe felt on top of the world.

Maybe I'll pick up some flowers tonight for Nina. Just because, he thought, while flagging down a cab.

"54th and Clark please," Joe told the cab driver. *I definitely need some wheels to take care of this business and make sure I get back in time for my meeting,* he thought, while taking a peek at his watch.

"No doubt," the older, Black man said from the front.

"On my way." Joe sent a text and sat back to think over his key points for his upcoming meeting.

"Thanks. I'm already here," Earl responded.

Twenty minutes later Joe arrived in front of an old, broke down structure that resembled a warehouse but was actually an apartment building.

"Aye, man, I'm only gon' be here for a sec. Can you wait around a bit?" Joe asked the driver, sending him a hopeful look.

"I'll give you 15 minutes. If it's longer than that, you gon' need another cab." The older man was looking around nervously, and Joe understood his urgency.

"Aight', man. Thanks." Joe slipped him some extra cash and glanced around. He saw a parking lot across the street with a few cars in it. Nobody was hanging in this neighborhood, and he could see why. He would have preferred to make the drop somewhere else, but time was short and Earl was already there. Joe's senses were alert and he realized he probably should have brought some protection, just in case, but it was too late now.

Lord, be with me! He said a quick prayer.

Joe took in the graffiti and grit that decked the halls when walking inside. He almost tripped over a bulge on the floor. When the bulge rolled over, he saw the face of a man who had seen one too many hard times.

"Sorry, sir!" he said quickly. The man grunted and went back to sleep.

"What room did he say again?" Joe mumbled to himself, pulling out his phone and regaining his balance. Scrolling through his texts he saw 222 listed. Being careful to avoid the few missing steps, Joe carefully went up the stairs. Just as he was about to knock, the door swung open. A large, mean looking brother looked him up and down.

"YouJoe?" he asked. But it all came out one word, and it took Joe a second to realize what he said.

"Yea, man–" But before he could finish his sentence the man had pulled him inside. Joe shook his gray, Tom Ford suit, and straightened his tie while stifling his temper. He was going to have to keep his cool to make this quick.

"Sitdown," the tough, big man said. Joe looked around. There was a sunken, yellowish couch with a seemingly unconscious female, and a few dusty crates to choose from.

"Where's Earl?" he asked, trying to figure out if he should even be there.

"Hebeoutinasec." Joe heard some noise coming from a back room and figured Earl was in there. He risked his suit and chose one of the crates. After about 10 minutes Earl emerged with a black eye, a split lip, and a couple other dudes who more than likely had given him his presents. His one good eye lit up when he saw Joe.

"Dawg, thanks for comin'." Earl succumbed to a series of coughs and hunched over to steady himself.

"This yo dude?" one of his assailants asked.

Joe sized him up and figured if need be, he could take him, though the man was probably carrying, and therefore had the advantage. He looked at the other dude and knew he was outnumbered. Better to just go with the flow.

"Yea," Earl responded, once he caught his breath.

"Where's the money?" the outspoken one asked, looking directly at Joe.

Joe opened his briefcase and pulled out a thick manila envelope. Earl strode across the room to take it from him. He passed on the coveted item and the other brother, who was silent up until this point, started counting. Joe looked at his watch, wondering if the cab was still waiting for him.

"It's all here," the money counter said in a gruff tone.

"We straight then?" Earl asked, wiping blood onto his t-shirt.

"Yea, we straight," the outspoken guy responded, even having the decency to crack a smile. Joe was feeling relieved and grateful this whole ordeal was over when, boom! The door was kicked open, and before Joe could even get his thoughts together, he saw several large figures dressed in all black with vests and large guns pointing at them.

"Police! Put your hands in the air! Everybody! Now!"

Fear and shock flooded him and Joe didn't even remember complying, only that his own hands were already on top of his head when a cop got to him.

"What's going on?" he couldn't help but ask, even though he knew it was the dumbest question in the world. In answer, Joe was slammed on his face by a policeman and heard the others go down with him. Cuffs were being placed while firearms were extended.

"Look what we got here!" Joe heard one cop say. He lifted his face a few inches off the dirty floor to see one of the cops holding up a large bag full of a white powdered substance.

"And there's so much more where that came from!" The man sounded excited, pointing to the back room. Joe groaned as the officer that cuffed him dug his knee into his back. They were being raided.

* * *

Nina came to bail him out. Joe didn't even know how to look at her in the face, he was so ashamed. He hung his head and stared at the concrete, taking slow strides as they walked to her house.

"I'm glad I wasn't working when you called," she said, following his pace. "I couldn't fathom you staying in there all night."

Joe

"Nina, I'm so sorry for this. I had no one else to call. My cousin Chuck wasn't available, and you were the only person I could think of." She looked at him thoughtfully. He had shared with her his side of the story on the way home and she had listened without interruption.

"Joe, I admit, this situation took me by surprise, and at first I was confused. I had to really pray about it." She sighed and pursed her lips. "But I know I have seen your heart and character during this time. I *know* that whatever this is, it has nothing to do with your character." She sounded as if she were speaking to herself as much as she was speaking to him. He was grateful for her support. He didn't know how she would fare with this when they were just getting serious.

"What's happening with work?" she asked. She sat on the front steps of her apartment and rested her hands under her chin. He joined her and stretched out his long legs, loosening his tie.

"Wendy told me Dick is pissed that I missed our meeting. She covered for me and said I had an emergency, but didn't give him any details. I'm supposed to call him later and fill him in."

"What are you gonna tell him?" Nina's face was filled with concern and she rubbed a hand on his knee in an effort to sooth him.

"I don't know." Joe let out a deep breath. How did he get into this mess? "I thought I was doing the right thing, you know?"

93

"Yea. I guess your heart was in the right place, but we need wisdom..." Her voice trailed off and she looked away. Joe couldn't agree more. Hindsight was 20/20.

"When's the court date?" Nina asked after a moment. "Next

week. I already called my lawyer. He's a friend of my family's. I'm hoping attorney-client confidentiality keeps him from telling my mom," he said, half joking, half serious. "He's gonna fly up here to New York just for me, so I'm definitely grateful."

"That's good. I'm just concerned about you being seen as a Black man and not just a man. How often do our people go to jail for crimes they didn't commit? And you were actually there!" She shook her head vehemently.

"You right. You not saying nothing I haven't thought myself. I'm really just trying to trust God in this situation. That's really all I've got right now." He let out another deep breath.

"It will definitely be a miracle. I have a cousin who's serving time right now and swears up and down he didn't rape that girl. Yet his damn lawyer was appointed by the system who doesn't give a damn about us anyway." With every sentence Lisa's voice swelled in anger, and Joe's heart ached for her.

"Yea. My boy Tone did time and he even had an alibi," he agreed. "But my lawyer thinks I'll be ok since I have no priors and no real connection with these people. Just at the wrong place at the wrong time, so to speak."

"Right. Well, I'm going to be praying and hopefully I'll be able to be there," she said biting her lip.

Who was this woman? *She is ride or die*, Joe thought, and he wished it were under better circumstances that he could see these amazing qualities she was demonstrating.

"You don't have to do that, Nina. It's bad enough I needed you to bail me out." He looked at her sheepishly.

"Oh, you definitely paying me my money back!" She grinned at him, causing joy to bubble up inside of him in the midst of the pain.

"Is that right? Maybe I shoulda just let you leave me in there overnight then!"

"Ha! You wouldn't make it one night!" She playfully punched him on the arm.

"Girl, I'll have you know I'm no joke on the street!" He swiped her hand away like she was a fly on a hot summer day.

"Yea yea. I'm sure. But I wouldn't want you to be in that environment one minute longer than you would need to be," she said quietly. Joe pulled her near him and she laid her head on his shoulder. *Lord, even though this situation is crazy, I'm grateful you brought me this woman to walk with me through it,* he thought to himself.

He who finds a wife finds a good thing, Joe heard in response. It was the first time Joe had a word regarding his love life, and he felt the message comfort his heart in only a way that God's words could.

* * *

Joe had never been to court and didn't know what to expect. The judge was an older gentleman; chocolate with a large demeanor. His gaze was friendly, but serious. Joe felt some relief to know he was a brother, but still, he was nervous. He sat, twiddling his hands in his lap and tried his best to not look like a criminal.

"How do you plead?" he was asked.

"My client pleads 'Not Guilty' your honor," Joe's lawyer responded.

"Proceed with your evidence." For one hour the prosecutor and defendant went back and forth. Joe's pastor, Wendy from work, and the manager from the Young Urban Youth Center where he volunteered, all testified of his character. Joe snuck a peak at Nina who was sitting next to Chuck. She offered an encouraging smile and just the sight of her warmed his heart.

Lord, if you get me out of this, I promise to ask You for wisdom in every life circumstance going forward!

Joe was nervous. He wasn't sure what road he would be called to walk; he only knew that he would have grace to walk it.

Joe

"I sentence you to six months community service," Judge Jackson's voice snapped him back to attention. Was it over already?

"You seem like an outstanding individual and community member who just happened to be at the wrong place at the wrong time. Is that correct, Mr. Banks?" The judge was having mercy and giving him an out.

Joe quickly nodded in agreement. "Y-yes, sir. That's correct."

"And, Mr. Banks, I NEVER want to see you in my courtroom again." Judge Jackson raised his full brows that graced his round face. "Court adjourned!" He hit his gravel and relief and peace simultaneously flooded Joe from the top of his head to the soles of his feet.

"Thank you so much, Frank!" He pumped his lawyer's hand up and down, standing to his feet.

"No problem, Joe. I'll send you my bill. And uh, not tell your mom." He chuckled before turning to leave. Joe was surrounded by support from his pastor to his girl, and he couldn't thank everyone enough for being there for him. Now he didn't have to worry about things at work, and he would be able to go back to his normal life. He looked down at Nina and kissed her forehead before leaving the courtroom, loved ones in tow.

* * *

97

Joe dribbled the ball between his legs, switching them back and forth to rattle his opponent, all the while looking for an open man on his team.

"Yo, Joe!" Dave shouted, while outrunning his man. Without thinking twice, Joe passed him the ball.

Dave drove to the hole and made the basket. Yes! They were up by 4 but there was still 10 minutes left to the game. The tournament was set up so that each team played for a full half hour and whoever was in the lead was the winner. The winners of each game moved on to the next round to play each other. There were three rounds total and this was the final round.

"Go, baby!" Joe heard Nina scream from the stands, and he shook his head grinning, his pearly whites on display. Mrs. Cole sat by Nina's side, looking tired but overjoyed. Focusing his attention back on the game, Joe hustled his way to get open, but his opponent was a lot faster and intercepted the ball when Ricky tried to pass.

"Shoot!" Joe ran after him, but they had already scored.

"Aight', y'all! Let's go to work!" He yelled to his team.

Chuck, who was standing in for Earl, ran behind him and slapped him on the butt. "No worries, baby! We got this!"

The other team had the ball and Joe stayed on his man as best he could. He watched Duck make the steal and shoot, but miss. Joe went in for the rebound and so did Big Rob. It was a close call and he almost got elbowed in the face. Rob came up with the ball, and Joe slammed it out of his hands just as he was going for the shot. Dave caught the ball and took his shot, sinking it into the hole.

"Yes!" Joe yelled, and gave Dave dap.

Two minutes left. Dave made a play for the steal, but his opponent did a behind the back pass and one of their members caught it. Ricky wasn't able to stay on him and they scored. Joe's team was only up by a bucket. One minute left.

"Chuck! I need you, man!" Joe said to his cousin.

"I got you, bro!" The hustle was on. Joe stayed on his man, playing defense like Scottie Pippen in the good old days. Chuck's opponent had the ball and Chuck was all in. Left, right, left, right, they danced from side to side. The crowd was so quiet Joe forgot anyone was even in the stands.

*If we can just hold him...*Joe thought.

And before he knew it, the buzzer went off. They won!

The crowd cheered, and Joe was swarmed by his team.

"Did you see that?"

"That brotha was on fire!"

"I'm saying, who run it?!" Was all he heard as Gatorade and water drenched him.

"Good game! Good game! Good game!" Each man said to the losing team and nodded their respect. It had been close.

"Baby, you did so good!" Nina said, running onto the court.

"Yea, honey! You were pretty slick out there!" Mrs. Cole added, following more slowly behind.

"Thank you! But I definitely had a good team behind me!" Joe grinned, and wiped himself with a towel before giving Nina a hug.

Victory is always sweetest when you fight together, he thought happily, and embraced his loved ones even tighter.

* * *

Joe was about to head over to Nina's for a barbecue but decided to get the mail as a last-minute thought. He was surprised to find a letter from Manhattan Correctional Facility. It was from Earl.

Joe, I hope this letter finds you well. It's been a few months since we spoke and I appreciate your willingness to reach out. Truth is I didn't respond until now because I felt bad about putting you in that situation. I'm grateful you got out though. I'm hoping we can still be cool.

I found some brothas in here who remind me of you. They talk about God and having values and standards for yourself. I probably wouldn't listen too hard if I wasn't in here but to serve this time, I need all the help I can get! Anyways, I just wanted to thank you for showing me so much love that you were willing to sacrifice your own freedom. That is what I'm learning to be called agape love. Love is sacrifice and I'm hoping to be able to demonstrate that kind of sacrifice in my life.

Anyways I don't want to get too deep. Just want you to know I'm doing well, mentally, emotionally and spiritually, and that even though our time together was brief, you made an impact on me man.

Stay blessed and keep in touch.

- Earl

Joe looked up at the sun and let the rays kiss his face. He had heard God after all.

VANESSA

"Nessa, did you pack your laptop?"

"Yes, Momma. I got it!"

"You sure, girl? Cuz I'm not driving no two hours back home to bring you that thing!"

Vanessa rolled her eyes and double-checked her Michael Kors messenger bag. Laptop–check!

"Yep, I got it!" she yelled back down the stairs over the banister to an anxious looking Mrs. James.

"Woman, stop worrying!" She saw her father appear out of the kitchen and stroke his hands up and down her mother's arms. "We've raised a responsible, dependable, *intelligent* young woman. She'll be fine." He gave her a forehead kiss, and a lopsided grin covered Vanessa's face as she headed back to her room. She was going to miss this place. It was only two hours from school so if she got really homesick, she could always visit, but she didn't see that happening too often.

"Hey, Buddy!" She patted the family's golden retriever who was lying on her bed. Even *he* looked upset about her departure. "I'm gonna miss you too!" She fondled him behind the ears and scratched him in his favorite spots. He nestled on her lap in response. "But I'll make sure to ask mom how you doing when I call!" Buddy raised his eyebrows and let out a low sound from the depths of his belly.

"Why you gotta leave, Nessa?" Her little brother stood in the doorway, holding his blanky and poking out his lower lip; the epitome of pitiful cuteness.

She sat up and looked at him adoringly. "Cuz, Bry. I gotta go to college."

"But why so fa away? Why can't you go *heya*?" he said, not able to say his "r" sounds yet. He eased his little 4-year-old body through the door until he was standing in front of her. Vanessa's heart filled and she pulled him onto her bed next to the dog.

"Cuz, Bry, I want to major in psychology, and this school has the best psychology program, remember?"

He nodded his head and a tear escaped.

"Aww, Bry, you'll get used to me being gone! And you are gonna looove visiting! I'll show you all around the campus and

Vanessa

take you to the events for Sibs Weekend! Just wait! It's gonna be great!" Her eyes were wide with excitement, as she grabbed him into a bear hug, but he stiffened at her touch and stubbornly popped his thumb into his mouth. "And guess what?" she continued with a new idea. "I'll get tickets to the basketball games, and get you a Michigan State basketball cap!"

For the first time his eyes lit up. "Fa weal, Nessa?" he asked.

"Yep!" Vanessa patted his little back with her free hand and the dog with the other.

"Oh aight'. That'll whok." Vanessa couldn't help but laugh.

"Boy, you a trip!" She shook her head and pulled him close.

"Alright, you two! The car is loaded! Let's move!" Vanessa's mom shouted from downstairs, and Vanessa knew she meant business.

"Alright, Ma. Here we come!" She drew out her phone for a selfie, then, licking her fingers, she wiped Bryan's tear-stained face. "Come on Bry, let's take a quick pic!"

Bryan perked up. "Ok!"

Vanessa bent her head low and got the three of them, Buddy included, in one take. Bryan ran out of the room, his sadness temporarily forgotten, while Buddy trotted happily behind him. Vanessa sent a text to her friends: **"Me, Bry and Buddy. Last day home**," along with the picture she had just taken and a sad face emoji.

She grabbed her messenger bag, swinging it neatly over her shoulder, and took one last glance around her room in the entryway. This was the last time she would live at home. Everything was about to change.

"Text us when you make it, V!" her friend CeeCee texted her. She only knew a few other people who were accepted into Michigan State from her school, and two of them just so happened to be good friends of hers. She was not looking forward to carving out a whole new crew, but figured she wouldn't have any problems if it came to that. Vanessa had always gotten along with people in general. She was smart, athletic, and a natural leader.

"Yep. Will do!" she sent back.

"Girl, you gon' spend yo last hours at home with your nose in that phone, or you gon' spend time with yo family?" Vanessa's mom looked back from the passenger seat of their four door SUV with raised eyebrows.

Vanessa sighed. "Sorry, Ma. I was just letting the girls know we on our way." Vanessa felt a stab of guilt, but also slight annoyance. Independence was calling her name!

"Don't be so hard on the girl, Regina. She has a life outside of us, you know." Her father smiled at her through the rearview mirror.

"Thanks, Daddy."

"I'm not hard on her, Darnell. I just want her to remember what's important." Her mom's tone softened. "Anyways, what are you looking forward to most, honey bunches?"

"Umm, probably the academic program," she said, playing it safe.

"Mmhmm. You know you thinking about what cute boys is there," her mom said, knowing better.

"Maaaa, why you gotta put me out there like that?" Vanessa slouched down low in her seat and smothered her hands with her armpits.

"Nessa, you goin' to school fa boys?" Bryan asked, looking up at her from the back seat. Up until that point he had been more interested in the game he was playing on her iPad.

"*Now* look what you done, Ma. You confusin' the boy! And Bryan don't need to be knowing my business like that anyway!"

Her father laughed. "Any business you got with boys is all our business, Nessa. And if he comin at chew', he gon' *have* to get through me!" Vanessa sunk lower in her seat, embarrassed that her love life was the topic of discussion. *It's bad enough Keenan broke up with me right before prom, and I had to go with a friend, now my whole family is putting me on blast!*

"Whatever happened to Keenan anyway?" her mom asked, as if she were secretly monitoring Vanessa's thoughts.

Dag, they are all up in my stuff! she thought to herself. "We cool. Just chillin' on things. You know..." Vanessa tried to keep it brief. *The way Keenan played me still feels fresh*, she thought, feeling a tinge of sadness. They had been dating for almost six months, but in high school, that felt more like a year. She was the captain of their drill team, and he was one of the star basketball players. They were one of *those* couples. Everybody thought they would continue on after high school, but Keenan had other plans.

"Vanessa, I like you and all, but when I get to college, I'm tryna do me. You know what I'm saying?" They were seated in his Ford Escape with the windows down, parked in her driveway. He had picked her up after both of their practices and driven her home as usual.

"What chew' mean you tryna do you? You don't have to cut me off just cuz you wanna do you," she responded. She didn't see it coming, and maybe she should have. After all, he was getting frustrated with her not wanting to take their relationship to the "next level" as he put it.

"I'm sayin', you going to Michigan State. I'm going to Ohio State University. How we gon' really see each other?" He switched uncomfortably in his seat, leaning away from her, more towards the door.

"You good, Keenan. You go 'head and do you, cuz I'm definitely gon' do me. In fact, I'm gon' do me at the prom. You don't need to be trippin' on us goin' together!"

Keenan looked surprised. "Aye, I didn't say we couldn't go to prom together. I'm just thinking about after *school. I don't wanna string you along having you thinking it's gon' be one way and it's not. I'm tryna look out for* you*."*

No he was not tryna manipulate her! "You know what Keenan, I appreciate the concern. I really do. But now you don't need to be concerned any longer when it comes to me. Goodbye." She jumped out the car and slammed the door.

"So, you a free agent then, huh?" Vanessa's mom's voice brought her back to the present.

"Yep, Mom. Free as a bird." She scrolled through her phone and saw there was one last picture she hadn't deleted of her and Keenan. Without a second thought, she hit the trash can button.

* * *

"Girl, look at this room! It is *small*!" CeeCee had her hands on her hips, shaking her head with an attitude, her pretty face contorted into a slight frown.

"I know, girl, but we gon' get it together! You know we can make anything fly." Vanessa put the finishing touches on her bed and moved her armoire to a better position. Her twin bed was stationed along the wall with a window located between her and Cee's Cees' twin bed, which rested against the other wall. Her armoire barely fit, but was a needed essential since the closets were so small. CeeCee just fit most of her belongings into her own closet, located near the entrance of the door. She also had her bed on bed risers with containers stuffed full of clothes underneath. Both girls' desks were tightly squeezed side by side across from Vanessa's bed next to her closet.

Vanessa's family had left over an hour ago after helping her unpack and taking her to lunch. Bryan had cried, her mother had cried and even *she* felt emotional, but also excited at the same time.

"I don't know. Even *yo* skills may not be up to par for this project, boo!" Diane was sitting on the floor, supposedly helping, but Vanessa hadn't seen her lift one acrylic fingernail.

"Girl, you'll see. We gon' have the most lit place and everybody gon' be tryna kick it here!" Vanessa was determined her friends would not bring down her mood. She was finally at college!

"Yea, you probably right. I mean, even if it's small, it can be cozy." Diane switched her tune quick.

"All I'm saying is, when are we gon' walk the campus and see who's who?" CeeCee asked in a serious tone.

"Girl, you are so boy crazy!" Vanessa said.

"Hey, I need to explore *all* my options! School is cool, but I came here for fun too!" CeeCee did a little dance to infer what kind of fun she was referring to. Vanessa shook her head while grinning, once again humored by her friend.

"There's a freshman meet up today behind the student center. They gon' be bar-b-cuing and have games and music," Diane announced.

"Sounds good to me!" CeeCee swiped her purse and ran over to their large, shared hanging mirror positioned above both desks. Her doe-like eyes, full lips and caramel complexion reflected back as she expertly applied a new coat of pink lip gloss and ran her fingers through her soft curls.

"Dag, it's like that, C?" Vanessa decided she needed to up her game too and went for her own makeup. She re-applied a coat of lip gloss and sprayed the cologne her mom had gotten her as a graduation gift.

"Sheesh, V! You got that grown woman stuff!" Diane said, picking up her petite frame off the floor and rushing to the mirror. "Them dudes gon' think you a senior or somethin'!" Vanessa laughed. She was tall, but she hardly looked like a senior in college. Her even-toned, chocolate skin sparkled with youth, and her almond-shaped eyes still held a look of innocence to them. She tended to walk with confidence, and whenever she entered a room, her demeanor commanded attention.

"Yea, well, age ain't' nothing but a number!" CeeCee said with a smirk. The other two girls looked at her in the mirror and laughed.

This is going to be too much fun! Vanessa thought to herself.

* * *

The girls finally made it to the student center, though it had taken them a while. They had to use the school's online map and asked three strangers to get there. CeeCee had even flirted with one of them.

"Welcome, ladies!" They were greeted by a young woman in her early 20s who held up a sign that said, "Welcome, Freshman class!" She was wearing a Michigan T, a pair of jean shorts, and a bright smile.

"Thanks!" they replied in unison.

"I love your hair!" the girl said to Vanessa, as they moved forward into the crowd.

"Aww, thank you!" Vanessa said, running a finger through her thick tresses. She was natural, but made it a point to straighten her hair daily. She kept it full and long and it framed her pie-shaped face nicely.

"Dang, there are so many people here!" CeeCee said. The lawn was packed with kids standing and talking, or eating bar-b-que on the grass, while others were playing games.

"Yea, this is cool," Vanessa replied. She looked around, searching for a sense of familiarity, but came up empty.

"Aye ladies! Y'all want y'all pic taken for the school website?" A young, short brother with long locs showed up holding a professional camera. CeeCee was already posing and Diane followed suit.

"How we know you really workin' for the school?" Vanessa asked, half joking.

"Aww, come on now. How many dudes gon' be kickin' it at a freshman school event tryna take pics?" the young man asked, flashing her a saucy smile. He was cute, but too short for her.

"I'm saying, it's a lot of crazies out here!" she said, warming up to him. She knew her mom was all up in her head, but still, her mom was no fool.

"Aight', girl. Let me show you my school I.D!" He whipped out a card from his back pocket, and all three ladies leaned in to inspect it.

"Ok-Tony. I guess you legit!" Vanessa said, nodding her head in approval.

"You a trip, girl!" He laughed, and put his I.D back. The three ladies posed and inspected the shot afterward.

"Look, even though you gave me such a hard time, I'm a let chew' know about a party happening tonight. It's not just for *freshman* either." He looked directly at Vanessa and she smiled.

"Oooo, sounds like we gon' be there then," CeeCee said with excitement.

"Yea? I'll text you the info then!" Tony pulled out his phone to give the ladies his number. CeeCee took his picture to remember who he was. She had a few Tony's in her phone.

"See you later, Tony!" she called after him in a sing-song voice. He turned, flashing another killer smile, then made his way to a different group of students.

"Tony was cute!" CeeCee gushed.

"You think everybody is cute!" Diane said. Vanessa laughed.

"Cuz they are!" CeeCee said, then led the group in the direction of the food. "Come on y'all, I'm hungry!"

The girls settled on a spot near an oak tree and risked staining their designer jeans on the grass. Vanessa took a deep bite of her hot dog. She was hungry from all of the activity that day.

"Y'all think classes is gon' be hard?" she asked her friends, wrinkling her brows. Classes started Monday, and she wasn't sure about her course load.

"Girl, you the smartest one. I know if *you* worried, I need to just drop out now!" CeeCee said, only slightly kidding. Vanessa shook her head and laughed.

"I'm not worried, I just want to be realistic. I took a few A.P classes, but how does that really compare to college classes?" Creases became etched into her smooth brown skin when she thought about the start of the school year. Her concerned eyes dropped down to her plate, and her half eaten hot dog stared up at her forlornly.

"Well, I know they have tutoring sessions and mentoring programs. Remember they was tellin' us at orientation?" Diane asked.

"Yea, but I don't even want it to get that bad. I'm not used to strugglin' in school." Vanessa felt butterflies in her stomach, so she set the hot dog down and took a drink of her water bottle.

"I heard a lot of the freshman classes ease you into your course load, and they give you a syllabus to help you plan out your study time and stuff," a voice said from behind the tree. All three girls looked to see a young woman with brown skin, a thick frame, and the latest fashions.

"Hi, I'm Tina!" she said, coming out further from behind the tree. Vanessa assessed her. The girl's cheetah print tank was stuffed inside a pair of light, ripped, fitted jeans that caressed her black platform sandals at the ankles. Her matte shade of pink lipstick popped in the sunlight.

Vanessa could tell the girl was nervous as she fiddled with her fingers at her sides. S*he must have been chillin' behind that tree for a while,* Vanessa figured. "Hi, I'm Vanessa, and these are my girls, CeeCee and Diane!" She motioned for the girl to come closer. "You can sit with us!"

"Thanks!" Tina sat on the grass with her plate, completing their circle.

"So, what are you majoring in?" CeeCee asked Tina, sizing her up.

"I don't know yet. I have a few interests and I want to wait until next semester before I decide."

"That sounds smart. I'm only majoring in psychology because of the class I took in high school, but if it doesn't pan out the way I want it to, I'm open to changing," Vanessa shared with a shrug.

"Yea, I don't really know what I want to do either, but my dad has put all this pressure to major in business. I come from a long line of entrepreneurs," Dianne added. She played with the bag of chips partially opened on her paper plate, before finally deciding to pop one into her mouth.

"That's cool. But what would you want to do if *you* could choose?" Tina asked her, picking up her hamburger. When the sandwich met her lips, she carefully chewed without smearing one ounce of her lipstick. Vanessa was impressed.

Diane paused. "Umm, I really love to draw. If I could, I would do something in the arts." She sucked the salt off her fingers, while thinking intensely about her options.

"Then you should definitely take a few art classes, just in case!" Tina advised, after swallowing her burger.

This girl is a bucket of knowledge, Vanessa thought. She leaned her back against the tree and looked at Tina approvingly.

"Thanks. I'll keep that in mind!" Diane smiled, appearing grateful.

"You know about this party happening tonight?" Vanessa asked Tina, wondering what else she knew.

"Yea, my brother told me about it. Some upperclassmen are kickin' it, and they usually invite freshmen to see who is gon' be what they call, "fresh-bait.""

"Dag. These dudes are a mess!" Vanessa said, her face registering disgust. She took another bite of her hot dog, her previous nervousness about classes forgotten.

"Yea, my brother just graduated and schooled me to all the games. But I wouldn't mind still checkin' it out just to see what the hype is. It's still supposed to be a good time," Tina said.

"So, you down? Cuz we rollin' tonight!" CeeCee said with a mischievous smile.

"Yep. Say less!" Tina nodded and smiled back.

"Cool. I'm looking forward to seeing how these upperclassmen think they gon' get *me!*" Vanessa announced. She finished her hot dog and crossed her toned, chocolate arms. "I ain't nobody's bait!"

* * *

It was almost 8PM, and the girls left their dorm room meeting. Their RA, Jenny, was the perky, in your face type, and Vanessa wondered how well they would fare.

"Let me know if you ladies need anything," she had said to the 20 young women while they all stood in the hall, shifting from insecurities and acne. "I'm right down the hall and look forward to getting to know you each individually!" She had made little contact cards for everyone, her short, blond hair bouncing as she passed them out.

I'm not really feelin' Jenny's vibe, Vanessa thought to herself, but figured she would try to give the girl a chance.

"What chew' think about Jenny?" CeeCee asked, once they were back in their room.

"I don't know, C. I'm wondering how *real* she is. People who are *that* chipper, can't be for real." She looked suspiciously at the contact card her RA had provided.

"Mmhmm. I was thinking the same thing. But then again if you got it like that, you probably got no worries to be trippin' over," CeeCee said, falling backward on top of her twin bed.

Vanessa knew where she was coming from. CeeCee's dad had left them a few years back, and her mom was raising her and her sisters on her own. The only reason CeeCee made it into college was because of the loans she took out.

"Yea. Anyways, what chew' wearin' tonight, girl? You know we gotta be ready in an hour to meet Tina and Di," Vanessa said, flopping down on her own bed.

"Umm, I was hoping to borrow something from you, girl. I'm sick of all my stuff." CeeCee's face twisted in disgust, and she sighed dramatically.

"Well, let's see what we got here then!" Vanessa got up and started pulling outfits from her closet, then laid them on the bed vertically; shirts near the top and everything else on the bottom.

"Oooo, this sparkly top will look great with my jeans from Forever 21!" CeeCee squealed. She was already squeezing the top and holding it up to herself in the mirror.

"That's cool. I think I'm a wear this off-shoulder Puma, pink crop top." Vanessa joined CeeCee in the mirror and both girls posed, then giggled. Vanessa heard her phone ding and looked to see a group text from Tony. "Ok, we got the location! Now we just need to get ourselves together!"

"I wonder what a college party is like, V? You think these dudes are really as bad as Tina was sayin'?" CeeCee looked anxiously at Vanessa while still clutching her items.

"Girl, I don't know. But I know my daddy will *kill* a dude if he tries to jack me up!"

CeeCee got quiet. "Yea. Wish I could say the same."

Uh oh. Vanessa hadn't even thought about her comment until it was already out of her mouth. She put her shirt down and placed her arm around her friend.

"You got me, C, and I got your back!" CeeCee attempted a small smile and leaned in to receive her friend's comfort. At least they had each other.

* * *

"That's cool, they did it in a basement like an old school party," CeeCee said into Vanessa's ear after they had made it inside. The downstairs room of the fraternity house was spacious with a large area being used as the dance floor. Some chairs and a few tables were set off to the side. Strobe lights flashed throughout the venue, enhancing the facial features of any young man wanting to get lucky that night.

"Yea, this is raw!" she responded. The music was loud and bodies were everywhere. Tina, Diane, CeeCee and Vanessa were hurled forward like cattle on a farm from the crowd pressing in behind them.

"Yo, Drake! Give me some of that urban fire, man!" A young man with shimmering, dark skin and a distinguished looking goatee, stood in front of the girls trying to get the attention of another guy who was serving drinks.

"I got chew', Al!" The man tending drinks gave a head nod while handing another student a drink.

Vanessa

"Umm, excuse me, but me and my girls were trying to get through here," CeeCee said to Al in an authoritative tone. She crossed her arms in front of her and shifted her weight while looking at him in expectation. Diane, Vanessa and Tina were shocked by CeeCee's boldness, and each looked around the room as if there was something more interesting to see.

"Oh. My bad, shawty. I didn't even see you!" Al put his hand over his chest and looked CeeCee up and down. "Mmm-mmm-mmm! But now that I do, I *have* to ask you to dance!"

CeeCee flashed him a flirtatious grin. "I thought you'd never ask," she purred, then let him lead her onto the floor.

"Dag! Yo girl don't play!" Tina said to Vanessa and Diane.

"Yea, she is something else," Vanessa said with a chuckle. "I see a few seats over there if y'all wanna sit down." She pointed to a corner with a table and a few chairs set aside.

"Sounds good to me!" Diane said. They navigated through the crowd and stole some chairs.

"Yo! I see you made it!" Tony popped up in front of them while they were talking, holding a girl's hand.

Vanessa noticed the girl didn't seem too happy he was talking to them. *Dag, she that insecure?*

"Yo, Tony. Wuz up?" Vanessa responded, nodding her head his way.

"'Bout' to turn up! But let me introduce you to my girl. This is Rox." He pulled the tall, leggy girl closer to him and tucked her waste into his arm. The girls nodded a greeting, but it was clear Rox wasn't too keen on conversation. She looked down at them in distaste beneath her thick lashes, forming her thin lips into a greeting no one was able to make out.

"Cool. Well, y'all have fun!" Vanessa responded, dismissively. Tony shot her a grin, seeming oblivious to his woman's hostility, before making his exit.

"Man, that chic was stank," Diane said. She made a face once the couple left.

"Yea. I guess she wasn't feeling her dude having female friends," Tina added.

"Well, that's *her* problem. Ain't nobody got time for that," Vanessa said. The music changed to the "Wobble" and people got on the floor to line dance. Vanessa ended up next to a light-eyed brother who kept "accidentally" touching her behind when it was time to do the turn.

If this dude don't chill out! Vanessa fumed to herself, but she didn't have to be frustrated for too long.

"Aye, man, you touch my girl again, we gon' have some problems." Vanessa looked up to see a tall, brown skin dude with a baby face and wavy hair.

Vanessa

"What? Oh, I didn't even notice, Rico. You good!" Light eyes said. Clearly her knight and shining armor was well-respected.

"Uh, thanks. I didn't know I was yo girl though," Vanessa said to the stranger. The song ended and he glued his hand to her back while leading her off the floor in one smooth gesture.

"Yea, I didn't know either 'til I realized how upset that dude was making me when he kept grabbing yo ass!" He laughed brashly, and she joined in, unable to resist the charisma he so easily exuded.

"I'm Rico," he said, in a self-assured tone. His smile spread wide like a Cheshire cat's, as his dark eyes pounced on her, taking her in from head to foot.

"You mean like Rico Suave?" Vanessa had to ask.

"Yea, I guess you could say that." He chuckled lightly. "And what about you, beautiful? What's yo name?"

Vanessa half-smiled at the compliment. "Vanessa."

"Cool. So now that we know each other's names–and you my girl–is it cool if I get you a drink?" he asked. He pointed to the area where drinks were being served.

"Umm, yea, I guess that's cool. I just want some water though." She was hot from all the dancing and was hoping to God her hair was holding out.

"Be right back then!" Rico took off towards the drinks, and suddenly, Vanessa realized she hadn't seen her friends in a while. She looked around the party but still couldn't spot anybody. She decided to check her phone and saw some missed texts.

"Nessa, I'm outside kickin' it with Al. Let me know when y'all leave, and I'll meet you."

"Ok, girl! Be safe!" she responded.

Text from Diane: **"We at the bar set up out back chillin'. Saw you with ol' boy, didn't want to mess up yo vibe."**

"Here you go, mama." Rico handed her a clear cup of liquid, and she took a sniff to make sure it wasn't alcohol.

"Oh, you don't trust me, huh?" Rico called her out.

"I don't even know you," she responded, then took a sip.

"Well, I want that to change. So, you a freshman?" He looked at her as if he already knew the answer, and for the first time in life, she felt a little self-conscious about her age.

"Yea. What about chew'? What year are you?"

"I'm a junior. I actually took a year off, so I'm a year older than I should be. Why don't we have a seat?" Rico eyed two free chairs and posted them against the wall so they could sit, straddling one across from her to face her.

"So, why did you take time off?" Vanessa was curious.

"I had some stuff I was goin' through, and school wasn't a priority at the time. But I got through it and came back to finish up."

"Oh. Ok. Cool," she said, nodding her head. "What are you majoring in?"

"Bio-Chemistry. I'm hoping to go into the medical field." Rico gulped his water then lightly brushed his chin.

"Sounds heavy. What made you want to get into that?"

Who the heck majors in Bio Chem? she marveled to herself.

"I've always been into science. My brain just works that way. What 'bout chew'? You know what chew' want to major in?" He seemed genuinely interested, and Vanessa felt a little important to be getting so much of his attention.

"I'm thinking psychology right now. I really liked the classes I took in high school, so we'll see…" She sipped her water, finally feeling cooled down. The music changed and some of the fraternity guys started strolling.

"Aye, let me get back to you. I gotta join my bruhs. Save my seat, ok?" Rico was already standing up before Vanessa could process what was happening.

"Oh, ok." She pulled his seat closer to hers and placed a leg on it. She watched him do their steps and had to admit, seeing him step made him even more attractive.

"Yo, Rico hollerin' at chew'?" Tony came up to her, but this time he was alone.

"Wuz up. Yea, we just talkin'." Vanessa was surprised to see him. "Where yo girl at?"

"Man, she was trippin', so I dropped her." Tony shoved her leg off the seat and turned it around, straddling it.

Vanessa busted out laughing. "Dag! I guess y'all wasn't serious!"

"Man, she always be trippin'. I only mess wit' her when I'm in between relationships." Tony smiled at her, and she noticed, once again, what a cutie he was. She was also surprised he was being so blunt with her.

"Dag. Well, do *she* know that?" she asked, raising an eyebrow.

"Please. She do the same thing to me! She only call me when she want it." Tony crossed his arms over the top of the chair as if he was 'the man'.

Boys and their egos, Vanessa thought to herself.

"Well, at least y'all have an understanding," she said, cocking her head and letting her long tresses dangle.

"Yea, it's cool. I mean, I'm not tryna be serious right now 'til I get outta school. Ain't nobody tryna settle down without a plan, you know?"

"Yea, I guess that makes sense. But um, that is Rico's seat, and he will probably be back soon." Vanessa tilted her head in Rico's direction and Tony followed her gaze.

"Oh, so you his girl now, huh?" He was obviously joking but Vanessa was intrigued. She smiled in response, and Tony looked at her strangely. He seemed like he wanted to say more, but didn't.

"Well, I'm a do my thing then. But chew' call or text if you need something," he said, while getting up to leave.

Vanessa was both touched and surprised by his offer. They barely knew each other, but already Tony seemed to be becoming a good friend. "Cool, I appreciate that."

"Hey, beautiful. Let's get some air." Rico was done strolling and cupped her hand, so Vanessa let him lead her out of the party. She briefly saw both Diane and Tina on the floor dancing.

The night air was soothing, and she was grateful to be away from the crowd, though there was still a line out the door and people were loitering outside. She felt grown. No mom, dad or little brother to keep tabs on her. They walked and talked for a long time. Rico told her about his dreams and aspirations and what he wanted to do after school. Vanessa told him about her family, interests and what she hoped would be her future. She had never connected with a guy who had so much vision before. She wondered if all college guys were like this, or if Rico was unique.

"I'm going places, Vanessa. I'm not tryna' waste my life. I want to make a name for myself," he said to her. His views made her think about her own. Where was she going? What did she want out of life? Could she even measure up to a guy like Rico? These were her thoughts for the rest of the evening. Even as she regrouped with her friends and they made their way back to the dorms. Even as she laid down to sleep in her new twin bed, all she could think about, was Rico.

* * *

The semester started in full swing, and Vanessa hardly had time for anything other than classes. She quickly developed a rhythm of class, studying and practicing for the dance team tryouts, which were soon. She wanted to be at the top of her game, so she was taking some time to hit the gym.

While running on the treadmill, her eyes met his. Rico. She didn't even realize he was there lifting weights. Should she acknowledge him? He hadn't reached out to her since the party other than a few texts, and she wasn't one to chase a guy down. She upped her speed on the treadmill, deciding it was better to focus her energy on running. A few minutes later, she felt a presence at her side.

"Hey, beautiful. I see you keepin' it tight." Vanessa could feel him studying her like one of his chemistry textbooks. She smirked and peeked at him out of the corner of her eye. Rico was drenched with sweat, wearing a tank shirt, long basketball shorts and a pair of grey Lebron's. His waves were curled up from the perspiration, and she was pleased to see how well-defined his arms were.

Dag he is fine! she thought.

"Yea, you know. That's what I do," she responded, after catching her breath.

"I definitely like that about chew'...Among other things..." His eyes painted over her again as if he were creating a masterpiece.

She was glad she wore her workout capris and cropped top. *Let him know what he missin'!* she thought.

"So, how you been?" Rico lowered the speed on her treadmill and rested his arm on the machine.

Oh, he think he runnin' me huh? Vanessa thought to herself. She raised the speed and kept up her pace. "I'm good. You?" she puffed out between breaths.

Rico laughed. "Ok, I see how it is. I know it's been a while, but–baby girl–don't think I ain't been thinking about chew'. With school and my extracurriculars, I just haven't had time to reach out." He lowered her speed again. Vanessa slowed down, then dropped her gaze and gripped the arm of the treadmill. She figured she could use the break, so she took a swig of her water and gently patted her face with a towel.

"That's cool. You don't owe me nothin'," she said, turning her head to look out the window in front of her treadmill to hide her hurt.

"Hey, don't be like that." Rico leaned his face into her space and flashed his most attractive smile. "I'm being honest, Vanessa." His voice grew serious. "I take my time in getting to know people, and I definitely don't want to rush nothin' wit chew'." She felt torn with what he was saying and how she had previously interpreted his actions.

"Well, if you feel that way, then you know what to do," she finally said, then stopped her jog altogether, meeting his gaze with one of her own. He smiled and shook his head.

"Girl, you are something else. Alright, I got chew'. I'm a come correct, and you gon' see!" He straightened up. "I'm a let you get back to your workout." Vanessa was pleased she had stood her ground. These college dudes were another animal, but they didn't know who they were messing with!

* * *

"How you gon' skip class and school *just* started?" Tina asked Tony, popping a fry into her mouth. They were at the campus' main dining hall, and Vanessa was glad she had this free time in her schedule to hook up with her friends mid-day. Tuesday's and Thursday's were her long days, and lunch with them was a nice break.

"Trust me, 'The Discovery of a Black Man' is *not* that difficult, at least, when you *are* a Black man!" Tony laughed, and stole a fry off Tina's plate.

Vanessa shook her head. "Why you taking it then, Tony, if you know so much?" she asked.

"Cuz, it's still interesting! It just don't require a lot. Plus, I needed a fine arts course credit."

"Ah, the real reason!" Tina remarked. "You ain't really tryna learn nothin', brotha." She swatted away his hand from stealing another fry.

"Why you tryna play me, *sista*. I know my roots. I know who I am and where I'm goin'!" He smacked his teeth and rolled his eyes simultaneously.

"Is that right? Then you should come to Bible study and enlighten us with your knowledge," Tina countered.

"Aww, here we go!" Tony leaned back in his chair, putting his hands behind his head. "I done' told you, girl, I already *have* the truth. I don't need no *white* man named Jesus telling me I need to *change* to fit the culture's definition of acceptability."

"First of all, Jesus ain't white, and if you knew your history, you'd know that. And second of all, there are so many cultural standards that you implement *daily* of which you don't even realize; from your clothes, music *and* food choices."

She gestured to the fries to accent her point. "Why do you think we eat french fries for lunch instead of beans and rice? Because our culture tells us to!"

"Alright, y'all, chill out! Why we gotta be all deep at two in the afternoon?" Vanessa said to diffuse the heated discussion.

"She started it!" Tony shook his head, sounding more like an adolescent than a 20-year-old. Vanessa laughed and Tina joined in.

"I'm just spittin' truth," Tina said, pushing her fries towards Tony. "You can have the rest."

"Hey, I ain't never one to turn down a meal!" Tony eagerly pawned her peace offering and started doctoring it with salt. All was clearly forgiven. Vanessa smiled at the two.

"Girl, look who is coming in here!" Tina nodded her head in the direction of the entrance. Both Tony and Vanessa immediately turned their heads. A group of young men dressed in fraternity apparel were walking in a singular line from shortest to tallest. Rico was at the end of the line. Everyone but Rico started marching and chanting, seizing the attention of the whole diner.

What is goin on? Vanessa thought to herself.

"Girl, I think they comin over here!" Tina sounded excited, and she was right. The group made a B line for their table, not pausing in their chant or step. All of a sudden, they stopped marching and stood to attention.

The first man in line shouted, "Three reasons why you should date my man Rico! One!" The men stepped. "His grades are siiiiiick!" (He dragged out the word and ended on a high note while stepping.) The group stepped again. "Two! He keeps his money tiiiiight!" More stepping. "Three! He is a part of the best fraternity on this cam-pus!" More stepping. Vanessa was shocked. What in the world was this guy doing? Rico stepped up from the side of the line, where he was watching his fraternity brothers, then dismissed his line.

"Y'all good." He nodded to them. "Thanks, bruhs!" The boys relaxed from their pose and watched in expectation. Rico then turned to Vanessa and took her hand in his. She was grateful she was dark-skinned or her face would have been on fire!

"Vanessa, would you please go out with me?" His shadowy, brown eyes looked up at her as if she were the only one in the room, and she couldn't resist the emotions that were surfacing. He did all that just to ask her out? In front of the whole dining room?

"Girl, say yes!" somebody shouted at another table in the diner.

"Girl, if you don't, I will!" somebody else said, and students started laughing.

Vanessa smiled, feeling giddy. "Boy, you are crazy," she muttered to him under her breath.

"Is that a yes?" He grinned.

"Yea. That is a definite yes."

* * *

Things got serious fast. Rico was intense, and Vanessa loved his intensity. She soon learned that whatever Rico wanted, Rico got. Whether it was his grades, his girl, or his respect on campus; he was very intentional about accomplishing his goals. As she grew closer to him, she discovered he was also intentional about how he wanted to be perceived. Although many respected him, she wasn't sure if he had any close friends. The more she learned about him, the more she wanted to be that person for him.

"How you think you did on midterms?" Rico slanted his head to the side, questioning her. They were sitting in his black Pontiac Firebird in front of her dorm and had just seen a movie at the student center's theater. She saw Tony there and spoke, but he kept his distance. Vanessa let out a sigh.

"Hopefully good. My parents will kick my ass otherwise!" They both laughed.

"It's good your folks have yo back like that. Not everybody has that." His eyes clouded over, and Vanessa ran her hand on his knee to comfort him. "*I don't have that as you probably may* have guessed," Rico finally said. She studied his face and saw the pain embedded into his features.

"My dad rolled out while I was still in diapers, and I never got along with my mom, whether she was using or not," he said. "But especially when she was using." He paused, and Vanessa felt the fall breeze roll through the partially lowered window from outside. "It was really just me and my brothers lookin' after each other. Well, really me, since I'm the oldest." Rico looked at her for the first time since he started sharing, playing with her fingers in his. "I did a lot of growing up quick. I had to." Vanessa finally understood why he didn't let people in easily. She felt privileged he would confide so deeply to her.

"I'm thinking about the future all the time Vanessa. I'm planning and making moves and always on my toes cuz that's the only way I'm gon' make it. Nobody's gon' do it for me. Nobody's gon' have my back." She weighed her body across the armrest and wrapped his arm around her shoulder, their fingers still intertwined. She looked up at him with compassionate eyes then, and he kissed her fingers softly, sucking on them, in the way that drove her wild.

"You got me, Rico," she said, with unabashed certainty. "I'm not going nowhere."

* * *

Homecoming was a night to remember. Ladies dressed in their finest. Young men struggled to keep up. It was the first dance of the year, and everyone wanted to show how good puberty had been to them.

"Girl, you are killin' it!" Vanessa said to a sultry looking CeeCee. Her curly hair was sassily piled high on top of her head, while her nude dress, laced with sequins, hugged every curb God gave her. She posed from side to side, her date standing proudly behind her.

"Yea yea, I know. I done' did it again!" CeeCee threw her head back in a naughty laugh. Vanessa grinned as she slipped out of Rico's hand to join her girl.

"But umm, I must say, you definitely doin' yo thing!" CeeCee looked her up and down and made Vanessa spin around to show off a pink, fitted, strapless dress that sparkled and hit just so at mid-thigh. Her long chocolate legs were accentuated by four-inch silver heels. Not that she needed them; her legs already ran for days. She had gotten extensions added, making her hair fuller than normal. It sped like a gazelle, straight down her back.

"Y'all ready?" CeeCee asked. Vanessa shot a glance at Rico who was greeting some other students.

"We'll be there in a sec," Vanessa said. She didn't want to cut Rico off from his conversation. CeeCee grabbed her date and the poor guy shuffled behind her into the entrance of the dance.

"Baby, I want you to meet Kevin and Jake." Rico circled her lower back with his arm.

"Dag, Rico! You didn't say she was *that* fine!" the short one said, his eyes shifting eagerly over her.

"Hey, man. Watch yo self," Rico responded in a strained tone. Vanessa saw him immediately clench his jaw.

"Aye, bruh, no disrespect!" The man quickly turned to Vanessa and shook her hand politely, "I'm Kevin."

Vanessa smiled, still aware of Rico's tension. "I'm Vanessa."

"I'm Jake." Jake held out his hand as well. After the introductions, the boys turned to each other and started chatting. Rico pulled Vanessa closer to him and kissed her forehead.

"You wanna' head inside?" he asked. Just when Vanessa started to agree, they both overheard the boys' conversation.

"Man, he betta not mess that up or I'm comin' for her," Kevin said with a loud laugh. He couldn't even start his next sentence, however, because in two seconds Rico had the young man pinned against the nearest wall.

"Aye-aye-man! I'm just jokin'!" Kevin choked out, struggling to remove the arm Rico had pressed up against his neck. The brother's feet were literally off the floor and a crowd had formed to see the commotion.

"Rico! Chill out! Let him go!" The other young man said. Cautiously, he stood next to Rico, too afraid to physically intervene. Vanessa was shocked, and she felt like everything was happening in slow motion.

"Babe, what are you doin?" She slowly landed a hand on his shoulder, and his face, that was just contorted in anger, immediately softened. Rico seemed to come to himself and shook his head, while simultaneously dropping Kevin to his feet.

"Yo, Kev. My bad, man. I'm trippin'." Kevin coughed and rubbed his hand over his neck. People recorded the incident with their phones, but everyone stayed at bay.

"Kev, let's bounce," Jake said to his friend. Neither looked at Rico before turning to leave. Vanessa caught Rico by the arm, leading him to the hall away from the crowd. She searched his eyes, but all she saw was shame.

"Nessa, baby. I'm sorry. I don't know what came over me." Vanessa bit her lip, struggling with her own emotions. *What the hell got into him?* she wondered. *I've never seen a dude flip like that before.* Rico dropped to a nearby chair and dropped his head into his hands. Not sure what to think, Vanessa stood there, waiting for more.

"Baby, I just want chew' to know, that's never happened before." He looked up at her, meeting her almond eyes with his large, round ones. She saw they were watery and instantly moved in front of him, propping his head against her stomach. She started rubbing his neck back and forth gently, as he held on tightly to her hips.

"It's gonna be ok," she said. "Everything's gonna be ok."

* * *

Vanessa stared intently at the screen while typing fiercely on her laptop. The library was her favorite spot to study, and there was a cubicle on the third floor that she considered to be her second home.

"Hey, girl! I thought I saw you over here." Tina stood nearby, holding a huge Biology textbook in one hand and a bulging embroidered jean book bag in the other.

"Wuz up, T! I guess you know my spot, huh?" Vanessa smiled at her friend and took a break from typing. She was almost done with her paper.

"Yea, you know you be on it with the studying." Tina shifted her weight, and gripped the book bag tighter. "So...how was homecoming?" Tina asked. It seemed like a loaded question to Vanessa, but she figured she would just play it cool.

"It was good. Too bad you couldn't make it, girl." She looked at her friend sympathetically.

"Yea, I was sick as a dog!" Tina rolled her eyes and shook the large, bouncy curls on her head. Vanessa suspected it was a wig, but it also looked like it could have been a sew-in. Apparently, her friend was gifted with hair styling. Everybody started going to her to keep their mane together. "My first college dance and I missed out." Tina made a fake pout with her full lips. "And I was too sick to do anybody's hair, so I missed out on making dough too!"

"Yea. We had fun though," Vanessa said. "CeeCee did her thing as usual! Girl, do you know she dropped her date for another dude at the dance?" Vanessa laughed, and rolled her eyes comically.

Tina's eyes got big. "Nooo. That is hilarious!"

"Yea. She said her date was a freshman and just wasn't on the level. So, I guess she found somebody who was." Vanessa was always entertained by her friend's antics. Tina laughed some more, then paused, licking her lips.

"So, umm, I heard about what happened with Rico," she ventured.

Vanessa stiffened while dropping her eyes low. "Yea, well, you know. He kind of lost his temper, but it's all good."

Tina nodded her head slowly. "Yea, but it sounds like he *really* overreacted. I mean, there's a video out there and everything…" She let her voice trail off.

"Oh, you know how dudes are. He was just overprotective." Vanessa waved a hand. "That dude Kevin ain't have no business saying what he said. And anyways Rico and I are really getting serious. So, I mean, he hasn't felt this way about a girl before. He just didn't know how to handle his emotions." Vanessa felt like she was rambling, but she couldn't stop herself.

"Oh, ok. Well, I just wanted to check on you, girl," Tina said, trying to lighten her tone. "So anyways, I gotta hit these books like you. I'll catch you later!" Tina held up her book bag before turning away.

"Yea, girl. I'll see you." Vanessa turned back to face her computer.

Dang, I can't believe there's a video out there. People are trippin' about one little incident? she thought to herself, while resuming her work. *"I guess you gotta expect the haters when you got respect like Rico do.* She definitely felt Rico's behavior was inappropriate, but after he explained it was due to his feelings for her, she understood. She also had never felt this strongly about someone before, and that was why she decided to offer her body to him the night of the dance.

* * *

Vanessa was playing catch with Bryan and Buddy in the garage when her mom popped her head inside.

"Dinner's ready!" she yelled from the door of the house that connected to the garage.

"Ok, Ma!" Vanessa and the crew hurried inside and washed up. When she reached the kitchen, Vanessa's mom had on her apron and was chopping up veggies while old school music played in the background. Some guy named Smokey Robinson crooned through the speakers. Vanessa checked her phone before joining to help her mother and saw that she had two missed calls from Rico. She didn't want to call him back since she couldn't talk long and decided she would wait until after dinner.

"Man, it's good to have you back!" Vanessa's dad beamed at her between bites of his chicken pot pie as they sat and ate their meal.

"Yea, you just want me here cuz mom goes overboard with cooking when I'm home!" Vanessa said to her dad jokingly.

"Yea, that's true too!" Both her parents gave hearty laughs and Vanessa looked around the table, taking in the love she had.

"I saw you did well on midterms! How you feeling about finals, honey?" her mom asked. She sliced up Bryan's chicken nuggets into little triangles the way he liked it. He didn't like chicken pot pie.

"It should be cool. I got a good study schedule goin'. The only class I'm annoyed about is my Lit class. I just can't seem to get an A on my papers." She rolled her eyes while twisting her fork in her hand.

"Maybe you should get a tutor?" her mom suggested.

"Or talk to some other kids in the class?" her dad chimed in.

"Yea, it's kinda hard to be tutored on writing, but I'll see if some other kids have tips." She looked at her parents appreciatively.

"I'm lewning to white, Nessa! I could help you!" Bryan offered, with ketchup smeared on his chubby brown face.

Vanessa smiled at her little brother. "Man, Bry, that's dope of you. I'll have to call when I'm working on a paper and get your input!" He nodded his little head, very seriously, in agreement. They're conversation got interrupted by her ringtone, "Boo'd Up" by Ella Mai.

"Whoops! I forgot to put it on silent. But umm, let me take this real quick." Without waiting for a response from her parents, Vanessa answered the call and moved to the living room.

"Hey, babe," she answered, still feeling the warm and fuzzies from her little brother's remarks.

"Girl, what's up wit' chew? I done' called you like five times. You wit' somebody?" Rico sounded angry.

"What? No, I'm having dinner with my fam!" she hurried to explain. Her heart slammed against her ribcage in fear.

"Yea right. I can't believe this shit. I know you playin me, Vanessa!"

"Rico, I'm telling you the truth!" But he had already hung up. Vanessa stood there, wringing her lip in and out with her teeth. She felt tears in her eyes and tried to make sense of what had just happened. Her mother stood in the entryway of the living room with her arms folded, observing her; a concerned expression covering her face.

"Honey, you ok?" Vanessa shook her head and her mother embraced her. "You want to talk about it?

"Maybe later, Ma. I just want to be excused from dinner, if that's cool."

"Oh. Ok. Why don't you take a nap and we'll regroup later?" Grateful for her mother's understanding, Vanessa made her way to her room and did just that. She knew it was no use calling Rico back. Whenever he got like this, she just had to wait it out.

* * *

It was a week later and Vanessa had made her way back to her dorm for a floor meeting after spending time with Rico. He really wanted her to stay, but she knew she couldn't afford to miss this one since she had missed the last one at his insistence.

"Ladies. Thank you so much for joining! I hope everyone had a great holiday! If you haven't stopped by my room to catch me up, then please do!" Jenny said to her residents. Vanessa and CeeCee looked at each other and rolled their eyes. Vanessa noticed some of the other girls snicker. "I have had a topic on my heart for a while now and wanted to address it with you ladies." Jenny flashed a bright smile that rivaled a Colgate commercial.

She must have had braces growing up, Vanessa thought to herself, while crossing her arms in front of her in annoyance. Jenny passed a stack of handouts to the nearest girl and had her distribute them.

"So, one very important topic on campus that some of you will come across is the issue of domestic violence." Jenny paused to clear her throat. "I know as teenagers you can think you're exempt, but the truth is, domestic violence is not limited to marriages; it can occur in dating relationships too. This is known as dating violence." Vanessa shifted her weight from one foot to the other as she unconcernedly leaned against the wall. She was passed a pamphlet and peered down to see a woman on the front, once a previous victim, but now smiling large with hope. Her head was slightly tilted backward, and her tan skin was kissed by the sun's rays.

"On the inside of this pamphlet you will see warning signs of abusive behaviors in a dating/marriage partner," Jenny said. "I know a lot of you feel like this stuff only happens on tv, or maybe to other people, but I want to share something with you guys." She cleared her throat again, and for the first time, actually looked human to Vanessa, as her blue eyes took on a vulnerability to them. "I have been in a domestic violence situation." Jenny briefly looked down at the floor, but then roamed the room to search each girl in the eye. Her voice ringing with sincerity, she said, "If you feel like you have noticed any of these signs in your partner or your relationship, please come see me, contact local campus security, or even the counseling center. We are here for you, and I want you to know that you have support and resources." After her full presentation, Jenny dismissed the girls and Vanessa and CeeCee made it back to their room.

"Well. That was interesting!" CeeCee announced while plopping down on her bed. They had finally gotten the room just the way they wanted and Vanessa had been right; it was fly. The girls had color-coordinated their comforters, opting for violet and pink. Large overstuffed pillows in a variety of textures such as fur, glitter, and microfiber, decorated each bed, while thick cream curtains draped the windows. They chose a white faux bear skin rug to spread out on the floor, giving it a grown and sexy feel. At least, that's what CeeCee had said when they found it on Craigslist. Vanessa sat at her desk and stretched her long legs in front of her, feeling somewhat subdued and quiet. "What chew' think about the meeting, V?" CeeCee studied her with raised eyebrows.

"I don't know. I thought it was kind of weird. I mean, what teenager goes through domestic violence?"

"Well, she said it can be with dating couples too." CeeCee opened the pamphlet while laying on her back and read out loud the information. Vanessa listened out of respect, but really didn't want to hear it. Yea, maybe she had experienced some difficult moments in her relationship, but it hadn't gotten *abusive*.

I've just got to learn to stop pushing Rico's hot buttons, she told herself and tossed the pamphlet in the very bottom of her desk drawer.

* * *

Vanessa concluded the first semester with flying colors. She got A's in everything but English Lit.

"Can you believe that chic gave me a B+? Like she just couldn't at least give me an A-," Vanessa huffed to her friends as they walked to the gym. "And the sad thing is, I got to take her again this semester for another English class!"

"I mean, V, how many A's do you need in your life?" Diane asked completely out of breath. She was struggling to keep up with Vanessa's long strides.

"Right. Girl, you still have the rest of your college career to kill it in!" Tina added. She was also having a hard time with the pace. Vanessa realized her friends were a little behind, so she slowed down, but when she did, CeeCee ran smack into her.

"Dag, girl. My bad!" Vanessa said.

CeeCee laughed. "V, you are on a mission!"

"I know. But Rico is supposed to meet me there, so I don't want to be late." The other girls looked at each other.

"Umm, we thought this was just girl's time," CeeCee said. Vanessa instantly felt bad. She hadn't realized she had double-booked herself until she got her boyfriend's text to confirm their meeting a half hour ago. She knew he would be upset if she backed out for her friends.

"Yea. I know it was, but I had made plans with him too and totally forgot." She shrugged and adjusted her workout pants as a distraction from the guilt.

"Dag. So you just ditchin' us then, huh?" CeeCee crossed her arms and stopped walking. Diane and Tina stayed silent, looking from one girl to the other.

Vanessa folded her arms too and faced CeeCee. "Look, I didn't do it on purpose. We'll just rain check it. No big deal."

"Nessa, wuz up wit' chew'? You got yo head in the clouds when it comes to that dude. You haven't been yourself since you started dating him. You always asking his permission to do x, y, and z. You spend *most* of your free time with him. You even quit the dance team because of him!" CeeCee's voice was rising with each sentence.

"First of all, I didn't *quit* the team because of *him*. I *quit* the team because I was doing too much! And who are you to judge when it comes to dating?" Vanessa put her hands on her hips and rolled her neck. "You wouldn't know love if it smacked you in the face!"

"Whoa. Alright y'all, just chill," Diane intervened.

"Yea, y'all trippin. Don't do this," Tina added.

CeeCee let out a breath. "Vanessa, I thought I knew love," she said, her voice shaking. "I thought I knew love through *you*!" She pointed a finger for emphasis. "But chew' right. Maybe I don't know what love is. Maybe the sisterhood I *thought* we had, doesn't really exist!" She pivoted in her Nike's and stomped away. Vanessa called after her, but it was too late. She knew her friend well enough to know her pride wouldn't let her turn around.

"I'm sorry, y'all. It's hard tryna' balance everything sometimes," Vanessa said, her brown eyes full of regret.

"We understand you're in love, Vanessa, but you have many different loves in your life. CeeCee is definitely one of those loves," Tina said.

"You right. I'll make it up to her," Vanessa promised, then resumed her pace. She couldn't really worry about CeeCee right now. Rico was waiting.

After their workout, they went to get hot chocolate at the cafe near campus. Vanessa looked at Rico, admiring the way his wavy hair curled up from sweat.

"I don't even want you hanging around that girl anyway, babe. She is bad news." He sipped on his drink as they sat in the car with the heat on in the parking lot. Vanessa had filled him in on her fight with CeeCee. She hadn't been able to shake the sadness, even after their workout.

"CeeCee and I have been friends forever. It's just a lot of change happening. Plus, she's had a lot of loss in her life." Vanessa played with the lid on her cup, admiring the winter landscape through the window. Rico put a hand on her thigh, and she immediately felt warm inside.

"I'm serious, Nessa. She's all over the place with different dudes all the time. It's not a good look for you." He caressed her leg and gazed at her with affection. She never seemed to be able to resist his charm, but in this instance, she couldn't do her friend like that.

"Well, I'm not giving up on my girl. She's had too many folks do that."

Rico looked at her silently. "I guess that's what I love about you. Your loyalty." She smiled and covered his hand with hers.

"That's right!" She let her mood lighten and ran her fingers through his curls, playfully wrapping a few tendrils around her finger.

"But if it were down to me and CeeCee, you know what you would need to do," he said. He leaned in and kissed her neck gently, then breathed slowly and rhythmically beneath her ear. Everything seemed fuzzy and all she could feel were warm sensations on her skin and in her belly. She gave in to all those sensations.

* * *

It was a week before either girl spoke, and it was the longest week of Vanessa's life. It was hard enough being distant from her best friend, but to also share a room with her in silence was even more difficult.

"I know you still mad, but CeeCee, you have to understand my position," Vanessa said, while sitting at her desk one evening. CeeCee was on her bed typing on her laptop, but stopped when Vanessa started speaking.

"Vanessa, I'm not saying you don't have a lot goin' on, but for you to play me like I haven't been here for the last 10 years for a dude that's been in your life for less than a year, man. I mean, that shit hurts." Vanessa turned around, pushing her textbook out of the way and facing her friend.

"I really wasn't trying to play you, C. I just had a mix up and I didn't know how to admit it to y'all. I was hoping to just play it off when we got to the gym."

"I mean, I get it. You never felt this way before. But honestly, V, I'm not sure about Rico. I was looking at that pamphlet we got last semester from Jenny, and I never thought I would be saying this, but I think the girl may know a little somethin'." She nodded her head towards the pamphlet laying open next to her laptop.

"Girl, you trippin on a pamphlet?" Vanessa smirked.

"Look, I'm just saying, look at this list and tell me if you don't see some stuff on here you can relate to." CeeCee looked at her friend pleadingly and shoved the pamphlet in front of her.

Vanessa quickly ran her eyes down the list of characteristics of domestic and dating violence. She started to blow off her friend until she got to the third one: "Isolates you from community." She felt a weight in her stomach. The memory of Rico trying to talk her out of her friendship with CeeCee just last week surfaced. She pushed the memory away, but others replaced it. She was always on a clock with Rico. If she didn't respond fast enough to texts and phone calls, he thought she was cheating. If she hung around Tony too much, it made him jealous. There was a long list of "don'ts" with him, and she was trying her hardest to keep up with it. She let out a sigh, then lowered her eyes.

"I don't know, C. I love Rico, and I have never seen myself in somebody's future the way I do with him." CeeCee walked over and knelt before her friend, taking both hands in hers.

"Vanessa, I love you, and I know you're in love, but domestic violence is serious. It could seem like harmless behavior now, but it's bound to escalate. You have to talk to someone." She rubbed her hands over Vanessa's and looked up into her eyes with concern.

"Wow. When did you get so mature?" Vanessa joked. CeeCee laughed.

"Maybe you been rubbing off on me! Plus, I been goin' to Bible study with Tina. They're teaching on Psalm 139 and relating it to self-worth." She shrugged. "So, you know, if God could value us and love us that much, surely a man should be able to." Wow. Vanessa was surprised and impressed. CeeCee in Bible study, growing and maturing?

And here I thought I was going to be the good influence on her, Vanessa thought.

* * *

Vanessa sat in her psychology 101 class near the back. It was her first class in her actual major, and the large auditorium was full of students.

"I have been a practicing clinical psychologist for 15 years now. I love the field so much that I want to help others discover the beauty in this particular science," Professor Redmond shared on the first day of class. Today she stood in front of the 100-something students looking flawless. From her diamond earrings, red cardigan and black and white patterned pants, to her black Dolce & Gabbana heels, she embodied how Vanessa saw herself in the future. Vanessa listened intently as Professor Redmond discussed the ins and outs of healthy relationships and how to notice warning signs in unhealthy relationships. She tried to ignore the weird flip-flops her stomach was producing.

"Remember, I offer personal counseling sessions for anyone interested, so feel free to use the cell on your syllabus," Professor Redmond informed. "Also, we will have a quiz on the reading, so be ready!" Vanessa took notes, highlighted her syllabus, circled the cell phone that was listed, then hurried to get to her next class across campus.

The day flew by with one class after another. Breathing deeply, Vanessa crashed her back to the wall and closed her eyes when she finally made it to her room later on that evening. When she opened them, she was shocked to see Rico waiting for her. He stared at her silently, a grim expression on his normally attractive face.

"How did you get in here?" She frowned, thinking CeeCee must have forgotten to lock the door.

"I have my waysh," he answered sluggishly.

He looks awful, Vanessa thought to herself. Rico's eyes were bloodshot and his hair was disheveled. *He must have been drinking,* she deducted.

"Why you not anshering my callsh, Vanesha?" he slurred. She slowly closed the door behind her and puffed out a sharp sigh.

"Rico, you know Mondays are my busy days this semester. I didn't even have time to breath, let alone call you." She sat down, took off her shoes and started unloading her books on her desk. Rico moved fast and had a firm grip on her wrist before she could even respond.

"Ow! You're hurting me!" She caught his hand and looked up at him with a pained expression.

"Don't blow me off! You lyin' to me ain't chew'!" He stared at her and she fought to free his hold.

"Let me go!" she said, but he only held her tighter. Her heart started beating fast and the beautiful brown eyes she had come to love glared angrily back at her.

"You think you gon' do me like dey did don't chew'? Huh?" He jerked her and she fell on the floor. "Give me yo phone!" he commanded. She rubbed her wrist, trying to relieve the pain.

"What? Why?" She looked up at him confused.

"Shooo I can sheee yo texts!" He reached for her messenger bag and rifled through until he got what he wanted.

"Rico, you trippin', and you drunk. Stop actin' like this!" She looked out the side of her eye, trying to figure out how fast she could get to the door. He was standing over her, and she didn't think she would make it. He grabbed her face and placed it in front of her phone screen to unlock it.

"You shtill talking to Tony, huh? What did I tell you about that!" he said, while reading through her texts. He then yanked her off the floor and made her stand in front of him.

"Me and Tony are *just* friends! It's nothing between us!" Vanessa breathed heavily and frantically searched for something, anything, she could use to protect herself.

"What is goin' on in here?" CeeCee stood at the door looking confused. Rico immediately let go of her arm, and Vanessa stepped away from him. She locked eyes with CeeCee and didn't have to say a word.

"Get out of here, Rico," CeeCee said, holding the door open. Rico's face softened.

"Nessa, I'm sorry. I just had too much to drink." He looked at her apologetically, then rubbed the back of his neck. Vanessa looked down at the floor, massaging her wrist.

"Get out now, before I get the RA," CeeCee said, now more firmly with her hand on her hip. Rico smacked his teeth at her and left.

"Girl, you ok?" After locking the door, CeeCee hurried over to her friend, and they both collapsed on top of Vanessa's brilliant, violet comforter.

"No. No, I'm not." She leaned her body against her friend's and let the tears flow. CeeCee held her tight and rocked her as if she were rocking a child.

* * *

In the following weeks Vanessa's schedule included counseling with Professor Redmond, talking to her family about her relationship with Rico, going to Bible study with her friends, and even connecting more with her RA. She decided to end things with Rico, though he had begged her not to. She almost caved, but her family was adamant that she needed to let things go.

"He needs to get help," her mother had told her. At first her father was too angry to even speak. She felt like she had disappointed them, but they assured her otherwise.

Vanessa

"Vanessa, we understand you are learning and growing, and the only way to do that is to make mistakes," her father finally said.

"Thanks, Daddy." She blew him a kiss over their video chat.

"How are things?" Tina asked. She crossed her legs on the floor Indian style while they waited for the pizza to arrive. It was Friday night, and they were having a girl's night. CeeCee and Diane were late, so Vanessa had a chance to catch up with her friend.

"It's been hard. I miss him so much, and often I have to remind myself why I had to let him go." Vanessa looked down at the bruise tattooed on her wrist where Rico had held her. It was fading.

"You are brave, Vanessa. Not everyone gets a chance to walk away."

"I know. But it's a battle every day." She thought about the last time she had seen Rico. His eyes were stained with regret, but he hadn't made any mention of getting help. "The only thing that keeps me is that he hasn't changed, and I know it will happen again if he doesn't get help." Vanessa played with the ring on her finger her dad had gotten her. It was a purity ring.

"You will always be my baby girl, Vanessa, but I understand you are becoming a young woman," he told her when they went for a walk one evening during her visit. "I just want you to know your value, and that you are never too far out of God's reach for His love,

157

or mine." He had embraced her then, and she couldn't stop the tears from flowing.

"Yea. That is wise," Tina said, bringing Vanessa back to the present. "I know it doesn't feel like it now, but this will work for your good, Vanessa."

Vanessa nodded, remembering that was a scripture they had read about in their last Bible study. "Well, one good thing that has happened recently is, I finally got an A in my English class!" she said, her chocolate face lighting up.

"Wow, foreal? That's awesome, girl!"

"Yea, I know! Here, I'll read to you the comments Professor Lewis made." She rustled through some papers on her desk before pulling out the paper she was looking for.

"Ms. James, after having you a second time I can definitely see improvement in your writing! That depth I was looking for last semester seems to have snuck up on you! Good writers need life experience to really manifest genius. This, Vanessa, is genius. A+"

"Wow! That's awesome, V! Before you were just smart! Now you're a genius!" Tina said. Both girls fell into laughter.

"Yea. When I first started school, I was so excited for the freedom and independence and I had so many questions on identity and purpose. But now I feel like some of those questions are being answered. I just didn't know they would be answered in the way that they are." She put the paper back on her desk and sat on her bed.

"Hmmm. Yea, I'm sure everyone feels that way. And I'm sure no one has all the answers." Tina looked up at her thoughtfully while squeezing a large pillow with grey tassels in her arms.

"Yea. And I used to think I was untouchable in certain ways. Now I know better."

"Well, sister, it's good that you know. Some people don't learn that lesson 'til much later in life." Vanessa smiled at her friend, grateful to have met someone with such a good head on her shoulders. There were so many around her that loved her dearly. She couldn't fathom learning her lessons apart from these people.

Vanessa stretched out on her bed and glanced out the window at the greenery peeking through. A blue bird landed on a branch that brushed up against her window. It was finally spring.

CALVIN & MONICA

"This is *not* how it was supposed to be." Calvin shook his head in disbelief. He twisted the hem of his t-shirt like doing so could change things. Like *he* could change things.

"I know." Monica dropped her neck low; any lower and it would have hit the curb. What was the point? She had run it over in her head a million times of what she did and why she did it and she just didn't have a reason. At least, that's what she told herself.

"Can't you give me an answer? I mean I need something, Mo. Two years..." Calvin stopped fiddling with his shirt and laid his hands on the steering wheel, staring straight ahead. Even though it was dark outside, Monica could see his eyes looked ice cold.

"I know. You're hurt. I know I hurt you. And you have every reason to be..." she choked. She couldn't finish. What had she done? "I deserve this. I deserve however you feel. I don't have a reason," she tried. Or did she? Did she really not have a reason? *Maybe I was just bored, or lonely,* she thought to herself. But how could she say that out loud? How could she offer such a shallow reason for a man who meant more to her than life itself?

"Get out," Calvin said flatly. He was still staring straight ahead, but now he was gripping the steering wheel of his 1967 Chevy Impala. It was a collector's item. His grandfather gave it to him on his 22nd birthday, right after he graduated. He was the first person to finish college in three generations. The first to get a full-time gig at a Fortune 500 company. The first for so many things.

"I'm sorry. I'm so sorry, Calvin." Monica laid her well-manicured hand on the passenger's door, the pink nail polish shining in the darkness. "Please know that I do love you. I do…"

Silence. What was she expecting, for him to agree? To say that even though she cheated on him with his best friend of 10 years, she was forgiven? He would ride with her through whatever? If that was her expectation, it was swiftly expelling out the car door, she now had standing open. She saw her stiletto-heeled foot hit the ground more than she felt it, shocked that her body was moving, even though she hadn't told it to.

"I'll keep my phone by me if you want to talk tonight," she offered, pathetically. She was standing by the car now, and stole a glance at him through the window, but he refused to look her way. She supposed it was enough that he hadn't pulled off while she was still exiting the car.

After all, that's what I deserve, she thought, while continuing to stare at his shadowed profile through the rolled-up windows. It started to rain.

Calvin turned the ignition on along with his windshield wipers and Monica took a cautious step back, shoving her hands in her fitted jeans. She let the rain drops fall, unable to move. Just like that, he was gone, and the rear lights of his navy-blue Impala flashed behind him. She turned to her apartment building and looked upward, her short, wet hair falling limply into her eyes. Suddenly, living on the 12th floor didn't feel so appealing. Having a penthouse suite was usually a luxury. Hosting rooftop parties with her friends and serving romantic dinners to Calvin had been the opportunity when other neighbors were fast asleep, or would even join in on the fun. Now, she slumped her shoulders in the rain and kept her head bowed as she entered inside, hoping her neighbors were fast asleep.

"I just want to be in my bed," she said with a heavy sigh, wiping the moist bangs from her face.

The elevator was full of mirrors which normally appealed to Monica. It was her last chance to check her figure and her makeup before running downstairs to meet Calvin for an evening out, or meet her girls before they hit the mall. Now, the images reflecting back, showed her someone she didn't recognize.

A betrayer, she thought to herself, peering through her beautiful brown eyes. Mascara and eyeshadow ran together from the rain and her hair was a curly mop. She shivered and ran her hands along her arms, hugging her Coach bag closer to her. Moments later, the elevator jolted to a stop, causing her to jerk slightly.

Even the elevator is against me, she thought with disdain. Sighing, she pulled out her house key when it reached her floor, and the cream and grey décor of her small living room greeted her upon entrance. Automatically, she removed her strappy shoes, placing them carefully to the side, then headed for the kitchen.

Herbal tea, Monica thought, but she found herself staring at the Keurig. Her arm, no matter how hard she tried to lift it, wouldn't budge. She gave up and made it to the master bedroom. As soon as her feet crossed the threshold, she fell to her knees and curled into a fetal position, not far from her plush, queen-sized bed.

"God," she cried. "What have I done?" She let the tears she had been holding in all night, decorate her pretty brown face. The agony of her sin weighed on her heart, and she cried herself to sleep.

* * *

Calvin

"Aye, man! Where you at?"

Calvin shook his head to get back focused. He was on the court with some of his boys and couldn't seem to stay present.

"My bad, Dre. I'm here. I got chew'!" Calvin assured his friend, while running to get open. It was a casual game of two on two and really only Andre (who went by Dre) was his friend. The other two guys were associates from work. He had invited them there to his house that weekend before he knew his whole world would be turned upside down.

"Dude, you just gon' let him check you like that!" Dre shouted, after one of the guys, Tom, who worked in Accounting, faked Calvin out by pretending to pass the ball to his partner, Eric, who was a Finance Specialist. But when Calvin went for the fake, Tom shot it, making nothing but net.

"Dag, too easy, Calvin!" Eric said. He gave Tom a hi-five and they both laughed. Calvin sighed. He knew he was not at his best. Basketball was his game and there was no reason he couldn't take these dudes from work. They were the preppy, suburban types, and he was used to street ball.

"Aww, you know I just figured I would show y'all some hospitality, being y'all never visited before!" Calvin tried to play it off.

"Yea, yea, that's what you say!" Eric responded with a huge grin. Calvin made up in his mind not to let it happen again, and even though he and Dre still lost, he did step up his game.

"Man, it's hot! I'm ready for some refreshments!" Dre said, once the game was over. Everyone agreed and the four men, sweaty and tired, strolled into Calvin's apartment. His complex was well-plenished. It had a pool, gym and basketball court. There were even some grills in the common area, and miniature golf was set up for the residents.

"Bruh, I know you got some Gatorade in this joint!" Dre said. All four young men eagerly stepped inside the air-conditioned unit. Calvin was immediately grateful he had listened to Monica. When he told her he was inviting the guys over, she harped on him about getting groceries, especially Gatorade.

"Now, Calvin, you know you are ravished after you play and yo boys are no different. Make sure you don't leave 'em hanging!" She had said while she fixed a salad for them to munch on. She was always making sure he ate vegetables.

"Hey, they get what they get! And, babe, why can't we have regular salad dressing? Why you gotta skimp on the salad? It's already nothin' but veggies!" He held up his bowl in front of her so that she could see he was being jipped.

"It does *have dressing! Just not that thick, creamy stuff you like!"* Monica smiled sweetly while handing him a fork. *"It has olive oil and lemon juice!"*

"Babe, when you put a fruit on top of a salad and call that dressing, you have gone too far!" he protested.

Monica laughed. *"You will thank me when we are old and gray and still lookin' this good!"* she said, then eased down on the couch next to him, placing her bowl of salad on her lap.

"Girl, we only 25! We got time!" he said, laughing at her.

"Yea, well, if God allows, we gon' look this good in 25 more years!" She elbowed him, and he pushed her away playfully.

"Yea. I can't be mad at that!" he said, then kissed her forehead affectionately.

At the time, even though he didn't say it, he was internally thankful she was thinking about their future.

I can't believe how much has changed, Calvin thought to himself, while standing in his kitchen preparing the food. The guys made themselves comfortable in the living room and had the game on.

"Calvin, you need some help?" Dre walked into the kitchen, his short fade and tall frame looming in the entryway. He and Calvin had been friends since they were teenagers, but their relationship had usually centered on Jamal. It was rare they spent alone time together without him.

"Sure, man. That's cool." Calvin was pouring chips into a bowl. "Can you put salsa in that bowl?" He pointed to the small plastic container on top of the counter.

"Yea. Aye, you heard from Jamal?" Dre asked, while reaching for the bowl.

Calvin stiffened. He knew it was a perfectly normal question, inevitable in fact. Yet and still, hearing his best friend's name set off something deep inside him.

God, please help me, he said a short prayer, then looked at Dre and shrugged.

"Naw, man. He's been MIA." He proceeded to roll up the chip bag, imagining it was Jamal's thick neck.

"Yea. I been trying to get a hold of him. I thought I'd see him here today. I was shocked he didn't come over." Dre looked around in the fridge until he located the salsa.

Calvin busied himself by making sandwiches. *How can I say the real, when Jamal is Dre's friend too?*

"Yea, I think he's had a work thing going on at the shop. A project," he tried.

"You think? I thought he was done with that car he was working on?" Dre stopped pouring the salsa and looked at his friend with a perplexed expression.

Calvin shrugged again and kept his eyes on his task. "Yea, well, it's his loss."

"Maybe we should hit him up after your boys leave?"

"Maybe not," Calvin shot back, and instantly regretted his harsh tone. Dre looked at him, surprised. "I didn't mean it like that. Look, man, can you get the beer out the fridge?" he added, hoping to distract his friend.

"Dude, what's up? Something happen wit' y'all?" Dre had completely disregarded his request. Calvin knew it wasn't the time, but could tell Dre wasn't going to drop the topic until he gave him something.

"Yo! Where's the food?" Eric yelled from the living room.

"Yea, man, we get better service at McDonald's!" Tom added.

"Chill out! Y'all act like just because you won *one* game you own me!" Calvin said, but sped up his pace with the sandwiches. "Man, can you get the beers and help me out?" His eyes begged Dre to comply. Thankfully he did.

The rest of the afternoon was filled with light banter and some work talk. The Heat played the Celtics and won. Eric made a bet, but lost to Dre who was an avid Heat fan. Calvin was feeling somewhat distracted by his company, until he checked his cell. Two missed calls from Jamal and three texts from Monica. They were blowing him up, but he had his phone on silent. He just wasn't ready. He hadn't talked to Monica since the night she told him. He did however confront Jamal, and that didn't go over well at all. He should have waited until his temper subsided.

"What the hell was you thinkin'?" Calvin had Jamal pinned against the outside wall of the movie theater. Calvin knew Jamal's shift, and that he would be at his second job that night. He was waiting for him to leave, not really knowing what he was going to say, but found himself sitting in the parking lot anyway.

"Calvin, I'm so sorry. I really am. I was so drunk. But I know that's not an excuse!" Jamal had his hands up, and even though he

was physically stronger than Calvin, he allowed Calvin to keep him pinned. He didn't have the heart to fight back.

"For real. You gon' pull that card?" Calvin was choking his friends' work shirt, wishing he could strangle his thick neck. Jamal was solid and when he wasn't working, he was lifting. On top of that he was a good three inches taller than Calvin. Still, Calvin was at the peak of his anger, and felt he could take him.

"Man, I promise to God I never meant for nothing to happen. You was on your work trip and she wanted to hang out. We've hung out before. You know that! But I think we just got too comfortable. I think the alcohol made us forget..." Jamal was heartbroken, and it was written all over his dark complexion but Calvin refused to feel pity for him.

"You my best friend, man." Calvin released his friend's shirt as his voice shook. "And I love this girl! You know I love this girl! You know I was thinking about proposing!" He clenched his fists, trying to gain his composure. He refused to cry in front of this traitor!

"I don't know how I can ever make this up to you, man. How can I ever regain your trust? I been goin' through a lot. You know. I been struggling with everything and I let myself get weak. I let myself forget that what I have, is more than what I lost."

Calvin knew Jamal was referring to his recent financial setbacks and his grandmother's passing. His grandmother was his closest family in the world and had raised him when his mom got locked up when he was a kid.

"I'm not making excuses, Calvin. I just want chew' to know where I been at. Where my head's been at," Jamal pleaded with Calvin and Calvin stepped back.

"I need time. I need time to think." Calvin looked away while capturing the back of his head with his hands. He started rubbing his neck back and forth, and sighed deeply.

"I understand, man. I understand. I know this sounds lame, but I am prayin'. I been prayin'. I knew this was gon' mess you up. But know, nothing is happening with me and Monica. It was one time and that's it. It wasn't ever supposed to be. We were stupid." He shook his head with regret, eyes glued to the ground in shame.

Calvin heard his friend but it sounded like his words were a thousand miles away. That's how much pain he was in.

"I'll holla," was all he could offer. He turned and made his way to his Impala. How could he possibly forgive his friend for such a betrayal?

"Father, what is happening right now? How is it that everyone around me has hurt me this deeply?" he asked aloud, while sitting in the driver's seat. He didn't really expect an answer, but one came anyway.

"I will keep him in perfect peace whose mind is stayed on Me," said the still, small voice.*

One thing was for sure, Calvin knew he would need this peace in the coming days to function in his normal life.

* * *

Monica

"I'm not one to give advice, you know this, Mo. But girl, you have *got* to get it together!" Sonya looked at her friend with concern.

Monica sighed. "I know, girl. I know, but I am so *jacked.*" The two were walking in the park that was located near Monica's apartment complex. They often walked or ran the trail. Today was definitely a walking day for Monica. She didn't have the heart to run.

"I just keep replaying it. Why didn't I ask him to leave after the first kiss? Why did I think we would be cool in the apartment by ourselves anyway? Why did I think we were above basic human nature of men and women?" She looked up at the sky in exasperation, her hands gesturing wildly.

"Girl, you have *got* to give yourself a break. You are human just like the rest of us! I know you struggle with perfectionism, but it simply does not exist. You and Jamal had a real friendship. You trusted him. You were comfortable. You thought it was safe because nothing had ever happened before. It was a blind spot." Sonya's voice was colored with compassion as she touched her friend's shoulder. She was the perfect person for Monica to confide in because she was the opposite of Monica. Whereas Monica was more reserved, Sonya was the free spirit. She saw life as an ebb and flow of opportunity for growth.

"Most growth comes through mistakes," she had once told Monica. At the time, Monica knew it was true, but it still annoyed the mess out of her. Why couldn't growth come through always making the right choices?

Monica dragged out a breath as they walked their final mile. Joggers passed, mom's pushed babies in strollers and dog walkers let their beloved canines lead the way. It was a beautiful, sunny day, but that did nothing for her disposition.

"It just feels like my world has ended. And it feels like I caused it, which makes it worse." She folded her arms in frustration. "Like there's nothing I can do to reverse it. I can't change the past." She looked over at a dog playing catch with his owner.

If only life were that carefree again, she thought to herself longingly.

"The past can't be changed, but it can be forgiven," Sonya said in a soothing tone. "That's by Lysa Terkeurst." She smoothed a hand on her friend's back and stroked it gently.

"Hmmm, that's good." Monica sighed, but this time it was less heavy. "I can see that," she said, reflecting on the woman's wise words.

The two were quiet for a moment, and the light breeze seemed to calm her.

"Daughter, your sins are forgiven," she felt God say to her heart. And though it wasn't the first time she had heard that

message, it felt like it was the first time she could actually receive it.

"I wish I could make Calvin see I love him. I want to be with *him*. I don't want anyone else." She walked a little less hurriedly this time, and her friend's shorter legs more easily fell into step.

"You are going to have to trust God with your future, Mo." Sonya said, turning to her and lifting her wavy black hair from her neck. "I know it's gonna be hard because you feel like you're responsible for the hurt you caused, and there are consequences to our actions, but you have to believe, it will work for the good. If you are meant to be with Calvin, then it's not going to destroy your relationship, it will be used for your purpose together." She looked at her confidently, her small, round eyes shining with care.

"I know. I know. I just wish I could speed things up. Like I could *do* something." Monica bit her lip and let out a breath.

"Girl, you have done *enough*. You just gonna have to wait." Sonya resumed their pace, and Monica fell into step.

Monica knew her friend was right. She had texted Calvin three times already and he wasn't responding. She had let a week pass before reaching out, hoping that was enough time for him to process enough to at least want to have a conversation. Clearly that was not the case.

"Let's get some ice cream," Sonya suggested after they finished their walk.

"Girl, I have had my share of ice cream and wine this whole week. I need to lay off it!" Monica admitted.

Sonya laughed. "Mo, where do you put it? Cuz I don't see it at all!" She looked her friend up and down and squeezed her own full hips.

Monica knew she was right. Her petite frame rarely held on to the calories. She gave thanks for her high metabolism every day.

"You right, girl. I guess I can afford to indulge," she joked, and the two drove over to the ice cream parlor. Spending time with Sonya really lifted her spirits and Monica was grateful she had reached out to her friend. She was so ashamed, and so afraid to tell anyone about her indiscretion, and yet knew she needed an outlet. They even went to a movie after getting ice cream, and by the time Monica got home, she was ready to wind down.

Just as she was running water for a bath, Monica's phone rang. She was shocked to see his picture pop up.

"Hi," she answered gingerly.

"Hey. Can we talk?" Calvin's voice was soft also and she could hear the freshness of his pain, even though she was sure he was trying to hide it.

"Yea, just let me turn off this water. I was running a bath." Monica hastily turned the knobs on the tub with one hand while gripping the phone with the other. She couldn't believe he called!

"How are you?" she asked. She sat on the sofa Indian style and hugged a pillow to her chest.

"I'm ok. How 'bout chew'?"

"Doing ok. I hung out with Sonya today." She tried her best to sound normal. Like this was their everyday. Like she hadn't just destroyed all trust in their relationship with her stupidity.

"That's cool. What was she talkin' 'bout?"

She could picture him lying on his bed on his back, the way he did when he was relaxing. Sometimes they would Facetime and he would be in that position, even though it seemed awkward to her, because he would be holding the phone in the air like that.

"She's trying to go to this Summer Walker concert next month, but I'm not sure if I wanna go. You know she always trying to kick it. She met this dude who gave her free tickets, but the concert is in Chicago and that is a little drive. I don't know if it's in my budget." Her voice sounded extra bubbly, even to her.

Chill, girl. Don't try so hard, she reprimanded herself.

"Oh yea? Sounds dope. You should go. I mean, it would be fun." His voice was sincere.

Typical Calvin. Always wanting her to enjoy herself. One of the things she loved about him was how free he was about their time. He always gave her space and let her do her thing.

Maybe he gave me too much space, she thought, while gazing out the large window on the side of the living room. The sky was overcast, unlike earlier in the day when she had gone for her walk with Sonya.

"Yea. I may. But anyways, how was your day? Didn't yo boys come over?"

"Yea, they did. It was cool. We lost at a game of b ball-"

"What? You lost?" Monica said, interrupting him. She was shocked. She knew Calvin was amazing on the court.

"Yea," Calvin said. "And they wouldn't let me hear the end of it. I know I'm 'bout to hear all about it at the office this week." He sighed, and his voice sounded heavy.

"Man, you must have really been off your game, babe." Whoops. Was she still allowed to call him that?

He paused. "Yea. Well, you must know why…" he finally responded. They were both silent.

"Calvin, what do you need? What do you need from me?" She pressed her face against the phone and bowed her body over her legs, while taking in the fleeting moments of him.

"I think I just need *time,* Monica. I can't say I'm in a place to still be wit' chew'. I can't be wit' chew' if I don't trust you. And right now, I don't trust you," he said in a gruff tone.

Monica felt her gut contract with each word.

"Oh," Monica said. The truth hurt. "I understand." She wrapped her arms tightly around her body, then laid on her side, keeping the phone smothered against her ear.

"I didn't want to leave you hangin', but truth be told, I'm not even ready to have a polite conversation wit' chew'. I'm mad as hell and I know I need time to let God heal me." His voice hardened on the other end; his pain now blatant.

"Yea. I get it. I do. I know I was being selfish reaching out to you earlier today. It's just been hard being away from you." She felt her voice catch. "But I respect what you need. I want to give you what you need." She said the words in a whisper, and heard the rain start to beat against the glass of the large picture window set in the middle of the wall by the dining area.

"I need for us to not be together, Monica. I need space." His tone was flat and each word tore Monica apart. She heard a whirling in her brain, and struggled to speak.

"Child, let him go," said the inner voice she knew so well.

"Ok," she heard herself say. "I understand. I'll be here when you're ready." A thick lump formed in the middle of her throat as the tears started streaming.

"Thank you. I'll call when I'm ready," he said, before the line went dead.

Monica laid on the couch for what seemed like an hour. She really had no concept of time, and didn't know that it had only been 15 minutes.

"Calvin called. He broke up with Me. He needs time. Please keep me in prayer." She typed out a message to Sonya.

Within minutes she got a response: **"I'm praying for you, sis. Remember all things work for the good."**

Monica didn't bother responding. She didn't have the strength. "God, help me see the good in this situation," she prayed, then decided to finish running her bath.

That night she had a dream, and in the dream, she was dancing. She was dancing so freely and it was exhilarating. She was not alone. Her partner was tall and strong and striking. He was whirling her around and she was surrounded by love. She knew that He was the perfect dancer and that she was the luckiest woman on earth to have such an amazing dance partner.

"I could dance like this forever!" she exclaimed, as He whirled and twirled her around on an immaculate dance floor.

"And you shall beloved! You shall!" When she looked up to see His face, all she saw was light. So much light, it filled the room, reflecting off the marble dance floor and glass windows.

"Jesus!" she said and woke up.

"Whoa!" Monica said. She laid there on her 800-count thread sheets before turning on the lamp by her night stand, then reached for her journal. She had never had a dream so vivid before and knew it had to be from God. She scribbled feverishly, not wanting to forget any detail.

"God, what does this mean?" she asked. After a moment of silence, Monica decided to go back to bed. Her curiosity was overcome by her emotional weariness, and she drifted off to sleep.

* * *

Calvin

Calvin wasn't the type that was easily impressed, therefore his extreme reverence for Carl Hill was unusual. The two had grown in their affection for one another over the last year after connecting at a church picnic. Carl was one of the ministers of the church and was well liked.

"Hey, Calvin. I'm so glad you called! You had been on my heart, man," Carl said. He strolled to where Calvin was seated in one of their favorite meeting places and embraced the younger man in his arms, before taking a seat.

"It's good to see you too, Carl. Thanks for taking the time to meet me." Calvin's heart warmed when they embraced. Carl had always been a safe place for him to confide in and even though he was 20 years his senior, he was super down to earth, and nonjudgmental.

"Hey, you know I'm always here for you, man." Carl flashed a wide, genuine smile. His salt and pepper beard always made Calvin want to let his own grow out, but Monica liked the smooth look.

Maybe I'll switch it up now, he thought to himself, feeling bitter.

The waitress came over and took their orders then they fell into small talk.

"So, how is work going?" Carl sat back, taking a generous sip of his lemonade, his large belly brushing the table.

"It's been cool, pretty intense though," Calvin admitted. His expression was pensive. "I'm working my butt off, but also trying to grow my relationships like you suggested." He slid his hands together back and forth thoughtfully.

Carl's eyes lit up. "Oh yea? How's that?"

"I've been having lunch with some of the guys, instead of alone in my office. I even invited them to the house a couple of times," he shared. "Being a sales rep, you can get caught up in competition, but I'm learning that my purpose is greater there, than just making sales."

"Well, good for you! I'm sure you'll find the most rewarding aspects of your job will be the people." Carl nodded encouragingly then took another large swallow from his glass. He drank eagerly, like a drowning victim gulping for air.

Calvin nodded his head in agreement, listening intently. "Yea. That's what I feel like God is saying to me."

"I remember when I worked at the bank and started climbing the corporate ladder. I was so focused on the money and status that I didn't realize I couldn't take any of that with me until my boss suddenly had a heart attack and died. Right there at the office," Carl shared.

Calvin's eyes widened in unbelief. "Wow!"

"Yea. He never recovered, and it was a blow to the whole division. That's when I changed my approach and started making more of an effort to get to know the people there." He crossed one leg on top of the other and stared out the window. "Man, it haunted me that I barely knew anything about my boss. I knew he had a wife and kids, but I didn't know what his hobbies were. What they liked to do on the weekends. And most importantly, I never knew his faith." Carl shook his head regretfully, his full lips set into a thin line.

The waitress approached then and set their food down. Calvin meditated on his friend's words as they began eating.

"So, you think it's ok to talk about faith in the workplace?" Calvin asked, eyeing his fries. He knew Monica would have wanted him to get sweet potato fries. Rebelliously, he popped the unhealthy carb into his mouth and chewed slowly. To his dismay, it wasn't that tasty.

"I think you should be led by God, but yes, I think the workplace is the perfect opportunity to connect with others, and build a relationship where you are comfortable in sharing your faith." Carl said, after taking a hearty bite of his burger.

"Interesting. I've never really talked to anyone openly about God at work." In fact, Calvin had always dodged the topics of faith and politics in public settings; that's what he had been taught to do growing up.

"Religion and politics are the most divisive subjects to mankind!" his mom had proclaimed when he was younger. Everyone in the family seemed to agree with her.

"Again, be led, son. But remember, 'the heavens is the Lord's but the earth He has given to man'.** All of the earth belongs to us through Christ's redemption and we have authority and dominion," Carl responded. He took another bite of his sandwich.

Calvin nodded, soaking up the other man's wisdom. He always enjoyed talking to Carl because he was constantly learning something from him.

"So, what else is new? How is Ms. Monica doing?" Carl's affection for Calvin's ex was obvious. He had spent time with the young couple many times, inviting them over for dinner where his wife served her famous fried chicken, greens, cornbread and homemade mac and cheese. Even Monica, who was pretty health conscious, made her plate full when they were dining over.

Calvin's heart ached at the question. "Well," he said slowly. Clearing his throat, he pushed around the food on his plate. "That's kind of what I wanted to talk to you about, Carl." He took a sip of his water and let his eyes drop to his half eaten grilled cheese and fries. "We broke up."

"Wow, son. I'm sorry to hear that!" And he genuinely was. "What happened? How did this come about?" Carl stopped eating and looked at his friend with concern.

Calvin dove into the story, sharing every detail; from the time she told him in his Impala, until their last phone conversation where he broke up with her.

"Wow, brother, that's heavy." Carl sat there, stunned and silent. Calvin knew he was praying, and was grateful he had shared with someone who's first response was prayer.

"I remember dating a woman in college I was so in love with," Carl said after a moment. "I swore I was going to marry this girl. Every time I saw her my heart did that pitter patter they talk about in movies. I couldn't seem to focus on my studies, I was so smitten." He laughed at himself.

Calvin observed the gleam in Carl's eye as his mind raced back in time. "Well, what happened?" He leaned forward, curious.

"She cheated on me. Man, it broke my heart. I never thought I would recover." Carl shook his head and played with a fry on his plate.

"Wow. But it seems like you did. What was your process?" Calvin's heart felt desperate for some type of guidance. He was so lost, and in so much pain.

"Time," Carl answered simply. "And a lot of intentionality. I had to be intentional about spending time with others who loved me and affirmed my identity. I had to work towards my own future and goals and being a whole person. And most importantly, I had to forgive her." He looked at the younger man with sympathy.

"Yea. That's what I'm struggling with. Because I feel betrayed by both her *and* Jamal. How can I ever forgive *them*? I mean, this was low." Calvin pushed his plate away and sat back, dejected, in his chair. Crossing his arms, he stared daggers at his plate angrily. He wanted to pick it up and bash the hell out of those fries for not being worth the indulgence! Instead, he opted to grab a nearby fork and started twisting it in his hand repeatedly.

Carl watched his friend, then gently took the fork from his hand, and laid it down on the table in between them.

"You're right, son. But who of us has not sinned? Who has not fallen short of the glory of God?* Besides, it will be *Him* in you that will forgive. You can't do it in and of yourself." He patted Calvin's hand.

Calvin pondered this. He knew his elder's words rang true and they resonated with his heart.

"Yea. It will definitely be God. But clearly forgiveness doesn't mean reconnection, right? I mean, you forgave this girl, but you didn't reconnect with her." Calvin sighed.

"I actually did reconnect with her. We dated for about a year after some time apart but God took our paths in different directions. She accepted a position out of state and I stayed home. It was circumstantial, but I knew it was Him using our circumstances to dictate our destinies," Carl said, clearly at peace with the outcome.

"Wow. How were you able to be back in a relationship with her after she cheated? How could you trust her?" Calvin was incredulous. How could he possibly go back to Monica?

"I loved her and I knew that she was sincerely repentant. I knew her heart, and that her actions did not determine her character. We had to work on rebuilding trust and it was not easy. I would say we did the best we could, and if we hadn't felt led to go in different directions, we probably would have gotten married." Carl shrugged and Calvin shook his head.

"Wow. That's amazing. Right now, I can't see past my pain, and I know as a result, I can't see being with Monica."

"Give yourself time, and, when your pain subsides, seek God. Ask Him if this relationship is seasonal, or if it's a covenant. He will direct your path. Lean not to your own understanding."**

Calvin nodded his head while sipping his water, mulling over his friend's words. What was God saying about the relationship? What was God saying about his friendship with Jamal?

Father, I need you like never before," he thought.

"Son, I will be with you like never before," came the reply in Calvin's heart.

* * *

"I love this class!" Monica exclaimed. She and Sonya were leaving the dance studio they attended twice a week.

"Yea, girl, it is such a great workout!" Sonya flipped her gym bag over her shoulder and watched for traffic. They were both parked across the street and made their way to their cars when there was finally an opening.

"You wanna meet at Billy's for a sandwich? I need replenishment," Monica suggested, warming her arms against a cool breeze.

"That sounds good! I'll see you there!"

Monica took the scenic route, hoping her friend wouldn't mind. She found herself slowing down a lot these days and didn't want to rush through life. Her cherry red Jeep Cherokee cruised through the city until she found Billy's. It was pretty packed and she was hoping they wouldn't run into anyone they knew. In particular, Calvin.

"Hey, girl! I got us a table!" Sonya was already seated and had her menu propped open. She waved to get Monica's attention when she entered the restaurant.

"Thanks, Chica. It's such a nice night out, I had to take a little drive." Monica plopped down into the booth and picked up a menu.

"No worries. I got you!"

Monica was so grateful for Sonya's companionship. Out of all of her friends, Sonya had been her closest confident. She felt she could tell her almost anything.

"Man, I wish I could get that one move down she be doin'!" Sonya said, referring to their instructor. She peeked over her menu and spoke animatedly. "I be practicing at home in the mirror, but it's a no go."

Monica laughed. "You mean when she arches her back and twists her leg?" Monica arched her back in the small booth, trying to imitate her instructor.

"Yea, girl. I be like, she must be double jointed!" Sonya put down her menu to watch her friend.

"Girl, I'm sayin!" After laughing, the two fell silent as they looked over the menu again until finally the waitress came over and took their orders.

"So, how are things *really* goin,' Mo?" Sonya looked at her with care.

"Oh, you know…it's tough. I haven't heard from Calvin in months and I honestly don't know if I ever will." Monica shrugged. "I can say, I *have* been hearing from *God* though, and that has been comforting."

"Really? How so?" Sonya folded her hands on the table, an expression of intrigue written on her sandy brown face.

"Well, I've been dreaming more. I feel like He's been speaking to me in my dreams. What I realize, is that even though I technically cheated on Calvin, I really cheated on God."

"Hmm. Wow, that's deep, girl." Sonya looked at her with wide eyes.

"Yea. I wouldn't have thought about it like that before, but now I feel like I'm getting this revelation of the Father's covenant with me, and His desire for me." Monica's face became pensive and her almond-shaped eyes were moist with tears.

"Wow, Mo! That's awesome! Scripture does say He is jealous over us," Sonya responded in awe.***

"Yea. I've been reading Songs of Solomon lately, and that is a book I've never read before. The crazy thing is, our pastor is doing a new series on Songs of Solomon and he started it right after I started reading it on my own!" Monica shared, her own face full of wonder.

"Wow, Mo. That's awesome! Great confirmation!"

"Yea. I just never viewed God so intimately you know? Like that He would feel like I cheated on *Him*? That is a new concept to me."

"Yea. I think often we think of Him as being this eternal being without feelings. We feel like He is far away and not intimately acquainted with us." Sonya paused and took a drink of her water. "But in truth He lives in us and we are made in His image," she continued. "We have emotions and feelings because *He* has emotions and feelings."

Monica quickly glanced around Billy's with her straw still in her mouth from drinking, and breathed an inward sigh of relief. *Whew! No Calvin!*

The waitress came by and placed their orders on the table and both women eagerly began eating, needing renewal from their workout. Monica knew she was eating spiritually also.

Her friendship with Sonya was so satisfying and sweet.

"It is like the precious ointment that runs down the beard of Aaron," she heard in her spirit. Monica smiled to herself, remembering that passage in the Bible. She knew God was confirming her relationship with her friend.

"Well, it sounds like you are growing a lot through this break with Calvin. Do you think you guys will ever get back together?" Sonya asked, once she had felt full enough to talk again.

"Honestly, I have no idea. I have asked the Father that question several times, and every time I ask it, I just feel His peace. He is giving me peace in the midst of the waiting." Monica said, feeling full herself. She wiped her face with her napkin then placed it on her empty plate.

"Well, that is good. I'm glad He is walking you through this, sis. I can't imagine how difficult it would be for me to love someone and not know if we will be together." Sonya reached across the table, placed a hand over Monica's, then squeezed it. Monica squeezed back and felt grateful, once again, for her friendship.

"Yea. It really is difficult. It goes back to me trusting the Father," she said after a moment. "I have to trust Him that no matter what mistakes I make, I cannot sabotage His path for me. He already knew, and worked it for my good. Just like you told me. Still, I do struggle, and so I have to submit to Him daily, trusting Him with my future daily." Monica looked at her friend with appreciation.

"Girl, you and me both!" Sonya said, waving a hand at her.

The ladies ended their time together and Monica found herself back in her apartment that evening. She was making some tea in her Keurig when her phone vibrated on the kitchen counter. She almost dropped the steaming hot mug she was holding when she saw his name on the screen. It was Calvin.

She paced a few times and took a few sips of her tea.

"Lord, what is he saying? I am so afraid of what he could be reaching out for! I am so afraid to read this message!" She stared at the phone out of fear, too nervous that she would accidently view the message by touching it.

"Be anxious for nothing Beloved,"* she felt God's response in her heart, and instantly she was at ease.

"Right, God!" she said out loud. "I have nothing to be afraid of! If Calvin doesn't want me, I have *You*. I will always have You!" She took a deep breath and slid open the message on her phone.

"Hi, Monica. I hope you are well. I apologize if this message is disruptive at all as that is not my intent. I just wanted to know if you could set aside some time to meet me soon. I would appreciate it very much if we could reconnect."

Monica knew her response right away, but she took a few minutes to sense what Holy Spirit was saying to her before she texted back.

"Hi, Calvin, it's good to hear from you and you are not disturbing me at all. I would really enjoy meeting up with you. Please let me know a day and time and we'll see what works."

Monica leaned her back against the counter and let her lips form into a small smile. Wow! She knew God was at work. But still, what would be the outcome? What was His divine plan for her and Calvin?

* * *

It was a cool evening. Fall had settled in, and the leaves were a vast array of colors. Calvin always liked the fall because he wasn't drenched in sweat like in the summer and he wasn't freezing like in the winter. He also marveled at how death could be so beautiful; all of the amazing colors of the leaves came from them dying.

"I never knew I'd come to appreciate the fall like I do now," Monica said. She was walking slowly beside Calvin on the boardwalk near the lake. It was a place they had frequented in the past. Initially he was hesitant to meet her there. Would it dredge up too many memories? But as soon as he saw her, he was at ease. She was the woman he had fallen in love with.

"Yea, I know you always liked summer the best. What brought on your love for fall?" Calvin was curious as to the changes he could see in her. Yes, physically she had grown out her hair and was wearing it longer now, but there was something else about her. Something he couldn't put his finger on.

"Hmmm. I would say that now I appreciate the beauty that can come from death."

Wow. Calvin was surprised that she had voiced what he also felt inside.

"Yea. That's actually one of the reasons I like fall," he said, looking over at her in surprise. He placed his hands in his jean pockets as they strolled by the lake.

"Yea. Before this season, I didn't know pain could bring something beautiful. I didn't know pain could cause growth." Monica paused, and began watching the other couples taking walks. The children playing. The birds begging for food.

That's what it is! Calvin thought to himself. He sensed growth and maturity in Monica.

"Calvin, these last six months have given me time to think and self-reflect. I know I have already apologized for my actions, but I was never able to tell you *why* I did what I did." She stopped and peered her brown eyes up at him beneath thick lashes, her grey pea coat clinging tightly to her form. He watched her draw it closer when a breeze hit.

Calvin waited, not wanting to interrupt her. *She looks so beautiful*, he couldn't help but think.

"I honestly didn't know *why* at the time, but now I do." Monica cleared her throat and pushed a few curly tendrils behind her ear. "I have never met a man like you Calvin Johnson. I have had men wine and dine me and take me out, I've told you those things. But I have never had a man who I felt really wanted me for *me*. So many times, I have had to *pretend* to be who I thought they wanted me to be. I had to be this *idea* of who they wanted, but with you, I could be *all* of me, and you accepted me regardless." She cleared her throat and licked her lips, gathering her nerves.

Calvin could tell she was nervous and he fought the urge to comfort her. He needed to know if she was really ready to take full responsibility for her actions.

"So, I self-sabotaged. I didn't think that I deserved someone as good as you. A successful, driven, intelligent, faithful, not to mention good looking, Black man..."

Calvin broke into a grin when she complimented his looks. She had smiled at him when she said it.

"I didn't think I would really find someone who wanted me for *me,* and that I deserved that. That I deserved *you.* I knew I put Jamal and I in a dangerous situation that night. I reached out to *him.* I invited him in. I didn't stop him, and I know it was because I wasn't ready. I wasn't ready to receive all that stood before me. I wasn't ready to receive *you.*" She looked up at him, her eyes full of hope. "But now I am. I now know my value to God. I now know what I deserve."

How many times had he enjoyed her company? How many times had he walked with her in this very area? She made him laugh when he didn't think it was possible. He admired so many things about her from her confidence, to her intelligence, to her beauty, and now to her faith.

Lord, I didn't know if I was really making the right decision, but now I know! I didn't expect this woman before me. She's changed*!*

"Thank you for sharing that, Mo. It still hurts to hear you refer to that night. I'm still hurting inside. But I know I have had some healing because I am able to continue my friendship with Jamal. I know he's in a vulnerable season and I feel like I have the grace to walk with him through that season." They had stopped walking now, and he faced her head on, his voice strong and self-assured. He looked like a man who had been through a storm, but had made it out on the other side, intact.

"That's so good, Calvin. I'm so glad you have forgiven him. He needs you." She leaned her back against the railing and looked at the ground behind him, playing with the white gold ring on her forefinger. He had given it to her on their six-month anniversary. She never did have the heart to take it off.

"Yea. I realize I need him too. I can look back at the history of our friendship and he's never done anything like this." He moved to her side and crossed one leg over the other, resting against the railing himself. His hoodie and jean jacket made crackling noises as he positioned himself. "I know it was out of character for him. We are rebuilding our trust."

Monica nodded her head and looked away. He wasn't sure what she was thinking, but he could tell she was biting her lip as she tended to do when she was nervous.

Calvin gently took her hand. "I know it hasn't been easy for you waiting for me to reach out. I wanted to be sure that I was hearing and seeing what I needed to hear and see." Monica turned towards him and he couldn't help but respond. He was still in love with her.

"And what did you hear and see?" she asked, timidly. There was a couple near them that walked by. Calvin waited for them to gain some distance before he answered. It seemed like an eternity to Monica.

"I heard God. And I saw you." Calvin turned her face to his and cupped her chin, lovingly. "I saw you when I thought of my future, Monica. I saw you when I thought of where I wanted to be, and who I wanted to be with." Monica let the tears fall and Calvin felt his own eyes burning.

"I heard God say it was my choice. He was allowing me to make this choice." Calvin let his fingers stroke the back of her neck, longingly. "I choose you." He moved his fingers, now rubbing her cheek, and she kissed his hand. "But I know that with this choice there will be work for us. I know it won't be easy," he said, heavily.

Monica embraced his fingers with her own, running his hand over her cheek, relishing in the feel of his skin on hers.

"I know," she agreed.

"But if you want to, I'm willing to do the work," Calvin said. His voice broke. He let his hands drop to her back, pulling him towards her. The night was quiet, other than a few crickets chirping in the distance. It felt as if the world had stood still to Monica. She was elated. The man she had hurt so deeply was willing to go the distance with her.

"I had a dream about us, Calvin, but I didn't know if it would come true," she revealed. He was holding her now, and she never wanted to leave his arms.

"Oh yea, baby. What was it?" he murmured against her hair and inhaled the sweet fragrance he had so missed.

"I dreamt we were running. We were running together, and nothing could stop us. We faced so many obstacles, but every time we faced them, we overcame them. The race was hard, but we were determined, and God was with us."

"I like that dream."

"Yea, me too."

The couple continued their walk on their new journey together, not knowing where it would lead them, only knowing their history of facing challenges. They had each learned the lessons they needed for the next stage of their lives, and, even though they were not promised an outcome, they were promised the ability to overcome.

* **Isaiah 26:3** "You will keep *him* in perfect peace, *whose* mind *is* stayed *on You,* because he trusts in You.

** **Psalm 115:16** *"The heavens belong to the Lord, but he has given the earth to all mankind."*

*** **John 8:7** "They kept demanding an answer, so he stood up again and said, 'All right, hurl the stones at her until she dies. But only he who never sinned may throw the first!'"

* **Romans 3:23** *"Yes, all have sinned; all fall short of God's glorious ideal."*

** **Proverbs 3:5-6** *"If you want favor with both God and man, and a reputation for good judgment and common sense, then trust the Lord completely; don't ever trust yourself. In everything you do, put God first, and he will direct you and crown your efforts with success."*

*** **Exodus 20:5** "You shall not bow down to them or serve them, for I the Lord your God am a jealous God, visiting the iniquity of the fathers on the children to the third and the fourth generation of those who hate me."

* **Philippians 4:6** *"Don't worry about anything; instead, pray about everything; tell God your needs, and don't forget to thank him for his answers.*

A REAL LOVE: ASIA

One month shy of her 31 birthday and Asia wasn't feeling too enthused. Why was it that her sister made such a big deal of birthdays anyway? Who said they were supposed to be so special you should start celebrating a whole month in advance? *Apparently everyone in the Black community,* she thought bitterly.

Hence, here she was, sitting at a table with her three closest friends, sister included. A stack of 20's stuck to the top of her dress, practically screamed that it was her "born day". Crossing her legs, the form-fitting black dress (which she'd found earlier that afternoon while shopping) clung tightly, tasting each luscious curve.

"'A', make sure you put on some high heels with that thing!" Samantha had told her in their shared fitting room. Her own voluptuous figure was clad in a white, skimpy thing. Asia shook her head, her thick auburn curls accentuating a heart-shaped face.

"Sam, I don't need heels. I'm already tall enough!" This was the constant discussion between the two. Asia, at 5 '8', hated to bring any added attention to her height, while Samantha, a petite 5' 3", envied Asia's long legs and frequently encouraged her to play up her height.

"I guess we gon' have to do backflips to get some service over here!" Samantha shouted over the music, bringing Asia back to the present. The club they were in was nearing capacity, and they were lucky enough to get one of the few tables that were available.

"Yea, maybe I should have shown more cleavage?" Renee, who Asia and Samantha had known since childhood, suggested. She poked out her perky breasts, each smooshed into a silver, pleather, something or other.

They're like two ripe cantaloupes, Asia thought to herself, catching a view of Renee's chest. Cracking a small smile at her own humor, she let her brown eyes drift back to the club scene.

"Clearly you are joking, my love. If you showed any more of your ta ta's you would be arrested for indecent exposure!" Samantha responded. She raised one brow for emphasis while a round of giggles subsequently hit the table.

"Finally, some service!" Renee piped. She was addressing a tall dark-skinned young man who had come over maneuvering a pad and pen.

"What can I get, y'all?" he asked the group, but his eyes were glued to Renee's boobs.

"I'll have the works. It's my girl's birthday!" she responded cheerfully. She leaned in to give him a better view.

"I'll have a Riesling," Asia said in a dry tone, once it was clear the young man would not be making eye contact.

"Aww, no shots, A? Come on now, girl! Get wit it!" Renee said. She reached over and gave Asia's arm a light, but encouraging shake. The others chimed in, but Asia wasn't interested.

"Leave her alone, y'all! She'll come around," Samantha intervened. She shooed a hand at their friends, then put in her order; a round of Tito's.

Asia leaned back to resume surveying the crowd. Bodies were grinding to the latest R&B groove, ("Talk" by Khalid), and she found herself being bored with the scene. Was this all there was? Men who went after women with tight skirts, large breasts, and Kim K asses?

"Hey, girl. Why you lookin' so glum?" Kelly asked, with her light blond streaks and honey skin; she nearly glowed in the dim lighting. "We here to celebrate *you*!" Asia cast her friend a small smile.

"You know I'm not the birthday type," Asia offered. "We might as well be celebrating for Sam." She nodded her head towards her sister who was eyeing the club and bouncing in her seat to the beat. "She drags me out to these things every year as it is."

"Now, sis, you know it takes you a minute, but you always end up having fun!" Samantha moved over and put her arm around her sister, pretending to smother her in kisses. Asia laughed and faked pushing her away. Sam was right, she did usually end up enjoying herself, but this time she wasn't sure if that would be the case.

"Girl, you need a night out with the girls more than anything! You know what they say, to get over an old love, you just need to get under a new one!" Renee chuckled, her coffee brown eyes sparkling with mischief. The other ladies nodded in agreement, but Asia wasn't so sure. She was fresh off a break up. Why was it that she couldn't seem to find the *right* guy? After investing a whole year in the relationship, Lance had the nerve to tell her he wasn't ready for marriage.

"But, you knew up front I was ready! That was one of the very first conversations we had!" Asia had yelled at Lance in her apartment's small living room, then stormed to her bedroom and started whipping out his clothes. Gucci this and Prada that, well he could have it all! She didn't need his crap lingering as a reminder of the time she had wasted!

"Look, 'A'. I thought I was ready, but I'm just not. You're an amazing woman, and I couldn't let the opportunity to get to know you pass by." He was on her heels, trying to catch the clothes as they flew across the bedroom.

"Ain't that some shit! If I'm such a great woman, then why the hell don't you wanna be with me?" She knew she was upset because she was swearing. She hated to swear. Lance ducked as she threw a shoe in his direction. She really didn't mean to hit him, she told herself, he just happened to be standing in the spot she was aiming.

"Look, I know you upset right now, A, but I don't think we need to call it quits just yet. Let's just take a few steps back." His arms were full of clothes and his tall, lanky frame had the nerve to look endearing. He was one of the few men she had dated that she could actually look up to. "I mean, why we gotta' get rid of the friendship?"

She rolled her eyes and pulled out the last of his things from the closet, finding a crate to dump them in.

"Please, at least do me the decency of not giving me the 'let's just be friends' line. In fact, let me just save you some time. You want a friend, and I want a spouse." Shoving the crate in his arms, she steered him towards the door. He stumbled a few times, but caught his balance. She was stronger than she looked.

"'A', I'm sorry. I really am." His eyes looked at her pleadingly while standing in the doorway, and she felt her heart melt. Was he really sorry? It didn't matter. She had to save her dignity.

"Goodbye, Lance," Asia said, then slammed the door.

"All I'm saying is, if Mr. Right comes in tonight and sweeps you off yo feet, you gotta give the man a chance!" Renee's voice interrupted her thoughts, causing Asia to snap back to attention.

Her friend was trying to support her argument on the need to rebound quickly.

"Mr. Right better look like Michael B Jordan, I know that much!" Sam added with a laugh, while tossing her long tresses to the side. Just then the drinks arrived.

"Girl, you know that's right!" Kelly said, reaching for her shot glass.

"Y'all, I am so not ready for another good-looking brotha who wants to take up my time, wet my panties, and leave me heartbroken." Nursing her wine, Asia fell back in her seat, feeling frustrated.

"But, was Lance really that good-looking tho?" Sam raised an eyebrow and grinned.

"Umm, that's all you heard?" Asia looked at her sister incredulously.

"I mean, he was aw-*ight*," Renee added, as if Asia hadn't said a word, "but really it was that job and his fit that was bangin'!" She threw her head back, swallowed her shot and immediately, her face scrunched up. Exhaling deeply, she grinned at the group, the fiery, tangy liquid doing its job.

"Yea, he was about a 7, but, girl, you could pull a 8/9 easy!" Kelly said. She gazed at her friend up and down and even had the nerve to have a straight face when she said it.

Asia burst out laughing. "Y'all are ridiculous. I'm not even going there with what, y'all have dated!" She crossed her legs and shifted uncomfortably under her friend's scrutiny.

"Oh, we've all been guilty of the squint your eye, look at him from the side, cock your neck and *maybe* he's cute, dude," Renee said, expelling a hearty laugh.

"Girl, or give him a haircut, put him in some nice clothes and *douse* him in aftershave!" Sam threw in, her large, oval eyes shining with humor.

Asia doubled over in laughter. Her friends always had a way of lightening her mood. Or maybe it was the wine? She was almost done with her drink.

"What's so funny?" A deep voice asked from behind her. He was so close she could feel his breath tickle the little hairs on her neck. Asia turned to see a chestnut-skinned brother with a bald head, holding a drink and a smile.

"Umm, you know. Girl talk," she managed. He was fine. And not just the squint your eye, cock your neck fine. He was fine fine! And his eyes made her think of two deep pools of chocolate.

"Is that right? I understand. Girl code." He chuckled lightly before taking a drink. "So, even though I can't know what you were talking about, can I at least know your name?"

Asia felt herself smile in spite of herself. *This dude is smooth.*

"Her name is Asia!" Samantha volunteered. Asia shot her a look that said, "Girl, you play too much!"

Mr. Smooth grinned. "Asia, huh? Nice. Can I buy you a drink for your birthday, Asia?" His eyes pointedly looked at the cash pinned to her chest, and before she could even respond, he was on his feet headed to the bar.

"Dang, do you believe this guy?" Sam commented with one raised brow.

"Yea, girl, and he look *better* than Michael B!" Renee announced. She was drooling over him from across the room like she was an inmate on death row, and he was her last meal. The group laughed.

Asia was shocked herself, and didn't know what to think. How did he even know what she was drinking?

Was he observing me the whole time? she wondered

"I'm watching him with that drink, girl, so you good," Samantha said to Asia, while staring intently over Asia's shoulder.

She's always on it. Asia thought to herself. "Of course you are, Sam." She looked at her sister appreciatively.

A few minutes later Mr. Smooth had another Riesling and pulled his chair next to hers.

"Umm, thanks. I guess..." Asia scooted over a little to make room and her friends all made their exit, claiming they had to go to the bathroom.

"So, what's your name?" she asked, still feeling caught off guard. She took the drink he had ordered and let the liquid play on her lips. She was definitely starting to feel the alcohol.

"Derrick. But my friends call me 'D'".

"That's cool, cuz my friends call me 'A'."

"Now isn't that a coincidence? We already have something in common. Maybe we are meant to be?" Derrick licked his lips and sized her up. She was happy she took her sister's advice on the heels since his perusal included a double assessment of her legs.

"Well, Derrick, what do you do when you're not hitting on innocent women in clubs?" Asia asked.

Derrick smiled and took a drink of some dark liquid he had swimming in a glass. "Hmmm, now are you really that innocent, Asia? I feel like you might be a little out of my league." He rubbed his chin, somehow managing to make even that small gesture look feverishly sexy.

Asia chuckled, warming up to him. "Yea, I'm a little high maintenance," she admitted. "I'll give you that. But I still enjoy simple things like biking, or a walk in the park—"

"Cool," he interrupted. "I like those things too. But I also appreciate the typical candle light dinner by a nice fire. I am definitely a romantic." Derrick ran his eyes over her again with a hungry expression. That's when she noticed the tan line on his ring finger.

"I'm sure that's a quality your wife would appreciate," she said simply, and took a sip of her wine.

Derrick raised an eyebrow but didn't miss a beat. "Well, we *are* separated, so she doesn't *really* get the benefit of my romantic gestures."

Samantha, Renee and Kelly reappeared and took their seats. "What did we miss?" Sam asked with a big grin.

She held her hand out in his direction as if he were a display on *The Price is Right*. "Oh, Derrick here was just telling me about being separated from his *wife*," Asia responded.

Sam frowned and the other girls glanced at Derrick. "Is that so?"

"Yea, well, you know. Things happen," he stumbled out. "Marriage ain't easy, so we have an understanding."

For the first time that night, Derrick didn't seem so smooth.

"Oh, I understand," Asia said. "I understand you and I are not meant to be because you belong to someone else." Sitting up a little straighter, she leaned towards him, placing her hand over his. Derrick looked surprised, but allowed the gesture. "Let me give you some advice 'D'. Because I'm going to be your friend right now, so I'd like to call you 'D'." She paused and measured her words carefully. "Go home to your wife. Work things out, and fight for your marriage. Fight like hell. Because any woman that allows you to walk around and hit on other women while you're still married, has probably been through hell and back with you and is damn sure worth fighting for."

Asia could tell her words were piercing Derrick by the look on his face. Sheepishly, he bowed his head to the floor while mumbling something that she interpreted to be an apology, before walking away.

"Wow, 'A'! I see you!" Renee said, giving her a hi-five.

"Yea, I mean you put the brotha on blast!" Kelly added.

Asia shrugged. "If I get someone else's man it ain't nothin' stopping him from doing the same thing to me down the line." She pawed a hand through her thick curls while watching Derrick find the club's exit on the other side.

"Amen to that! Sis, you are spittin' knowledge!" Sam said, standing up and giving her sister a squeeze.

The girls made their way onto the dance floor as Beyonce's *Single Ladies* blared and Asia let herself go free. It felt good not to play herself cheap and steal somebody's else's man. It reminded her of her own morals and values. Even if she was disappointed that she hadn't found Mr. Right yet, at least she wasn't at the place of settling for Mr. Right Now. And even though Lance had totally disappointed her, she was glad she held onto her self-respect and let him go.

"What chew' thinkin' about, sis?" Sam had been watching her, as was her normal. Although Sam was younger, she had always been the protective one.

"Oh, life, I guess. I'm just realizing the importance of valuing yourself, you know?" Asia kept her feet moving on the floor and turned to her sister to be heard over the music.

Sam smiled. "It must be that old age kicking in!"

Asia laughed and play-shoved her. "Hey, you not too far behind!"

"Yea, but you'll always be older!"

"Yea, older and wiser!" Asia piped back.

Laughing, the two women kept their bodies grooving through the next song.

They swayed and danced to the various rhythms of the beat. They would do the same to the varying rhythms of life. There would be ups and downs, heartbreaks and pains, birthdays and other celebrations, but through it all their sisterhood would remain.

It wasn't the love that the movies promised, or the love that Asia had read in the romance novels she used to sneak under her covers in bed, but it was still a *real* love.

And that's really all I need, Asia thought to herself, while looking at her sister and her two best friends, letting loose on the dance floor.

All I need is real *love.*

CARLY

Carly let out the breath she had been holding while watching Bruce leave her small apartment. She was scared he knew she was not being truthful about how she felt about things. About how she felt about *them*. She tangled her hands through the thick mop of twists on her head (dodging her colorful headscarf from Liberia) and straightened the area where he had been sitting. There wasn't much room elsewhere; cleaning wasn't her forte. Instead, she preferred her space to exude flavor and spark creativity.

Carly prided herself on her love of urban artistry, showcasing her abilities in her own safe haven; her home. She had everyone from Gordon Parks to Fabiola Jean-Louis' works dressing her walls in a mix of contemporary styles and old school flavors. One particular painting caught her eye as she flattened out the black and white throw Bruce had gotten her from Paris. The painting was filled with bright colors and cascades of light. It emanated hope, and that was what she was needing right now. Hope.

Carly decided to take a long, warm bubble bath to soak and relax in, hoping her mood would lift.

"I just don't know what to do," she muttered to herself while running the water and pouring in her favorite oils. The ring from her cell interrupted her. Carly hesitated, really wanting her alone time, but maybe it was Bruce? Maybe he had forgotten something in her apartment? She glanced at the caller i.d. Even better, it was Neece.

"Hey, girl! Where you been?" She could hear her best friend's eagerness on the other end and knew she was smiling from ear to ear.

"Hey, Neece. Oh, you know, it's been crazy since getting back." Carly glimpsed her reflection in the large, oval, bathroom mirror. Silky skin, large, worried brown eyes, and a slender frame stared back at her.

"Uh oh! I hear something in your voice. Girl, why are you not hype about this trip you just went on with your boo? And did he propose or not? And am I going to be maid of honor or what?" Neece's voice gushed a river of excitement over the phone.

Carly burst out laughing at Neece's game of 20 questions. It was just like her friend to run full-fledged into a story without having any details.

"Girl, I don't know. Paris was amazing. We took pictures at the Eiffel Tower. We saw the Luxembourg Palace. We attended

Carly

an opera at the Opéra Garnier and took a ride in a Gondola under the stars, while holding hands and drinking wine." Carly sighed and stopped the water from filling up her whirlpool tub. "It was all so surreal." While perched on the closed toilet, she reminisced on the trip with Bruce, then peeked down at her left ring finger. The full-carat, sparkling diamond set in bronze gold, beamed up at her. The part she didn't share with Neece, the part she intentionally left out, was that Bruce had proposed on that gondola ride. He had proposed and she had said 'yes'. But was 'yes' really the right answer?

"Girl, all that and you ain't call or text me as soon as you landed? I mean, Carly, why you holding back?" Neece questioned, and Carly could just imagine her Godiva chocolate face covered in confusion.

"My bad, Neece. Bruce literally just left my house like 20 minutes ago. I figured I would call once I got some rest."

"Oh, ok. I got chew', girl. You know I'm just hype about everything. I mean you've been waiting for a guy like Bruce for a long time! I mean *praying* for a man like him! And then poof! There he is! And I *know* he is the one! I mean, I just know it!" her friend said happily.

"Really? How do you know?" Carly was edging forward on the tip of the toilet now, gripping the phone, hoping that somehow, some way, she could experience the confidence her friend seemed to have about her own relationship.

"Girl, because of the way he *treats* you! And looks at you! And loves you! And what man has brought it like Bruce?" Neece carried on.

To that Carly, could say nothing. She knew Neece was right. She had not dated anyone of Bruce's caliber, his character, his heart! She knew he was a good man. But was he the *right* man?

"Yea, you're right. But there's something in my heart that isn't settled on a future with him." Carly bit her thumb nail as she wrestled with the lack of peace she was feeling. "It's like God is saying 'no'. Or maybe, 'not now'. Or maybe, 'not ever'," she finished, lamely. Was her feeling God, or was it fear?

"Hmmm, well I can't say anything to that, girl." Neece's voice grew serious. "If God isn't giving you peace, then you need to spend time alone and pray on it. He sees what we can't. He knows what we don't."

Words of wisdom. Carly knew she could count on her friend to deliver. Even though Neece was excited about the prospect of marriage, she would not have Carly go against her own conviction.

"You right, sis. I know. I have just had such an amazing time with him this past year! I've really enjoyed all of the experiences we've had. I just don't want it to end. And I don't understand." Carly's eyes anxiously darted to the tree bark texture gracing her cream ceiling, then swam along each brush stroke." I mean, Bruce has everything."

Carly

"Girl, who you tellin'? I am team Bruce all day!" Neese said. Both girls laughed heavily. "But seriously, you know what you have to do. So, I'm gonna' let you go do it and I'll check on you a little later."

Neece was right. Carly needed time to hear what God was saying to her about this relationship and why she didn't feel the peace she needed to move forward. She let herself soak in the bath for nearly an hour, listening to Janell Monae, H.E.R and her favorite, India Arie, sing about love, and life, and hope. When she was clean and dry, she pulled out her Bible, hoping something would stand out. It had been a journey of having loved and lost. And though often she had felt like it was mostly losing, ultimately, she knew that God had proven time and time again, His way was best.

"Father, what is it You are saying to me?" she said out loud, peering up at the ceiling. Immediately she sensed His familiar presence and felt the intimate connection that had been with her since childhood.

"Daughter, lay this down," was the response in her heart. She let out a painful breath, dropping her face into her pillows. Why was it that God seemed to be so vocal when she didn't *really* want to hear what He had to say? While squeezing the beautifully patterned pillows she had bought in Africa, she let the tears flow. She had visited there on a mission's trip in college and that was the trip that had changed her life. It was Africa where she had chosen to follow God with her whole heart and to not hold back any longer. Still, sometimes it felt like she didn't have anything left to give of that heart He kept asking her for.

"Father, please help me!" Carly spent a good hour crying and praying, knowing what God wanted from her, until finally she felt strengthened enough to do what He asked. Slowly, she dialed her boyfriend's number.

"Hi, Bruce." Carly sat up on her bed while holding the phone, knees pulled to her chin, feeling like a child.

"Hey, babe. I was just thinking about you!" he said, in an upbeat tone. "Did you get some rest?" Bruce's warm and caring voice made it even more difficult for Carly to move ahead, but she felt more peace about obeying what was in her heart, than not obeying. She used that to give her courage.

"Yea, I took a long bath and had some quiet time."

"That's good, sweetie. I'm definitely whooped. I had such an amazing time with you!" Bruce said, affectionately. "I already miss you!"

Carly's stomach twisted into a knot, but she pushed forward. "Babe, I was hoping we could meet tomorrow morning after church. Will you be free?" Carly normally went to church with Bruce, but had decided to let herself recoup from their trip. Bruce had already had a meeting at the church he needed to attend, so he was still going to go to their regular service.

"Sure. I should be free around one p.m. Let's meet at Alice's Café." He was referring to a local spot they both enjoyed. It was inexpensive and had great coffee.

"Ok. I'm gonna' get some rest. I'll see you tomorrow." Carly could already feel her eyes drooping.

"Ok, sweetie. Good night," came Bruce's sweet tone.

He was so unsuspecting.

Lord, please prepare his heart! Carly prayed fervently. She finally let the exhaustion of the past few days catch up to her, and drifted off to sleep.

* * *

The next day Carly arrived in the café 15 minutes before their meeting time. She wanted to give herself a moment to go over her speech, and pray, and get her emotions together. Her hands were shaking as she sipped the herbal tea she had ordered. She was too nervous to drink anything caffeinated.

"Hey, girl! Where's my boy at?" Tanya, the owner, sashayed over to the table and greeted Carly. Carly knew she was referring to Bruce. Tanya loved Bruce and was frequently engaging in banter with him about sports, politics or religion.

"He's on his way. I just got here a little early." Carly smiled at the older woman, appreciating her genuine friendliness. She was constantly talking to her customers and had excellent service to match the delicious items for purchase. Tanya had opened the café a year ago, right around the time Carly and Bruce had started dating. She shared with them that she named it after her mother, and it was to honor her legacy. Carly knew then that it was a special place and she would try to sow into it as much as she could.

"Ok, honey. Well, you just let me know if y'all need anything!" Tanya smiled back in her usual way before moving on to another table.

Carly loved her constant upbeat attitude. The woman wore joy like a cloak. She resumed going over her thoughts that she had typed out in her phone, and was intensely praying to remember it all, when she suddenly felt a presence behind her.

"Hey, babe. Sorry I'm a little late." Bruce touched her shoulder then bent down and kissed her on the forehead. "I see you already ordered. Pastor was holding me up some," he explained, while sitting down across from her.

"Oh no, you're fine. I had some spare time, so I got here early." Carly gave him a small smile and put down her phone.

Even now, Carly couldn't deny her attraction to him. Bruce was average height but very fit. He loved all athletics and kept in shape. One of their favorite things to do together was to go running. She knew there was more she was laying down then just someone she loved and cared for. She was laying down their connection and companionship.

Lord, help me!

And suddenly, that still small voice, *"I will never leave you nor forsake you. Where you are weak I am strong."*

Carly

She felt His peace. The peace that surpasses understanding.

"So, how was service?" she asked, hiding her left hand under her right and shifting in her seat. She didn't want Bruce to see that the ring wasn't on.

"Oh, good as usual! God is really moving. The sermon was about Abraham and him sacrificing Isaac. Pastor talked about how hard it can be to sacrifice to God, but in our obedience, God provides the ram in the bush. Whether it's returning what was offered as a sacrifice like with Isaac, or providing something better." Bruce spoke in a lively tone with round, bright eyes.

Carly felt her own eyes widen. "Really? Wow. That's amazing."

"Yea. I felt it was confirming some things God was putting on my heart." Furrowing his brows, he looked at her intently. "Like how important it is to keep Him first, you know?" he said thoughtfully.

"Hey now! I was waiting on you, boy!" Tanya came back to their table and said to Bruce.

He leapt to his feet to give her a hug. "Yea, I was running behind. How you doin', Ms. Tanya?"

"Oh, you know. Same oh, same oh. So, what can I get chew', son?" she positioned her pad and pen, ready to take his order.

Bruce ordered his usual latte and Carly exhaled.

Lord, this is so hard! she thought, as she watched the friendly interaction between Bruce and Tanya. Once Tanya left, Bruce gave her his full attention.

"So, what were we saying? Oh yea, keeping God first." Bruce smiled and Carly felt her heart speed up.

"Right. That's a great word. I can definitely say that has been on my heart as well," she offered, staring down at her tea.

"Yea. I'm so glad we have Him at the center of our relationship, Carly. I'm so glad He is first and that we can walk out our life together with that knowledge." Bruce gently placed his hand over hers, his small dimple making an appearance. She felt her heart melting at his touch, but knew this was her opportunity.

"I'm glad you said that. That is actually what I wanted to talk to you about, Bruce. Except, I'm really nervous," she started, and took another deep breath.

Tanya came over and set down his latte. "Here you go! Now, I made it with some extra almond milk this time, so you let me know how it tastes! I know *last* time you said it wasn't creamy enough." She grinned, while placing her hands on her shapely hips.

Bruce cupped the mug and took a sip. "Oh, this is perfect, Tanya!" He held up an "ok" sign with his fingers and smacked his lips. "Thanks!"

Carly

"And you, miss lady? You need anything else?" Tanya turned to Carly.

"No, ma'am. Thank you," Carly responded, her smile not quite reaching her eyes.

"You ok, baby?" Tanya's round, mahogany face looked worried while studying Carly.

"Uh. Yes, ma'am. I'm fine." Carly waived her hand dismissively.

"Hmmm. Alright. Y'all holla if you need anything!" she said, and was off to serve her other customers.

"Babe, you can tell me anything. I'm a safe place, remember?" Bruce peered at her, also seeming concerned.

Carly knew what he said was true. They had had many conversations regarding her issues with trusting men, and he had proven to be caring and confident. She had been hurt so many times in the past that it took her awhile to see that Bruce was a good guy.

"Right. I know. And I'm so grateful to have found you." She gave him an appreciative smile. "I'm so grateful to have a good man and that God has used you to help me heal and restore my faith in men, and in His promises." Absentmindedly, she used both hands to play with the unused napkin on the table while she spoke.

"Wait. Where's that fat rock I just gave you?" Bruce joked, seeing her naked ring finger, but she could tell he was confused.

"Right. So that's what I wanted to talk about." She toyed with her tea, looking away, then slowly met his eyes again. "God has put that same message on my heart... about sacrifice, I mean. He has not given me peace to move forward in marriage with you, Bruce." She smoothed her hand over his. "I'm so sorry," she said, feeling a tear roll down her cheek.

Bruce was still, but she could see his eyes cloud over with pain and it tore at her heart in the worst way. "What?" he said, his voice breaking. "Since when?" He sat back in his chair, looking confused.

"Well, I would say since I believed you were going to propose. And then definitely after I said 'yes'. I mean, I felt so excited and cared about you so much that I was high off my feelings." Carly's voice was shaky but she continued. "Then when the high settled, I felt God telling me to lay down the relationship." She lowered her gaze, unable to meet his eyes. "I'm so sorry," she said tearfully.

Bruce was quiet. Carly was quiet. She felt like time had stood still. Is this how Abraham felt when Isaac was on the altar? Did it feel like time had stood still and his whole world was changing every second that passed, while waiting for God to burn his son?

"Ok," Bruce said quietly. She had never heard him that quiet. She stole a glimpse in his direction, afraid of what she would see. He was physically composed, but she sensed his pain.

"I know it was hard for you to say this. I know it wasn't easy. Thank you for being honest," he managed. Carly moved her head up and down mechanically, then began digging through her purse until she found the small, white envelope.

"Here is the ring," she said, placing it into his hands. She let hers cover his for longer than necessary, hoping to comfort him, and perhaps, to hold onto him a little while longer. Still, she needed to let go.

"I need some time," he said, thickly. "I need some time to process." He removed his hand from hers, the gesture breaking her heart in little bitty pieces. "I'll be in touch." He didn't look up. Carly understood. This was her cue. She got up from their usual table and squeezed her bag like a drowning victim would a raft for life support.

Before leaving, she stole a glance behind. Tanya was back at Bruce's table, probably wondering why Carly was leaving without him.

Well done my good and faithful servant, was the response she heard in her heart.

She sped as swiftly out the door as she could before Tanya could ask her why she was leaving without her boyfriend of the last year. She didn't know if she herself could even answer why.

* * *

4 Months Later

"Ma, I don't know *why* you think we are the same size! I keep telling you, you cannot wear my stuff! You stretch it out!" Carly huffed at her mom. She held up one of her favorite sequined tops in the living room, examining it.

"Honey, if you saw how good that top looked on me, you would be *giving* it to me!" Mrs. Davis casually strolled into Carly's kitchen then pulled out a bottle of water. Smiling, she gave Carly a mischievous look. "That shirt got me a date for Friday night!"

Carly laughed. Her mom was forever getting dates and she highly doubted it had to do with her top. She was just a very outgoing person, which tended to attract the male species to her.

"But, Ma, seriously. You stretch my stuff out and then it fits different. When did you steal this anyway?" She eyed her suspiciously.

"Girl, how is it stealin' if I gave birth to you and brought you into this world? That means I *own* you! And if I own *you,* then I own everything *you* own! Including that shirt, those pants, those earrings, and everything in this house!" Mrs. Davis strutted her full hips to the living room then dropped down on the couch next to her daughter. She had to remove a few scarves and shawls before doing so. Carly shook her head. Evaline Davis was always right and Carly knew she was too much like her to be mad about it.

"Girl, you could at least straighten up when you know you 'bout to have company!" Mrs. Davis said, while moving around on the vintage sofa to get more comfortable, her face decorated with annoyance.

"Well, maybe if you didn't just drop by…" Carly mumbled.

"What?" Her mother pivoted her neck with the speed of a rabbit and gave her a sharp look. "What was that, girl?"

"Nothin', Momma," she said, just as fast.

"Girl, don't be tryna blame *me* for *your* messy habits!" Mrs. Davis took a drink from her bottle before returning back to her chipper self.

"So anyways, like I said, I have a date Friday night. But what about chew,' honey? What's yo dating life looking like these days?" She eyed her curiously.

Her mom was digging. The topic of dating and Bruce hadn't come up in months but Carly was still feeling tender. She had been thinking about Bruce a lot lately, but wasn't trying to reach out since they had broken up. In their last conversation they agreed to give each other space. Even at church, she was now attending a different service time.

"Well, I haven't thought much about it, Mom. I have been really just seeking God. I feel super focused spiritually and I think dating was kind of a distraction." To direct her from her discomfort, she played with the material from her tan, wide-leg pants.

"Mmhmm." Her mom nodded knowingly and gulped her water. "Well, I do agree, you have been more available to hang out with your old mom, so that's been cool. And I know your business has picked up. Did you sell that one painting I loved? With that beautiful, Black, voluptuous woman, who looked just like me?"

Carly laughed. "Ma! That was a portrait of Queen Sheba, and yes, I sold it." She shook her twists, humored by her mother's comment.

"Oh, ok." Her mom's tone softened. "And look, I hear you with the dating, Car, but I would be open to it again, sweetheart. You just don't know when your season will change." Her mom leaned over and brushed long strokes up and down her arm with her fingers, the way she used to when Carly would be afraid of the dark, or monsters, or some other childish fear.

Carly appreciated her mom's love and care, but wasn't so sure if she agreed. She had been growing a lot mentally, emotionally and spiritually. She had been re-visiting things about herself like her gift at drawing that she hadn't used since she was a kid (most of her work was sculpting and photography). She was healing from some other issues from her past, like her father's death, that she knew she had used dating to run from. Was she really ready to start dating again?

"Mom, how did you know you were ready to start dating after Dad died?" she asked, turning more to face her mother. Carly had never asked that question. She was always cautious of how it could make her mom feel and didn't want her to feel judged.

"Well, I would say, when I didn't want to continue living without companionship," her mother answered thoughtfully. "I knew your dad was ok with me moving on because he wouldn't want me to not enjoy my life. And I had peace about it." She looked sincerely at her daughter with eyes full of love. "An inner peace," she finished.

"Yea. I understand." Carly moved a few items out of the way and sat down next to her mom. She laid her head on her shoulder, and felt her mother's arms embrace her.

While mulling over her mom's words she felt that, for now, she was okay without male companionship. And, more importantly, she felt at peace.

* * *

"Thanks for meeting me here!" Neece grabbed Carly's arm and swung her into the nearest entrance to the mall.

"Yea, girl. I needed to get out. I've been cooped up in the house all weekend stuck on the couch, binging on Netflix," Carly confessed.

"You and your Netflix!" Neece laughed while shaking her cute little bob. "I don't know *how* people do it. They get so caught up in these shows!" Carly knew her friend couldn't relate because she was such a socialite. She figured Neece would be more prone to *being* in a reality show then watching one.

"Yea, I can get caught up for sure." The girls spent the afternoon shopping in their favorite stores, and trying to find new outfits for the change in season. Summer was peeking through.

"Hey, Car. What do you think about this skirt?" Neece held up a denim pencil skirt, stylishly ripped on the edges.

"It's totally you," Carly said, without hesitation. She watched her friend stuff it into her shopping bag and before long, they were in the checkout line. While Neece took her things to the register, Carly browsed the store. She hadn't found much, but wasn't too disappointed. She was having a good time just being with her friend.

"Carly. Hey…" a familiar voice sounded behind her. Was it really him?

Carly slowly turned in the direction of the sound and let her eyes roam up his frame.

"Hey. Bruce. How are you?" She knew he was well by the glow on his face. His brown skin was a tad darker; he had been in the sun.

Carly

"I'm good. My family and I just got back from Florida. How are you?" He was smiling, and looked genuinely happy to see her.

"Oh, that's nice! I'm good. I'm surprised to see you in *this* store!" She gestured to the young, feminine clothing store and grinned back, realizing she too was happy to see him.

"Yea." He laughed self-consciously. "I actually was walking by and thought I saw you. I didn't want to *not* speak," he shared, stuffing both hands in his pockets then rocking a little.

"Ahem." Neece was clearing her throat. Apparently, she was done with her purchase.

"Oh. My bad. Neece, you know Bruce," Carly said, nodding towards Bruce.

Neece chuckled. "Umm, yes. Hey, Bruce." Neece tossed him a wave.

"Hey, Neece. Well, I don't want to intrude. Just wanted to say 'hi'." Bruce awkwardly shifted his weight in his Air Force 1's.

"Oh. Ok. Uh, it was nice seeing you," Carly offered. She tried to ignore the disappointment in her heart. *Lord, why do I feel this way?*

Because he's your husband.

What? Carly wasn't sure if she heard correctly. Was God speaking to her, or was she hearing what she wanted to hear?

But then, as she glanced into Bruce's eyes, she felt peace. That same peace she felt when she laid down the relationship four months ago.

"Umm, well, I was actually hoping we could connect," he said. "I mean, I know we said we wouldn't for a while, but...it's been a while." Bruce's face drew into a hopeful look. "And I'm ready whenever you are." She could tell he was bracing himself for rejection.

"*Go,*" said the still, small voice. Carly could hardly keep her composure. God was saying "yes"? He was saying "yes" to Bruce?

"Umm, well, yea. That would be great. Text me later and we can figure out something," she said, smiling wide.

I can't believe this! she thought.

"Ok. You guys have fun!" Bruce turned to leave.

Neese gave her an excited grin. "Girrrrrl," she said, and Carly shook her head, not wanting to get too excited herself.

"Now don't start, Neece," she told her friend in a serious tone, while holding up a hand.

Instead of speaking, Neece cocked her head to the side and threw her a look that said, "It's going down!"

Carly

Carly felt like she had the rug pulled out from under her. Was it going down? Had this all been just a test?

* * *

"You look great!" Bruce complimented Carly as she entered the café. They had decided to meet at Alice's about a week after running into each other at the mall. Carly was wearing one of her favorite floral dresses that flirted at the knee with violet high-heeled sandals. Her nude head scarf drew her long twists upward and opened in the back, allowing them to cascade down past her shoulders. She loved being able to finally walk outside without a jacket.

"Thanks! So do you!" And he did. Bruce wore a green polo and dark jeans with clean, white Puma sneakers. His brown skin was smooth as a Hershey's Kiss and his smile was just as sweet. The sight of him gave Carly butterflies.

The two talked for nearly two hours, catching up on everything that had happened in their lives individually. They couldn't seem to get enough of each other and Tanya came by and commented on how nice it was to see them there together.

Bruce corrected her. "Well, we are not really *together*, Ms. Tanya."

"Is that so? I can't tell!" Tanya shook her head and smiled as if she knew something Bruce didn't. "Feel free to stay here, *not together*, as long as you want!" She cackled, then walked away.

Carly chuckled and Bruce fake rolled his eyes while smiling.

"I don't think she believed me," Bruce said.

"No. I don't think so. But that's ok. I kind of don't either," Carly said shyly while stroking her cup of coffee.

"Whaaaat? What chew' mean? You broke up with me *four* months ago in this same spot!" Bruce gestured at the cafe and shook his head incredulously. "Or was that all in my head?"

"I know, I know. But things have changed. It seems there has been a change in season." Carly proceeded to share what had been on her heart since she heard God say, "*Go*" at the mall.

"I think I needed time, Bruce. I think I needed to remember who I am and my identity outside of you." She bit her thumb thoughtfully. "I think there was some healing I needed, and most of all, I needed to remember that God was first." Carly looked at him, her eyes shining with emotion.

"Wow. Well, I can say I needed a reminder that He is first also. And I'm so glad you listened to His prompting. I'm glad you obeyed." Bruce paused, observing her with adoration. "It makes me respect and admire you even more that you were able to do such a difficult thing."

"And it makes me appreciate and respect you that you didn't try to fight me on it. That you listened and obeyed also." Carly cautiously placed her hands over his on the table.

Carly

"So, what does this mean?" Bruce looked at her with love in his eyes. He drummed his fingers under hers nervously.

He is yours, came the still small voice.

"It means, I am yours. If you will have me." Instead of responding, Bruce was on his feet, revealing an envelope from his pocket. He beamed at her and Carly felt her heart beat faster once she realized what was happening. In moments, he was on one knee, holding out the ring.

"I brought this just in case," he said. And then, "Carly Sharnese Davis, will you marry me? For real this time?" His face was hopeful. His eyes were wide. His extended arm was slightly shaking. Carly was elated.

"Yes! Yes! I will!" she nearly shouted.

People in the café started clapping and taking pictures with their phones. Bruce placed the ring on her finger and pulled her into his arms. Carly had never felt so happy and so at peace! She kissed him and was giddy with joy.

Tanya stood nearby. "Mmhmm. That's what I thought." She looked at the two with a huge grin. "Free coffee in honor of the newly engaged couple!" she shouted.

Wow, God. Wow. You do great things! Carly thought, and then embraced her fiancé as they celebrated their engagement.

I make all things new, He responded.

DANTE'S JOY

The clouds were rolling in quickly and Dante knew he only had so much time before the downpour would begin. He sped up his run, forcing his thick calf muscles to pound on the pavement even harder. "Man, I didn't know you had it in you, boy!" his homeboy, JR, shouted over the music in his earbuds.

"Oh, you didn't know? Don't ever underestimate ya' boy!" he threw back, while speeding up even more. JR, not one to be outdone, kicked it into high gear and stretched out his legs to match the pace of his friends'. The two men swiftly made their way through the neighborhood and right before they hit Dante's apartment building, the first drops of rainfall landed.

"Whew! That was close!" JR shouted after they had entered the front door.

"Who you tellin'? I didn't know your little scrawny legs could pump that fast!" Dante laughed and pulled out his key. He was secretly grateful he lived on the first floor. He didn't want his friend to know he couldn't have made it up a flight of stairs if he tried.

"Yea, whateva. You always gotta' throw yo height up in my face! But it's cool, cuz I still get more play than you!" JR tugged his Lakers jersey up over his head and threw it on the floor by the couch.

"That's cuz you thirsty!" Dante immediately picked up the shirt and folded it, placing it on the end table.

"Hey, everybody ain't Mr. "High and Mighty" like you, my man, and don't hate cuz I don't discriminate!" He sat back on the couch, then kicked up his Nike's on the coffee table, making himself more than comfortable. "I like my women in all sizes, shapes *and* skin tones!"

Dante shook his head while making his way to the bathroom to grab some towels. "There's water and Gatorade in the fridge, man. Help yourself." He knew there was no use in responding to his friend's remark. JR just wasn't ready.

Dante could hear JR rummaging around in the kitchen as he splashed water on his face in the bathroom mirror. Light, hazel eyes, medium, brown skin and a short beard that was dripping wet, occupied the mirror.

"Yo, dawg. What you doin' in there, takin' a dump?" JR shouted from the kitchen.

"Oh, my bad! Here I come!" Dante seized a couple of towels before heading back to the living room. For a man's pad it wasn't too shabby. He wasn't the best at decorating, but his twin sister Dana had given him some pointers.

"Now, don't be making it a pigsty after I do all this hard work!" she yelled at him while helping him move around the furniture.

"Dag, Dana. Why you gotta' come down on a brotha like that? You ain't got no faith in me?"

"Boy, I know you! And I've known you since we spent nine months together in the womb! You was a slob even then!"

Dante laughed. "Why you bringing up the past tho? Why can't a brotha mature, and grow up and change? Why you gotta' keep me boxed in?"

"Boy, ain't nobody boxing you in! I'm just sayin'!"

Dante smiled at the memory. She was right. He *was* a slob, but he was determined to keep it decent now that he was on his own again.

"Yo sister did a pretty good job decorating tho', homie." JR sat back down on the couch, wiping strands of sweat off his neck. "I mean, who knew you could actually have a nice spot?"

"First of all, put the towel on the couch before you sit yo sweaty, nasty, self down, and second of all, you right. She did."

Dante fell back next to his friend with a blue Gatorade container in one hand and a towel in the other.

JR smirked, but obeyed. "I'm just sayin'. I remember that other spot you had and you was horrible with it."

"Bruh, it was college!" Dante held up his hands in defense.

"Like I said..." JR let out a loud belch.

"I can't believe you judgin' me and you one of the most disgusting creatures alive!" Dante said, looking surprised.

"Hey! Takes one to know one!" JR retorted.

"Oh, very mature!" They both laughed. The men had grown up in the same neighborhood together and never did Dante expect anything less than what his friend gave; companionship, loyalty and fun. He knew JR did not have the spiritual depth he needed for a deeper, more intimate relationship. For that, he went to his men's group.

"So, you down this weekend or what?" JR asked. He took a swig of Gatorade and smacked his lips, making the "ahh" noise.

"Oh, you mean the music festival? Uh, I don't know. You know I'm doing my men's group Friday, so it would have to be on Saturday," Dante said thoughtfully. He played with the bottle of Gatorade on his lap, mindlessly swirling around the blue liquid.

"Yea, yea. I know. You all dedicated to the church now." JR rolled his eyes.

Dante's Joy

"Whateva. The service is cool, but what I really like is the small group meetings. I mean, you really should check it out J."

"Dawg, I'll check it out when I want to sit around on a Friday night with a bunch of old heads and talk about Jesus. But right now, I'd rather have me a good time with Candice, or Tish, or Stacie! You know, and engage in a more *physical* conversation!" JR laughed impishly and Dante threw a pillow at him.

"Yea, yea. I know." Dante kicked his feet up on his coffee table. It was wooden, and he was glad too because he didn't have to worry about any scratches. "So, maybe Saturday around 8. I'll have my sis come with us. I'm sure she wants to see the show."

"Bet. Dana is always a good time. I mean, one of these days I *know* she gon' give me the time of day!" JR said, grinning.

"Yea, bruh, keep dreamin'! Besides, she's dating Jerard now." Dante took a nice swig of his Gatorade.

"Man, I done' seen yo sister go through so many dudes over the years. I ain't worried," he said, waving a hand dismissively.

"I think this is different, dawg. I think she really feelin' him."

"Yea, I'll believe it when I see it. Nobody can put Dana on lock down!"

"Well, you check them out this weekend and I think you'll see otherwise. But um, what chew' think gon' be the attire? The flyer ain't really say." Dante was wondering if he should get a new outfit. *I know I need to upgrade my kickin' it clothes.* He looked down at his plain white T, and saw a few old mustard stains scribbled in.

"I don't know, homie, but you know it's gon' be some nice-lookin' females there! I mean, R&B always brings 'em in flocks!" JR said with another hearty laugh.

"Fa sho." Dante was thinking he wasn't necessarily going to look at women, but to enjoy time with his peoples. *Still, I just might hit up the mall beforehand.*

* * *

The week seemed to fly by, partly because of Dante's workload, and partly because he was always looking forward to his men's group. He had joined the group just a few months ago and found it to be so edifying he didn't ever miss a meeting.

"Hey, Dante. How's your week been?" Bill Jones, the leader of the group asked. Bill had been a member of the church for a while, and Dante really respected his wisdom and spiritual insight.

"Oh, it's been busy, Bill. It's like they are giving me more and more responsibility at work, but I feel like it's purposeful you know?" He met Bill's gaze and smiled. "Like God is saying, He is giving me an increase."

Dante's Joy

Bill's eyes smiled and Dante could tell he was excited for him. "Now that's awesome, Dante! I know it's been a struggle for you to stay in that position, and the fact that you can now say you are seeing an increase is nothing but a testimony!"

"Definitely! I have the men here to thank for their prayers for sure." Dante glanced around the small room and noticed several individuals who had been coming consistently. They were young and old and of different ethnicities, but had formed a bond that he hadn't experienced anywhere else. He was truly grateful.

"That's great to hear, son." Bill shook Dante's hand, covering it with his other one. "I'm looking forward to seeing how God continues moving in your life!" Dante returned his handshake and let Bill move on to greet some of the other men coming in. He found a seat next to the window and glanced outside, catching sight of a blue bird flying nearby. For the first time in what felt like forever, he had a moment to just be.

This is My Son in whom I am well pleased.

Lord, is that You? Dante asked the still, small voice.

Dante felt his heart swell with love, an indicator that it was. He started flipping through his Bible on a quest to find the scripture that was on his heart, but the meeting started before he could.

"Hi everyone! It's so good to see, y'all!" Bill began. Men responded in agreement and smiles. One of the younger guys sitting next to Dante patted his back and he smiled in return. "Let's begin." Bill and several of the men started leading worship, while Dante and the others joined. The room was saturated with baritones, tenors and everything in between. Sweet sounds of exaltation engulfed the group. Dante stood with his hands raised and eyes closed. He was One with his Creator and nothing else mattered. He didn't even realize that time had passed, until he felt someone standing in front of him. When he opened his eyes, he was staring eye level at Bill.

"Son, can I speak into you?" the older man asked.

Dante knew God was moving and that there was a word Bill had for him, so he nodded in agreement. "Yes."

"I hear the Lord saying 'get ready'. He has seen your faithfulness. He has seen that you are a good steward indeed. He has seen that you are trustworthy and He wants you to be fruitful and to multiply. What God gives, no man can take away. He has said, 'You are His son and He is well pleased'." Bill placed a hand on Dante's shoulder, and he felt the peace of God saturate his heart.

Wow. That was exactly the word God had given him when the meeting started! Dante was overjoyed.

Thank You, Lord! Thank You for Your great encouragement!

Bill embraced him and the other men gave God praises. Dante felt surrounded by love, beauty and joy. He never wanted to leave this place.

*　*　*

"I should have known it would be packed! This side of town is always lit on the weekend!" Dante said to JR. They were unsuccessfully trying to find an open parking spot at the mall. JR had said he would tag along while Dante shopped for an outfit for the festival, even though, as he put it, "I'm already fly, and don't need nothin' else!"

"Dude, you shoulda took that one! We could have made it!" JR said, pointing to an empty spot just as another car swerved into it.

"Naw, man. That ain't right. You saw that car was there first."

"Yea, but we could have swooped in there right before them! See, that's why you ain't making moves! Cuz' you too slow." JR held up his hands in frustration. "You let everybody pass you up, and don't get what's yours."

Dante knew JR was referring to more than just the parking spot he passed up. His friend was into some sketchy side hustles which wasn't too surprising given the neighborhood they grew up in. In spite of Dante's upbringing, he couldn't succumb to the fast life. His own mother was a victim of addiction, and he and Dana had been through so much just trying to make it in their own home. He swore to himself that if he ever got to college, things would be different for him.

"Look, man, I don't have to snatch somebody else's to get mine. Mine will be right there waiting for me if it's mine." Dante kept driving and searching for a spot to park.

"Mmhmm. Well, why you circling the lot everybody else is getting…"

JR's voice trailed off as Dante pulled into a space not too far from the mall.

"Ahem. You was sayin'?" Dante glanced at his friend.

"Yea, alright. You lucked up! But I'm telling you man, in life, you gotta go for yours!"

I'll just let it ride, Dante said to himself. *He'll see when he's ready.* Once parked, the two hopped out into the beautiful sunny day.

"I need some new kicks, so let's head to Foot Locker." Dante led the way while they fought through the crowds of people who were on their own mission to purchase.

"Those are *nice!*" JR stated, as Dante held up a pair of LeBron's' in the store.

"Yea, they cost a nice price too!" Dante quipped. Still, he held onto the red and black shoe, admiring the look and style.

"Bruh, you gotta try 'em on at least!" JR said. Dante agreed and found a bench where he slipped on the pair.

"Excellent choice, sir," a sales rep came by and commented, while Dante stood to his feet.

"Thanks, but um, I'm not so sure I've made the choice yet." He laughed.

The rep, a scrawny young kid with red hair whose name tag read "Ron," was persistent. "Oh, you definitely have to have this shoe! Look at the detail and design, and how it flatters your build and muscle development!"

Man, this dude is laying it on thick! Dante chuckled to himself. *He must get commission!*

"Man, he's right, dawg. You *need* these!" JR chimed in, motioning towards the shoe.

Dante wasn't sold. He had just moved into his apartment and while his savings was nice, he was cautious about purchases that weren't long term investments. Were these shoes really worth it?

"Yea, I'm a pass, but thanks." Dante started taking the shoes off and putting them back in the box. Ron shrugged his narrow shoulders.

"Ok. We do have a comparable, less *expensive* shoe I can show you if you're interested."

"Sure, why not." Dante followed Ron to a different wall of shoes on display but after several tries, didn't see anything that caught his eye.

Man, there's just nothing like that shoe, he thought to himself, feeling a sense of longing. "I appreciate your help, man, but I'm not seeing anything. Maybe another time," he said, fighting his own disappointment.

"Ok, sir. Next time then!" Ron headed towards another customer to assist.

Dante turned and saw JR standing near the door with a bag in his hand. He hadn't even realized his friend had made a purchase.

"Hey, man. Sorry for the hold up! What chew' get?" he asked, walking over to JR.

Dante gave him a half-smile and pushed the bag into his chest. "Don't say I never gave you nothin'."

Dante was confused. "What chew' mean?" He opened the bag, and, seeing the familiar box, said, "Naw. You ain't have to do this, man!" He looked at JR with his mouth wide open.

"Man, you loved that shoe, and you look almost as good in them as I would," JR joked.

Dante carefully lifted the shoes from the box and smiled, loving the way the red peaked through the black design. But he felt convicted. How could he take this gift when he knew how the money was made that purchased them?

"I'm sorry, man. I can't take em'. I appreciate it though, really. But chew' know I can't get down wit' yo hustle." He gave the bag back to JR.

JR shook his head. "Man, why you gotta be goody goody all the time? I mean, *live* a little! It ain't like *you* was on the block hustlin'. It's a *gift*!" JR held the bag back out but Dante shook his head.

"Like I said, man, I can't. But I appreciate it though." Dante stood firm on his conviction, assuming it probably hurt his friend's feelings, but knowing that his own peace was more important. JR smacked his teeth in frustration but didn't say anything.

Dante managed to find a few things in other stores and the two decided to have lunch in the food court. He was reading the items on the menu when he felt JR tapping his arm.

"Dawg, check out shorty over there." He nodded to the right of where they were standing.

Before Dante even thought about it, he followed his friend's gaze.

Wow. Who is that?

She was curvy and just below medium height with almond skin and a short haircut. Not his normal type, but he couldn't keep his eyes off her. She was wearing one of those jumpers that hugged her in the right places. Dante watched as his new interest tossed her head back, laughing at something her friend said. Then he noticed a guy standing nearby, his arm tattooed to her lower back.

"Man, if she wasn't taken, I'd be all over it!" JR said.

"Yea right. Like that's ever stopped you before!" Dante forced himself to look at his friend.

JR laughed. "Yea, you right!"

It was their turn to order, and after they did, Dante immediately looked to see if the young woman was still there, until he spotted her and her crew sitting at a nearby table.

"Uh, J, let's sit over here, man," he said. He pointed to a table that would allow him to observe her.

Man, what am I doin? She's taken!

"Ok, cool." JR went on to brag about how he was looking forward to the show tonight because of how many numbers he was going to get, but Dante could barely focus. He kept stealing glances at the girl. While the guy sitting next to her had his arm laying possessively on her chair, her body language seemed distant from him. Even distant from everyone at their table.

She misses Me, Dante heard God say.

What? Wow!

Tell her I miss her too.

What? Umm, are You sure, God? Am I really hearing You?

But Dante's heart was feeling heavy with the message.

"Aye, man! You listening to me? What's up, D?" JR's voice broke into his thoughts. "You not even eating yo food!"

"Yea, give me a sec. I need to do something." Dante got up before his friend could respond and before he lost his nerve.

Lord, please be with me! He quickly prayed before heading to his destination.

I am with you always.

"Umm, excuse me. I'm sorry to interrupt." Four pairs of eyes stared at Dante. He couldn't help but feel embarrassed as he had clearly interrupted a conversation.

"Yea, man, wuz up?"

It was the boyfriend. Dante sized him up and pushed the desire away to compare. He was not here to fight for this girl, but to encourage her.

"Hey, y'all. My name is Dante. I was just chillin' with my man and felt an urge to share something God put on my heart." His heart was beating fast and he watched the group's various facial expressions change as he talked. Two of the girls looked skeptical. The guy looked like he was humored, but his target, the one he couldn't take his eyes from, looked intrigued.

That was enough motivation for Dante.

"So, yea, I've actually never done this before." He laughed nervously. "Umm come up to a perfect stranger, but I can't shake the feeling that God has a message for you." He looked directly at her.

"Me? Umm, ok." She looked at him expectantly and the whole table seemed to be waiting.

"Umm, God says He knows you miss Him, and He misses you too."

The girl's eyes widened while both brows raised.

"What? Wow!"

"Umm, does that resonate with you at all?" Dante asked.

"Uh, yea." She swallowed, her expression pensive. "It does actually."

"Wow, girl, that's crazy!" one of her friends said. "Yea!" the other one added. Dante could see they were impressed and looking at him as if he had a gift.

"Thanks, man. We appreciate that," the guy said. Dante sensed he wasn't too happy about his presence, but didn't want to appear like a jerk in front of his woman.

"No, no problem." Dante knew when he was being told to leave, so he started to back up.

"Yea, it means a lot. Thank you!" the girl said before he could go. "My name's Joy by the way. And this is Tamia, Linda and my boyfriend, Nick." Dante nodded to each person as she introduced them.

"Alright, well, I'll see y'all." He turned before she could continue the conversation. He didn't want to cause any more of a disruption then he already had.

"Man, what was *that* about?" JR asked, when he got back to the table. "Don't tell me you shot yo shot right in front of ol' boy!" He leaned over excitedly and Dante laughed.

"Naw, man. You are a nut! I had something on my heart God told me to share with her."

"Who? The fine one?" JR looked in Joy's direction.

"Yea, man. Her name is Joy." Dante slid out his seat before grabbing his food.

"Dawg, you are on another level! You out here giving messages from God? I thought chew' was getting the digits!" JR laughed. "Man, you ain't gon' *never* get a woman at this rate!"

Dante shook his head while inhaling his burger. Maybe so, but nothing could compare to the feeling he had at that moment. The feeling of walking in purpose. The feeling that He has been used by God.

* * *

It was a perfect night. Summer was fleeting and the humidity had dissipated to a refreshing breeze. Dante was in all white and was still on a high by the way God had used him earlier that day. He couldn't stop thinking about it, and he had to admit, he couldn't stop thinking about Joy.

Man, what is up with me and this girl? She is taken!

Not for long.

There was that still, small voice again. But He couldn't be hearing right. How could God be leading him to someone who wasn't available?

"I see you, baby brother! Lookin' fly!" Dante's sister Dana sauntered up behind him with her beau in tow.

"Oh, you know I do alright!" He turned and embraced her in a hug, appreciating that he didn't have to reach too far down to grab her; she was only a few inches shorter than him. Even though they were fraternal, they were extremely similar to each other. From their skin tone and hazel eyes, to their athletic build and no-nonsense personalities.

Dante assessed his sister. She had on a polka dot tank with distressed denim jeans and tan sandals. Her brown skin sparkled in the sun, while her hair was tied up in a large curly bun with a headband. His sister was his best friend. She knew him through and through. They had both survived a difficult childhood and were determined to not repeat the same bad habits their parents had. While their mother struggled with drug abuse until her dying day, their father had simply walked out. Abandonment and addiction were in their bloodline, but they were both believing God had better for them, and the generations to come.

"Yo. Wuz up, Dante!" Jerard, Dana's boyfriend, gave Dante dap. Dante was impressed by Jerard. He was the first of Dana's guys that had actually seemed to have something going for himself and had his sister's best intentions at heart. He was hard working and helped his father with construction. Dante knew he was set up to take over the business soon, due to his father's failed health.

"Yo, man. What up. How you doin?" Dante greeted Jerard.

Jerard lifted his large shoulders while holding several blankets under his meaty arms. "Ah, man, you know, staying out of trouble. Grindin'!"

"Yea, I feel you! Same here!"

"Yea, Dana said you was up for that promotion. How's that going?" Jerard asked. When he shifted his stance to balance out the weight of the blankets, his football players-sized frame casted a shadow on the grass that nearly doubled in size.

"Workin' my butt off, but I think it's gonna pay off soon," Dante said, lowering the cap over his eyes to block out the sun.

"Cool. If anybody deserves it, bruh, it's you." Jerard looked at him with confidence.

Dante placed a hand on his chest. "Aww, man, thanks for that! I appreciate it!" He was truly touched.

"Oh, alright! Enough of the bromance!" Dana interjected. "Y'all making me sick." She made a face like she was puking and Dante playfully hit the back of her head.

"You know you love it!" he teased. He had never really hit it off with any of her boyfriends, so he knew she was pleased.

"Whateva. So, where y'all wanna sit?" she asked, looking around. The park was filling up quickly and pretty soon there wouldn't be any more good spots available.

"Well, JR should be here soon. How bout we go to that section and I'll text him to see his ETA." Dante pointed in the direction near the stage towards the left. The first group hadn't started yet, but nobody seemed to mind. People were busy socializing, drinking and eating. Many had blankets and fold out chairs, while some opted to stand. It seemed like everybody was trying to cling to the last bit of summer that remained.

"Yea, that's cool. I hope he don't bring one of those floozies, though," Dana commented. "I can't stand when they don't have nothin' to talk about but how good they look! Or how good *he* looks! Or how good they look together!"

Dante laughed. "Now they not *that* bad, Dana."

"Come on, D, that last one thought the last president we had was Bush."

Dante's Joy

"Well, everybody can't keep up with politics…" Dante tried to come to her defense.

"But Bush? I mean, Clinton would have been a *little* more current." She looked at him with an unbelievable expression, her hazels reflecting the diminishing sunlight. "And let's not even mention the fact that we had a *Black* president!"

Dante gave up and laughed. "Just sit and be nice!" he warned her. He knew his sister could be a bit of a mean girl and it was something God was dealing with her about. He also knew it stemmed from the drama she dealt with from the girls she grewup with in their neighborhood.

"Alright, J will be here shortly," Dante said. "I told him where we sittin'. I'm gonna go get a drink. Y'all want something?" Jerard had laid out a couple of blankets, and for now, they were going to sprawl out until the show started.

"Yea, get me a smoothie, bro, and some kettle corn!" Dana said.

"I'll take a soda, man, thanks," Jerard added.

Dante made a mental note and headed towards the food trucks. He was trying to balance everything in his hands while leaving his last stop, when he heard what sounded like an angel.

"So, are you stalking me now, Dante?" He raised his eyes to see a pair of beautiful browns, full pink lips and that smooth, almond skin.

259

"Joy. Hey!" He knew he sounded too excited, but he couldn't help himself. What were the odds?

"I mean, twice in one day? What is a girl to think?" Joy smiled with her hand tied to her hip and he felt his heart leap.

How did she do that to him?

"Well, I could say the same thing to you. You must have heard me and my boy at the mall talking about the festival and decided you had to come see me." Ok, so he was flirting. But wasn't she flirting back?

"Is that so? And I decided to come alone so we wouldn't have any distractions?" Joy threw him a cheeky smile, while crossing her arms and shifting so that all of her weight was on one side. She looked good. Her jean shorts hit at the knee and a fitted white tank with white sneakers completed her ensemble. Oversized, gold hoop earrings dangled from her ears whenever she bobbed her head.

"Well, you said it, not me," Dante kept up the banter. "So, you here by yourself foreal?" He looked around, expecting to see her boyfriend lurking by.

"Well, my girl Jennifer is supposed to be meeting me here, but she is forever late. She can also be super flaky, so for the moment, yes, I am."

"Wow. And no boyfriend, huh?" he asked curiously.

"Oh, so you remember I have a boyfriend?" She cocked her head, causing her large gold hoops to graze her shoulder.

"How could I forget? Dude had his arms pretty much chained to yo chair today!" Dante said, grinning.

Joy laughed. "Yeah, he can be a little extra sometimes. Well, a lot of times..." She let her voice trail off, and Dante noticed her eyes get dark. Was there something more to that statement?

"Well, you free to hang out with me and my fam until your friend gets here. We're sitting right over there." Dante nodded his head in the direction of his friends and the two fell into step together.

Dante introduced Joy and proceeded to hand out refreshments.

"So, Joy, you from the west side?" Dana asked. She was sizing Joy up and Dante prepared himself for her to go overboard with her questioning.

"Yea, but I'm hip to the east side too." Joy crossed her legs on the large blanket and met Dana's gaze, seeming perfectly unintimidated. "I actually moved around a lot growing up so I don't feel like I have a place that's really "home" per se."

"Hmm, that's interesting. I guess I could say the same, although we did stay in the same neighborhood all our childhood. It wasn't until college that we got out. But things were so crazy at home, we just wanted to leave." Dana flicked a bug off her arm and took a gulp of her smoothie.

Dante wished Dana hadn't mentioned that last statement. He didn't want to lay the heavy stuff out there on someone he had just met, but Joy didn't seem put off.

"Yea, I get that. My grandmother raised me because my dad was in the military, so we always moved around." Joy mindlessly rubbed an area on her knee that was red from a mosquito bite, while she seemed to be thinking. "What I learned was that being with my grandma *was* home. So even if our physical location changed, I always had *her*."

"Wow. That's perceptive," Dana said, and Dante could see she was impressed. He was as well.

"Yea. I never thought of a person as being home," Jerard said thoughtfully.

"Now, y'all did *not* get this party started without me!" JR appeared. Dante could see a smaller figure standing behind him, so he scooted over to make room for them to sit.

"Yo, man. Wuz up!" Dante said to his friend.

"Oh, I see you added to the group without my permission!" JR was looking straight at Joy with an appreciative smile chiseled on his round face.

"Excuse me," his female companion said.

"Oh, my bad. Aye, y'all, this is Candice. Candice, this is everybody!" JR plopped down next to Dante.

"Nice to meet you, I'm Dante," Dante offered, feeling bad for his friend's horrible manners. "And this is Dana, Jerard, and Joy."

The group nodded to the newcomers.

"Man, when is this thing gonna start!" JR piped up.

"Boy, you just got here!" Dana said.

"Right, I'm late, and it's still not poppin'!" JR said loudly, shaking his head.

Dana and JR went back and forth and Dante found himself sneaking glances at Joy.

Man, she sure is pretty.

He couldn't diminish the desire to get to know her more. He was so excited they had connected again. As if she felt his gaze, Joy looked his way and smiled, but before he could say something, the first band joined the stage.

The evening flowed with smooth R&B and even some hype classics like, "Can't Touch This" by MC Hammer and Run DMC's "My Adidas". The crowd moved and swayed, singing loudly with the bands' lyrics to old school and new. Dante was so happy to be with his people and treasured the time he was able to spend in Joy's presence. By the end of the show, he desperately didn't want the night to end.

"So, your friend Jennifer flaked, huh?" Dante asked. They were folding the blankets and heading out, but taking their time because there were so many people; rushing was pointless.

"Yea, she texted me about half way through and said she was hanging with her new boo. She is always dropping me for some dude."

"That's not cool, but I know the feeling." Dante cocked his head in the direction of JR who was fawning all over Candice. The two were lost in each other.

Joy laughed. "Yea. But it ended up being a good night after all. I appreciate you inviting me to hang wit' y'all."

"Yea, girl. You are more than welcome!" Dana said, coming up along beside the two. "I think we are going to head over to *Denny's* for food if you want to join." Dante was pleasantly surprised at how friendly his sister was being.

"Oh. Yea, that sounds cool!" Joy looked at Dante. "I mean, if you're down."

"Definitely. I could eat!" Dante was overjoyed.

"Ok, let me just check in with Nick. Umm, can you shoot me the directions and I'll meet you there?" she asked Dante.

Dante's Joy

"Fa sho." Joy rattled off her number and Dante quickly locked her in. He couldn't believe what was happening!

Go slow. He heard in his spirit. Immediately he paid attention.

Ok, God. I got you.

By the time they arrived, it was an hour later. It seemed everyone had the same idea and had headed from the concert to the diner.

"Man, it is *packed*!" JR said sloppily. He rested his arm over Candice and her small frame sank under his weight. Dante could tell his friend was intoxicated and must have inhaled something on their way to the diner. He was hoping Candice was driving, since she seemed to be sober.

"You think we should leave?" Joy asked Dante, her brown eyes worried.

"Nah, they move through the line pretty fast. Besides, we can talk while we wait." Dante led her to a seat on the bench and they began conversing.

In their 30-minute waiting time, Dante found out Joy grew up an only child but had three half siblings from previous relationships that her father had. Her mother had died in childbirth, which is how she ended up with her father and grandmother. She was a nail tech and makeup artist with her own independent business, and she loved kids. She loved God too, but hadn't been to church in a while. He felt even more enthralled after learning more about her.

"So, you think you'll have kids one day?" he asked when they got seated. Everyone settled in and waited for the waitress. The group seemed to be paired off with Dana and Jerard sitting on one side of the booth conversing and Ray and Candice on the other, cuddling.

"Yea, I hope to. But I don't know when that day will be. I'm not in any rush though," Joy answered, her leg slightly brushing his.

"Yea, me too. No rush here. I'm still trying to get myself situated to raise a family," Dante said. He steadied an arm on the booth behind her and tilted backward into the cozy red booth, getting relaxed.

Dante told her about the upcoming promotion, his new apartment, and even the men's group he was in.

"Wow, it sounds like a great support system. I wish I had something like that," she said wistfully.

"Oh, it is. I don't know where I would be without them! I have grown so much spiritually by having my brothers," Dante said excitedly. It felt so good to be able to share his faith with someone who understood.

"Yea. I used to have that when I lived in Seattle, but it's been a while. I haven't really found a place I feel like I fit in

Dante's Joy

spiritually with." Joy appeared saddened by the thought. "Oh, let me get this real quick," she said, looking down at her phone. Immediately, she stepped away to take a call.

"She seems nice," Dana cooed as soon as Joy was out of earshot, a small smile gracing her delicate face.

"Yea, man. She's cool," Jerard agreed.

"Yea, but she got a dude!" JR slurred. He was even more loud when he was high.

"Dag, y'all! We just met. I'm just getting to know her, so chill out!" But Dante knew it was a big deal that he was interested in someone. He hadn't found a girl he liked this much in a long time.

The waitress came with their plates and the group started digging into eggs, sausage, bacon, fruit and pancakes.

"Sorry 'bout that," Joy said, sitting back down. She took her silverware and began cutting, but Dante could tell something was wrong. She seemed—heavy.

"No problem. Everything ok?" he asked gently, his hazel eyes cloudy with concern.

"Yea, it's cool."

Dante noticed Joy didn't make eye contact.

Hmmm, he thought to himself. *I'll let it slide.* He figured since they were in public she may not want to share.

The rest of the evening went well. JR was his usually animated self, telling embarrassing stories about growing up with Dante, and the antics they used to pull in the neighborhood. Dana sprinkled in some of her own, and Dante pretended to be horrified, but couldn't hide the joy he was feeling being with his folks.

I love my fam, he thought.

"So, how did y'all meet?" Dana asked Joy. JR had just finished another tall tale of growing up in the hood.

"Oh, my man is slick over here!" JR piped up. "Dante up here givin' messages from *God* to get them digits!"

Dante was immediately embarrassed. "Dawg, that's not even how it went." He shot his friend a look.

Joy reached for his hand and patted it. Instantly he felt his heart leap and tried to calm himself. "Yea, Dante has been nothing but a gentleman. He *did* have a message for me, but it was something that was already on my heart," Joy said. "We were chillin' at the mall when he came up to me and shared it. It was pretty amazing, actually." Joy looked at him, her brown eyes full of admiration.

Dag, am I blushing? he thought, smiling from ear to ear. He felt his sisters' eyes on him and tried to cover up his grin by drinking his coffee.

"Wow, Dante!" Dana said. "Ok, I'm impressed!" She looked at him knowingly; he was sprung.

"Yea, I'm impressed too!" JR said. "I'm 'bout to have to start praying to Jesus too so He can tell me how to get them digits!" He threw back his head in raucous laughter, cracking himself all the way up.

Dana reached over and socked JR in the side with her little league pitch-throwing arm and he let out a groan. "Boy, you need to just pray He forgives you for being a fool!" she said, and the table erupted in laughter.

Dante gave Joy an apologetic look, but she seemed like she was enjoying herself.

The night eventually ended with the group calling it quits around 2AM-closing time.

"I had a great time!" Joy said. Dante was walking her to her car after the others had said their goodbyes.

"Yea! This turned out to be a great night. Sorry about JR tho." He looked at her sheepishly. "He can be a handful sometimes."

"Oh trust. I'm not concerned. I have dealt with plenty of JR's in my life!" She tossed him an amused smile. Dante jammed his hands into his pockets while kicking at a pebble nearby. He still didn't want the night to end, but he remembered the prompting he heard earlier.

"Cool. Well, I should probably let you go..." He lingered a little, then forced himself to take a step back.

"Yea, probably," Joy said. She also didn't want the night to end. "Dante, I have to be honest," she started hesitantly. Shyly, she hid her hands in her own pockets and peered up at him. "I find myself attracted to you, and I'm not sure what to do about it. I care about Nick a lot, but things have been topsy-turvy for a while now. I know he doesn't share my beliefs and he can be too controlling. He actually threatened to come up here tonight when I told him I was here wit' y'all."

"What? Wow." Dante said shocked.

Does her dude really not trust her that much? he thought to himself.

"Yea, and he has pulled really jealous stuff like that before. I was nervous he was going to actually show up." She played with the hem of her shorts, eyes glued to the pavement.

"Man. That's crazy," Dante said. He felt bad for her, and wished she wasn't in something so toxic.

"Yea. He struggles with trusting me. He can be really possessive. Anyways, I want to be honest because I don't want to mislead you. I don't want a relationship. I'm not in any position to even have one. But I do feel drawn to you. I want to learn more about your church. I know I have been longing for that connection I once had with God." Joy looked at him intensely while taking a step closer, then gently rubbed his arm. "He clearly used you today to affirm what was already in my heart."

"Yea, I'll say." Dante chuckled, feeling all kinds of emotions towards her.

"So, I believe there is purpose in our connection. But I don't want that to be misconstrued." She let her hand go and turned to face the restaurant, leaning her back against her Honda Civic.

"Yea, I get it," Dante said, not wanting her to stress. "Hey, don't worry. I understand your situation, and I'm in no rush. I have so many things I'm focused on right now before I feel like a relationship is on the table." Dante fell back next to her on the car and looked over at her. "But I won't lie, I'm attracted to you too and I want to keep getting to know you. So, can we at least do that and be friends?"

He saw relief flood Joy's eyes and felt God's presence.

"Yea. I would like that very much, Dante. Thank you for understanding!"

"Hey, that's what friends do." Dante smiled. "I see you getting sleepy, so I'm gonna let you go. Make sure you text me when you make it home!" He got off from the car and Joy did the same.

"Will do. Thanks again, Dante." Dante watched Joy drive away in her little blue Civic. While he was definitely disappointed there couldn't be more between them, he knew he was hearing God.

Lord, please help us to navigate this friendship, and help me to be what Joy needs in this season, he prayed. He made his way to his own vehicle to drive back home. Alone.

* * *

God did answer Dante's prayer, and the two began a friendship. Dante focused on his work, eventually receiving his promotion. He kept attending his men's group and would now see Joy at his church on Sundays. She seemed to be acclimated, and even had her own small group she faithfully attended. They texted sometimes, and even hung out in groups, but they were never out alone. Dante knew that would be too much temptation for him to handle and he was afraid he would get romantic. If anything, Joy and Dana had hit it off. He felt like his sister saw Joy more than he did.

"So, how did you like the service?" Dante asked Joy, one day after church. They were loitering outside in the cool air bundled in jean jackets, scarves and boots. The colorful leaves covered the grounds while naked trees swayed nearby. Other attendees were either leaving for home, or lingering in conversation themselves.

"It was good as usual! I'm so glad you told me about your church!" Joy said. Her eyes were shining, and Dante marveled once again, at his attraction to her.

"Yea, me too!" he agreed. "I was hoping JR would come today, but you know, it's like pulling teeth with that dude." He gave a sad smile.

"Yea. He will. He has you in his life to be the light. Sometimes when all people see is darkness, it's hard to believe that such a light exists." Joy smiled reassuringly.

"Yea. I know. I just get grieved sometimes thinking about his choices. I mean, we grew up in the same neighborhood, had the same life circumstances, but took different paths." He lowered his gaze, his heart heavy at the thought.

"Yea, it's like the parable about the seeds falling. Some fall on good ground, while others don't." She moved towards him to stroke his face, and he found himself surprised, but pleased by the gesture. "You are good ground, Dante," she continued. She studied him with certainty in her eyes, as well as a deep affection.

"Thanks, I appreciate that. Look at you 'strengthening the brethren'!" he teased, referencing a familiar passage of scripture.*

"Well, I figured I should sow into you and pay back the favor!" Joy said. "But seriously, thank you for your obedience with giving me that word at the mall when we met. I really feel like God used it to get me back on track. I was in a murky place in my life and I wasn't even sure He was still with me. I felt… lost."

"He is always with us, Joy. I'm so glad you found your way! But even with me giving the word, you still had to choose."

"Yea. There are some other choices I've been making too that I want you to know about, Dante." She sounded hesitant.

Dante listened intently. What was she talking about?

"I broke up with Nick about a month ago," she informed quietly.

"Oh. Wow. I see." Dante glanced at the church building. Most of the traffic had cleared.

"Yea. I felt like it had been a long time coming. I knew it wasn't going to work out given the direction I felt led in, but I wanted to make sure it was really what I was supposed to do." Joy began toying with the hem of her jacket nervously. "You know, that I was doing it for *me,* and not because I had met *you.*"

"Oh. Ok." Dante looked back down at her. He was a little confused. What exactly was she saying?

"I mean, I know plenty of girls that go from one guy to the next. I've actually done the same thing. So I didn't want the feelings I was developing for you to be the reason I broke up with him," Joy added.

Wow, she has feelings for me? Dante couldn't believe what he was hearing.

She bit her lip slowly before proceeding. "But when I knew I was doing it because it was about *my* identity and destiny, I knew I had to."

Dante didn't know what to say, so he just nodded. *Lord what is going on? What are You saying?*

"So, what I'm trying to say is, I'm making choices that are in line with my destiny, and I hope that you will be next to me as it keeps getting revealed." She stole a glance his way, her eyes questioning.

"Wow. That's deep." *Father, please guide me! he prayed silently.*

Dante studied Joy, trying to see if his feelings were worth trusting, but he couldn't ignore the intensity of them, and of what his heart was telling him.

"Joy, when I met you, I knew that you were special. I knew that I wanted you and that I wanted to be next to you. But I also knew it wasn't time," he began. "I appreciate the time we have had to get to know each other and develop a friendship." He stepped towards her, letting the back of his forefinger glide softly along her cheek. "Though I want to move forward, I still think there is more time we *both* need in getting prepared for the future."

Joy shook her head in agreement. "Yea, I know. I would love to take it to the next level, but I know I need more time. Still, I want to be honest with where I am." She gingerly placed a hand over his chest, her eyes locked with his. Dante moved in closer and grabbed her hand, their faces only moments away from one another.

"Joy, I am a patient man," he responded, huskily. "I told you once before, I am not in any rush. I don't need you to commit to me today, because I know that if there is a future for us, it will happen. Let's just continue taking one step at a time and see how the Father unfolds things." Instead of lowering his lips to hers, the way he desperately wanted to, he drew her into a bear hug.

Joy's smile was hidden in the comfort of his chest. "I would like that very much," she murmured, letting his fragrance engulf every one of her senses.

* * *

Dante stood in his tux and straightened his bow tie.

"You look good, bruh!" JR said, slapping him on the chest.

"Yea, man, so do you!" Dante responded. They were waiting at the end of the aisle. The wedding was a small affair, not much family, but lots of friends. Dante had learned that his friends *were* his family. He was learning that life didn't always turn out the way you wanted it to, but God always provided.

He looked around at the simple, but elegant decorations and held his breath for the bride. The music sounded, then everyone stood to their feet. The bridal party made their way in in hues of yellow, and that's when he saw her. Joy. His Joy. Walking down the aisle—not in the white bridal dress that she would wear in just two years' time, but in a yellow, maid of honor dress she was wearing in honor of his sister.

Dante smiled as she approached her spot across from him. She smiled back, and then, there she was—Dana. She was elegant and regal. Tall and lovely, and Dante couldn't help but marvel that the trauma of their past held no residue on her physical appearance. He was so grateful that God had spared them that at least. He looked over at the groom, his new brother-in-law, and saw that Jerard was crying. After handing him his handkerchief, he made sure he had the ring in his jacket pocket. Yep, still there.

"Thanks, man," Jerard whispered while wiping his tear-soaked face.

Before Dante knew it, Dana was before them, standing next to her husband to be.

"Who gives away this bride?" their pastor asked. Dante cleared his throat. This was it. This was the moment he had been praying about. Could he really give away his sister? She had been all he had for so long. She had been his home.

"I do," he managed to say, and caught eyes with Joy.

Yes, he could. It was a new season. It was a new day. And even though it was going to be different, it could still be good.

Well Lord, You have brought us this far, Dante prayed. *Take us the rest of the way!*

* **Luke 22:32** *But I have prayed for you, that your faith should not fail; and when you have returned to Me, strengthen your brethren."*

JASMYNE

"Hi! I'm Jasmyne Moore," Jas said. She stuck out her hand in an awkward fashion. First dates were already uncomfortable. Blind dates were even more so. The tall, yellow, slim guy standing before her, fondled her hand in his sweaty palm.

I hope that's just nerves and not his normal, Jas thought to herself with distaste.

"Hey. I'm Ray." Jas waited for more but Ray proceeded to take a seat and review the menu.

Um ok, I guess I'll get my own chair, she thought.

"So, Ray. Latoya says you're a truck driver?" she offered, after the waitress took their orders.

"Yep." Ray nodded, looking pleased with himself. "I've been with my company for five years now. Looking into some other options though for more pay." He puffed out his small chest, revealing a few chest hairs that had escaped the V-neck T-shirt he was wearing under a suit jacket.

"Oh, that's nice." Jas took a sip of her water and smoothed down her navy, polka dot skirt. After it was clear that Ray was not one to initiate topics of conversation, she mustered up enough effort to ask some other relevant getting-to-know-you questions. But when the waitress asked about dessert, Jas could no longer hold in her frustration.

"No dessert for me. Thanks. I'll just take my portion of the check." The waitress, a younger version of Janet Jackson, lifted one arched eyebrow before shooting a glance at Ray. Ray moved around restlessly in his chair and finally said more than two words during the date.

"Yea, I'll take my portion too," he mumbled, and looked out the restaurant window. Jas sighed inwardly as the waitress shook her head pathetically and walked away.

Why is it that every brother out here is on some other stuff? she wondered, and decided to give Latoya, a piece of her mind, as soon as she saw her at work on Monday.

* * *

"So, girl, how was your date?" Stephanie asked Jas as they prepared for their Yoga class. They had been attending for the last month, and Jas was still wondering when the class would get easier.

"Girl, why is it that I had to carry the conversation, seat myself *and* pay for my own meal?"

"What?! That is crazy!" Stephanie shook her thick, curly, shoulder length hair while pursing her lips. "I can't with these dudes." Stretching her legs out, she bent over and easily touched her hands to each foot.

"Yea, it's like I took *myself* out on a date!" Jas modeled her friend's move, feeling her muscles unwind as she, too, bent over. Her full figure was the perfect hourglass shape, but though her curves were an advantage in the dating world, in fitness, they could be obstacles.

"I'm sorry you went through that, girl. But I guess it's like what they say, you gotta kiss a lot of frogs to get to yo prince," Stephanie offered. She then contorted her small, delicate frame into a position Jas couldn't dream of doing.

"Easy for you to say, girl. You already have *your* prince." Jas was about to try Stephanie's move when the instructor, Mya, glided into the room and greeted them.

"Hello, beautiful queens! So glad you were able to make it on this lovely new day!" Mya was dark skin and slim with wide hips. She frequently exuded joy and peace, and Jas loved being in her presence.

"Now, let's get started!" Mya led the ladies in a 45-minute routine of sweat and strength. Jas had often tried to stay active, but this level of strength workout was something else.

"Girl, I'm *done*!" she exclaimed to Stephanie, once they were finally released from the grueling workout.

"Yea, me too!" Both ladies plopped on their yoga mats and eagerly gulped from their water bottles.

"Hey, y'all! We going to get smoothies, if y'all are interested," Kim, one of the girls in the class, came over and said.

"Hey, Kim. I'm with it. What about you, Jas?" Stephanie asked, looking at her friend.

Jas responded, "Sounds good to me."

The two gathered up their things and followed Kim, and her best friend Monique, out of the studio.

It was the perfect summer day with sunshine and not a cloud in sight. The ladies were chatty and talked the whole 10-minute walk to the smoothie spot. Frank's Smoothies was a common stop to many after a workout, but Jas hadn't been there before. She looked around and took in the mix of ethnicities gathered, waiting for their orders.

"Wow, this place is lit," she commented.

Jasmyne

"Yea, girl. We gon' have to wait a minute but trust, it will be worth the wait!" Kim said with a smile. Jas smiled back then took in more of the scene while the ladies carried on their conversations. That's when she saw him. Not that tall, but not too short either. Muscular build and a bald head. He was wearing basketball shorts, a jersey, and the new Air Force 1s. He cocked his head, smiling at something his buddy next to him said.

"Girl, you hear me?" Stephanie interrupted Jas' thoughts and Jas quickly tore her gaze away from the handsome stranger.

"Huh? Oh yea. You was talking about Leon's new gig."

"Mmhmm. I know you wasn't *really* listening, but I can see why you would tune me out!" Stephanie smiled and turned her head in the same direction Jas had been looking.

Jas grinned. "Hey, ain't no crime in lookin'," she said, giving a sly smile.

"Girl, get yours," Stephanie quipped, and they both laughed.

"Who we lookin' at?" Kim asked, turning her head in their direction. Prior to, her back was to them while she talked with Monique.

"Brown skin over there," Stephanie answered, before Jas could deny anything.

283

"Ohhh, yea! He know he look like L.L.'s fine self! That's Courtney," Monique informed.

"You know him?" Jas asked, a little too excitedly, even for her own taste.

"Yep! He used to date my cousin," Monique said proudly. She looked again over at Courtney, then licked her lips and shook her head. "Mmm, mmm, *mmm!*" The girls all giggled in response.

"Well, girl! Give us the tea!" Stephanie demanded. All eyes were on Monique in expectation, and Jas took in every ounce of detail.

"It was a while ago, but back then, he was working full time, *and* in grad school studying to be a *dentist.*" She emphasized the word "dentist" while making eye contact with each girl. "He was always busy and didn't really have time for a relationship, at least, that's what Juanita said." Monique shimmied a hand through her high ponytail that fell down her back. Jas was just wondering why she was fixing herself up, when she caught sight of her friend's view. The very topic of conversation was heading their way! Four pairs of brown eyes tried to look nonchalant, but Jas suspected that their previous attention had not gone unnoticed.

"Umm, excuse me ladies," Courtney said. His boy was right behind him, and Jas could see he was just as attractive as Courtney, but taller.

Man, the cuties are always together, she thought to herself. She licked her lips and wished she had reapplied her lip gloss after class.

"Do y'all mind if we share this table while we wait for our smoothies?" Courtney asked. "Y'all seem to have gotten the last free one." He gestured at the booth they had managed to get. Four beautiful, brown women quickly shook their heads.

"Oh no not at all," Kim answered in a rush.

"You can sit next to me," Monique eagerly volunteered. She scooted over in the booth to make room.

Dag, didn't she just say he dated her cousin? Jas thought to herself. *Thirsty.*

The ladies moved over and the two newcomers sat down. Jas ended up next to the friend, who introduced himself as Troy. She and Stephanie engaged Troy in conversation, and she learned he was a musician, but worked at a factory to support his music.

"Yea, my boyfriend is a musician too," Stephanie said. Jas could see the disappointment in Troy's eyes when Stephanie dropped the "b" word, and stifled a laugh.

"Oh yea?" Troy responded in a low, deep tone. Leaning back in his seat, he tried to look unfazed.

"Yea. He actually has a gig tonight I was just telling Jas about. Y'all should *all* come. It's gonna be at a new club that's black-owned downtown." Stephanie spoke excitedly while addressing the table.

"Cool. I'm in," Courtney said, moving in towards Stephanie to be heard.

"Yea, me too," the others responded.

"Good! Then it's a go," Stephanie confirmed.

Yep, and hopefully I'll get a chance to peep Mr. Courtney, Jas thought, as she watched Monique and Kim fawn all over him.

* * *

Jas had to make a stop at her mom's before she met her crew at the club that night.

"Hey, Auntie." She bent down to give her aunt, who was in the rocking chair on the porch, a kiss on the forehead. Aunt Milly was the eldest out of all of her mom's siblings and loved telling everybody what to do. Out of all of her aunts *she* was the one Jas was the closest to.

"Hey, baby! How you doin?" The older woman's eyes twinkled with love, as she gave Jas a warm embrace.

"Let me get a look at you! M-m-m! Looks like you been working out! I see those legs!" She made Jas turn around on the porch to show off her figure.

Jas had on a black bodysuit and a faux leather pencil skirt with black high heels. Her hair was pulled up into a big poof and loose brown tendrils framed her round, nut brown face.

"I see that baby hair is laid!" her aunt exclaimed with approval. "Where you goin' lookin that good?"

"Bout' to catch my future husband!"

"Well, he ain't gon' be able to say 'no' to you. I tell you that, honey!" Aunt Milly's boisterous laughter trailed Jas all the way inside.

"Hey, Auntie Rita, Aunt Pam, Ms. Carol," she greeted her folks sitting at the dining room table.

"Heeeeyyyy!" came in response as one chorus.

Jas gave a round of hugs to each woman, experiencing the normal adoration she received from her female relatives. She stood for a moment, watching the women sip their drinks and playing cards. It was Gin Rummy night, and normally her mom was hosting her friends and fam for card games and back talk.

Aunt Pam asked, "So how you doin, baby girl?" with a loose grin from the alcohol on her large, tan face.

"I'm good," she responded to her aunt. "You know where Mommy is?"

"She in the basement with Jimmy," Auntie Rita informed, then slammed down her card. "Gin!" she cried out and the table sighed, while money was tossed on the counter then subsequently grabbed by Auntie Rita as she happily squealed.

Jas passed through the small, but clean living room. One wall in front of the stairway was decorated with ample family photos of her and her brother, either participating in some sport, or receiving an academic achievement. Her dad's photos were taken down when the divorce happened, so she only saw the ones where her mom was present.

"Hey, knucklehead," Jas greeted her brother, Jimmy, once she made it down the stairs.

"Sup'. Why you all dressed up?" Jimmy glanced at her and then back at the TV to focus on his video game.

"Why you worried about it?" she asked, hitting him upside the head.

"Don't hit your brother!"

Whoops! "Hey, Mommy! I didn't see you." Jas quickly dropped her hand and turned to her mother who was behind the bar.

"Yea! Get her, Mommy!" Jimmy said, laughing.

"Shut up before I get you again," Jas whispered, before walking over to her mom.

Jasmyne

"Girl, why you come over here starting stuff?" Mrs. Moore was busy restocking the quaint little bar they had in the basement.

"I'm goin' out with Stephanie and them. Can you do my eyebrows real quick?"

"Umm, didn't I just do them last week? They can't look that bad." Her mom stood up and squinted her eyes to inspect her. Jas was her mirror image, except she had her father's coloring. Both women shared a thick build, large, light brown eyes, and full, pouty lips.

"Uhhh, yea, Mommy, but I'm tryna make sure I'm super on point tonight," Jas said, then started looking for the razor her mom used.

"Mmhmm. Who is he?" her mom asked. She put a few containers of 1800 Tequila on the shelves, barely looking at her daughter while she worked.

"Nobody!" Jas placed her newly manicured hand over her heart and batted her eyes innocently. "Can't I just want to look good for myself?"

"You know she tryna get *somebody's* attention, Ma," Jimmy said from the couch.

"Boy, why don't you mind yours?" Jas retorted. "And why you up here wasting your life on these video games? Get up and do something."

"Ain't nobody wasting nothin'. I'm waiting for Shantè to come swoop me," he said, as if he were proud of the fact.

"M-m-m. It's a shame you be doing these females like that," Jas said in a condescending tone.

"Ain't nobody forcing nobody to do nothin'," Jimmy said, rolling his eyes and turning back to his game.

"Yea. I heard it all before." She leaned to one side and put a hand on her hip, watching him with disgust. "Why don't you get your own and stop using people?"

"You just mad cuz Willie dropped chew'," Jimmy spewed, smacking his teeth at her.

"Hey! Now, y'all better stop!" Mrs. Moore said. "It's the weekend. I'm tryna relax, and y'all stealin' my peace!"

"She started it," Jimmy murmured.

"Jas, go sit in the chair and let me do your eyebrows." Mrs. Moore started towards the bathroom where she kept the razors. Jas did as she was told, but her brother's words had stung. She was still getting over her breakup with Willie from a year ago. He had been the first man she thought she would actually marry.

"Ok, ok! I see you, miss thang!" Mrs. Moore handed Jas the mirror when she was done and Jas admired the perfect arches.

"Yea, I guess you look alright," Jimmy said. Jas knew that was the closest she would get to a compliment from her brother.

"Thanks, Ma! Appreciate chew'!" She grabbed her mom and lightly kissed her cheek, not wanting to smear her makeup.

"You welcome, baby. Now have fun tonight! And make sure you post how good you look so Willie can see what he missin'!" Her mom winked, making Jas chuckle. Her mom didn't know the first thing about social media.

"Mommy, we don't even follow each other on there anymore. But I'll definitely post so everybody *else* can see."

"Ok, well, make sure somebody *he* know see it, so *they* can show him!"

Jas grinned, feeling tickled. Maybe her mom did know a little something? "Ok, Mommy, I got chew'."

* * *

The club had a gown and sexy vibe which Jas appreciated. She hated the hole-in-the wall "hood" spots her brother tended to frequent.

"Hey, girl," Stephanie called to her as she was making her way inside. "Here's your seat!"

"Hey! Where's everybody else at?" Jas asked, sitting down by her friend.

"The boys are buying drinks, and the girls are in the bathroom, and of course, Leroy is in the back with the band getting ready."

"Oh, ok." Jas took a second to reapply her makeup using the camera on her phone. "So, what did I miss?" she asked Stephanie in a conspiratorial tone.

"Well, Courtney has been cool, but I can't tell if he is into either girl like that, and Troy started talking to some female he met here. He literally has been talking to this girl since we got here."

"Dag, that's crazy."

"I know right. We invite *you* out and you talkin' to other people." Stephanie rolled her eyes and crossed one of her strappy heeled legs, her red mini dress dipping low with each movement.

"I guess he wasn't feeling nobody but chew'," Jas said.

"Well, *that* ain't happening," Stephanie responded, rolling her neck. Her face filled with an, "Ain't *nobody* taking me from *my* man," look.

"What's not happening?" Courtney was standing nearby, and Jas hadn't even seen him approach due to the club getting crowded.

"Hey! Let me help you." Jas stood up slightly to take one of the drinks in his hand and set it on the table. She felt their fingers briefly touch and was immediately excited.

"Thanks. Appreciate it—Jas, right?" Courtney hit her with a smile and slid in on the other side of her.

"Yep, short for Jasmyne," Jas said, pronouncing her name with a long "e" sound, then smiling back.

"Wow, that's a pretty name," Courtney complimented her.

"Thanks!"

Troy was right behind Courtney and Stephanie helped him with his drinks. "I got you a Margarita, Jas," Stephanie said, sliding the glass in front of Jas.

"Thanks, homie." Cupping her glass, Jas carefully took a sip, so she wouldn't smudge her lipstick.

"Aye, I'm gonna hit the floor," Troy announced, before swiftly making his exit.

"Dag! Sorry your boy just left you like that," Jas said to Courtney.

"You know how it is." He threw her a lopsided grin that was too cute for words. "Besides, I'm not. That means I get more time wit' chew," he added, before smoothly drinking his gin and tonic.

Hmmm, he is a charmer, Jas thought to herself. *And he really do look like a young LL Cool J!*

"Hey, Jas." Kim made her way to the table with Monique in tow.

"Hey," Jas said, still flattered by Courtney's flirting. The girls took their drinks and sat on the other side of Courtney. When he scooted closer to Jas, she took that as her cue.

Feeling a moment of boldness, she asked, "You wanna dance?" Courtney's eyes lit up.

"Definitely." He moved fast, and led her out to the floor. Jas barely had time to savor the jealous faces of Kim and Monique before she was flung on her feet by Courtney.

Courtney wasn't the strongest dancer, but Jas appreciated his effort. She eagerly admired him while they danced. Tailored cream pants, blue, silk collared shirt and brown and white Christian Dior shoes. A full goatee cut short rivaled his thick, full brows.

Dang. I don't know who's prettier, me or him? she thought, chuckling to herself.

"I see you got some moves," Courtney said to her when they ended their dance. They were posted together against the bar, cooling off.

"Well, I do what I can." Jas smiled and let him assist her onto the bar stool. It was the only one free, and he was forced to stand.

"I'm sure you do. So, Jas, tell me about yourself. What do you like to do for fun? Other than dance that is?" Courtney gave her his full attention, and Jas was elated.

"Well, I like to be social, but I like my alone time too. I do a little drawing and painting. I love working out. I do Yoga right now and a little bit of swimming. Oh, and I love spending time with my fam. We have card night on Saturdays. Normally I would be there." Jas felt herself rambling, and knew it was because she was nervous. She was so attracted to him!

"Ah, so you and your fam are close?"

Jas looked up at him, "Very. How 'bout chew'?"

"Lightweight. I mean, we ain't the Huxtables or nothing, but we aight'," Courtney said, and Jas laughed.

"Well, who is?" Jas took a sip of her water, and Courtney did the same, his eyes piercing hers as he looked at her over the glass. She felt like she was being studied, but in a good way.

"I guess you have a point," Courtney said after a while. "So, what do *you* like to do?" Jas felt excited. She hadn't really initiated with a guy before. *Nice to see it pays to be a little aggressive,* she thought to herself.

"Well, I'm finishing up graduate school, so a lot of my time is spent studying. But when I *do* have time, I like to chill in classy clubs like these." Courtney pointed around at the club, with drink in hand. It was now jam-packed with late 20-something and 30-somethings.

Jasmyne smiled in agreement. "Yea, I'm definitely about class. But that's not prevalent in our generation. So many are cool with the ratchet, hood spots." Jas' face filled with annoyance.

Courtney nodded. "Well, one thing you'll learn about me, Jasmyne, is, I am not the average young, Black man. In fact, many would say I have an old soul." He massaged his goatee, with a self-assured expression settling on his attractive features.

"Well, I can appreciate that. I'm tired of little boys," she said, half flirting, half serious.

"Then you're in luck, Jas," Courtney said. "Cuz I'm a grown man." He took Jas' hand, stroking it like it belonged to him. She felt a current shoot up her spine and was giddy beyond belief.

"Then we should be just fine," she said, with an unexplainable certainty.

* * *

Dating Courtney was a thrill. In just two months he had taken Jas to a play, the opera, and a Black art history museum. She was getting experiences with him she hadn't even had with Willie, and he had been her most serious relationship. She was on a high and felt like their relationship was meant to be.

"I'm having so much fun with you," she said. Looking up at Courtney in the moonlight on the back patio of his two-bedroom townhouse, she tugged her arms more tightly around his waist. His features were soft and endearing in the lighting. In

Jasmyne

response, he brushed her cheek tenderly with a finger, and kissed the tip of her nose.

"Me too," he said. "It's been hard for me to find the right fit for my lifestyle. I have very serious plans about what I want to do with my life. My schedule can be grueling, and I need someone who understands that." Jas nodded her head in complete agreement.

"Yea, I get it. I appreciate your goals and drive," she said. "I have my own goals and having someone who is comparable has been hard to find as well." Jas leaned her head against his chest.

I never want to let this man go, she thought. She tilted her head upward to view the night sky and smiled. The stars were shining brightly.

* * *

"This girl is taking all day!" Jas said under her breath. She was sitting outside the hair salon waiting for her cousin Brianna.

"**How much longer?**" she texted her, pounding the keys on her phone.

No response. Jas shifted in her seat and ran over her options in her head. A. leave Brianna, and make her call an Uber, which she felt bad about doing because Brianna was usually there for her when *she* needed something. B. see if Jimmy could have one of his females come swoop her, which also made her feel bad because she hated how he used women. Or C. wait it out, and hope she wasn't too late for her double date.

"**Girl, I'm comin**," came the response with the rolling the eyes emoji.

"**So sorry, babe. I'm prob gonna be a half hour late,**" Jas texted Courtney, hoping he wasn't too annoyed. She had learned quickly in their dating he was pretty Type A, and tardiness was a no-no.

Just then Stephanie called.

"Girl, where you at?" her girl asked, sounding irritated.

"Waiting on my dang on cousin, girl, at the freakin' hair salon. You already there?" Jas asked her friend, although she already knew the answer.

"Yea, and your boy is too. I think Leon is running out of stuff to talk about with Courtney tho. I mean, they just met forreal. How long you think you gon' be?" Stephanie's voice was tense.

"She sayin' she comin', and she's only 10 minutes from the restaurant, which is why I thought I could swoop her before our date, but you know, Black hair dressers..." Jas spoke rapidly, as if that would speed up her cousin.

"Well, hopefully you make it soon. Not sure how long he gon' wait."

"Girl, I gotta go. Here she come." Seeing her cousin leave the salon, Jas quickly ended her call and unlocked the doors to her dark blue Taurus.

"Girl, I thought you was ready when you texted for me to come get chew'?" she stated, as soon as Brianna sat down.

"Dag, girl! Hello to you too!" Brianna responded. Her light brown face stared back in surprise. Jas started driving.

"My bad, I just have something else goin' on, and I didn't know you was gon' be *that* long. Your hair is cute," she added. She assessed her cousin. Tall, light skin and heavy chested. Growing up, Brianna was the one the boys wanted, but finally junior year in high school Jas was able to give her a run for her money.

"Thanks." Brianna rubbed the shaved side of her do. It fell down mid-cheek in layers on the other side and was streaked with blonde. "She had somebody else pop up she forgot about, and that pushed me back. I swear one of these days I'm gon' find somebody who don't overbook."

"Girl, when you find 'em let me know cuz I ain't *never* heard of such a thing!" Both girls laughed, and it felt good to Jas. By the time she had dropped off Brianna she wasn't as anxious about her tardiness, even though Courtney had not responded to her text.

"Hey, sorry I'm late." Jas paused to hug Stephanie at the outside patio of their favorite Black-owned restaurant, *Sisters & Friends,* then tossed Leon a nod.

"Hey. Your boy *just* left," Stephanie informed her. Sighing heavily, Jas fell down into the chair across from her.

"Dag. He must be pissed cuz he didn't even respond to my text."

"Yea, dude is pretty uptight," Leon said. He took a swig of his lemonade. "I mean, you only what, 20 minutes late? And it ain't like you ain't let us know..." He scrunched up his almond brown face in disbelief.

"Yea, but I know he has a meeting to prepare for. Plus, I've been late a few times before, and I told him it was something I would work on," Jas quickly defended Courtney. Her friends were both silent.

"Well, we can always do a redo," Stephanie said optimistically. "Besides, it's a gorgeous day, and we at our favorite spot." She handed Jas a menu. "Let's enjoy." Jas tried her best to let the disappointment go from missing Courtney, but the feeling of regret stayed with her throughout her meal.

* * *

Courtney picked up Jas for a baseball game around 7 o'clock the following weekend. It was her first game, and even though she wasn't a big fan, she was excited to see Courtney. They had talked things out, and he had forgiven her for being late for their double date.

"Hey, babe," she said, leaning in for a kiss in his Jaguar. Even though it was an older model, it was still nice.

"Hey," he replied in a dry tone. He kissed her cheek, and she tried not to be disappointed it wasn't her lips.

Smoothing down her yellow sundress that hugged in all the right places, she put on her seatbelt. "How was your day?" she asked.

"Stressful. Arnold kept me on my toes all day. I almost thought about rain checking the game, but I didn't want to disappoint you." His well-groomed eyebrows were bunched together and she could tell he was stressed.

"Ahhh, well you should have told me your boss was trippin'. We could have done something more low-key, or even nothing if you wanted."

"Naw, it's all good. I love baseball. Once I get there it'll help me destress," Courtney assured her while turning down a side street.

"Well, maybe *before* you get there, I can help with that," Jas said sweetly. She grabbed his hand from the steering wheel and started to caress it, but he ripped it from her.

"Girl, are you crazy? I'm driving. You want me to hit somebody?" Courtney snapped.

"Dag. I was just trying to loosen you up," Jas said, feeling hurt.

Why is he taking his bad mood out on me? she thought to herself.

"Look. I'm sorry. Let's just get to the game, ok?" Jas didn't respond, and instead listened to the jazz station he had playing. One of the things she liked about Courtney was how well cultured he was. He exposed her to classical, jazz and even country music.

The drive to the game was quiet. Courtney seemed lost in his thoughts and Jas wasn't sure how to pull him out of himself. Finally, when they reached the ballpark, he loosened up.

"I'm sorry for the way I acted earlier." He turned to her and rubbed her cheek gently. She couldn't resist the sincere look in his beautiful browns. "You look really good by the way." He bent over her for a kiss.

In spite of herself, Jas was melting. She knew she shouldn't give in so easy to Courtney, but he was hard to resist.

Besides, you know how many chics would want to be in your shoes? she thought to herself. *Don't mess this up, Jas.*

* * *

"Momma, I want you to meet somebody!" Jas called to her mother when she walked in the house. Even though she knew her mom was expecting them, she didn't necessarily want Courtney to know how much she had talked about him.

Jasmyne

"Hey, baby girl." Mrs. Moore came to the front of the house and hugged Jas, then looked at Courtney who was standing next to her. "And you must be Courtney," she said, with a warm smile.

"Yes, ma'am. How are you?" Courtney's deep voice came out strong and sturdy.

"Oh, and well-mannered too! But you can lose the ma'am. Lena will do just fine!" she said, waving a hand. Now come on, y'all. Let's have a seat out on the balcony. Everybody out back." And by 'everybody' she meant just that. Jas had known an aunt or two would be there, but she didn't expect her cousins and their kids too!

"Dag, Ma. I thought we was doing a *small* family dinner," she said to her mom in a low tone, looking at the group with concern.

"Oh, honey. You know how word get around. Besides, your uncle is bar-b-queuing. You know everybody be wanting his bar-b-que." Mrs. Moore led them out back, and Jas gave Courtney an apologetic smile. Even though he smiled back, it didn't quite reach his eyes.

"Aye, y'all," she heard, as soon as they stepped on the back porch. Immediately, Jas was immersed in hugs and kisses. When she introduced Courtney, the looks in her female relatives' eyes expressed their approval.

"Wuz up, man," Jimmy greeted Courtney with a dap. Jas could see he was sizing him up.

"Hey, man," Courtney said. "Wuz up." He looked a little over dressed for the occasion in a pair of khakis and a collared shirt, and Jas kicked herself for not telling him it was more of a casual affair.

"I'm Jimmy, in case my rude ass sister didn't inform you," Jimmy said.

"How could he not know *you*, Jimmy. You the only big head in the family," Jas retorted, before she could think twice. Courtney shot her a surprised look.

"Hey, now. Y'all stop," Mrs. Moore intervened. "They been fighting like that since they were kids." She looked at Courtney apologetically. "You wouldn't even know they were twins," she commented, handing him a plate.

"Twins? Wow. Jas didn't mention it." Courtney looked at Jas confused.

"Just an unfortunate incident really. We don't have much in common," she said with a casual shrug.

Jas tried her best to be attentive to Courtney during their stay, but one relative after another seemed to pull on her. Aunt Milly wanted to know where she got her dress from, which led to Aunt Pam talking about taking a shopping trip to New York.

Jasmyne

Aunt Rita was adamant they should do Vegas instead. Before she knew it, Jas was lost in conversation for nearly half an hour.

"Umm, honey. I think you better check on yo man. He seems a little distant," her cousin Brianna came over and whispered. Jas hadn't even noticed that Courtney was seated in a fold out chair by the garage, staring at his cell phone like it was the SAT's. His beautiful face was set into a frown while his stuffy clothes made him look straight up uncomfortable.

"Oh. Good lookin'," she told her cousin before quickly leaving the group.

"Hey, babe. Sorry about that. I guess I got caught up," Jas said to Courtney. She bit her lip nervously. "Did you get enough to eat?"

"Yea. You ready to go yet?" Courtney sounded irritated.

"Babe, we just got here. We about to play some music and probably line dance," Jas said. She gestured to the patio area where most of her people were engaging in conversation. She didn't want to leave her family prematurely; they would be hurt.

"Well, I'm pretty tired. I didn't expect to have to be *this* social. I mean, meeting your mom and brother was one thing. But this..." He nodded to the slew of relatives covering the backyard. He didn't even know that there were still more on their way!

"Yea, my bad. I should have known. Can we stay one more hour? My mom will be disappointed if I leave this early." Jas knew she was begging, but she couldn't help herself.

Courtney sighed. "Tell you what, maybe your fam can drop you off? I really need to get some rest. You know I have work *and* school tomorrow."

"Alright, fine. I'll have somebody give me a ride." Jas didn't have the energy to argue, even though she really wanted to. Better to keep the peace. She also knew everybody was lowkey watching her interactions with Courtney.

Courtney looked relieved. "Cool. Hit me up when you make it home." He stood and pecked her on the cheek before making his exit. Jas dropped down into his still warm seat, feeling disappointed, and watched him go.

"What? Prince Charming leaving Cinderella at the ball?" Jimmy towered over her with a plate and bar-be-que plastered all over his hands.

"Didn't mom teach you not to chew with your mouth full? Dag, boy." She narrowed her eyes at him in disgust.

"Yo, have you seen how *you* eat? Anyways, he comin' back?" Jimmy wouldn't let up.

"He has work *and* school tomorrow unlike *some* people I know. He's doin' something with his life, so no, he needs to get up early." Jas crossed her arms in the chair and lifted her chin in arrogance.

"I'm just saying. He was only here a minute. That's not cool, Jas." Jimmy's tone softened before he busied himself by licking some sauce off a finger.

Jas shrugged with indifference. "Like I said, you wouldn't understand."

"Hey, maybe you right," he responded. His tone was uncharacteristically considerate, and Jas felt unnerved by the sudden sympathy. "But what I *do* know," he continued, "is that when a man doesn't prioritize a woman into his schedule, he doesn't value her. And from what I hear, this ain't the first time ol' boy has left you hangin'." He grabbed another chicken wing and started working at it.

"Well, I don't know what you *heard*, but whatever it *was*, it was just a misunderstanding," Jas huffed. "Anyways, don't you have one of your little *floozies* around here to entertain?" Jimmy shrugged his shoulders before strolling away.

Dag, since when is Jimmy concerned about my dating life? Jas thought.

The answer was never. And Jas couldn't help but feel that the fact that he was, meant something.

* * *

"Aunt Milly, how did you know Uncle Reggie was 'the one'?" Jas inquired. She was seated between her aunt's legs on the floor while she braided her hair. It was rare that she had her aunt's undivided attention; usually one of her cousins was stopping by for something.

"Well, I would say, it was like he made me feel safe, and secure. No man had ever shown me he was able to provide and take care of me in the way that Reggie had. I was smitten by his swag too," Milly added with a smile.

"What chew' know about swag, Aunt Milly?" Jas laughed. She mistakenly looked back at her aunt, who immediately pushed her head down to the side, while still gripping her curly tresses.

"Girl, I had swag before you knew how to spell swag," Milly said, laughing.

"But, Aunt Milly, how do you know *for sure* that a person is the right fit for *you*? I mean, just because they can *provide*, is that really enough?" Jas asked, her voice tainted with frustration. She glided her hands over the dark blue carpet she was sitting on, comforted that it had been there since she was a kid.

"Of course, that's not enough. I mean, they need to value you and love you and endure with you also," her aunt quickly said. "I'm just saying that for *me*, Reggie was the full package. I didn't have to settle in any way." She paused while pulling more strands of her niece's hair together. "Now, what I *will* say, is if you have to question if someone is for you, then they probably are

Jasmyne

not for you." Milly stopped braiding her niece's hair then lifted her chin lovingly to face her.

"And, honey, you are worth more than the minimum. I don't care if he checks *all* your boxes, he needs to create new ones you ain't even thought about as far as *I'm* concerned! You are just that valuable!" Jas smiled and turned to hug her aunt.

"You know you my favorite auntie, right?" Jas said, her heart full.

"Sweetie, you ain't tellin' me nothin' I don't know!" Her aunt put a hand on her hip and rolled her neck.

Jas laughed and spent the evening bonding with her aunt. By the time she got home she was exhausted.

"I think I'll run a bath," she mumbled, and was just starting the water when her phone rang.

"Hey, I was just thinking about you," Jas said to Courtney after picking up.

"Hey. I'm glad you answered. I wanted to let you know I'm going to be traveling for a little bit. I need some time to get away and decompress," he said. He sounded nervous, and that gave her pause.

"Oh. Ok. Where you goin'?" Jas was confused. Why was he not inviting her on this getaway?

"I have an uncle in Florida I'm gonna visit. His health isn't the best, so it will give me some time to hang out with him while I unwind." Courtney spoke rapidly and Jas wasn't feeling it. Something was up.

"Oh. Ok. Is anybody going with you?" Jas felt her temperature rising and fought to keep her voice steady.

"What's that supposed to mean?" he asked, quickly on the defensive. "I just told you what I was doing and why I was doing it. What do it matter if anybody else is goin'?"

Why was he not answering the question? Jas could tell Courtney wasn't being fully honest by the defensive nature of his tone. She sighed and looked at the bubbles forming in her tub.

"You know what, Courtney, you right. What does it matter? Because clearly you and I are not a good match. Have fun on your trip." And before she could lose her nerve, she ended the call.

Wow. I can't believe I just did that! she thought, surprised at her own actions. But suddenly the anxiety and fear she had regarding the relationship was dispersed. Immediately Courtney called her back, but she declined the call. She turned up Queen Naija's "Pack Lite" on her playlist, and let the water massage her limbs.

* * *

Jasmyne

"So, you quit Courtney, huh?" Stephanie asked. They were packing their stuff up after their workout class.

"Yep." Jas smirked. "Fired his ass!" She tidied up her hair puff from the workout. Even though she knew she looked like a wet dog, it felt great to work her body.

"Well, Jas, I'm proud of you. I mean, really, that took guts." Stephanie looked at her impressed.

"Thanks. But, girl, what else could I do? Clearly Courtney wasn't treating me right, as fine as he was," Jas said, folding up her yoga mat.

"Yea, I agree. He was fine!" Stephanie grinned and both girls giggled.

"But you know how many women would have stayed to be with a freakin' dentist?" Stephanie added, while folding her own mat. Jas smiled, but she knew her friend was right.

"Yea, but I need more than that." Jas popped the mat under her arm and picked up her water bottle. "I need the full package."

"Ladies, great workout today!" Mya, the instructor called to the girls, as they walked by her on their way out of the studio.

"Thanks!" they responded in unison.

"Yep! And Jas, I see your improvement! You are really getting stronger!" Mya gave her a light pat on the back.

311

Jas beamed at her instructor. "Wow! Thanks so much, Mya! I can say it has not been easy, but it has definitely been worth it!

"Well, isn't that life, Jas? I mean, tests and trials can be painful, but it's always once we endure the storm that we see our own growth." Mya smiled and Jas was blessed by her words.

"Wow, I never thought of it that way. But yea, I guess you're right!"

"Listen, ladies, I'm having a small gathering with some young, bright, women like yourselves this evening if you guys are up for it. We talk about life, love, spirituality and anything else that's on your heart. It's such a great support, and I think you guys would find it very encouraging." Mya looked at both women warmly, and Jas felt a prompting on her heart that this meeting would be something special.

"Wow, I would love to!" Jas looked at her friend. "What about you, Stephanie?"

"Yea, I'm in!" Stephanie agreed.

"Great! I'm looking forward to having you guys! And just be ready ladies! There is greatness in store for you both!" Mya's lips tilted into a confident smile, and Jas felt a peace she couldn't describe.

Jasmyne was in awe. She hadn't figured she would have an opportunity to connect with Mya (a woman she had admired from afar) on a deeper level, but she was excited at the prospect.

Wow, I wonder what's in store? she thought. *Well, whatever it is, I'm definitely ready!*

For Ahmaud, George, Breonna, Trayvon, Michael, Philando, Eric, and so many more, whose names are too plenty to list. We fight for you.

FOR GEORGE (A POEM)

I. Can. Not. Breath.

Because your knee is on my neck.

And your heel is on my back.

And the more I try to break free and be great, you stump me down and tell me, I'm still a slave.

Yes 200 years have went by, and we had a Black man in office, but we all know that was just a pity toss.

So that we would sit down and shut up.

So you could pat yourself on the back, and sleep a little better at night, and tell yourself, "I'm not a racist".

Oh, but you are.

You are when you are quiet and calloused to the repetitive atrocities that keep happening to Black men in America.

When you bury your head deeper in the comfortable quaintness of golf outings and tea parties, shopping sprees and fake body.

Parts.

And to the church.

Where have you been?

Because now your sudden upheaval over George, lets me know you *do* have a voice.

But why did you not use it before?

For Trayvon, or Mike, or Ahmaud, and so many more?

But I digress.

The truth is you don't want to see.

You would rather walk blindly in a slew of delusional hypocrisy.

You say America is the land of opportunity.

But what you fail to realize is that the very constitution that said we all had rights only meant those rights were for someone who looked like you.

And even today when you navigate the world you never once think about the color of your skin.

For George (A Poem)

But I do.

I have to wonder will I face discrimination today when I go to the dentist office?

Will the doctor treat me with the best level of care if my skin doesn't look like theirs?

And I make sure to use the language you'll understand.

That proper language.

That king's language.

But that was when I could speak, because right now, I can't even breathe.

And my lack of breath is not due to some virus.

No.

Because regardless of the coronary report, my death will not come from natural causes or earthly means.

Instead, my life will be eked out slowly,

on the concrete,

prematurely.

Senselessly.

From some ignorant ass man's knee.

TYRONE

Tyrone was in his third year of college, and although he was an excellent student, he wasn't so sure he was majoring in the right subject. As much as he loved Economics, his heart seemed to be yearning for something more. But what was it?

"Aye, man! What chew' think about going to Kristine's tonight? She having a party to celebrate the end of the quarter," his homeboy, Alex asked him. They were wiping down tables at the dining hall where most of the students were still milling around, or eating dinner.

"Oh yea? I still got one more midterm exam to prepare for, so I don't think I'm gon' make it." Tyrone slapped the dish rag over his shoulder and started emptying dishes into his bin.

"Dawg, you gon' miss the biggest party of the semester! I can-not let you go out like that!" Alex shook his head as he busted down his own table. As soon as he was done, a couple of underclassmen sat down giggling and sneaking looks at the boys.

Tyrone laughed. "Alex, you say that about every party!"

"And I be right!" Alex indulged the girls with a head nod and flirtatious smile, before joining his friend to help him finish his work. The two shuffled to the back to dispense their dishes in the kitchen sink.

"Man, last time I listened to you I ended up oversleeping for my 8AM!" Tyrone said. "I can't let that happen again! My moms will *kill* me if I lose this scholarship."

"Hey, Ty," Janet said, interrupting the boy's conversation. She strolled into the kitchen and started looking for ingredients for her dish on the back pantry. Tyrone glanced up from the dishes he was washing and noticed Janet's figure was looking extra nice in her white apron.

"Sup', Janet." Tyrone responded. "They got chew' cookin' again, huh?"

"Yea, but I don't mind. I like being in the kitchen." Janet grinned.

"Dag, it's like that, Janet," Alex jumped in. "I don't get no love?"

Janet laughed and shook her head. "Wuz up, Alex."

Tyrone

"You, girl! And when you gon' go out wit' me?" Alex said, asking as if her previous rejections were irrelevant. Alex never missed an opportunity to shoot his shot. Janet tossed her head back and looked up at the ceiling in exaggeration. Her long, thick locks gently brushed her shoulders.

"I done' told you, Alex. We *just* friends." She gave him a knowing look, then proceeded to grab the sugar and flour from the pantry. Alex did his best impression of Redd Foxx while clutching his chest, pretending to be in pain and stumbling backwards.

"Dag, Janet! Why you gotta do me like that?" Tyrone laughed.

Alex is a trip! He should know better than to think Janet would give him the time of day, Tyrone thought to himself. Everybody knew she was super focused on her studies and hardly ever engaged socially. In fact, Tyrone had never known her to date *anyone* the three years he had attended school there.

"You'll be alright." Janet smiled while she glided past the boys to get to the stove.

Tyrone rubbed his full beard unconsciously. "Well, my shift is over and I need to hit the books," he announced.

"So, I'm gon' see you tonight at Kristine's thing?" Alex tried again, looking at Tyrone hopefully.

"What's happening at Kristine's?" Janet asked.

321

"She having an end of the quarter situation outside the rec center. You should come!" Alex said.

Janet looked thoughtful. "You gon' be there, Ty?"

"Probably not. I still got one more exam." He unrolled his sleeves and removed his apron. "If I get enough studying done though, I *could* make it."

"Yea, I feel you. Well, maybe if you go, I'll go," Janet said. She had turned her head slightly to look at him, and Tyrone was surprised, but pleased to hear it.

"Oh, yea...then bet. I'll definitely be there," he assured her.

"Cool," Janet responded. She started preparing her dish, smoothly mixing her ingredients with a pleasant combination of skill and joy.

"Yea, text me when you on yo way!" Alex said with a huge grin. He turned his back to Janet and mouthed to Tyrone, "That's all you!" while pointing to her over his shoulder.

Tyrone shook his head while chuckling at his friend. "Alright, y'all. Later!" he called, before making his exit.

Taking long strides, Tyrone crossed the quad to get to his dorm. It was a warm evening and he was feeling good about Janet possibly being at this party tonight. He had had his eye on her for a while now.

"Aye, man. Wuz up," he said to Jerome. The young student was running towards him, shirtless and dripping with sweat. Jerome had his music playing but paused his workout when he saw Tyrone.

"Yo, bruh." Jerome gave him dap before removing his earbuds. "How you been?" The sun smiled upon his skin, dark as the night, and highlighted the muscular build he worked so hard to keep.

"Not much. 'Bout to knock out these books so I can hit this party tonight. I see you putting in yo own kind a work!" Tyrone gestured at his toned friend.

"Yea, you know, I need to make sure I keep it tight," he joked. "So, you talking about Kristine's party? I heard it was something happening outside the rec." Jerome swept away small beads of sweat from his forehead while squinting in the sun.

"Yea, man. It's supposed to be hype."

Jerome's midnight face broke into such a wide smile that his pearly whites gleamed in the sunlight. "Cool, maybe I'll see you there," he added, then put his earbuds back into place and started moving.

"Bet!" Tyrone jerked his chin up to his friend before proceeding to his destination. *Man, I really need to start running with Jerome and get my stuff toned*, he thought to himself. He squeezed a love handle and made a mental note to hit the gym more during break.

That evening Tyrone worked hard to finish his reading and finally felt confident in the material around nine o'clock.

"Where you at?" Alex was blowing him up via text. **"Yo girl here, and she is looking goodt! I must say!"**

"Just got done. On my way!" Tyrone texted back speedily.

He leapt out of his desk chair and started removing clothes from his body. It was a luxury to have a single room where he didn't have to worry about interruptions from a roommate. After taking a few whiffs of his underarms, he decided a shower was definitely in order. By the time he was dressed and ready, it was nearly 10 o'clock.

"Man, I thought you was never gon' make it!" Alex said to Tyrone at the party when he arrived. Tyrone scoped the crowd and was impressed. Kristine had hired a live DJ, and students were scattered all over the quad, dancing and having a good time. His eyes ran across a sea of beautiful browns. He loved attending an HBCU.

"Yea, I just hope I don't fail this midterm messin' wit' chew'!" Tyrone joked.

"Hey there! You lookin good, Ty!" Kristine stopped by to greet Tyrone, noticing his entrance. Tyrone was glad he had chosen his dark blue Tommy shorts that displayed his athletic, thick calves. His yellow crew-neck Champion T shirt shone vibrantly against his dark skin tone.

Tyrone

"Oh yea? Well, I can definitely say the same!" Tyrone bent his 6-foot frame to reach down and squeeze her, and when Kristine held on a little longer than necessary, he took note.

Man, something must be in the water, he thought to himself. Kristine was another one he had had his eye on for a while, but she always seemed to be with somebody. Short, thick and in-shape, she was definitely a catch. Alex had been cheesing while watching the two, but then his smile suddenly crumbled.

"Yo, man. Five o'clock," he alerted Tyrone under his breath.

Tyrone forced himself not to look over, but snuck a peak out of the corner of his eye where he spotted Janet. Immediately, he put some distance between himself and Kristine. He definitely did not want to mess his chances up with Janet.

"Kristine, save a dance for me ok?" he asked. "We 'bout to check out the refreshments."

Kristine nodded then went on her way to speak to some other guests.

"Smooth, playa." Alex laughed, while they walked to the food. Since it was a college party there wasn't any alcohol, but Tyrone didn't mind. He wasn't a big drinker anyway. Alex on the other hand...

"Yea, well, you know I learned from the best," he said, with a light chuckle. Tyrone loaded up a plate while Alex danced with a slender, tall girl Tyrone recognized from his Ethics class. He

325

didn't realize how hungry he was until he scarfed down his plate and was thinking about seconds.

"I guess you finally made it," a soft voice said behind him. He turned to see Janet, wearing a fitted jean number. Her even, brown skin tone was radiant as a playful look decorated her young face.

"Yea, I couldn't miss an opportunity to see you." Tyrone pitched her his most confident smile.

"Well, I guess we don't get to see each other enough at work," she said shyly.

"Yea, we definitely gon' have to do better." He hesitated, fondling the empty plate in his hands. "So, you want to dance?"

"Yep." Her response came fast. The two made their way to the grassy area where they released all the stress from the academic challenges they had endured that quarter. While they danced, Tyrone was surprised by how much Janet seemed to be into the music.

"I see you got my cuz' out here having the time of her life!" Jerome approached Tyrone when he went to get a couple of waters.

"Yea, bruh. Janet is pretty cool. I never seen her this loose before tho," he said, with a surprised look. Jerome nodded in agreement.

"Yea, it definitely seems like she is feeling you! First off, she don't ever be at nobody's party." Jerome drank from the cup in his hand. "Second of all, she don't be dancing all like that either." Tyrone couldn't help but smile. He brushed the tip of his beard with a few fingers, while he eyed Janet waiting for him with some friends.

"Forreal, man? I been feelin' Janet for a minute, but I didn't think I had a chance, so I never stepped to her."

"Yea, and you was right!" Jerome laughed loudly. "But clearly, you got *something*. Cuz Janet ain't the one to waste her time," Jerome said, and finished his drink. "Aye, man. I'll holla at chew'!"

"Bet! And fa show, we gon' run soon too, cuz I'm tryna be on yo level, man!" Tyrone said, pointing a finger at his friend.

"Oh yea? I got chew'!" Jerome gave him dap before going off to meet his female companion.

Tyrone found Janet leaning against an outside patio table, talking to a couple of her girlfriends. He knew he must have been the topic of conversation since they immediately stopped their chatter when he approached.

Females are something else, he thought to himself, but felt proud that he had their attention.

"This one's yours." He handed Janet her cup, as the girls made themselves scarce.

"Thanks," Janet smiled. She was even prettier when she was laid back.

"You wanna take a walk?" Tyrone suggested, hoping for some alone time.

"Sure." Tyrone led her out of the rec area and they strolled in silence for a few moments around the campus.

"So, how are midterms treating you?" he asked, finally breaking the silence.

"So-so. I mean, I struggle with anxiety when it comes to testing, and even though I do ok, I never feel like academics comes easy to me," Janet answered, smoothing her locks over one shoulder. "It takes a lot of work."

Tyrone was surprised. "Yea, standardized testing can be difficult in general for our people, since the tests can be biased against minorities. But I'm honestly surprised you struggle. I always thought you were a brain and school was easy for you. You are so serious about your studies and..." He was searching for the right word so as not to offend her. "*Focused.*"

Janet chuckled. "Yea, *focused* is about right. I mean, my parents are on me tough, so I have to be. But honestly, I don't enjoy working that hard. I'm just trying to get to where I need to be," she said with a shrug. Another couple passing by smiled at them, and Tyrone assumed they were heading to the party. Young love seemed to be in the air. Tyrone tugged on Janet's waist to let the other couple pass by, pulling himself close to her. He savored the moment.

"So, where do you need to be, Janet?" Tyrone looked down at her attentively. He was genuinely interested.

"Well, I really want to open a nonprofit for youth. I love kids, and there are so many atrocities happening in the Black community that affect not just our generation, but the next. I want to help them with *their* current struggles. I mean, how could we have overcome slavery only to be faced with systemic racism and more subliminal oppression for Black people?" Janet spoke passionately, and Tyrone was intrigued.

"You're in the Student Coalition, right?" he asked, searching his mind for extra details he knew about her.

"Yep," Janet stated proudly. "I'm so glad to have that outlet to voice the concerns and address the community of African Americans and even other minorities on campus. I also appreciate attending an HBCU where administration helps prepare you for racial experiences you can possibly receive in the working world." She kept her face forward as they walked and talked, and Tyrone admired the way she carried herself.

She walks with such class, he thought appreciatively.

"Yea, I agree. I was thinking about going to a meeting next semester. My schedule has been packed, taking 18 credit hours and working at the dining hall. I haven't had a chance." Tyrone continued admiring Janet's profile while enjoying the night air. It was the perfect night for a walk.

"Yea. You should definitely check it out. I've been a part for two years now, and I'm one of the chairmen. We always have events we're hosting to help empower students and even faculty, to be vocal about our community's issues." Janet looked at him excitedly and her gaze caused an electric current to shoot through him.

Man, this girl is fire!

The path they were walking had ended where Normandy Woods began. Students often cut through this area to get to the other side of campus, or even hide in it, to make out.

"Hey, look!" Tyrone pointed a finger towards the woods, and Janet's eyes followed his prompting.

"Wow, it's amazing!" she exclaimed. Lightning bugs dressed the trees, blinking in and out sporadically throughout the forest.

"It looks like Christmas tree lights!" Tyrone said in awe. Both stood in silence, touched by nature's gift.

"It's like a dream," Janet commented, as she let her fingers find his. Tyrone started cheesing from ear to ear. After a while the couple walked hand-in-hand and headed back towards the party.

"So, back to our earlier conversation. I would like to check the BSC out for sure," Tyrone informed.

"Cool!" Janet said. "So, what about you, Ty? Where is it that you see yourself going after college?" Janet looked at him curiously, and he realized how much they really didn't know about each other. He was excited that he finally was getting the opportunity to change that.

"Well, that is the million-dollar question," he answered honestly. "My major is Econ, and I did an internship last year for a Financial Analyst position. I've been thinking that is probably the route I'll take, but I'm not 100 percent sure that's the route I *should* take."

"Hmmm. Well, what is it that brings you passion? What is it that you just can't live without?" she asked, her brown eyes wide and sincere. Tyrone was quiet. They had approached the rec center, and he could see the party was dissipating.

Stuffing his hands into his shorts' pockets, he hesitantly shifted his weight to the side. "You know, Janet. I'm gonna have to get back to you on that," he finally answered. He didn't want to make up something just to impress her.

"No worries. I think that's good that you're being honest with yourself. I know people who are majoring in a field just to please their parents and end up working a quote on quote *"great"* job by society's standards, but they're miserable." Janet peered up at him with an understanding smile, and he was grateful for her support. They talked for a while about their different interests and what they were looking forward to in their futures.

"Yo, Janet, we 'bout to leave out!" one of Janet's girlfriends called with a few others. Her friends were standing at the edge of the party and had been waiting for Janet to return before leaving, since they had all come together.

"Oh, ok. Give me a sec!" she called back. "I guess I need to be getting out of here," she said, turning back to Tyrone.

"Yea, I really appreciate your time, Janet. Is there any way I can get your number? I would love to continue getting to know you."

Janet smiled shyly. "Yea, that would be nice," she said, before rattling off some digits.

"I need to get up early and do some studying anyway before this last exam," Tyrone said.

"Ok, cool." Janet touched his arm and he felt that electricity again. "You got this!" she said, as he pulled her close, embracing her, and letting his nose nuzzle her neck for a little bit. She responded by squeezing his hand before heading off to her friends.

Tyrone felt elated as he made his way back to the party which was pretty much over. Alex was sitting and talking to Kristine at a patio table. It was quiet since the DJ had left, other than a few students engaging in some small talk.

"Yo. I'm about to bounce. I got my exam tomorrow, man," Tyrone said to his friend after greeting Kristine.

"Aww, you leavin', Ty?" Kristine pouted her thick, pink lips. "You didn't make good on your promise to dance with me, though you had time to with Janet." She cocked her head to the side, while making a sad face. Alex shook his head with a humorous smile, watching the interaction.

"Aww, yea. My bad, Kristine. We gon' have to do a raincheck on that one," Tyrone said quickly. He placed his hand over his chest, his face apologetic.

"Well, the least thing you can do is walk me back to my dorm, boy, dag." Kristine was already hopping up from the table, clearly ending her conversation with Alex. Tyrone stole a swift glance at his homeboy.

"Yo, man. That's cool. I'm 'bout to hook up with Jackie anyway," Alex said, referring to the young woman Tyrone saw him dancing with earlier.

"Aight' bet." Tyrone gave him dap. "I'm gon' hit you up after my last exam."

Tyrone watched Alex leave before accompanying Kristine to her destination.

"That was a dope party, Kristine," he offered. They walked side by side towards the east part of campus.

Kristine smiled proudly. "Thanks, Ty. I figured people needed to let out some steam since midterms are winding down. So, what's your plans for break?"

"Oh, I'm actually gonna stay on campus and work. My mom is doing a trip with some friends, and I didn't see the point of going home when nobody was gon' be there."

"Really? I'm actually gonna be on campus myself. There's a volunteer program I'm a part of, and I need some community service hours to get the position I'm trying for."

"Word? That's cool. So, what's the position?" Tyrone looked at her curiously. He hadn't known Kristine was the community service type.

"I'm hoping to be Secretary. I've been working with a hotline for abused women. I'm pretty administrative, so having that position will give me more experience," she said, while rubbing her arms. Tyrone followed her movements with his eyes, momentarily fixed on her jean skirt and white netted top that were glued to her voluptuous form. He tore his eyes away from the hot pink bra that was visible through the netting.

"Nice. Yea, I was hoping to find some other interests myself," he shared, not wanting to mention that Janet was his reason for doing so. Brushing through her short, honey-colored hair, Kristine turned towards him in front of her dorm.

"Yea. I've really enjoyed getting to help others overcome such trauma." She paused. "Especially when that type of trauma has hit close to home." She lowered her gaze, and Tyrone took note of her statement. Still, he didn't want to pry.

"Cool. Well, I'm gon' let you get inside," he said instead, cocking his head towards the front door.

Kristine frowned, looking disappointed. "Uh ok. Well, hit me up over break. I mean if you bored and not doing nothin'." She laughed nervously.

"Oh, yea. Fa sho." Tyrone saved her number in his phone and watched her make her way into the dorm.

Dag. Two numbers in one night. I'm on a roll! He thought to himself, and grinned the whole walk home.

* * *

Pleased, Tyrone reviewed his final grades with a large smile. 3 B's and 3 A's. His perseverance with studying for his midterms had paid off. The fall break was a time of rest other than when he was at work. He was calling Janet a lot, and was loving getting to know her less serious side. He was also determined to give Jerome a run for his money and found himself at the gym almost daily. This particular day would be no different, and he made his way to his normal workout area in record time.

"He ain't gon' have nothing on me!" Tyrone mumbled under his breath while lifting a 50lb dumbbell at the rec center. There were a few students there, but not as many as there would be when the break was over.

"Yo, Ty. Why you working so hard?" He saw her more than he heard her since Jay-Z spit fire into his ears.

335

"Oh, yo! Wuz up, Kristine! Yea, I got goalz you know!" Smiling, he removed his Beatz headset.

"Well, from where I'm sitting you meeting those goals." She tilted her head to the side and smiled. Kristine was wearing a blue razor-back tank top that allowed her bright, yellow sports bra to peek through, snug cut off capris, along with a pair of black Nikes with a white logo. Tyrone threw her an appreciative smile.

"Oh, yea. Well, I got to keep up wit' chew', you know?" he said. He gingerly removed the sweat from his eyes with a towel embossed with their school logo. "So, how has your break been going?" They had texted a few times but that was about it. Kristine took a seat on the bench near him and started handling her own, lighter-weight dumb bells.

"It's been good. I been doing my volunteer work and working at the student center. It's pretty slow though since nobody's around." She did a few bicep curls, and Tyrone marveled at her definition.

"Ok, girl! I see you with the muscles!" he joked, but he was really impressed.

Kristine laughed. "Hey, I learned after freshman year, if I don't stay on it, I'm gon' be walking around here with the freshman 15 for four years!" They both laughed easily.

"Yea, I got so caught up working and studying I fell off myself, but I'm back on it, fa sho!" Tyrone picked up his weights

Tyrone

and enjoyed having Kristine there for the rest of his workout. She was even able to show him a few back workouts that he wasn't aware of.

"I think I'm about done," Tyrone announced. He fell back against a bench, buried with exhaustion.

"Yea, me too. You got it in tho!" Kristine said, encouragingly.

"Yea, I'm about to get it in with some food now!"

Kristine let out a sharp breath, while dropping her weight on the floor. "I feel you. I can definitely eat."

"It's too bad Bush's Dining Hall is closed. They be having the best fries," Tyrone said, licking his lips.

"Now, boy, you don't need to be messin' up yo workout with those fries anyway. Besides, Larry's Subs is everything," she informed. "They have that down south flavor in their meat, and you can load up your sub like you at a buffet." Kristine put her weights up, then dried her face with a towel. "Shoot, if you gone' do it, do it right!"

Tyrone sat up and looked at her. "Oh yea? I'm not hip."

Kristine's eyes grew wide. "Foreal? Ok, I'm a have to show you!" The two cleaned up their areas, then hurriedly packed up to leave, since, at that point, they were both starving. Tyrone then followed Kristine to her car since he didn't have one on campus. He watched her whip out the key fob to a black-on-black Range Rover with tinted windows and sparkling, 28-inch rims.

"Ok, girl! Get it!"

Kristine laughed while letting him in the passenger side. "Yea, my dad has a thing for cars and gifted this to me on my 16th birthday."

"I see!" Tyrone looked around the interior, impressed.

Kristine sped off, and Tyrone laid back to enjoy the ride. Drake blasted through the speakers, as they both sang the versus word for word to his latest hit.

* * *

Tyrone found himself spending more time with Kristine and was surprised at how much he enjoyed her company.

"I really thought she was just a pretty face, but she's cool people," he admitted to Alex, while laying back-flat on his bed. His small room was a little snug for his large frame, but it was worth it. The first couple of years as a student he shared a room and learned quickly it was not his thing. His former roommate was always bringing a female to the room, which would have been fine if he had given him a heads up about it. Instead, Tyrone had had one too many encounters witnessing his roommate in action under the sheets.

"Yea, but chew' know she done' got around, dawg. Be careful with that one," Alex said in a warning tone on the other end of the line; he knew his boy was a softy.

"Yea, I know. I'm just sayin'. She's surprised me, that's all."

"So, what's the news with Janet? You still on it wit' her?"

"Yea, we talk every day and video chat. I wanna take her out when she gets back." Tyrone smiled, thinking about Janet.

"My man. Pullin' all the chicks out here! And you don't even be tryin'!" Alex sounded excited on the other line. "It's gotta be that beard game!" Tyrone chuckled while rubbing some scraggly hairs from his beard.

"I'm as shocked as you. I'm just rollin' wit' it."

After his call with Alex, Tyrone decided to take a nap. He awoke to a missed video call from Janet.

"Hey, beautiful. How is everything?" he asked. Hastily, he cleared lumps of sleep out of his eyes, then straightened his white T-shirt and basketball shorts, both disheveled from his nap.

"I'm good. I just got done having dinner with the fam. It was my turn to cook." Janet's smooth brown face flashed on the screen. Her hair was tousled into a ponytail. She wore a purple top with a light gloss on her lips.

"Yea? How did it go? Everybody still alive?" he teased, still wiping sleep from his eyes.

Janet laughed. "Boy, you know I can throw down in the kitchen!"

"Is that right? Now how would I know? You ain't never cooked *me* nothin'," he said, giving her a hard time.

"Well, maybe that will change if you play your cards right." She tilted her lips into an impish half smile.

Tyrone enjoyed his conversation with Janet until she had to get off to play a board game with her younger brother. Just when he was picking a movie on Netflix, his phone vibrated.

"Wanna watch a movie?" It was a text from Kristine.

"I was just about to do that," he responded, surprised.

"Cool. Want some company?"

Although Tyrone wasn't as aggressive with women as Alex, he wasn't one to miss an opportunity either.

"Yep," he answered, without hesitation. A slight feeling of guilt surfaced, but he pushed it away. *It's just a movie*, he told himself.

Twenty minutes later Kristine was at his door dressed in a snug, pink cardigan, and ripped, skinny blue jeans. Her honey-blond hair was dazzled by her light brown skin.

Whew! Her curves is poppin'! he thought, as he forced himself to look at her face.

"Hey, you. How are you?" Tyrone bent down to give her a hug before letting her in.

Man, she smell good!

"Hey," Kristine smiled, then let her eyes roam. "So…this is you? Nice. I got stuck with a roommate, so I don't have it like you." She unabashedly plopped down onto his twin bed. The only other place to sit was the office chair at his desk.

Tyrone shrugged, trying to appear casual, but felt as nervous as a virgin on prom night. "Yea, the roommate life is not for me. If I can pay to have extra space, I'm all for it." While sitting next to her, he clutched the remote, stifling feelings of excitement by how close they were.

"So, what are you in the mood for?" he asked, hoping she didn't say a romance movie. He didn't need any encouragement from romantic images.

"Oh, whatever you want, Ty. I'm easy to please." She fell back against the wall while licking her lips thoroughly. Tyrone had to fight visions of what he could do with those lips, and turned on the TV instead. He settled on an action film, thinking that was safe.

"You not gon' cut the lights, Ty?" Kristine purred, while slipping her tan pumps onto the hardwood floor to get more comfortable on his bed. "I mean, it's real bright in here."

"Oh, yea. My bad." Ty quickly went to turn the lights off and found that when he turned back around, the girl had spread out on top of his comforter.

"Now, that's better," she said. She looked up, while smiling eagerly at him in the dim lighting from the TV. Tyrone knew he had a decision to make as to how this was going to play out. He didn't want her to feel rejected, but he also wasn't so sure he could be the perfect gentleman with her sprawled out on his bed like that.

"Umm, you want me to sit in the chair so you can relax?" he tried awkwardly, and started moving in that direction. Kristine giggled.

"Boy, there is plenty of room for you on this bed." She scooted up to make more room between herself and the wall. "You just gotta lay behind me."

"Oh, ok." Tyrone said, knowing he was being set up, but liking it too much to resist.

He made his way onto the bed and positioned himself behind her. She wrapped his arm around her waist and pushed her backside against him while they watched the movie. Tyrone felt himself responding and knew she could probably feel his response through the thin material of his basketball shorts.

Damn. What have I gotten myself into? he thought to himself. But he didn't have too much longer to think about it, because

Tyrone

Kristine rolled over and pressed her lips against his. His body was now in the driver's seat, and the two found the rest of the movie watching them instead.

* * *

"Don't tell her," Alex told his friend. They were out for a run and had taken a break near the edge of campus. The weather was turning, and students were now forced to wear hoodies and jackets.

"Man, I've *got* to. I mean, Janet is a sweet girl." Tyrone started stretching to loosen his quads and calves.

"Dude. If you tell her you smashed, she gon' make a bigger deal of it than it is. You *not* in a relationship yet, so really it don't count." He shrugged his shoulders as if to solidify his argument.

Tyrone shook his head. He didn't expect differently from Alex, and if he were honest with himself, he was hoping this would be Alex' response to him sleeping with Kristine. He was hoping that somehow his guilt could be removed and his actions validated.

"Yea, I got chew'. But I think Janet should know. If she wants a relationship with me, then she should know." Tyrone was struggling with what he felt was right, and what he wanted. He wanted Janet. That was the girl he knew he could have something real with, but He didn't know if she would still want to be with him if she knew about Kristine. Did he really want to mess up what they were building?

"Man, I done told you what *I* would do. I don't know *why* you think her knowing is going to help you in *any* way." Alex shook his head in pity for his friend. The fall breeze hit them both, and Tyrone stroked his arms over his hoodie. Instead of responding, he proceeded to run while Alex followed his lead. They headed to the student center where they had started, only to see a large group of students gathered out front.

"Man, wuz going on?" Tyrone said to Alex.

"I have no idea." As they got nearer, they could see Principal Williams speaking through a megaphone and addressing the crowd.

"Alright, everyone, alright. We know this is disturbing news, and we know everyone is upset. We have counselors and professionals that are available. We are going to get through this time. We want to be able to honor Jerome in the right fashion, and that is *not* through violence."

What? Honor Jerome? Tyrone turned towards a girl he recognized from his Econ class. "Shelly, what's he talking about? What happened with Jerome?" Shelly looked up with a tear-stained face and shook her head, emotional.

"Some-some body k-killed him while he was out run-running by his house over b-break," she sputtered out.

Tyrone's eyes grew big. "What!" he shouted. "What are you talking about?"

"He wasn't even armed!" she whaled. "They k-killed him, and he wasn't even armed!"

Tyrone frantically looked around and saw how distraught the students were. Realization dawned on him.

"Yo, man. This is crazy!" he said to Alex. Alex nodded quickly in agreement, wearing a similarly shocked expression.

"I can't believe this shit!" Tyrone watched as various students connected with outside counselors and faculty. Some were so distraught they were breaking down, sobbing in the counselor's arms.

I need to check on Janet, he thought.

"Bro, I'm a holla at chew'. I gotta call Janet," he said to his friend. He left to find a quiet place to talk, and settled for a large maple tree nearby.

"Janet. What are you doin'?" he asked breathlessly, when she answered the phone. He felt his heart literally racing.

"Ty. Have you heard?" She was emotional, and he could tell she had been crying.

"Yea. Where are you?" He looked around frantically as if he could randomly see her outside.

"I'm in my dorm," she said tearfully.

345

"I'm on my way." Tyrone didn't think twice and started running towards the west part of campus.

"I can't believe this shit," he said, over and over the whole way there.

* * *

The Student Coalition had been a resource for the school for decades. Students found advocacy and support for various issues that affected their community. It was truly a legacy and vital at a time like this. Tyrone sat quietly while waiting for the meeting to begin. He fidgeted uncomfortably in his chair. Many students were there, including Kristine, whom he hadn't spoken to since their last encounter in his dorm room.

"So, how long you think this is gonna be?" Alex asked him from the seat next to him. He kept checking his phone impatiently.

"Janet said usually it's an hour, but given what's happened, it could be longer because they want to set aside time for an open floor." Tyrone had been wanting to attend one of their meetings, but surely not under these circumstances. It had been a week since he heard the news about Jerome, and he had barely slept since. Visions of seeing Jerome running on the quad kept haunting him, and every time he saw a brown brother running in a hoodie, he thought it was him.

"Ok, thank you all for your patience and for taking time out of your evening to attend," Janet announced. She was seated with a few others at the table in front, looking emotional, but poised.

"I know we normally open with the minutes, but I actually would like to open with a moment of prayer." She glanced out into the crowd and was met with quiet nods, then led the group in a short, but heartfelt prayer. Tyrone felt eased just hearing her sweet voice.

"Now, let's get started." Janet shared with the group the updates she had received from Principal Williams in regards to Jerome's death. She and the other leaders of the BSC had met with him to get instructions on what would be appropriate for how the student body was to respond.

"Also, we have been in communication with Jerome's mom, who, as many of you know, is also my aunt." She paused, then resumed her speech. "As a result of that meeting, we have decided to host a prayer vigil in honor of Jerome this Friday evening at 8PM. Minister Brown will lead and all are welcome." She sat with her hands clasped and her gaze poignant, looking out into the audience.

"Well, is that all?" A voice interrupted from the crowd. "I mean, we not gon' march?"

Janet searched the room but didn't find the speaker. "Normally we would wait until the end of the meeting to address these concerns, but I understand we are all grieving." She took a sip of her water before continuing and breathed out a deep sigh. "We do have permission to march, however, we have to guarantee the march will be nonviolent. We cannot afford any violence, or else the police will say that *we* are the cause, and that could attract the media who have already had their presence on campus. Anything that makes Jerome look violent, could throw his case, and we cannot afford that," Janet responded, her voice laden with authority.

She seemed so in control, and Tyrone was proud of her. Still, he knew the difficulty she had been having from losing her cousin. They were usually on the phone for hours in the middle of the night, due to one of them not being able to sleep. Sometimes she would even come over, and he would just hold her, until she could fall asleep.

"So, how are we going to get our point across if we don't say anything? We can't just be quiet!" another student said, this time standing so everyone could see him. Tyrone understood where they were coming from. He was angry too and knew they needed some type of release for their grief.

"How about we run instead of walk? At least that will let us release some of this energy," he heard himself suggesting. All eyes were on him. "I mean, since Jerome was a runner, it would only be right to honor him that way," he added. Janet's eyes brightened and she smiled at him gratefully.

"Thanks, Ty. We will discuss with Principal Williams to verify, but a run would be nice." The other members of the BSC nodded in agreement.

A short, brown girl with glasses, spoke up. "And everyone isn't into running, so maybe we can walk, jog or bike ride!"

"Yea!" other students chimed in. They were excited.

The rest of the meeting consisted of others sharing ideas on how to honor Jerome and how they could be of service to his family.

"Bruh, I gotta get back to studying, but I'll see you," Alex said, as soon as the meeting ended.

Tyrone nodded and stayed seated, intending to wait for Janet. She was engaging in some last-minute dialogue with the other BSC leaders.

"Hey there." Kristine came over, sitting down in Alex' empty seat.

"Kristine...hey. How are you?" Tyrone asked. He quickly looked over and was relieved Janet wasn't paying attention. Kristine caught his glance and rolled her eyes.

"Yo, Ty. I get it that maybe we ain't datin', and maybe you heard some stuff about me, and made some assumptions, but forreal, I really did like you." She stopped talking, and looked at him with hurt-filled eyes. "I thought you was different. To not hear from you, I mean, dag..." She let her sentence hang, and Tyrone felt like a jerk.

"Kristine, I'm sorry I didn't reach out and I haven't returned yo calls. Honestly, I didn't know what to say. Things between us just kind of happened at a bad time. I'm kinda talkin' to Janet right now," he explained, briefly meeting her eyes.

"Yea, I figured, but if it was really *that* serious, would you have gotten wit' me?" she pushed back. Tyrone hadn't realized how much she liked him, and therefore how much his actions had hurt her.

"You right. I shouldn't have been wit' chew'. I wasn't thinking. But you know, can we talk about this another time?" Tyrone noticed Janet starting to pack up and wanted to put an end to this conversation ASAP.

"Well, I was trying to talk to you before, but you keep avoiding me. But yea, whatever." She got up and left. Tyrone shook his head.

Idiot! he thought to himself.

"Hey, you ready?" Janet was in front of him, holding her book bag and books in hand. He stood up fast and took her books.

"Yep." The two walked hand in hand to her dorm in the brisk, evening air. All the while, Tyrone's head was full of his conversation with Kristine.

"What chew' thinkin about?" Janet asked.

Tyrone

"Oh. Uh. Nothin'. I'm good," he said, not wanting to get into it right then.

"Oh. Ok. Well, I really appreciate your suggestion about the run to honor Jerome tonight." She smiled at him, looking happy for the first time since the news of her cousin's murder. "That was dope."

Tyrone smiled back. "Yea. I mean it's not a lot, but at least it's something." He shrugged, his large frame magnified next to Janet's small one.

They had reached her dorm. "Well, Ty, I wouldn't say it's not a lot. The community having *something* to look forward to, and a way to share their heart in a nonviolent manner, is *exactly* what we need." She leaned her head back and reached up for a kiss, while steering him close.

"Wow, I need to make more suggestions then if that's my reward!" he said, his lips still touching hers. He rested his chin on the top of her head, and stroked his beard against the roots of her locks, while she tightened her embrace around his wide waste.

"Oh yea? Well, my roommate isn't going to be home until later, so we can continue your reward inside," she murmured, looking up at him suggestively.

"Oh. Um. You know, Janet, I would love to normally, but um…" He was struggling. He hadn't intended on telling her right then, but knew he couldn't move forward in their relationship otherwise.

"What's up, Ty? You don't think I'm pretty anymore?" she teased, batting her eyelashes at him.

"Of course. It's not that. It's just...It's just that. I've been with someone," he blurted.

Janet stiffened.

"What? What do you mean you've *been* with someone?" She took a few steps back from him, her facial expression an even blend of shock and pain.

"I mean, I've been with someone. It-it didn't mean anything. It just happened, and I really care about chew'. I know we just gettin' to know each other, and I didn't want this to mess things up." He sighed and looked down at his feet, studying his Timberlands.

"You mean, you *slept* with someone?"

Tyrone nodded quietly.

"Wow. Well, if you didn't want this to mess things up, then why did you let it happen?" Janet shook her head in disbelief. "So, who was it?" she demanded after a moment.

Tyrone was silent. He dragged his eyes along the pavement, then finally said, "It doesn't matter."

Janet drew a deep breath while tightening her hands at her sides into little balled up fists. "Dag, Ty. I thought we were friends," she said in a low tone, hurt wrapped around each word.

Tyrone

"We *are*." Tyrone sighed. "I'm sorry, Janet. I really am." He swam one hand through the deep waves in his hair, all the while keeping his gaze down.

"Yea, Ty." Janet said with regret. "Me too."

* * *

Tyrone was getting ready for the run. The BSC had decided to do it that Saturday after the vigil. For some reason he couldn't find his headset, but figured he probably didn't need it.

I'm just gonna spend this time being with my folks, he thought to himself.

"Yo, bruh. You ready?" Alex was waiting at his door, decked in a black Adidas hoodie, grey Nike jogging pants, and a scuffed-up pair of Jordans.

"Umm, I don't know *now*! We lookin' like twins!" Tyrone looked down at his matching hoodie and sweats then shook his head. Alex laughed.

"I been around you too long, man!" Alex said. "Come on, we gon' be late. It's cool if everybody think we the double mint twins." He socked his friend in the arm and Tyrone grinned. Grabbing his student ID, key and phone, Tyrone jammed all items into his pockets. On his way out he gave Alex a loose hug.

"Aww, don't get too mushy on me, Ty." But Tyrone couldn't help it. He was truly grateful to have his boy, especially when tomorrow wasn't promised.

353

"Hey, I'm just glad I got my peoples. That's all."

Alex nodded. "Bet. It's crazy out here in these streets. A Black man can't even go for a run without getting killed."

Tyrone and Alex joined a large crowd of runners positioned at the student center. Behind the runners were the joggers, then the walkers, and some bikers. Janet was the spokesperson, and seeing her made Tyrone's heart ache.

"So, y'all talked yet?" Alex gave Tyrone a questioning look, noticing his friend's gaze.

"She said we would talk after the run," Tyrone answered, feeling frustrated. "She said she needed time to think."

"Ok, cool." Alex looked like he wanted to say more, but Tyrone was glad he didn't. He didn't need an "I told you so speech". That wasn't going to help anything. Tyrone couldn't fault Janet. On the one hand he was grateful he had told her the truth. On the other, he wished he hadn't.

I just miss her, he thought, but decided to focus on Jerome. His friend was gone. No longer would he see his easy-going smile or meet him for a workout session, and the circumstances of his death were so *senseless*.

Tyrone looked around at the crowd. Many held up signs that said, "We miss you, Jerome!" and "Running with you, Jerome!"

He thought of the last time he saw his friend at Kristine's party and how much of an influence he had been. Even now, in his death, Jerome was his motivation for staying in shape. He wanted to make this run count.

* * *

While playing with his mug on the coffee table, Tyrone stirred in too much sugar.

"I see you still like coffee with your sugar." Janet loomed across from him with her own steaming mug; her long locks pulled up high on her head in some type of jazzy concoction, her smooth brown skin shining with only a hint of lip gloss.

She looks like a goddess, Tyrone thought.

He stood to help her with her jacket, and she revealed a thick, purple sweater dress with gray knee-high boots.

"You look good," he said, smiling softly.

"Thanks. I just came back from visiting with Auntie Kim. I was able to update her on how everything went this weekend." After cupping her hands around the mug, she brought the steaming liquid to her lips.

"How is she?" Tyrone asked. He didn't know if it would be appropriate for him to approach Mrs. Jefferson, but he had flowers sent. His mom wouldn't think anything less.

"As good as can be expected," Janet stated while still hugging her mug. "We have a large family, and she hasn't been alone since everything happened. Jerome's dad died a few years ago, so she has definitely been through a lot. Thankfully she also has a strong church community."

"That's good. I couldn't imagine." He stopped, sipping from his own sugar-filled drink. "How have you been holding up?" he asked, looking at her with concern.

Janet shrugged, appearing saddened. "So-so. I mean, what can you do but pray and keep pushin'? I just wish I could have said 'goodbye'. That is what hurts the most right now." She drew from her mug, her eyes downcast. "I didn't get to say 'goodbye'." Tyrone nodded quietly and just listened.

"The last time I saw him was a few days before it happened," she continued. "I was at Auntie Kim's, picking up some candles she had gotten me from Bath & Body Works. You know they have the best candles?" she asked, and Tyrone nodded, not really knowing that they did, but figuring it was the easiest response. "Jerome was on his way out, about to meet his boy. I didn't think twice when we said we would see each other later. I didn't know there wouldn't be a later…"

Tyrone reached for her hand, but she pulled it away. "I'm sorry, Janet. For everything…"

How could he have been such an idiot? How could he have caused her even more pain? He licked his lips nervously when she didn't respond, then veered his eyes to the window of the cafe. The colorful leaves adorned the trees and the sky was overcast.

"Thank you for meeting with me," he finally said, peering back at her. "I know things aren't great between us right now, but I want you to know how much I've enjoyed getting to know you. I value our friendship, and I don't want to lose you." His voice cracked on that last statement, and he took a drink to swallow the lump in his throat.

"Ty, I appreciate that, but I guess it's just shocking that you could step out so quickly on me if you felt that deeply about me. I mean, we *just* were getting close." She looked away and gazed at a couple who sat at a nearby table, pain etched staunchly into her features.

"I know. I know. But I know after this experience I can tell you without a doubt, it will *never* happen again," Tyrone hurried to assure her, following her gaze to the couple.

"I agree," Janet said adamantly, looking back at him.

Tyrone was surprised. Had she forgiven him? Were they back together?

"Really?" he asked.

She nodded. "Yes. You see, Ty, I take relationships very seriously. I take my future seriously. I take my academics seriously. I took a chance on you and let you in prematurely. I had promised myself not to get too serious with anyone until graduation. I saw something in you that caused me to change my mind. But I have to be honest with myself. I need to get back focused and make sure I'm on track for my destiny." She caressed her mug and took a long drink, then inhaled and exhaled deeply.

"See, that's what I love about you, Janet. I love that you are driven and focused and so self-assured. Dating you has helped me to learn more about myself. Remember the question you asked me when we were at Kristine's party?" He looked at her, excited. "About what brought me passion?"

"Yea, I remember," Janet said, her expression blank.

"Well, I know now. Attending the BSC's meetings these last few weeks, participating in the events to honor Jerome, and seeing you in your element. All of those things have helped me see that I want a larger role in the fight for justice in the Black community. After graduation, I'm going to Law School." Tyrone spoke proudly, his eyes brimming with joy.

Janet's own eyes grew big. "Wow, Ty, that's great! I really am happy for you," she said sincerely. She couldn't help but feel happiness for her friend.

"Yea. I can't believe I never saw it before, but now I see so clearly." Tyrone's whole body felt energized.

"That's how it is when God shows us our purpose," Janet shared, before sipping from her mug.

Tyrone thought about her words. "Yea. I guess so." He was pensive, and wondered what else God wanted to show him.

"So, does this mean I get another chance?" Tyrone asked hopefully.

Janet formed a small smile. "This means that right now, I don't think either of us are ready for anything serious. I think our friendship is more important than anything. Don't you?" Tyrone couldn't argue. Not having Janet romantically was tough, but not having her at all, especially after losing Jerome, was even worse.

"Yea, I understand. You know, one of the last conversations I had with Jerome, we talked about chew'." He sat back in his seat, picturing his friend at the rec party.

Janet's eyes lit up. "Really?"

Tyrone nodded. "Yea. He was looking out for you. He was happy to see you happy and lettin' loose. I could tell he really respected you."

Janet's eyes filled with tears. "Thanks, Ty. That means a lot."

"And you know what? I do too. I definitely want to continue our friendship, Janet," he said, wanting to comfort her. "In fact, girl, I'm gon' be the *best* friend you ever had!" he joked.

Janet laughed and Tyrone enjoyed her company for the rest of the evening. Whenever he was around her, she gave him life.

He had meant it when he said he did not want to lose that. He had meant every word.

NIKKI

Nikki rolled over and peeked one eye open to look at her phone. Relief flooded her; she had fifteen more minutes. Drifting back into a coma, she let her 1000-thread cotton sheets caress her dark, chocolate skin. Fifteen minutes later she was jerked awake by the alarm.

"Coffee," she mumbled. That was her only motivation for an early morning. She was not a morning person but neither was she a night owl. If anything, she liked sleep so much she preferred to nap once a day like her best friend's three-year-old.

"What is it about mornings?" she thought. She slipped on her silky, black robe, a gift from Africa from an ex who was Ghanaian. She hadn't liked him too much, but she definitely liked his gifts. Slowly, she made her way to the kitchen after washing up and started her favorite podcast.

"Today we will discuss the unique challenges of Black marriages in America," the host said.

"Hmmm," Nikki mumbled to herself, intrigued. While listening, she expertly mixed her breakfast ingredients (all the makings of a good frittata): eggs, cheese, and an assortment of veggies, along with her favorite seasonings.

"Many of us know that Black Americans were formally slaves and as slaves they experienced the segregation of families in a way that other races simply did not. A Black man could marry a Black woman and then be sold to a different master, leaving his wife and children abandoned and neglected. Black marriages were simply not considered respectable and valuable because Black people *were not respected or valued. How could they be in an era where Black people were viewed as property and not people? And this segregation, which led to systemic poverty, false allegations resulting in Black men being imprisoned, the lack of resources in urban communities which limited their options and resulted in further incarcerations, is the foundation of the Black family."* The podcast was interrupted on her phone through an incoming call.

"Hey, Mommy. I was just about to call you," Nikki said, switching the phone to speaker.

"Good morning, honey pie. Are you ready for your big day?"

"Yes, ma'am!" Nikki responded, her heart warming to the childhood nickname. "Ready as I'll ever be!" She had her first big presentation today in front of the owners of a small marketing firm she worked for. She had been there for about a year and was rising quickly within the company. It seemed everyone loved her except for one particular executive, and that caused her some concern.

"Good. You know I've been praying, and you know God has your back," her mom replied with sincerity. Nikki's heart swelled. She was always being supported by her mother, and the words were definitely needed.

"Thanks! I know, Mommy. I'll text you when it's over and let you know how it goes." She ended the call shortly after so she could make sure she didn't waste any time. After her shower, she checked her cell and saw she had received several texts from many of her close friends. These women were more like sisters, and they were all wishing her well on her big meeting.

After fixing her hair into long, thick, wavy tresses (her signature style), Nikki stepped into her walk-in closet. *Carrie Bradshaw has nothing on me.* Nikki laughed to herself. With only a few moments of debate, she emerged wearing a gray striped pencil skirt that said "chic but professional", a fitted cream cashmere sweater and her favorite black high-heeled shoes. Her black blazer was the final touch. One look in the mirror confirmed her inward thoughts.

I look GOOD.

She sprayed her Chanel, donned her pearls and headed out the door without a second glance. Today was her day.

"Girl, you are 'bout to kill it!" her best friend DeeDee said through her car's Bluetooth speaker.

"Thanks, lady! I've been waiting for this moment. I'm a little nervous, but I feel prepared." Nikki switched lanes in her black SUV, and navigated the Cleveland traffic on I-480.

"Yea, you got this. Let's just hope ol' girl don't try to play you."

"I know. But I really think she learned her lesson the last time she tried to cross me." Nikki instantly thought of the female higher up, Kaitlyn, who had been gunning for her since she had started with the company. It was obvious to Nikki it was out of jealousy. The woman had spent several years sucking up to the Partners of the firm, and while it may have gotten her to where she was today, she didn't seem to have the grit and ambition Nikki had to keep pushing.

"It's a shame, too because you would think that a woman in that position would use it to help bring other women up, not keep them down," Dee Dee said.

"Oh, she working on grooming *her* girl, but you know it's about color," Nikki swiftly responded. "She ain't trying to help no *Black* woman." She tightened her grip on the steering wheel while eyeing her exit up ahead.

"Yea. Ridiculous," Dee Dee said, being the typical, supportive best friend that she was.

"Aye, girl. Dre is on my other line. Call you later." Nikki's ebony eyes sparkled as she saw the incoming call on her other line.

"Ok," Dee Dee didn't hesitate in her response. She knew what it was.

"Good morning, beautiful," Dre's deep voice broke the line, and Nikki's face burst with a smile.

"Good morning, yourself." Nikki swerved into the parking space in front of her job, and saw she was 30 minutes early, just as planned.

"I just wanted to make sure I caught you before your big meeting." Dre's voice could bring warmth on a cold winter's day in Cleveland, and he looked just as smooth as he sounded. Not too tall, but just enough for her short stature. Perfect caramel skin, two deep dimples, and a swag that couldn't be taught. When they first met, he had her at "hello".

"Yea, I was wondering where my text was," Nikki said. She was referring to her normal "good morning text" she had been receiving the last six months they had been dating.

"Well, today you deserve more than just a text," Dre said in a spirited tone. She could just picture a sexy smile on his lips, one dimple showing when he said it.

Nikki's smile widened. "Well, I'll have to get all that I deserve later when we celebrate my big win." Switching the phone from the car to her air pods, she removed her belongings.

"Oh yea? I got you on that!" Dre's laugh enclosed her heart like a mother with a newborn child. She knew he thought she was "too much", and that was one of the reasons he was so into her.

"I'm gonna let you go, babe. I'll call you later," Nikki said. She straightened up her outfit and used her phone's camera to make sure her hair and makeup were intact.

"Later, babe. Knock em' dead," Dre said before hanging up.

"Hey, girl, hey!" Nikki turned her head and saw Lakeisha holding the door of the building open for her. Lakeisha was an intern and the only other Black person in Nikki's division. They had clicked instantly, even though she was 10 years Nikki's junior.

"Heyyyy!" Nikki carefully made her way to the door while juggling her briefcase, files, coffee and purse.

"Let me help you with some of that," Lakeisha offered, holding out her arms to be filled.

"Thanks, girl." Nikki dumped her files into her hands, then led them into the building.

"I see you here early. You ready for your presentation?" Lakeisha asked. Nikki really appreciated Lakeisha's maturity for an intern. She didn't know too many college students who were as driven or focused on achieving their goals the way this one was, and it made her stand out even more as a person of color.

"Yep. I got this," Nikki said, as they entered the elevator. A few others joined them before they got to their floor, so the conversation was halted. The two women then strolled in an easy silence until they reached their department.

"Well, make sure you update me when it's over, and let me know where the after party is. You know I'm trying to turn up wit', chew'!" Lakeisha said, setting Nikki's stuff on her desk. They were in "cubicle land" so Nikki appreciated that Lakeisha was speaking in low tones.

"I got you, girl. Have a good day!" Nikki watched Lakeisha's curvy form sashay to her area, then proceeded to prep for her meeting. Time went fast, and before she knew it, her boss was calling her to request her presence in the conference room. "Whew." Nikki exhaled a short breath, said a short prayer, and walked to her destiny.

* * *

"To my girl for SLAY-ING the corporate and KILL-ING that ladder!" Dee Dee shouted over the DJ. She raised her drink for everyone to follow suit.

"Yassss, honey, yasss!" Nikki said, smiling ear to ear. She was with her crew celebrating, and couldn't be happier. They were at her favorite spot, Benny's, where it was always live and seldom any drama.

"Girl, you did that!" Lakeisha chimed in after all had taken a swig.

"Yea, my girl don't play!" Dre added, nestled behind her. He squeezed her by her small waist. She was happy she had changed into a more relaxed outfit, choosing her high-waisted, distressed black denims, black baby Tee, and low pumps. She arched her back while beaming at Dre.

"Thanks, y'all! I'm so blessed by how well the meeting went. I mean, I felt confident it would go well, but I couldn't have fathomed *how* well!"

"Yea, I can't believe the execs were so receptive to your proposal," Shannon said. She was petite, with light brown skin, large almond eyes and a beauty mark on her chin.

"Yea, it really was just that one I was concerned about, but even *she* didn't seem too opposed to my data. In fact, she seemed uncharacteristically chill," Nikki said. She took another sip of her Malbec. Much like Olivia Pope, she was a red, dry wine kind of girl.

"That's cuz you already put her in her place!" Dee Dee exclaimed. She was referring to a previous issue where Nikki went to the Partners and pointed out some errors the exec Kaitlyn had made. Nikki really didn't want to do it and normally if it was anybody else, she would have gone to them first, but every interaction she had with Kaitlyn previously was fruitless. The woman couldn't stand her and heeded none of her advice when she actually tried to assist her with different projects they worked on together. In the end, she left Nikki with no choice but to go to her superiors.

"Yea, but it's in the bag. I mean they do have a day to discuss and give me the final approval, but once it's approved, I get a *fat* bonus, *and* I get to lead my own team to execute the new marketing program!" Nikki looked around her circle and grinned.

"Yassss!" Dee Dee said. She held her drink in one hand and snapped her finger in the air with the other. "But, girl, I'm gonna have to head out early cuz little Chris is going to need dinner, and my babysitter ain't getting paid enough for all that."

Nikki laughed. "I appreciate you coming out! I know you don't be getting down like this on the regular." She tossed a hand to the club scene.

"Oh, you know I wouldn't miss it!" Dee Dee swarmed Nikki in a warm embrace that reflected their 20-year friendship.

"Now it's time to hit the floor!" Lakeisha announced, demonstrating every ounce of her youth by pretending to gyrate by a stranger near the bar. Nikki tossed her head with a laugh, then let her young associate lead the way. The dance floor was packed and the music was perfect; mostly throwbacks with a few new hits. It was Friday night, and everyone was ready for the weekend.

Lakeisha and Shannon had captured two poor victims to dance with, and Nikki found herself happily staring up into Dre's eyes. Even though the song was fast, she was in his arms, two stepping in the minimum space they had.

"I'm so proud of you," he breathed into her ear, and she snuggled a little closer, smiling hard into his neck.

"Thank you!" Nikki had never felt so elated. How was it that she was so blessed? Her job was on the up, her girls were there, and this man was into her something serious. She had been waiting for a guy like Dre. He was working on his own business and still had a 9-5. She could talk to him about anything, and they connected on so many levels.

"I mean it. I've never met a girl like you before, Nikki." Dre looked down at her and ran a finger under her chin. "I want you to know I don't take you for granted."

Nikki lifted up her face in response. "Me either," she mumbled, and laid one on him, so he knew she meant it.

* * *

After working hard all week, Nikki was grateful for the weekend. She spent it working out at the gym, and with her mom. They caught a movie, then went to dinner on Saturday.

"Man, I can't believe she was letting that dude dawg her like that," Nikki said, referring to the character in the movie. Her mom put down her fork and finished chewing the food in her mouth, pondering her thoughts for a moment.

"Well, you know women can feel like they need a man. They can feel like their self-worth is so low, they will take anything they can get," she finally said. "We all have our own journey in life where we grow and have to learn our value."

"Yea, I know. It has definitely taken me time, and I am still on my own journey," Nikki replied. Her face also grew thoughtful as she reflected on her various lessons in life on dating and relationships.

Nikki's mom smiled and looked at her adoringly. Nikki was an only child, and the closest family she had left in the world. Her own story of evolution was a difficult one. Growing up in the ghetto of Toledo and dealing with abuse, poverty, and a teenage mom just trying to make it, she had fought for her daughter to experience better than she had. She was grateful she had won that fight.

"You are doing so well for yourself, honey pie, and I'm so proud of you!" She reached over and patted her daughter's hand.

Nikki smiled. "I know, Mom. You tell me all the time."

"Because I want you to know. Now there is something I need to share with you." Nikki's mom cleared her throat then took a drink of her water. Nikki wasn't sure what the change in her mom's mood was due to, but she figured it couldn't be too serious. Her life was a dream.

She leaned in and clasped her hands on the table in expectation. "Ok, what's up?" she asked, giving her full attention.

"As you know, I had a doctor's appointment yesterday." Her mother licked her lips and took another drink. Nikki waited for her to continue.

"Umm, they found something, and it doesn't look good." She lowered her gaze, and Nikki felt confused.

"What? Found something? Something like what?"

Her mom started playing with the napkin on the table while shifting in her seat. "Like a tumor. And they are saying they caught it really late." Nikki's stomach felt queasy.

"What does this mean? What are you saying?" she asked, removing her hands from the table then letting them drop, forgotten, into her lap.

Her mom swallowed, now fighting back tears. "They don't know how much time I have left." She looked back up at her daughter, meeting her eyes again. Nikki sat in silence. She was in shock. Why was this happening? What did this mean?

"Are you saying you are dying?" Nikki asked, feeling bewildered. Her mom reached a hand over across the table, and Nikki met it with one of her own.

"We are all dying, baby. And every day we are all getting closer and closer to heaven. I'm just a little bit closer today then I was yesterday."

Nikki felt the tears begin rush down like the Niagara Falls and her mom instantly came over to her side of the booth. She fell into her arms and let her mom cradle her the same way she did as a child. Never mind the people milling around the restaurant; the guy across from them, sitting with the 5-year-old who was pretending his french fries were toy soldiers, the waitress who kept asking if they wanted anything else every 10 minutes, because she was new and nervous about not getting her tip. These were normal people, and their lives were normal, and nothing had changed for them.

But for Nikki, everything had changed, and she so desperately wanted things to stay the same.

* * *

"I can't believe it!" Dee Dee said. She leaned back into her vintage, green couch and wrapped her soft, cream fleece more tightly around her slender frame. They were in her living room, and Nikki had just gotten done filling in her childhood friend on what her mother had shared.

"Yea, me either," Nikki said, while handing little Chris a Lego. She was sitting cross-legged across from him, attempting to help him build a tower, but every time she added a piece, he would push her hand away.

"No, Auntie Ki. Lemme do it!" Nikki couldn't help but smile. With golden brown skin and short curly hair, he had her heart. She would hand over the Lego every time.

"I mean, did she say what options for treatment they are providing?" DeeDee asked, tugging on a strand of long, curly hair. She worked on her bottom lip with her teeth, which was always a sign she was in deep thought.

"Yea, but they are saying it's really late in the game," Nikki answered in monotone. She kept her gaze on Chris, afraid to look at her best friend. She knew they were experiencing the same thing. Her mother had been Dee Dee's mother. She had been there cheering them both on at every milestone, every accomplishment. It was both of their losses.

"Well, I'm gonna look into some natural remedies. You know the government don't want us to be healed. They just about making money, stuffing us with this medication that's keeping us dependent and killing us at the same time," DeeDee fumed. She crossed her arms, her face set in resolute determination.

Nikki nodded silently.

"Auntie Ki, why you cwyin?" Little Chris' voice jerked her out of her thoughts. She hadn't even realized she was.

"Oh, honey!" Dee Dee fell to the floor and Nikki let herself, once again, lean into a loved one's arms. Wiping the tears, she sat up, trying to be strong.

"I'm ok kiddo, just processing some things," she said to little Chris after a moment.

"Ohhhh!" Little Chris' eyes widened in understanding, and he nodded as if he knew exactly what she was going through. Dropping his Legos, he moved to her lap and put his tiny arms

Nikki

around her shoulders. That gesture just brought back the tears and Nikki covered him with her body. DeeDee hovered over them both, swaddling her loved ones into her arms.

* * *

Sunday morning Nikki dragged herself out of bed. Dre would be there in the next hour to pick her up for church. They had started attending regularly together a few months into their relationship, and she was grateful. It was so difficult to find a man who shared her faith and had the depth that she did.

Nikki popped on Fred Hammond's "No Weapon" and set her mind on her Creator. "Father, I don't think I can do this," she whispered with a heavy heart.

"I've got you," said the still, small voice.

Nikki was moving slower this morning, her heart heavy, but somehow was dressed and ready when Dre texted her that he was outside.

"Good morning!" Dre greeted her when she sat in his 2016 Dodge Challenger. She respected the fact that he wasn't the type to lease and overspend on something he couldn't afford. Instead, he had his car paid off and was working to invest the extra money he was making on his business.

Nikki attempted a smile. "Good morning." She had filled in Dre on her mom's diagnosis the night before, and he was supportive as she assumed he would be. His own mom had

375

passed a few years ago from a similar illness. Dre leaned over to kiss her cheek, then gently patted her hand before pulling off. The ride was quiet, and Nikki was deep in thought.

God, where are You? she kept wondering, searching her heart for that familiar sensation of His presence.

Dre held her hand as they walked in the building and led her to their usual seats. Her church wasn't a traditional group. They were small and intimate, and felt more like family to Nikki then many of her blood relatives. Her pastors had been doing life with her since she came to faith.

"Honey, I'm going to get us some coffee. I'll be right back," Dre said, once she was situated. Nikki moved her head up and down automatically. They were meeting in a gymnasium one of the members had access to through their job. Their group had been meeting there for a few years, and everyone seemed to be content with it, even though the chairs were fold-out and not as comfortable as maybe a church pew.

"Hey, Nikki. How are you?" Hearing the familiar voice, Nikki lifted her eyes. It was her pastor who had been a strong mother figure to her for the last 10 years.

"Doin' ok. Just trying to figure out life I guess." She gave the older woman a hug and appreciated the compassion that always emanated from her.

"Yea, that is most of us in this season." Her pastor took a seat next to her and fingered the tips of her long, dark locs.

She had been growing them since the 70s, when Black power was the rave and the Jesus movement took the culture by storm. Her and her husband got swept up in both, and their lives were never again the same. "What's up?" she asked Nikki in her usual knowing tone.

Nikki updated her and was immediately glad she had. Her pastor had lived through so many things, yet still had so much life and love brewing in her heart. Nikki knew many others who had been hurt and jaded by life, but somehow this woman kept this sweetness about her.

I hope to be like her one day, she thought to herself.

The word came forth and was encouraging. Nikki eagerly drank in the fellowship, worship and love. At one point she looked over at Dre, and saw that his head was bowed in prayer. She felt peace overwhelm her, and for the first time since her mom gave her the news, she had hope.

* * *

Mondays were never her favorite days but today Nikki was grateful for the distraction. Work was keeping her mind challenged, and she always loved a good challenge.

"Nikki, please come to my office." The chat window popped up in the middle of Nikki's work screen.

"**Ok**," she replied, feeling slightly annoyed by the interruption.

Hmmm, I wonder what this is about?

Nikki smoothed down her skirt after saving the document she was working on on her work computer. In no time she made her way to her boss' office and took a seat in the chair facing him.

Larry was tall and slender with a small pouch in the place of his stomach, and dark brown hair that surprisingly wasn't receding in spite of his 50 plus years on the planet. His habit of looking over his glasses at her instead of through them indicated that he was really listening, and she always took that as a good sign. Overall, he was a good boss, even though he was wet behind the years in management.

"Hi, Nikki. How are you?" Larry asked, as he left his seat to close the door.

Nikki instantly felt on guard. This was clearly a closed meeting.

"Doing well. How about you, Larry?" She eyed him curiously.

He cleared his throat and took back his seat. "Oh, you know, Mondays. Always chaotic around here." Lightly chuckling, he shuffled some papers on his desk.

He seems nervous, Nikki observed.

"Well, I first want to thank you for the presentation you gave on Friday." He gestured with a hand, then clasped both in his lap.

Nikki smiled, feeling proud of the work she had done. She crossed one leg over the other, and got more comfortable in the chair.

"I know you brought up some great points and new ideas on how we can increase revenue for our largest client by implementing a new marketing strategy," Larry continued.

"Yea. I did a lot of research and the numbers don't lie," Nikki said, nodding confidently.

Larry cleared his throat.

"But actually, they do," Larry said, squinting at her. He shifted in his seat some while loosening his tie.

"Huh?" Nikki said.

What is he talking about? she wondered.

"After reviewing the information this weekend, we found some errors in the figures you reported. Once we revisited the calculations, we discovered the correct solutions actually show a significant *decline* in sales, not an increase."

Nikki was at a loss for words. *What? A decline in sales?*

"Well, that can't be right. I mean, I've been working on this project for about a month, and I can't imagine I didn't provide the right analysis." Nikki sat up, rigid as the back of her chair, and laid both hands on its arms. "I went over those numbers a million times," she said, starting to rub the wood beneath her fingers back and forth anxiously.

Not to mention I had Lakeisha work on them, she thought.

Larry assessed her through his glasses. "Well, as a result of our findings we are *not* moving forward with the program. The Partners were very disturbed by what they found, and one of the execs even pointed out that the information you gave had been copy and pasted from the internet."

"What!" Nikki was pretty much suffocating the chair arms now. Was she being accused of plagiarism?

"Yes," he continued. "Our policy at this company is not to tolerate such behavior. Now, since this is your first instance, we are not going to give an immediate termination, as we normally would."

Well, I guess I should be glad about that! Nikki thought sarcastically.

Larry looked at her with his mouth set in a line, his jawline firm. "We *are* however going to put you on a two-week suspension as we continue researching this topic."

"What! This is crazy." Nikki was struggling to keep her composure. "You haven't even given me a chance to review the information and defend my work," she said through gritted teeth. She couldn't believe what she was hearing.

Larry held up his hand. "You will have an opportunity at the end of your suspension to review with the executive management your findings. We will determine the final outcome of your employment here based on the outcome of that meeting."

Nikki was silent. It was obvious to her, leadership had already made up their minds and whatever she said would not be taken into consideration.

"Fine. Just let me grab my stuff and go." She started to get up from her seat, but Larry spoke quickly.

"Hailey from HR is waiting for you at your desk," he said. "She will be there to escort you out." He cleared his throat, then moved around some papers on his desk as a sign of her dismissal.

Nikki felt her stomach drop. She stopped in her tracks momentarily, and stared at her boss, then slowly planted her Jessica Simpson nude pumps on the floor.

"Ok," she said softly, resigned. The feeling as if her whole world had turned upside down in a matter of moments engulfed her for the second time that week. Walking out of her boss' door, her legs felt as heavy as led, but she never looked back.

* * *

"Babe, you want your veggies sautéed or broiled?" Dre asked.

Nikki looked up from her phone and met his eyes. "Whatever you want," she responded half-heartedly. She loved Dre's cooking and was normally super excited when he was in the mood to do his thing, but today was a different deal. She poured her glass of red wine into her mouth before retreating back into social media land. What was it about everyone's posts that made it look like their lives were so damn perfect anyway?

Dre didn't let her off the hook so easily. "How about I serve 'em raw?" he cocked his head to the side and tossed her a mischievous smile. A small smile crept along her face in return.

"You're the chef," she threw back sarcastically.

Dre winked at her and proceeded playing with the pots and pans on the stove. Nikki let her head rest on the back of the couch cushion while listening to the sounds of H.E.R fill the small one-bedroom apartment.

> Set the tone, when it's just me
>
> And you alone, and we're lonely
>
> In the room, breathin' slowly
>
> Oh, you know me, yeah

Nikki sighed. Her soul was heavy, and she didn't know how to get out of this space she was in.

"Dinner will be ready soon," Dre announced. He came over to refill her glass before moving to the couch next to her and piling her feet on top of his legs. When he began softly massaging them, she became thankful she had recently gotten a pedi.

"I just can't believe those A-holes," she vented. "I have been there for a whole year, working my butt off, showing them who I am, and what I'm capable of, and this is how they repay me." A plump tear escaped and started to cruise down her cheek.

Dre stopped his job of massaging and wiped it, rubbing her cheek with care and concern.

"I know, babe. I know." He was quiet, and she could tell he was being sensitive to what she needed.

"I reached out to Lakiesha to see if she had changed any of the numbers when I had her add in some of the info she researched, even though I *know* I checked *everything* when she gave me back the files, and of course she said she hadn't. That girl is a smart one, so I don't think it was her." Nikki chewed her lip while narrowing her eyes, deep in thought.

"But, babe, anybody can make a mistake. I mean, she is an intern. You sure she didn't *accidentally* put the wrong numbers in? Maybe you weren't able to catch it in your review."

Nikki was silent. She didn't want to accuse the girl when *she* was the one who gave her the opportunity.

If Lakiesha did jack up the numbers, she thought, *what does that say about my own judgement in entrusting her with some of the research?* Nikki downed another drink of her wine.

"Well, how are you going to proceed? You said they are giving you two weeks to defend yourself?" Dre was back to rubbing her feet.

"Yea. They are supposed to send me over their findings for me to counter. But forreal though, this whole situation has given me such a bad taste in my mouth. I don't even know if I want to continue working for them." Nikki peered into what was left of the glass of wine and swirled it around. I've already started looking for other jobs," she confided.

Dre lifted up an eyebrow. "Oh yea? What are you looking for?"

"Anything that will let me be more in control of my work. I'm so tired of others having the authority to just let me go at the drop of a dime and not valuing the work I'm putting forth."

"You sound like an entrepreneur to me." Dre tilted his head to the side, studying her.

"Yea. Entrepreneurship has always been the plan, it's just about the timing." Dre carefully put her feet down and pulled her to him.

"Nikki, I want you to consider this. You know I've been doing my hustle part-time, and the big reason for that is because I need help. I can't leave my 9-5 right now, but if I had someoneI trusted who understood the vision, and could give it the time I can't, then I could grow it to where I want it to be. I could finally pursue it full time."

"Dre, what are you saying?" Nikki looked at him surprised. "You want me to come work for you?" They had been dating only six months, and this was a major commitment.

"No, babe. I want you to work *with* me. I want you to be my partner." Nikki sat up, and folded her legs over one another Indian-style. Dre started stroking them as he peered at her intently.

Whoa. What was happening? Just a few days ago she thought she was going to climb the corporate ladder, then today she finds out her job is in jeopardy, and now she could possibly be going into business with Dre?

God, what are You saying? Nikki was quiet, pondering this new opportunity.

"But, I mean, what if things don't work out between us?" she asked timidly. She really liked Dre. In fact, she felt she loved him. But she was trying to follow his lead and not jump the gun. She didn't want to presume anything until he said it.

Dre set her glass of wine down on the table, then locked both of her hands in his, before lifting them to his lips. He raised her chin tenderly and said with all of the certainty in the world, "They will."

* * *

Her favorite season had finally emerged, hence the leaves were changing. Nikki loved this time of year simply because of the fashion. She also no longer took the change in seasons for granted, realizing other geographical locations did not offer such beauty, and just how fleeting seasons were in general.

"Let's rest at this bench," Nikki's mom suggested, pointing to a bare wooden one standing in the shade.

"Ok." The pair ambled over in their thick, colorful scarves and matching UGGS boots before perching side by side. Both were quiet for a moment, soaking in the brevity of life.

"What's the update with work?" her mom asked, finally breaking the silence.

It had been two weeks, and Nikki had faced the execs head on. Once she received the files they sent, she saw where the discrepancies were. Someone had changed the figures, and she realized, because the files were saved on a public drive on her work computer, it would have been easy to do.

But who would do it? she pondered.

Lucky for her she had a contact, Scott in IT who was always flirting. She hit him up via text.

"Aye, Scott. Wuz up?"

"Wuz up, Nikki. Not much. How you been?

"Hanging. Tryna figure out something with a work file."

"Yea. I heard you was on leave, but didn't know the details."

"Yea. They saying I submitted some false information in my report, but I know that's not the case. I was wondering if you could do me a favor and see if anyone went into my files other than me, and maybe Lakeisha?"

"Sure, Nic. I got you!"

Sure enough, Scott found that Kaitlyn had been in the system on the dates right before Nikki had submitted her information to the board. He was even able to find a newer version that was updated after she had left the system. Nikki filled her mom in with this info, and her mom was steaming.

"I can't believe that wench!" Nikki's mom started going off.

Nikki looked at her in disbelief. "I know, Ma! It's crazy right?"

"Didn't you say she was real chill during your presentation?" her mom asked, with accusatory eyes. She turned slightly to Nikki and started stroking her back.

"Yep. And now we know why."

"So, what did management say when you brought this to their attention?"

"They was trippin'. They were stuttering all over themselves and apologizing. Kaitlyn was trying to defend herself, but what could she say? It was in the system. Basically, they put her on a two-week leave and said they would further investigate, but they offered me my job back on the spot." While taking in the view, Nikki felt a breeze hit, so she eagerly tightened her mustard-colored scarf around her neck.

Her mom removed her hand from Nikki's back, doing the same, and scrunched a large plaid, wool scarf to her face. "And what did you say?"

"I said they could keep that job, I'm done. And I walked out," Nikki responded, while watching a blue jay land near their feet.

"That's my baby! Good for you!" Nikki's mom beamed.

"I know it was crazy. I just left and didn't look back," Nikki said, marveling at her own actions.

"Well, you know you're in the right and you know God will provide." Her mom bobbed her tan, slender face up and down with confidence.

"Yea, and I think He already has." Nikki met her mom's gaze and updated her on the business opportunity Dre was proposing.

"Hmmm, you sure this is the right move, Nic? I mean, have you prayed on it?" Her mom looked worried.

"Of course, Ma, and all I feel is peace." Nikki's mom was quiet for a moment, but then swallowed her daughter's hand in her own. The two observed the birds and the squirrels going about their business, not worrying about a thing.

"Well, I know one thing, honey pie. God has you. He has never let you down, and He won't start now."

"Yep." Nikki looked at her mom with love.

"You and God, I'll always have. No matter what."

THE END

LISA'S LESSONS

Lisa is a new (Christian) Believer and has found faith primarily through her beloved Aunt Sylvia's demonstration of love and support, and then from an unexpected relationship with a new love interest, Joe.

Lisa is able to capture a man like Joe because even though she was not raised in a faith, she still has similar values. She engages in conversation with Denise, sharing that she should not use men. I have Lisa intentionally do this to show her standard and that she has class so that the reader knows the type of woman she is. I also make it a point to have her meet Joe that very same night, who asks for her number, when earlier in the evening Denise brags that no man is going to do so if Lisa doesn't "play the game" the way Denise advises. I wanted to show the reader that having a standard and doing things the "right" way does still yield results (even speedily).

Along with Lisa's standard, she had lived her whole life believing that working hard would yield the life she wanted (as was taught by her parents). Like most of us, she found that life had unexpected twists and turns, one of them being a divorce from her husband, Michael.

After the divorce, Lisa was still in love. She wrestles with her feelings for her ex as we see in her dialogue with Sylvia; her desire remains for Michael. Joe's pursuit seems to be just the ticket for moving on, but when she finds Joe, she finds God. Lisa learns an important lesson when she finds God, and that lesson is that being a follower of Jesus Christ will cost something. In other words, she learns the lesson of sacrifice. We see this discussed in **Philippians 3:7-8 (NKJV)**:

"But what things were gain to me, these I have counted loss for Christ. Yet indeed I also count all things loss for the excellence of the knowledge of Christ Jesus my Lord, for whom I have suffered the loss of all things, and count them as rubbish, that I may gain Christ and be found in Him..."

When Lisa lets go of Joe, she appears to lose something, but in that situation, she learns a new lesson: God is a Restorer! He does not ask for something that He does not intend to replace. He gives her back her husband, Michael, the very desire of her heart! We see God's ability to do this in the following scriptures verse:

Matthew 7:7-11 (NKJV)

"Ask, and it will be given to you; seek, and you will find; knock, and it will be opened to you. For everyone who asks receives, and he who seeks finds, and to him who knocks it will be opened. Or what man is there among you who, if his son asks for bread, will give him a stone? Or if he asks for a fish, will he give him a serpent? If you then, being evil, know how to give good gifts to your children, how much more will your Father who is in heaven give good things to those who ask Him!"

Lisa's journey is just beginning as a Believer, but she is learning quickly that believing in Christ, and following Him, go hand in hand. Thankfully, she met Joe, another, more mature Believer. Joe was able to respond to what she needed. Joe's ability to keep boundaries with Lisa made her decision to obey God a little easier.

God always provides grace and strength, especially when we have to do very difficult things, and He is faithful to give us the desires of our hearts, when we first delight in Him.

Proverbs 37:4 (NKJV)

"Delight yourself also in the Lord, and He shall give you the desires of your heart."

JOE'S LESSONS

When we find Joe, we know that Joe is a man of faith and integrity, even from the glimpse that we got of him in Lisa's story, but now, we get to see him in other venues. Joe's integrity is further demonstrated when he refuses a woman with seductive ways in the club. He is spiritually mature enough so that his environment does not negatively impact his own morals and values. A key scripture that touches on this is **John 17:14-16.**

"I have given them Your word; and the world has hated them because they are not of the world, just as I am not of the world. I do not pray that You should take them out of the world, but that You should keep them from the evil one. They are not of the world, just as I am not of the world."

Joe is in the world, but he is not of it. He stands apart, and his ability to illustrate this standard influences a young brother named Earl. Joe's friendly demeanor, which stems from his own roots in Black culture, is what opens the door for Earl to reach out. Joe's social class standing is relatable to many Black Americans who may be "middle class" but are exposed to more "urban" street backgrounds through friends and family. Hence, the dialogue later between him and Nina before he goes to court. In this dialogue they touch on their loved ones, who were faced with injustices in the court system.

This standing in middle class America also produces "code-switching" which is practiced by many in the Black community.

This ability to switch the type of language used is often dependent on one's environment. Joe speaks one way when he is at work, another when he is engaging with a romantic partner (both Nina and Lisa) and another when he is with "his boys". He may even speak a certain way when he is talking to God. I wanted to demonstrate the use of code-switching using Joe's character and showing how his language changes in these different environments, and even how it changes when he is speaking to himself through internal dialogue.

By giving Joe a Black judge, I wanted to show the need to have people of color in positions of power in our society. If we have people who are able to see our side, then we can have a greater chance of experiencing advocacy, instead of biases and prejudices that rule against us. I also wanted to show Joe's heart for his community by having him be a volunteer at the Urban Youth Center and having the basketball team play for funding for this organization for urban youth.

Even though the club scene isn't Joe's normal scene, he greatly benefits from that decision, not just because he was able to be a light to Earl, but also because he meets a new love, Nina. I wanted Joe to meet his next love in an unlikely place for a Christian to show that God is not confined to a church building, but He is everywhere and in all things, especially concerning His children. Nina is the first person to catch Joe's eye since Lisa. He was so impacted by the relationship ending with Lisa, that he did not even re-visit Devon's since the breakup! Often after a breakup we have venues that represent our time with our exes, and we may not feel comfortable attending those places again.

Joe was finally in a good enough place emotionally to patronize Devon's, and he made sure he and Nina were looking good! Their outfits complimenting each another showed that they were now a "couple". Their debut as a couple in the very place that Joe had met his ex, symbolized that he was healed and had moved on. But even healing doesn't mean there wouldn't be some discomfort. This is the reason that he was relieved when Denise mentioned that Lisa would not be there that evening.

From Joe, we learn to be relatable as Believers. We learn to stay involved in our communities, and we learn that there is love, even after a breakup. After introducing Joe in Lisa's story, I had to write his own to show this. Lisa had hit it off with Joe, but because she was called back to her husband, it left him alone. I couldn't do that to Joe when he was such a good man! I couldn't let his story end and his desire was still not met. That was ultimately my main reason for writing "Joe"; to give him the desire of his heart: a mate. But there was so much more that came from the story. The greatest part for me, was seeing his mentorship and impact on Earl, a young Black man who had a criminal background, but who was trying to make better choices. I hope that Joe's story encourages other young men to offer that same support for Black men in our community.

Key scripture:

Matthew 5:13-16 (NKJV)

"You are the salt of the earth. But if the salt loses its saltiness, how can it be made salty again? It is no longer good for anything,

except to be thrown out and trampled underfoot. You are the light of the world. A town built on a hill cannot be hidden. Neither do people light a lamp and put it under a bowl. Instead they put it on its stand, and it gives light to everyone in the house. In the same way, let your light shine before others, that they may see your good deeds and glorify your Father in heaven."

VANESSA'S LESSONS

Vanessa is a young adult from a close-knit, Black, middle class home. She's self-assured, popular, athletic, and it doesn't seem like anything can get in her way. She's one of those rare individuals who acquires this kind of confidence at a young age. I personally did not have this experience growing up, but saw others who did, and I desired that. It was fun to be able to embody those "young, popular people" I observed, into Vanessa, and live it out through her, in a sense. I also was intentional to make her dark-skinned. Colorism is a prevalent issue in the Black community, however, there are some darker skin people who actually do cross over into the "acceptance" category in the class ranking system that silently exists in high school (or in pop culture). Unfortunately, they are often viewed as the "exception to the rule".

Vanessa's so confident that she chooses to end things with her high school sweetheart and go to the prom with a friend! We know that her making such a bold move like that (and it not impacting her popularity) shows just how much of a secure individual she is! Yet, even with her great family structure, intelligence, attractiveness and self-confidence, she finds herself entangled in an unhealthy, toxic relationship.

Vanessa is raised "right" and she clearly respects her mom, often practicing the guidance her mother gave her, even when she is unsupervised. At the freshman welcome party, she quizzes Tony on who he is and even requires proof (he then whips out his

I.D). At the fraternity party she sniffs the drink Rico offers her before drinking it, leery that it could be alcohol. She is on guard and thinks over and over again that she is above being caught up by "some dude". But with all of the precautions she takes, she is not able to see everything. Rico is older, he has more life experience, and as confident as Vanessa is, she feels insecure with him. I intentionally had Rico take a year off school to show that he is even one year older than the students in his class. Vanessa marvels at his intelligence and wonders if she could ever measure up to someone of his quality. One of the messages I wanted to get across in her story was that as much knowledge as we may have, we can only know so much, and we need people, and God, to help us see the rest. This is a lesson I have learned, and continue to learn, in my personal journey with God.

Vanessa was the leader of her crew, and her best friend CeeCee was her constant companion and comparison. CeeCee came from a broken home. She was dealing with her own pain and dealt with it by moving from one guy to the next. Vanessa laughed at CeeCee's shenanigans and unknowingly looked down on her friend. In contrast, one would think that *CeeCee* would be the one to fall prey to someone as toxic as Rico! But I wanted to capture the individual's story who had a strong family structure but who still found themselves in a toxic situation. In Vanessa's case, what made her susceptible to this relationship wasn't a broken family background, but partly, it was that she had *too much* self-assurance, and that excessive confidence led to pride.

Romans 12:3 (NKJV)

"For I say, through the grace given to me, to everyone who is among you, not to think of himself more highly than he ought to think, but to think soberly, as God has dealt to each one a measure of faith."

Sometimes we compare ourselves with those who are not (in our eyes) doing as well as we are. Vanessa's comparison to CeeCee was foolish, causing her to elevate her own view of self. We should never compare ourselves with others. *"For those who compare themselves with themselves are not wise."* **(2 Cor 10:12)**.

Vanessa was surprised when CeeCee started showing interest in Bible study and learning about self-value. That is because she just assumed CeeCee would always stay where she was, but we never know a person's outcome and what God has in store for them.

Vanessa is helped along in this new phase of her life by a new friend, Tina. Tina is very mature for her age, and this maturity is not just due to her personality, but to her walk with Christ. She is relatable to her peers, and her wisdom is able to help influence them positively. She is someone who also demonstrates being *in* the world but not of it. I had a "Tina" I met in college. She was only a year older, but to me and several of my friends, she was several years older. Her maturity and personality was that of a big sister, even though we were in the same age group. I attribute this to her having the Holy Spirit and attempted to manifest this same maturity in Tina.

Vanessa is also supported by her RA. Initially she doesn't think her RA is relatable because of the color of her skin, however, I wanted to show with Jenny's character that you can never judge a book by its cover. This was influenced by one of my closest friends sharing that her own urban background caused her to believe that white, middle class people did not have hardships. In college she learned that they had their own source of problems and were not exempt from emotional or even physical pain, even if they were financially supported.

In addition to pride, another component that led to Vanessa's entanglement with Rico was her tendency to enable. She was used to enabling CeeCee's acting out with different men, (she only laughed at her friend and never encouraged her to be healthier) so when Rico needed a crutch, she was there. She wanted to be the one person he could trust and did not understand that his lack of close friendships was a red flag.

The final lessons from Vanessa are that we are all susceptible to dysfunctional relationships, and we all need help in making it out of bad situations.

Key scripture:

1 Cor 10:12-13 (NKJV)

"Therefore let him who thinks he stands take heed lest he fall. No temptation has overtaken you except such as is common to man; but God is faithful, who will not allow you to be tempted beyond what you are able, but with the temptation will also make the way of escape, that you may be able to bear it."

CALVIN & MONICA'S LESSONS

Monica and Calvin are the couple no one wants to be. Monica's affair was heartbreaking enough, but to find out that her lover was her boyfriend's best friend makes the betrayal ring even louder. The scene opens with Calvin's response to her telling him. His pain is evident and so is hers, but it's not until the end of the initial scene that we find out Monica has a relationship with God.

So often in the church we paint a portrait that Christians are not as "messy" as Monica. Yet the Bible discusses so many stories of men and women who were far from perfect, but who still loved God. We see Abraham, who had a child outside of the will of God (Ishmael), yet God said he was a man of faith.

Romans 4:1-3 (NKJV)

*"What then shall we say that Abraham, our forefather according to the flesh, discovered in this matter? If, in fact, Abraham was justified by works, he had something to boast about—but not before God. What does Scripture say? "Abraham believed God, and it was credited to him as righteousness"...***(Genesis 15:6).**

We see David who committed murder and adultery, yet God said he was a man after God's own heart.

1 Samuel 13:14 (NKJV)

"But now your kingdom shall not continue. The Lord has sought for Himself a man after His own heart, and the Lord has commanded him to be commander over His people..."

God looks at the heart, and his view of our identity is not predicated on our works. It is by grace that we have been saved.

Monica does some soul searching, and God uses this betrayal to move in her life like she had never experienced before. He comes to her in a dream and reveals his desire to know her more intimately. This expression of God's Spirit is verified in scripture:

Acts 2:17 (NKJV)

"And it shall come to pass in the last days, says God, That I will pour out of My Spirit on all flesh; Your sons and your daughters shall prophesy, Your young men shall see visions, Your old men shall dream dreams."

I have experienced this type of move of God often since I laid down my life for Him at age 19, and it was important to me that I share these manifestations of Him in my writing. I believe God has sent me dreams because my mind and consciousness can't get in the way of His voice with doubts or fears that could deflect His truth while I am asleep. Usually, He moves in this way when I am going through a hard thing or right before I am about to, and always it is to bring me closer to Him and to remind me of His love and care.

Monica's time separated from Calvin gives her an opportunity to discover that God is her Lover, and her decision to go outside of His will and sleep with Jamal wasn't just an adultery against Calvin, but was an adultery against her first Husband.

Isaiah 54:5 (NKJV)

"For your Maker is your husband, The Lord of hosts is His name."

I have also experienced God showing me that *He* is my Husband and my shortcomings were against Him. In scripture David shares a similar experience, saying that his sin was against God alone. **(Psalm 51:4)**

I also showed Monica's personal development symbolically by having her so distraught and emotional at the beginning of the story that she couldn't even make a cup of tea, or even make it into her own bed, before she collapsed at the threshold. Later on in the story when she is less emotional and has grown spiritually, she is making a cup of tea when Calvin reaches out via text. When he reaches out, she is in a much better place emotionally, mentally and spiritually. I have experienced God move this way in my own life. When I have let something go and grown in my character, he has given it back to me.

Calvin's time apart from Monica shows his own relationship with God, and thankfully, his mentorship from an older man in the faith, Carl, aids him during this difficult time. I wanted to include this element of Black men needing older Black men to guide and counsel them. Often there are more women than men in the church and Black men may not have access to the relationships that women do. Calvin seeks Carl's counsel which is helpful but doesn't dictate his ultimate decision. This shows Calvin's sensitivity to the Spirit. Leaders are not to choose for you but help you make the choice for yourself. Their discussion also touches on Calvin's experience in the workplace, and Carl is able to help guide him in being more effective spiritually at work. After college, my own spiritual journey was reflected in my career. God showed me that I would be a minister in the business arena and not in the four walls of a church building. We see Calvin is also maturing in his faith by taking these steps to share the gospel through building relationships outside of work and inviting his coworkers to his home.

Another lesson Monica had to learn was how to wait on God. She wanted so badly to fix things with Calvin, but she had to release the relationship and trust that if it was meant for her, God would give it back. Much of my spiritual journey has been in "waiting on God", primarily with my career and with relationships, and the result has always been growth in my own character development. Since waiting has been such a huge life lesson, I needed to demonstrate that in my writing.

In the end Calvin chooses Monica and that could only happen by the supernatural working of the Holy Spirit. The ability to forgive has to be supernatural, as his mentor Carl shared with him. Through Calvin and Monica's story, we learn that nothing is impossible with God.

Key scripture:

Luke 1:37 (NKJV)

"For with God nothing will be impossible."

ASIA'S LESSONS

Asia's story is short and sweet but still pertinent. We find her on her 31st birthday, out with her girls, one of which is her sister. We learn that she is fresh off a break up and navigating the club scene. This is her normal, and she is bored with it. This is me! So much of my social life is this: out with my girls. We have a sisterhood that is sweet, but still we desire the right relationship. As much as I love my girls, too many girl's nights out gets to be boring!

In the process of being forced to celebrate her birthday, Asia meets, what appears to be, a new possible love interest, but it is quickly revealed, he is not the man for her because he belongs to someone else! The statistics are there. There are more men than women, and that means more men are going to be married. Even though Asia makes the right decision, there are many who do not. I wanted to create a character who did what was difficult to do to give hope to this generation not to settle for something toxic. In a sense, Asia is a female heroine.

Though Asia doesn't profess a faith, her morals and character are admirable. Instead of choosing to be entangled with Lance, who offered to be friends after their breakup, she chooses her respect. Instead of being a "side piece" to a married man, she chooses to be alone. In the end, she realizes the value she has in her sister and friends, and for her, at least in this season, that is enough.

So often Black culture, in music and media, says you are not "winning" if you're single (not boo'd up). We are inundated with messages from culture that being a "side-piece" is actually glamorous, but Asia goes against the culture, even when her friends pressure her to do otherwise.

We can learn from Asia how to uphold our value and respect in the midst of temptation and opposition. We can learn how to be the standard.

CARLY'S LESSONS

Carly wrestles with the decision to marry her boyfriend who has proposed in Paris. It is everything she has been wanting, for so long, but she did not have peace after accepting the proposal. Any woman desiring marriage would find it a difficult situation. I personally have had to let go of several relationships due to not having peace, and I know others who have the same experience. I knew this lack of peace was God speaking to me, but often I could not see the reason for the lack of peace. I had to learn that when God said 'no' it was for my protection.

Carly experienced something similar. How could she say "no" to her heart's desire? But God did not say "yes". She obeys God, and learns the cost of following Christ as I, and others like me, have had to learn in these situations. She is encouraged by her good friend Neece that she needs to obey, and still, her friend expresses her own desires for Carly to marry Bruce! Through Neece, I wanted to show that friend who wants to see you happy, but also knows the importance of listening to God. I have been surrounded by those friends, and it is comforting when others empathize with you. It can even help in doing the hard thing.

Carly learns after her own obedience that the time away from Bruce was purposeful. There was some healing and character development God wanted to do in her, and He wanted to do it in her before marriage. He also wanted to remind both her and Bruce to keep Him first. These were lessons I have learned in my own personal life and wanted to share with the reader.

Ultimately, God rewarded Carly's obedience and gave her back what she had given up. From Carly's story, we learn that God will test us, but He is also a rewarder. I cannot say His reward will come speedily, or even look the way we want it to, but I have been greatly blessed in my own personal life from heeding God's voice. And I have reaped in so many areas as a result.

Key scriptures:

Hebrews 11:6 (NKJV)

"But without faith it is impossible to please Him, for he who comes to God must believe that He is, and that He is a rewarder of those who diligently seek Him."

DANTE'S LESSONS

Dante is a young, maturing Christian. His background is urban, and his close friend JR is someone he is close to but is unable to share his faith with. Still, he does not allow their different beliefs to separate him from his friend. He remains a light in JR's life in hopes that one day, JR will have his own revelation of Christ. Throughout the story we see Dante's desire for JR to come to Christ, however, Joy encourages him to believe that he is planting seeds and when JR is ready, he will. Dante also leaves room for JR to be JR. He doesn't try to change him, yet he sticks to his own convictions and beliefs.

Dante is in a season where God is speaking prophetically, and the plans God has for him are being revealed. The theme of reaping is evident, and God wants to reward Dante for his faithfulness. I too have had these experiences. I remember receiving a word about promotions, bonuses and elevation in my career after a period of stagnation and testing. Everything came to pass just as I was told it would, and God taught me about His principle of reaping and sowing through that experience **(Gal 6:7).**

Dante's own prophetic gifts are used when he gives a word to Joy in the food court at the mall. I wanted to demonstrate how God is everywhere and not reserved to a church building by having Dante do this. The word God has is of love and not condemnation. Prophecy should be for edification as confirmed in scripture:

1 Corinthians 14:3 (NKJV)

"But he who prophesies speaks edification and exhortation and comfort to men."

I'm grateful to have received so many words rooted in love, especially when I have been in pain or felt I was in a "murky" place, just as Joy did. Receiving these words taught me that behavior does not define identity. As a friend once told me, just because a diamond falls on the floor and gets dirty doesn't mean it is no longer a diamond. It does not lose its value or change its identity.

Joy is in a relationship and even though they are attracted to each other, she and Dante decide to just be friends. Dante kept boundaries and this allowed Joy to grow in her faith and her own identity. She eventually gives up her relationship, not for Dante, but for herself and *her* purpose. This teaches us to be whole and healthy people before entering into a relationship. In real life things aren't usually so smooth when trying to keep boundaries with the opposite sex. Emotions and desires are involved. However, I felt writing was an opportunity to encourage readers that it is possible to navigate these kinds of circumstances, even if it's difficult.

Additionally, from Dante, we learn the benefit of being patient and once again, how to be a light through relationship in a non-Believer's life. From Joy, we learn we are never too far from God's love, and His heart is always near us!

Key scripture:

Romans 8:38-39 (NKJV)

"For I am persuaded that neither death nor life, nor angels nor principalities nor powers, nor things present nor things to come, nor height nor depth, nor any other created thing, shall be able to separate us from the love of God which is in Christ Jesus our Lord."

JASMYNE'S LESSONS

Jasmyne (pronounced Jaz-meen) is a young woman navigating the dating scene. She experiences something so many young, Black women do with dating, and that is, the difficulty in finding a partner who is comparable to them. Her luck seems to turn around when she meets Courtney. He's good-looking, educated and has a job! All her girls are on him and having him is a good look. Yet he isn't all he seems cracked up to be. As the honeymoon period fades, she finds out he is rigid, selfish and devalues her. Still, she struggles with seeing these red flags because she desires a good man, and he has so many other great qualities!

Jasmyne's story is one I know too well and so do many of my friends. The statistics show that Black, educated, professional women outnumber their male counterparts. It's not easy finding love in the Black community, especially when navigating these numbers. I wanted to show the outnumbering of women to men by having four attractive Black women engaging with two attractive Black men and having Monique and Kim "fawn all over Courtney".

I also tried to show the Black male perspective from Courtney's character. He was a Black, educated man but struggled to find someone who fit his lifestyle, and I'm sure there are men out there with this experience.

I know from personal experience the excitement with finding someone and then getting to know them. It seems the closer you get to a person, the more you see their flaws and shortcomings and the reality dismantles the "ideal". Thankfully, Jasmyne has a strong family and good friends. She makes the tough decision to let Courtney go and chooses her own self-value. She is a great demonstration of the importance of having self-worth and not letting others mistreat you. I have had to practice this myself a few times, and it is never easy. The support of my loved ones and God's strength has greatly aided me in these "valley of decision" moments.

Another prominent occurrence in this story is Jasmyne's interactions with her twin brother Jimmy. For the most part Jasmine seems like a grounded, loving, confident and fun individual, but every time she interacts with her brother her immaturity is revealed. I wanted to include this part of her character to show her own need for growth. I also wanted to depict the type of young Black male that is so prevalent in the Black community, and that is, "the womanizer". Several times I have seen a brother and sister raised in the same home, receiving the same resources, having the same family life experience (their parents' divorce) and yet the sister seems to land on her feet and excel academically and professionally, while the brother does not. Even though Jasmyne's occupation isn't revealed, we know she has a job, drives her own vehicle and feels superior to her brother who spends time playing video games and using women for rides. Unfortunately, this is the case for too many young Black males.

Near the end of the story, we find that there is something waiting around the corner for Jasmyne and more than likely it is a move of God that couldn't have happened in her life had she held onto that toxic relationship with Courtney. In my own journey, I have seen God move and give me something better, once I let go of something toxic, and I wanted to share this through Jasmyne's story. Again, the message is that God will fill the gap and restore what was lost.

TYRONE'S LESSONS

Tyrone is a young Black male who attends an HBCU. He's intelligent and gifted but has questions about his future. I had a similar experience in college. I knew I wanted to major in business, but wasn't sure specifically in which field. At one point I became a journalism major, but with God's leading, I switched back to business. Even with that major in business, I didn't know that ultimately it would be used to build a career in Accounting. Although I was accepted into an HBCU, I didn't attend one because God had other plans, so writing Tyrone's character gave me that opportunity to "participate" in the Black college life. I did some research and reached out to friends who did attend one to get additional info I could include in the story.

Tyrone connects with Janet and this connection inspires him to seek his purpose. Janet is self-assured, grounded and intelligent, which are all attractive qualities, but there is another woman he finds himself attracted to—Kristine. Tyrone does what so many men do and found himself in a situation where he got involved with someone he didn't really want to be with. He let his hormones lead him. Unfortunately, this hurt himself, Janet *and* Kristine.

College is generally a time to explore, and I wanted to capture this in the story by having Tyrone be sincerely interested in Janet but also desire Kristine. Most college students are in that "in between" period where they are being prepared for adulthood but do not yet have the responsibilities of an adult. I wanted to

423

show characters in that age group who often make poor decisions based on their desires.

I was more like Janet in college—very loyal and serious about my dating relationships, however, I knew of the "Kristine's". But even with Kristine's character I wanted to show that even though she had a "reputation", she still had some depth to her as shown by her ambitions to help others dealing with sexual abuse. In addition to this, I wanted to show that even though she was the pursuer of the relationship with Tyrone, she had *real* feelings for him and wasn't just after a sexual relationship. She only used the tools that she knew to use to get close to Tyrone, and that was her body. I always want there to be hope for my characters. Even if Kristine wasn't in a healthy place at that time in her life, her desire to help those facing sexual abuse shows potential for growth.

Alex's response to Tyrone sleeping with Kristine is something I wanted to include to demonstrate a "typical" (less mature) male's response. In contrast, I wanted Tyrone to demonstrate a young man who had a good heart and some morals. This shows that not every young male is immature in their dealings with women. Even though technically Tyrone was not in a committed relationship with Janet, he deeply cared about her, and in my experience when a man cares and respects a woman, they are honest with them, even if it costs them the relationship.

Tyrone learns that an education is good, but it doesn't define purpose. Part of his purpose is to use his education to help the Black community. That is a lesson I too had to learn.

As previously mentioned, I majored in business, but that did not keep God from giving me an opportunity to write. My education was a platform for my purpose, but it was not all encompassing of it.

Although my fondness for my own college years is incorporated in this story, the greater inspiration for it was the brutal killing of Ahmaud Arbery. When I heard about Ahmaud, I was in tears. I could not believe another young man's life was taken from him for no reason whatsoever! I laid on the floor crying out to the Father and was heavy with grief. I too am a runner. I too could have been running innocently, unarmed, and some random racist white citizens could have taken my life for no reason at all, other than for the color of my skin. How could this have happened? I was still grieving Ahmaud when George Floyd was killed. It was all too much.

My heart was to be able to release some of this pain through writing this story.

NIKKI'S LESSONS

Nikki's story is loosely based on my own personal life. There was a period of time where a lot of hard things happened that greatly affected my life perspective. These hardships pertained to my career, the loss of a loved one, my dating life and even my own ability to have children. I felt like I was getting hit on so many large areas in my heart, and I'm honestly still in a period of recovery of that season, even as I write these words.

I wrote this story to revisit that period and release the pain. It was great to rewrite some of the things I wish could have happened (like becoming a business partner to my boyfriend). I also wanted to capture some of the beauty in the things that did (like spending time with loved ones and enjoying life).

While in Nikki's story there is only one best friend, in real life I have several. I tried to combine some of their personalities into one person to make the story more efficient. These women have all been like sisters, and I am so grateful for each one of their roles in my personal story.

There was a time in my life where I was frustrated with the standstill, frustrated with the waiting and sacrifice. *I could write a better story than this!* I thought to myself. Of course, God knew my thoughts, but He did something I wouldn't have expected Him to do. He moved! He moved in such a way that He showed me that He is the great Author of Faith for a reason (Heb 12:2), and that reason is because **He writes the best stories!** He proceeded to give me many of my heart's desires, and I wanted to exhibit that in Nikki's story.

From Nikki, we learn that there are various seasons of life. There are highs and there are lows, and sometime they can happen all in the same season. She has a great support group, a strong spiritual family, an active dating life, a loving mother and close friends who are like sisters. She has hard things happen, but she is able to overcome because of this provision in her life. Most importantly, she has God, and when one door closed in her career, He opened another one.

These are the truths I have seen in my own life, especially pertaining to my career. After feeling rejected and even persecuted, God provided another avenue. What the enemy meant to take me down in my career only became a springboard to catapult me into a future into entrepreneurship.

Key scripture:

Genesis 50:20 (NIV)

"You intended to harm me, but God intended it for good to accomplish what is now being done, the saving of many lives."

A NOTE FROM THE AUTHOR

Dear Reader,

I hope you found yourself immersed in the midst of a throwback 80's/90's house party, "getting it", on the basement dance floor, with the guy you had a crush on in middle school who wouldn't give you the time of day. Or maybe your soul was fed by the soothing sounds of Jill Scott as you sipped your favorite cup of joe and poetry oozed over Jill's lyrics in the background. Perhaps, you lazily enjoyed a glass of Chardonnay, while gazing up at the stars on the back patio with a new lover. But most importantly, I hope you felt the arms of your Creator wrap around you warmly, embracing you in a way you were only used to that lover doing on the back patio. I hope these things for you because I have felt them all myself. Ok, ok, maybe I didn't get to dance with that boy from middle school, but I have definitely had my share of partners on the dance floor (wink). I have had my share of so many things that have been the very desires of my heart all because I found favor by the One who is always faithful.

It took me a while to realize that my Creator was not a color, though He was a Person. For a long time, I viewed Him through the lens of White culture, unknowingly so. I thought *their* music and *their* language and *their* way of worship was *the* way. Yes, I found gospel as a way to express this worship, but in my maturity, I have learned that God is not limited to a style of music. In fact, He can be found in so many things. Fashion, music, creativity, and most importantly, in the vast expression of

His people. As I evolve in my faith, one of my greatest pleasures has been seeing how intimate He is in the very nuances that make me, me. Whether it is my fashion, hairstyle or music choice, He is there, finding joy in what I find joy in. Finding joy in me.

My hope is that you will find the same thing. That you will find there is joy in Him. There is life in Him. And He is always there.

Blessings,

Nicole

Made in the USA
Middletown, DE
30 April 2022